This is a work of fiction. Names, characters, and places are products of the author's imagination.

Edited by Sarah B. & E. L. McNicholas

Cover design by MiblArt

Illustrations by Dragon Quill Art

Published by True North Press

www.mhwoodscourt.com

Paperback ISBN: 978-1-959619-00-0

Hardback ISBN: 978-1-959619-01-7

To those who strive to break the cycle—
Your battle inspires me.

And to Laura A. Barton—
Your steadfast friendship means the world.

CONTENTS

NAKANIA

Neminar
KryTeer
Tivalt
Vylam
Clanslands
Keep Lunorr
Amantier
Kavacos
Shing
Bahadronn
Lily River
Kyon Taro
Snowblinds
Tild
Frostfire Canton
Kilitheer
Keep Falcon
Lormenway
Drifting Sands
Snow Wastes

DEAR READER

This book stands on its own as the first installment in the *Mark of Valliath* trilogy. That said, it is technically a sequel to what has been called, until recently, *Crownless*. That book has since been re-released under the new title: *The Storyteller True*. It is a high fantasy stand-alone novel which chronicles the life of a certain wandering storyteller with a knack for getting himself arrested. As such, *this book does contain spoilers for its predecessor.*

I've taken great pains (as have my alpha/beta readers and editors) to be certain you don't need to read *The Storyteller True* in order to immerse yourself in the characters and settings found in *The Shattered Arch*. What you need to know from the previous story is carefully woven into the pages. Consider that novel a prequel, which can be read before, between, or after this trilogy. Bearing this in mind, proceed at your own discretion.

Thank you for picking this book up! If you enjoy it, please consider leaving a review. Reviews are more helpful than you might suspect.

—M. H. W.

CONTENT WARNING

Along with fantasy violence, this book does contain human and animal death. Sensitive hearts, beware. It also contains brief mentions of rape and seduction, though nothing explicit is shown. PTSD is represented on page.

—M. H. W.

CHAPTER 1
DARK DREAMS

Sunlight flashed across his opponent's sword hilt. Prince Jetekesh flinched and staggered back, raising his broadsword in defense. Beneath the merciless noon sun, everything shone: the pond, the broken bottles crowding one corner of the ruins, the crumbling granite walls.

I need to see my surroundings.

He set his jaw and bounded into the meager shade painted by a leaning pillar.

Master Ivam anticipated him. The man swung his sword hard enough to make it sing.

Jetekesh blocked the blow. A dull thud sounded as covered blade met covered blade.

"Good! Better, Your Highness. Much better." Master Ivam lowered his blade. "That's enough for one day."

Jetekesh shoved back his damp golden hair, plucked a handkerchief from a vest pocket, and mopped his brow. "Let's go a little longer. I'm not tired yet."

Master Ivam's smile drew crow's feet around his eyes. "You

say that now, my prince, but tomorrow you'll feel what you've already done."

"That's fine." Jetekesh rotated his wrist until his pommel caught a sliver of sunlight and gleamed. "I need to get much stronger."

Master Ivam rested a hand on his shoulder. "You are strong, my prince. Your progress has soared in recent months, and your father is pleased. Very pleased."

Jetekesh's cheeks warmed as he grinned. "Thank you, Master Ivam. But I'm not where I wish to be just yet." His eyes strayed to the mountain range beyond the Ruins of Glayn. The lush green verdure of late spring wrapped the mountains in a bright tapestry, promising a fertile year for farmers across Amantier. The rains came frequently enough to color the world without drowning it.

It'll be a good planting season.

His chest constricted.

His eyes drifted from the north, then he slowly wheeled to face the south and the rolling hills leading down toward Kavacos, Royal Capital of Amantier. The walled city shone, roof tiles bright and clean after the last series of storms. Prosperity reigned across Amantier, and reports from KryTeer and Shing suggested they, too, flourished in this new age of peace. The White Death, a persistent plague in Shing, had vanished nine months ago.

All moved like a potter's wheel, steady, fluid. All were content and happy.

All but Jetekesh with his heavy heart.

His eyes drifted past the Rose City and its myriad sights, sounds, and smells, toward the southern desert far beyond view. His memories crawled over the wearisome paths he'd trod in company with some he would never meet again.

Sir Palan, the legendary knight without equal. Silent Tifen,

Jetekesh's faithful protector. Jinji Wanderlust of Shing, the renowned storyteller with a price on his head. All dead.

"Your Highness?"

Jetekesh ducked his head to blink back a sudden mist, then pressed a smile on his lips as he turned to the swordmaster. "Perhaps we *should* stop for the day, Master Ivam. I'm more exhausted than I believed if my thoughts wander so far."

The middle-aged man narrowed his brown eyes. "You appear rather melancholy, my prince. Do you wish to unburden your soul? I'm a fair listener."

Jetekesh shook his head. "Thank you, but no. It's nothing." How could he speak of those he'd lost in KryTeer? How could he articulate his guilt? Nine months weren't sufficient to shed his grief and move on. A hunger clawed at him to become strong enough that he wouldn't lose anyone else through his helplessness.

Nor my temper.

He strolled beyond the ruinous structure and sat in the tall grass to unwrap the cloth around his blade. Master Ivam followed, crossed his legs in the grass, and worked in silence to unbind his own sword. A breeze teased their fair hair and tugged on their shirts.

Finished, Jetekesh climbed to his feet, sheathed his sword, and brushed every speck of dirt from his britches.

The swordmaster rose, slid his blade into its sheath, and squinted down at Kavacos. "Beautiful day. The weather is finally taming, I think."

Jetekesh nodded faintly. "Just in time to plant crops."

"We're blessed by the One God this season."

Jetekesh didn't bother answering. He'd never known how to juggle small talk. "Shall we return?"

Master Ivam started to nod, then pressed his hand against his forehead to shield against the sun. "Is that the banner for Sage Province?"

Jetekesh cupped his hands across his brow and searched the far westside gates of Kavacos. Approaching them, a group of horsemen rode along the King's Highway in military formation. Rippling above the contingent, a banner bearing sage leaves clutched in a black hawk's talons boldly stood against a silver field. Wisdom and Might: the motto of Sage Province.

"By the saints, I think it is." His heart stuttered. A smile graced the edges of his lips despite himself. Cousin Rille had come to visit. Energy surged through his limbs. "Come along, Master Ivam! Make haste."

He bounded down the north hill toward the capital. How long had it been since he'd seen his cousin? Rille had turned eleven years old last autumn, shortly after they'd returned from KryTeer. After that, she'd gone back to her fallen estate to restore her dead father's duchy. In the winter snows, she'd returned to Kavacos only once to celebrate the Holy Nocturne. Her stay had been brief.

Jetekesh couldn't say why excitement now carried him like he had wings on his feet. He and Rille had never been close. They'd spent most of their journey south bickering. Yet together they'd experienced something few royals ever did, and she understood better than anyone—except perhaps the Blood Prince of KryTeer—the painful depths of losing Jinji Wanderlust.

Not Blood Prince. He's the Blood King *of KryTeer now.*

Jetekesh crested the second, smaller hill and paused to catch his breath. Master Ivam pulled up beside him, puffing for air.

"Why the urgency, Your Highness?"

Jetekesh brushed back strands of his long honey-blond hair while he gulped more air. "Haven't...the faintest...notion." He inhaled, drinking in verdure and the damp of a nearby brook, then he sprinted onward. He'd chosen not to ride his stallion out to the ruins. He loved riding—particularly to spite Mother who had rarely let him near horses—but he'd decided after his adventure with Jinji that he needed to increase his stamina.

Soon he reached the northside gates of the Rose Capital, puffing only a little. A few trumpet notes blasted the news of his return as the portcullis lifted to give him passage. Master Ivam caught up, and together they entered Kavacos near the palace walls.

A company of knights saluted as the two passed, then they pivoted to flank Jetekesh. The escort crossed one of many thriving market squares, with its mingled scents of leather, ironworks, and roasting mutton, to reach the sandstone palace walls. Jetekesh ignored the hawkers who called out to him, begging royal favor.

The knights ushered him between the tall palace gates while guards stationed to either side saluted. He hurried through the northern rose gardens where the first buds peeked out among the thorns. His eyes roamed the paths, expecting to spot Mother among the rose beds, cooing at her precious, growing flowers.

A forlorn sensation swept over Jetekesh. *Mother is gone. Let her rest. You hated her anyway, didn't you?*

A liveried servant turned the corner and stepped into view. Relief softened the man's face. "Ah, Your Highness, excellent. Your Lord Father wishes you to meet him in the throne room. Lady Rille has arrived from Sage Province and claims her arrival is of a most urgent nature."

She'd really come.

Of course, it would take something urgent to chase her back here.

Jetekesh tacked a smile to his lips. "Thank you. I'm on my way."

The servant bowed and vanished around the corner. As

Jetekesh reached the same bend, he glimpsed the servant trotting toward the sandstone Rose Palace cut like a great solid square. The prince's gaze lifted to find the Crowned Rose pennant—gold against a red field—snapping in a growing wind atop the highest turret. His stride quickened.

His Majesty, King Jetekesh the Fourth—along with Cousin Rille—waited upon the raised dais in the throne room. Lord Father wore his fine court apparel, and his long mane of light brown hair hung in loose curls around his scarlet surcoat. His blue eyes shone in a ray of sunshine, bright and kind, though lines of worry strained at his mouth. He still looked a bit fragile since his years-long illness, but each month brought improvements. Someday, he might have his old strength back.

Father and son didn't look much alike. While the king had a solid, tall frame—despite his prolonged illness—Jetekesh was lean and of average height for his sixteen years. Mother had also been tall, with platinum hair and hazel eyes. The prince, meanwhile, had honey-colored hair, turquoise eyes, and delicate features. He was almost pretty, but he hoped to one day grow into a man's figure with the authority and fortitude of Father or the iron will of Sir Palan. Mother would have hated that.

The prince gave the vaulted chamber a cursory glance as he entered, taking in the polished stone floor, the Crowned Rose banners hanging from the rafters, the swaths of red velvet draping the throne of Amantier, and the absence of gentry and nobility. His steps echoed as he crossed to meet his cousin.

Rille smiled down at him from the dais, amber eyes cat-like in the colors streaming from high, stained-glass windows. Her pale blonde hair had been piled and coiffed on her head, and she wore a gown of green velvet and gold satin.

Jetekesh climbed the dais steps. "Hello, Rille."

"Salutations, Lord Cousin." She dipped into a graceful curtsy. As her grim eyes lifted, fear flashed through them.

Jetekesh frowned. "Not that I'm unhappy to see you, but your unannounced appearance does instill a sense of anxiety."

Her smile stretched thin. "Astute, Lord Cousin. I'm not here to socialize."

Movement in his periphery snared Jetekesh's notice. He glanced left to find Sir Yeshton near the dais, cloaked in the shadows of a sunless corner. The knight looked much more polished than he had on the road last year. His long, dark blond hair was half pulled back; his scruffy dusting of whiskers had turned into a respectable, trimmed beard; and his brocaded clothes were tailored and costly. Rille doted on the knight, there was little doubt of that. But then, Sir Yeshton had saved her after her household had been slaughtered by the Blood Knights of KryTeer during their march on Amantier. Jetekesh suspected she had unofficially adopted Yeshton as a surrogate father.

The knight's gray eyes collided with Jetekesh's—grim, pensive—then Yeshton bowed at the waist.

The prince inclined his head, then turned back to Rille. "It must be quite a sensitive matter for my lord father to dismiss his court this time of day."

"I fear it is." Rille sighed. "A bad dream awakened me yester week. A dream like none I've had since Jinji's passing."

Jetekesh flinched. How could she use those words so bluntly? He drew a quick breath. "I thought your Sight had failed when magic fled Nakania."

"Precisely my point, cousin. It did. But now I *See* again. My gift has come back. Yet I fear the reason for that."

A shiver jolted up his spine. "What was your dream?"

Rille opened her mouth just as footsteps approached beyond the throne room—dozens of them, pounding, scraping, as armor clattered. Lord Father stepped to the edge of his dais, silken cape rippling. The far doors flung open to reveal Captain Frebe of the palace guards, eyes wide and searching.

"Your Majesty!" Frebe cried. "Strangers at the northern gate." He scurried forward, guards at his back matching his pace.

Lord Father nodded, calm despite the alarm in the soldiers' eyes. "Expound, Captain."

"Sire, they...they're...not Amantieran."

The king's lips twitched down with stifled impatience. "Go on."

Captain Frebe took a moment to collect his breath as his eyes danced from the king to the prince, to Rille, to Sir Yeshton, to the empty room. Back to the king. "Sire, they're from the Clanslands."

Jetekesh started and glanced toward Lord Father.

The king's eyes narrowed. "How many?"

"Two, sire."

"Two dozen, two hundred?"

"No, sire. Two people." Frebe looked over his shoulder toward the half dozen guards at his back. He cranked his head back around to eye the king like an owl blinded by the sun. "I've never seen their like before. Skin dark as ebony. Strange hair. Nasty-looking spears."

Lord Father nodded and strode down the dais steps. "Are they waiting outside the gate?"

"Yes, sire. They requested to see—"

Lord Father marched across the chamber. "Lead me." He glanced back. "Stay here, Kesh."

"Please, sire," said Frebe. "They requested to see *Prince* Jetekesh."

The king's steps faltered. "Did they say why?"

"No, sire. Only that it was imperative."

Rille moved from the dais. "Let them, Lord Uncle."

"I'll come with you." Jetekesh slipped past Rille and trotted to Lord Father's side.

The king's frown deepened. "No. Captain, escort our guests here. We had best do this in proper fashion and within our halls." He glanced at Jetekesh. "I won't risk you in the open until we know what they want, my son."

As Captain Frebe bowed and waved his men out of the throne room, Jetekesh's heart quavered.

"Am I in danger, sire?" he asked. "I've never met anyone from the Clanslands before."

The king shook his head. "That, I couldn't say. But I'll take no chances. The Clanslands are full of peculiar, wild places. Some clans are friendly. Most aren't. But very few are openly hostile." He strode back to the dais, spun to face the chamber, and sat upon the throne. "Rille, we've a few moments before they arrive. What is your dream's warning?"

Rille paced to the dais steps and stared up into the king's troubled face. She drew a breath. "I dreamt that the darkness that possessed Emperor Gyath had returned from its banishment in the depths of the sea. *Erisyrdrel* walks this world again."

Memories of the KryTeeran emperor's court surged across Jetekesh's thoughts. Mere months ago, he'd stood before that wicked man, alongside Jinji and the rest of his traveling companions. Jinji had mustered enough strength to summon Prince Sharo from the magical realm of Shinac, and the fae prince had struck Gyath down upon his throne. The darkness possessing

Gyath had slipped away like black sand, banished back to its confinement in the ocean.

Prince Sharo had claimed the dark thing wouldn't return in Jetekesh's lifetime.

What happened to change that?

"You're certain it wasn't a mere nightmare, niece?" asked the king.

Rille shook her head. "The difference between Sight and dream is substantial, Lord Uncle. Something broke *Erisyrdrel*'s chains. I couldn't say what. Something...horrible."

Sir Yeshton slipped from the shadows to stand at Rille's side. "She awoke screaming, Your Majesty." He folded his wrist over his sword. "She never screams."

Jetekesh could well believe that of his cousin. She was too pragmatic and proud. The prince stepped onto the dais. "What should we do, Lord Father?"

The king shook his head, eyes riveted on something beyond the floor at his feet. Something far, far away. Silence enveloped the chamber until the distant sound of a bird outside the stained-glass windows penetrated the stillness.

Jetekesh let his eyes wander over the windows. The images set into the colored glass depicted Cavalin the Third, hero of Nakania; Driodere, grim Death himself; the saints of ages: Vashi, Kilith, Norgric, Peratha; and others, so many others. Martyrs, heroes, warriors.

Jinji should be up there.

Jetekesh lowered his gaze and turned to find Rille watching him.

"I dreamt of *you*, cousin," she said.

Jetekesh grimaced. "Not dying at the hands of darkness, I hope."

"No. Not quite that."

He rolled his eyes. "Always so cheery."

"I have little reason for cheer. We haven't the means to slay such a monster as *Erisyrdrel*."

Jetekesh turned his gaze from Rille as his heartbeat quickened. He willed his face to keep a neutral expression, but knew he'd failed.

What can we do against a threat like this?

Footsteps pounded against the flagstones beyond the chamber doors Captain Frebe had left open. A swell of guards poured into the throne room and parted to let the captain lead the strangers across the elongated chamber. The two clansfolk walked behind him, their strides long and graceful.

Jetekesh's eyes widened. Never had he seen such people. Their dark skin shone in the window light. Thick woolen hair in many braids twisted atop their heads, black but for streaks of outlandish colors: bright green, orange, and pink. Patterned cloth, including leopard spots, swathed their lean, tall figures. Both wore spears with jagged tips, decorated with feathers, sheathed across their backs. One stranger was male, the other female. Captain Frebe brought them a dozen feet from the dais, turned, and motioned for them to stand still. They obeyed without a word. The captain marched to the edge of the dais and positioned himself near Sir Yeshton and Rille.

The male foreigner took a single step forward. "King Jetekesh, I presume?" A slight accent laced his words, but otherwise he spoke the trade tongue flawlessly.

"You presume correctly," Lord Father said, switching from Amantieran to the trade tongue. "Whom do I have the honor of addressing?"

The stranger inclined his head. "I am Dakarai of the Karanki Tribe in the eastern realm of what you call the Clanslands. This is my companion Anenyasha. We have traveled to your fair city on a mission of terrible importance." His dark eyes drifted to Jetekesh. "Is this your son and heir?"

"He is," said Lord Father, a note of strain threading through his tones. "My captain of the guard mentioned you came here seeking Prince Jetekesh. I'm surprised you know him by name."

So was Jetekesh. The Clanslands had long kept out of western politics, keeping to themselves in their deep, dangerous jungles. Little was known about the folk who lived there, and the prince's tutors had assumed that the Clanslands cared little about other countries. Only a few of the clansfolk ventured south across a wide bay to trade with Shing.

Dakarai's lips lifted in a smile. "You would be surprised by much that we know, Your Majesty." He extended his free hand toward the prince. "Your Highness, we have brought a gift for you if you will accept it."

Jetekesh threw a furtive glance toward Lord Father, who nodded faintly. Squaring his shoulders, Jetekesh inhaled and moved from the dais to stand before the strangers. He met Dakarai's gaze. The stranger was well over six feet tall and almost willowy. His eyes were a vibrant brown, keen and sharp, above high cheekbones and full smiling lips. He was no more than thirty years old.

The young woman, Anenyasha, stepped forward and extended her hand in a fist.

Jetekesh held out his palm. She dropped something onto it. He flinched like the object scorched his flesh—but something cool settled against his skin. Heart hammering, he dared to look: a sapphire, winking in the colored light from above.

His heart cartwheeled. "I... It's beautiful. Thank you. But, if I may ask, why are you giving this to me?"

The stoic woman stepped back and looked at her companion.

Dakarai answered. “It is our custom to bring our host a gift. Please accept our humble offering.”

Jetekesh resisted an urge to seek his father’s guidance, though why they gave *him* the offering rather than the king, he couldn’t fathom. He curled his fingers over the sapphire and tugged his lips into what must look like a bemused smile. “Thank you again. I accept your gift heartily.”

Dakarai smiled. Anenyasha mirrored him, though her expression was far more reserved.

“Now to business,” the clansman said. “We have come to Amantier at the behest of our watchwoman. She bade us to make haste seven days ago after she awakened from a terrible dream.”

Rille’s intake of breath echoed in Jetekesh’s ears as his face drained of blood. He shivered.

Lord Father rose from his throne. “What was the essence of this terrible dream?”

Dakarai’s eyes lanced Jetekesh, never wavering. “She saw a glowing arch burst asunder. Then a great watery demon rose from the western seas. It slithered into the shadows and became lost to her. Just after this dream, dark things attacked my tribe and slew many of my people whilst they slept.”

The man took a shuddering breath. “We come, Prince Jetekesh, to aid you against the fell things creeping across our world. The watchwoman has declared you Marked—one who has been touched by truth.”

CHAPTER 2
SNOWSTORM

Wind snatched at Kajsa's hood, trying unsuccessfully to unleash her long white-blonde hair. A gust flung snow in her eyes. She shuddered and huddled deeper into her fur-lined cape as she trudged through the knee-deep snow, a cloth bundle of dried herbs clutched in her arms. The glow of the firelight within the distant turf house compelled her onward.

Only a few more yards.

Her boot caught a buried rock. She lurched forward and plunged into a snowbank, losing her herbs in a sea of white. Kajsa lay stunned as ice kissed her cheeks. Setting her jaw, she drew herself upright and dug into the snow until her mittened fingers found the bundle. A few herbs had spilled out. She swept them back into the pack and pulled herself to her feet. Only a few more paces to the front door.

A frosty gale howled in her ears, laughing. She ignored it and slogged onward as her nose tingled. The feeling in her toes had faded to a distant thing, like a memory of spring.

Kajsa staggered the last few feet to the porch. She pounded as hard as her frozen arm would let her through the cushioned mitten, too numb to clutch the doorknob.

"Ingrid, it's me! Open up, please!"

The door swung aside, and Kajsa stumbled into the cheery room. Warmth slapped her face. She steadied her feet and turned to smile at her friend.

It wasn't Ingrid.

Instead, a tall, comely young man held the carved door.

"Axel!" An urge to throw herself into his arms flooded her limbs, but she swayed back to stop herself.

The young man grinned and his pale green eyes twinkled. "The hunt ended early. No sense dying in this blizzard." He pointed to the ornately engraved hearth. "Brought some fowl for my supper."

Kajsa spotted the birds plucked and strung up. Curled up beneath them, Axel's black and silver wolf, Raum, slept near the open flames, nose tucked under his bushy tail.

Nodding, Kajsa shifted her pack. "I'll start cooking right away but first..." She dodged around Axel to find Ingrid in the wise-woman's favorite corner, rocking in her chair, a mangy cat curled up on her lap. Kajsa held up the bundle. "I brought what you needed, Ingrid. My stores are a little low, but we've plenty of feverfew."

The old woman lifted her blue eyes from the cat and smiled, drawing new lines into her craggy, papery face. "Thank you, Ky."

Kajsa brought the herbs to the table where other dried plants lay in neat piles. She slipped her mittens off, untied the pack, and carefully separated each root and leaf into its proper pile while Axel looked on beside her. His nearness brought a fire to her cheeks, and she avoided glancing at him until she set the last herb in its mound.

Turning, she wiped her hands against each other as she stared at Axel's feet. "I'm glad you're back safe, Xel."

He caught her chin and tilted her head until their eyes met. His gaze, warm and friendly, melted the last specks of ice from Kajsa's blood. His platinum hair fell around his chin, but for a long lock trailing down his shoulder, caught in a beaded clasp. She longed to finger his hair, to press herself against his well-sculpted frame, and drink in the security he exuded.

"You're thinner," Axel murmured.

Kajsa eased back from his touch and moved to the hearth. "I'll start on supper." She shook her layers of woolen skirts to dislodge the clinging chunks of snow, then hung her short cape on a peg near the fireplace and knelt beside the slumbering wolf.

Axel's footsteps thudded across the floor behind her. "Are you taking care of yourself?"

She nodded faintly as she examined the fowl. He sat beside her, crossed his legs, and rested a hand on her shoulder. She dipped her head further.

"Ky."

She sighed and angled herself to face him. "Don't worry so much, Axel. I'm getting by well enough."

He scoffed. "You're thin as a reed, tiny for your sixteen years, and pale as the driven snow. I'll worry if I like, thank you." His hand slipped from her shoulder to catch her wrist. "You've got to stand up for yourself, Kajsa. You can't let the village use you up."

She shrugged and stared at the floor.

"That's not an answer. What am I supposed to read in that? Look at me."

She hefted her eyes.

Axel's smile could banish a blizzard. "You deserve respect, Ky. Most especially from yourself."

She let her lips curve upward. "You're an angel, Xel."

He snorted. "*Right.* But I mean what I say." He climbed to his feet. "Now, get that supper on. You need it as much as I."

As she set to work seasoning the meat, moisture gathered in her eyes. She wiped at them before Axel could see. He mustn't know how she felt. She was already such a burden without that.

An hour later, Kajsa sat with Axel on the floor of Ingrid's turf house and picked at her meal. Ingrid had fallen asleep. The cat prowled close to examine the bit of meat Axel proffered to lure him.

"What's his name?" asked Axel.

Kajsa shrugged. "I call him Mouser, hoping he'll start earning his keep if the name sticks. Ingrid calls him Nuisance, but she likes him all the same."

Axel grimaced. "Those aren't names. C'mere, Tatters. C'mon. Get the meat."

The cat's yellow eyes slid from the hand holding dinner to Axel's face, a look of mild offense punctuated by a backward flick of his ragged ears. His tail lashed back and forth in a slow rhythm.

"He won't come," Kajsa said between mouthfuls. "You'll have to throw it. He's too proud to beg."

Axel chuckled. "Don't be like that, Tatters. Some things are worth the begging."

The cat yawned and sat down on his haunches, content to wait.

Axel shrugged and tossed the meat. "Fine." He turned back to his plate, lips turning down. "There's another reason we came back from the hunt early."

Kajsa pushed her meat away from her turnip juices. "Was someone hurt?"

"Well, yes."

Her eyes jerked up. "Who?"

"Not anyone we know. Relax."

She let her shoulders slouch. "A stranger? At this time of year?"

"Must've been caught in the storm. He was half frozen but still breathing. We'd been debating turning around anyway. Finding him settled the argument. We'll know more if he wakes up."

"Is he hurt badly?"

"Dunno." Axel prodded at his turnip with his fork. "I'd hoped you could look at him. I don't want Ingrid going out in this weather."

Kajsa sprang to her feet and nearly lost her grip on her plate. "Is he at the Elderhouse?"

"Yeah."

"Xel, you should've spoken sooner."

He rose and crammed the last bite of meat into his mouth as he shrugged.

Kajsa threw on her cape, still damp but endurable. "Hurry."

"A couple minutes won't make much difference. Slow down."

She shot him a scowl. "A couple minutes and an hour besides!"

He chuckled. "So assertive. You might try being more like this about other things. You'd fare better in the village."

Kajsa's fingers fumbled over her soggy mittens. The village. "H-how many will be at the Elderhouse?"

"Probably half of Tuksa by now. Word travels fast, even in this weather."

Kajsa snatched Ingrid's herb kit off its peg on the wall. "Can't worry about that. I'll endure it."

"Sorry, didn't catch that."

"It's nothing." She turned to find Axel chewing the last of his turnip. Kajsa's expression softened. He stood there, a full eighteen years old, looking like a child caught with a fresh-baked strudel. But his childlike moment vanished as a smile swept over his lips and the warm firelight caught in his pale eyes.

"I'm ready." He shrugged into his fur coat. "C'mon, Raum."

The wolf's ear flicked, then he raised his head. A whine issued from his mouth as he yawned, stretched, then rose to his paws.

THE FRAGRANCE of woodsmoke and pipe tobacco lingered in the air as Kajsa steeled her nerves and pressed her way into the Elder-house. Axel was right behind her. Raum stayed outside. Kajsa stifled a sneeze and danced around a gaggle of women deep in conversation. They offered no more than a perfunctory glance as she plowed further into the crowd.

Voices droned around the large room. More than half the village had indeed braved the cold night air and sleeting snow.

Axel slipped ahead of her to cut a path. People parted like snowy drifts beneath a sled for him, and soon Kajsa reached the head of the lodge's main hall. Elder Viggo stood before the large hearth, hands cupped behind his back, head bowed in reflection. Axel strode up to him and cleared his throat.

Viggo turned a vacant glance on him, then blinked. "Ah, Axel. Did you bring her?"

"Yes, Elder."

Kajsa slipped up beside her friend and bowed her head. "Greetings, Elder Viggo."

"Never mind that, never mind. You've a patient in the next room. Step softly. Help him if you can."

Kajsa padded into the adjoining chamber. The death room, most called it.

Her steps faltered but she willed herself to plunge ahead. Axel followed her and shut the door in their wake.

A single candle illuminated the confines of this room of horrors. Kajsa hadn't come back here since she bade farewell to Fa...or what had been left of him. Bile burned Kajsa's throat as the memory of Fa's torn body and the odor of death closed over her mind.

Run. Go. You can't stay here!

She cast a glance around the room: the curtains shrouding the window, the cold fireplace—dead like everything that dwelt in this room.

A gentle hand caught her shoulder. "Easy," whispered Axel. "Breathe out the bad, Ky. You're here to save someone, not say goodbye."

His words eased her racing heart back into a steady beat. She let her breath out and tiptoed to the bed set against the leftside wall. In the flickering candlelight, she could make out a pale face and hair.

"I need more light, Xel."

He retreated from the room with the silence of a skilled hunter, then prowled back inside moments later, a lit lantern swinging from his hand. He shut the door with a soft snick, then crept to the bed. The flame illuminated the room, dampening the sterile feel a little.

"Set it there." She motioned to the nightstand.

Axel rested the lantern on the polished wood surface, then

stepped back as Kajsa pulled the heavy quilted coverlet from the unconscious figure in the bed. Like everyone else in this forsaken wasteland, the man looked Norvian, with fair skin and pale hair, yet something in the structure of his bones unsettled Kajsa as she ran her fingers over his frame. Nothing broken. No indication of blood loss. A few bruises. No fever. No sign of a head injury.

She tipped her head as she considered the sleeping man. His flesh looked almost like ice stretched over sharp features reminiscent of a fox.

"I don't see anything wrong with him." She turned to Axel. "He's just sleeping."

Axel's brows knitted together. "You're sure?"

She nodded. "There's no sign of injury. Nothing." She glanced at the sleeping man and tensed. His eyes were open now, their color molten gold in the lantern's guttering light.

"Oh, hello." Axel stepped up beside Kajsa. "How do you feel?"

The man's gaze slid to Axel's face. A strained smile twisted his lips. "W-where...?"

"You're in Tuksa, one of the mountain villages. From where do you hail, stranger?"

The man considered Axel for a long, silent moment. He drew a breath, then spoke in soft, silken tones. "Where is Tuksa in relation to Amantier?"

Kajsa blinked. *Amantier?*

Axel laughed softly. "That's *leagues* away. I doubt anyone in Tuksa—or indeed, anyone in *Norva*—could give you better insight than that. Are you from beyond the mountain, friend? Or did you dare attempt to travel up the Snowblinds in this blizzard?"

The man's eyes closed. "I...will rest a while longer."

Axel pulled Kajsa away from the bed. "We might have a madman on our hands, Ky." His voice hung on its lowest notes.

She glanced at the bed. "Let him rest. When he's regained his strength, he might better know what he's about."

Axel grinned and ruffled her hair. "Can't always give people the benefit of the doubt. Time will tell, I suppose. Best report to the Elder."

"First let's start a fire."

"Good idea."

Kajsa grabbed the lantern and followed Axel from the room in search of kindling. Nearing the door, she glanced back and a shiver ran down her spine. The man had opened his strange gold eyes, and they were pinned straight on her.

CHAPTER 3
ALTERATION

Prince Liu pounded on the hut's shabby door, shattering the birdsong within a cluster of nearby cypress trees.

No one answered.

He struck his hand against the wood harder until the door shuddered, then stepped back and glanced around the muddy yard as sheep bleated on the other side of the rutted highway. A vein twitched near his eyebrow.

A boy of about thirteen years stood with the sheep, eyeing Liu wordlessly.

Liu picked his way through the mud toward the edge of the road. "You, boy. Do you know who lives here?"

The boy nodded.

"Is it a woman—a shepherdess named Song?"

The boy held still as a statue.

Liu let out a growl. "Are you slow-witted?"

"No," said a cool female voice directly behind Liu. A sharp point met his back, nipping flesh. "Merely cautious."

Liu's heart missed a beat. His hands shot up in surrender. "Are you Lady Song?"

"No."

Liu's hands drooped above his head. "Do you know the Lady Song?"

"What if I did? Why do you seek her?" The unseen blade pressed a little closer.

Liu flinched, fingers itching to snatch the sword hanging at his hip. "That's between her and myself."

The shepherd boy across the road inched nearer, dark eyes riveted on Liu and his assailant. The sheep kept on clipping the wild grass.

"You're from the capital," said the cool voice, breathing ice against his neck.

Liu cleared his throat. "Yes."

"Then your purpose here—and with anyone living in this valley—is now my business, and you will answer my questions."

Liu rolled his eyes. "This is ridiculous. Whatever you people think, the war is over. The occupation is over. You can trust—" He cut off. The irony of his words rang like a hollow note in his mind. She could trust whom? Hadn't Liu come here because *he* couldn't trust those he loved most? He huffed out a breath. "I've been sent by a knight to find Lady Song of Crimson Lilies. He calls her friend."

"What is this knight's name?"

"Sir Kousa."

Silence. The blade tip vanished.

"Turn around."

Liu lowered his tingling arms and turned to face a woman of barely more than twenty years. She held her weapon—a fine Shingese sword—before her, ready to pierce him at the first foolish move. Despite her homespun tunic, calf-length pants, and sun-kissed complexion, she exuded the confidence of a lady of the emperor's court. Her slanted black eyes considered him, sharp, suspicious. Her slight frame suggested speed rather than fragility. Long straight black hair hung down to her waist. She was more beautiful than even the wildest rumors had painted.

"You are she," Liu said. "You're the Lady of Crimson Lilies."

Song's mouth twisted into a scowl. "Once, perhaps. Tell me why Sir Kousa sent you to me."

Liu's admiration dimmed in the rise of recent memories. "I need your aid. I must find the storyteller true—the one you met while Sir Kousa camped on your land. He...he's the only one who can help me."

Song's eyebrows shot up. "You seek Jinji?"

"Yes."

"I've not seen him since that night along with Sir Kousa. That was a year ago, maybe longer."

"But you know what he looks like and where he walks." Liu took a step forward. "Lady Song, it's a matter of terrible importance."

Song's scowl slipped into a grimace. "He's not in Shing. He crossed into Amantier. There's a price on his head in that country. I'm not certain he's even still alive, and if he is, he might be imprisoned."

Liu folded his arms. "I still have to try. I must have his aid."

Her eyes narrowed. "Why? Tell me all, or I can't and *won't* help you. I wield little trust for nobility in this age, and you reek of that caste."

The scuff of footsteps jerked Liu around, and his eyes fell on the shepherd boy striding toward him, a curved staff in his hands. The boy's black hair was pulled back in a tail, and his dark eyes were sharp and focused.

Liu started. "Ah, you must be Song's brother Yin. Sir Kousa mentioned you."

The boy nodded. "I am."

"Go inside, Yin," said Song.

The boy trudged past Liu to slip inside. The door snicked shut after him.

"Well?" Song slid her short sword into the battered sheath she clutched in one hand. "Explain or leave us alone."

Liu's mare nickered where she stood at a sagging sapling, her reins looped around a wilted branch. The heat of the midmorning sun was already crusting the mud from last night's storm. Liu sighed and swiped a hand over his brow. "It's a delicate matter."

Song shrugged. "So is intruding on my privacy."

It was hardly the same, but she didn't know that yet.

"Very well. I am Prince Liu of the White Lotus. My father is Jung Tep, nephew of Emperor Majinglee and third in line to the throne. My mission concerns my Great Uncle."

Song's narrowed eyes softened. "In that case, come inside, Your Highness." She padded to the door and pushed it open to give him passage.

Liu slipped through the doorway. Brushing past Song, he caught the woman's scent: wool and loam, with an undertone of saffron. Song stepped to one side and shut the door behind him. Liu blinked until his eyes adjusted to the dim interior. It was a tidy one-room hut with two sleeping pads rolled up in a corner and a leaning table near the fireplace. Yin was crouched before the remnants of a sputtering fire, stirring the contents of a pot blackened from its life in the coals.

"Is the emperor in danger?" Song asked.

Liu hesitated. How much should he explain? Despite Song's reputation and service against KryTeer six years ago, she'd been exiled from court. When the emperor had sent an invitation for her to reclaim her family's titles after KryTeer pulled its forces out several months ago, she'd refused.

Can I really trust her? He eyed the slight woman. *Do I have a choice?*

He pressed his hands together and bowed. "Please hear me out to the end, Lady Song." The words seared his tongue. In his seventeen years, he'd seldom bowed to anyone, let alone a stranger within a backwoods hut in a border province of Shing. His pride rankled, but his mission mattered more.

"Sit." Song gestured to the table.

Liu strode over and sat on a worn embroidered cushion. Song took another for herself across from him. Yin maintained his place by the bubbling rice. Steam curled from the old pot.

"The emperor is not himself." Every word provoked lancing pain. Liu swallowed and continued. "An...incident occurred six days ago at dawn. My Lord Uncle had risen early and taken a walk alone in his gardens. When a servant went to retrieve him for the morning meal, he discovered that his liege lord had collapsed. The emperor was taken at once to his bed, and his healers were summoned. At his age, any fall is of great concern, yet they found nothing that could have caused this. Even so, he slept until the following day." Liu hesitated. "When he stirred, he seemed fine. Yet his actions since that moment are not in keeping with his kindly disposition."

"How is he altered?" asked Song.

"He is..." Liu's fingers flexed. He stared at the grains of wood in the table, seeking the right word. "He is cruel, my lady. He has bouts of temper I've never seen before, doling out extreme punishments for petty offenses. He demands lavish entertainment and great feasts each night. And more, Lady Song. He has ordered an army to be gathered. Its purpose, I suspect, is to invade Amantier."

Song's eyes narrowed. "Why seek Jinji?"

"By Sir Kousa's report," Liu said, "the storyteller can see truth in ways others cannot. He knew things about yourself and your kin that no one, not even at court, would know. And he also knew things about Sir Kousa. Could he not also discover the reason for the emperor's extreme alteration?"

Song sat in silence and considered him for a long moment. The pot rattled as the rice roiled faster.

Liu glowered at the table. Frustration surged through his veins and he pounded the wood. "I *must* do something to help my Lord Uncle!"

"Breaking my table won't do it, Your Highness." Song's glare cut like a dagger. "I will help you. We will seek out Jinji if it's possible to do so."

Yin set the pot on the table and handed Song two chipped bowls. "Am I coming?" asked the boy.

"You're too young," Liu said above Song's response.

The woman lifted a brow. "That isn't your choice to make, Your Highness. Besides, he's little younger than you." She considered Yin. Silence rose, as though unspoken words passed between brother and sister. At last, Song nodded. "Yes, you'll come. Your skills with a bow may come in handy." She dished rice into one of the bowls and handed it to Liu. "Eat up, Your Highness. We leave after lunch."

Liu accepted the bowl and stared at the plain rice. *This is lunch? It's not yet noon.*

Exiled nobility-turned-peasants had strange notions, it seemed—even about mealtimes. Despite that, relief trickled through him like cold water on a blistering day. He could handle the mission on his own, but a guide familiar with Amantier would make the matter easier.

"I'm pleased that you grasp the seriousness of my mission." He prodded his food. "But I must be clear on two points: I sneaked out of the palace with all possible care, but I might've been followed even so. The emperor is mistrustful toward all his kin at present. I fear his knights might try to stop us."

Song nodded, unphased. "That just means we'll need to be stealthy."

"The second matter is this: While I need your help, the fact remains that *I* am in charge. Sir Kousa entrusted me to find Jinji. You're simply my guide. Is that clear?"

Song's lips lifted in a dark smile. "Perfectly. But I don't accept those terms, Your Highness." She looked him up and down. "You're how old—sixteen?"

Liu's cheeks burned. "Seventeen!"

"Why did Sir Kousa send you?"

Liu's shoulders squared. "I'm a skilled fighter regardless of my age. As I understand it, you were younger than I when you took on the Blood Knights and killed them."

"Exactly my point. I've been at this longer." Her mouth softened into a lighter smile. "Why don't we work together rather than insult one another? I'll guide, you'll follow. We'll make decisions together."

Liu snarled. "With all due respect, I hardly know why your guidance is necessary. Sir Kousa led me to believe you *knew* where Jinji is, but you yourself claim otherwise. What guidance can you provide? What use are you to me?"

She slammed her sword sheath against the floor. "I am blooded, O prince. Are you?"

Blood rushed in his ears. He glowered at the woman. "I, too, have killed in combat. Perhaps not as many as you—but while you've been cowering in your pastoral province, we struggled to free Shing from KryTeer's control. *We* never gave up!"

Song sprang to her feet, black eyes aflame. Her body trembled as her hand gripped her sword hilt, ready to unsheathe her blade.

Liu resisted an urge to flinch back. He was a skilled swordsman, but the Lady of Crimson Lilies was legendary. "Forgive me, my lady. I've barely had a moment's rest since the incident, I forget myself."

Song's eyes shut. Her shoulders shook harder, then slowed. Stopped. She exhaled through her nose, then peeled her eyes open. "It's a rare and foolish person who makes me lose my temper. I will say this only once, Prince Liu. No one who calls me coward will live to regret it. Do I make myself plain?"

He offered a hasty nod.

Song plopped back onto her cushion. "Good. Now eat."

WHILE SONG and Yin packed essentials for the journey, Liu fed his mare and surveyed the rustic fields. Sheep still grazed across the highway. What would happen to them without their shepherds?

His gaze swiveled to the opposing fields dotted by cypress trees, then traveled the wending path of the nearby stream where a stand of bamboo trees jutted up along the bank. His eyes traced the stream toward the hut, until they settled on a tall stone at the edge of the hut's muddy property.

A grave marker.

Sir Kousa had mentioned that Lady Song lived with a younger brother and her grandfather. The old man hadn't been inside. Song and Yin had said nothing of leaving anyone behind.

The hut's door banged open, drawing Liu's gaze. Yin sprinted outside, a satchel slung over one shoulder, a bow and quiver of arrows in his other hand. He stooped to set his things beside the door, then straightened and darted past Liu and into the field with his sheep. They bleated at the boy as he raced toward a distant thicket of trees reaching toward the wide blue sky under the sweltering sun.

A moment's noise had done little to shatter the stillness of the countryside.

It's so quiet. Liu turned back to the stone. *Not a bad place to live out one's old age, I suppose.*

Song's voice broke into his thoughts. "We can go once Yin returns."

Liu's heart jumped into his throat. He growled. "Don't sneak up on me."

She shrugged and adjusted her grip on a bundle in her arms. "I'm not responsible for your ambling thoughts."

The prince turned to double-check his saddlebags. "Where did Yin go?"

"To ask our neighbor to watch the sheep in our absence."

"Won't your neighbor be suspicious of your departure?"

"No. Our grandfather passed away one month ago. I told Yin to explain that we're visiting family to heal from our grief."

"Where will we start our search?" Liu fiddled with the reins.

"In Amantier."

He scowled. "I know that much. But *where*?"

"Villages. We ask the locals. How is your fluency in the trade tongue?"

"Impeccable."

"Good. Mine is as well, though Yin's is not. This will be good practice for him." Song's eyes flicked to the mare. "Leave your horse. She'll draw too much notice. We walk from here."

Liu stiffened. "I can't leave her out here."

"Our neighbor will watch her."

He folded his arms. “She’s a thoroughbred. I *won’t* leave her behind.”

“Her bloodline is exactly why you must.” Song glanced across the field. “Yin’s coming back. Decide quickly, but if you choose to bring her, you risk exposure, and the villagers won’t be disposed to speak with nobility.”

Liu’s mouth snapped shut. Never had he encountered a more infuriating woman. “Fine, I’ll leave her. But just you wait. We’ll need her before the end, and you’ll regret your recommendation.”

Song shrugged. “And that will be on me, Your Highness. One more thing. From here on, we must drop any titles. No ‘prince’ or ‘lady’ or any derivatives thereof. All right?” She shoved her bundle at him. Peasant clothing. “I almost forgot. Put these on. You stand out too much in those rich trappings of yours.”

“As you *wish*.” He glowered at the gray tunic and pants, likely her grandfather’s.

She set a hand on Liu’s shoulder and offered a tight smile. “I don’t mean to upset you. I realize the pride of your House bristles at these directives. But please trust that I’m protecting you as well as my brother. We must do this right. Despite any truces between Shing and Amantier, our blood has been bad for years—and a country’s memory lives long in its people’s hearts.”

Her eyes strayed to the gravestone. “If the emperor hungers for war, no matter the reason, we tread now into an enemy’s domain with ill tidings. We must go unnoticed.”

CHAPTER 4
THE SENTINEL

Whether the king had intended this evening's feast to celebrate Rille's visit or to welcome the guests from the Clanslands, Prince Jetekesh barely cared. Throughout the rowdy ordeal, as jugglers and jesters entertained Dakarai and Anenyasha, Jetekesh's thoughts lingered on the clansman's words.

Touched by truth. Marked.

His hands wrung under cover of the table, and his stomach churned. Fell things crept into the world. Dark shadows had murdered most of Dakarai's clan.

The world is supposed to be better now. Jinji died to prevent darkness from spreading.

A courtier's boisterous laugh jolted Jetekesh upright. A jester landed with easy grace despite his haphazard tumble into a juggler. Not a single plate used in the juggler's act crashed to the floor. Applause smattered along the tables lining the throne room.

Jetekesh cast a glance at his cousin. Rille sat beside him in repose, eyes bright if glassy. On her other side, Sir Yeshton poked at his dinner. Jetekesh leaned forward to grab his wine goblet and glimpsed Dakarai and Anenyasha in private conversation, seemingly incognizant of the floor show. Even Lord Father bore the signs of polite indifference, his smile slipping at the edges of his mouth.

This was no time for frivolities.

Yet the part must be played, and Jetekesh willed himself to sit still and endure the foppish humor of petty court life. His gaze traveled over the royal banners fluttering above, past them to the darkened stained-glass windows. He imagined the star-crested sky dancing with light and heard the memory of a fairy's voice from when he'd visited the fae realm of Shinac. Had that been real? Had he truly met Prince Sharo, that legendary fae warrior with snowy hair and a magical sword bursting with light? The death of Sir Blayse, the lost knight, felt real enough.

Jetekesh fingered his goblet but didn't take a sip. He'd imbibed too much when his world had crumbled last year, when Mother had sold out Amantier to the KryTeer Empire in order save her own neck—all while poisoning her husband to free herself for a more tempting crown. Only King Aredel's knowledge of *traveria*, and how to cure it, had spared Lord Father's life. At the time, Jetekesh had been leagues away, convinced the king was dead. Convinced he was the last of the line of kings dating back to Cavalin the Third. Convinced no one suffered more than he did.

Yet Jinji had been dying of a deadly illness, and Rille had been grieving the loss of her father as well as the duke's entire House. No one in their ragtag company had been spared heartache and pain.

On the heels of Jinji's death, Jetekesh had made a vow not to drown his guilt in strong drink ever again. He'd failed a few times, but not tonight. This night he would honor Jinji, no matter how fear clawed at his insides—no matter what Dakarai claimed about magic markings or dark things hunting people down.

Even if *Erisyrdrel* had returned from the black regions of the sea.

Rille let her fork drop onto her plate with a clatter. "This is pointless." Her tones were clipped and low.

Jetekesh shrugged one shoulder. "Yet here we are."

"Don't be glib, cousin."

He shook his head and stabbed a strip of meat. He nibbled and savored the juices before he answered. "You know, Rille, you're right about many things—and I respect your sensibilities. But in court matters, I think you should trust the king to know his business, even if it looks pointless."

"I—I do. But it's frustrating. With all the ill news we've heard today, *how* can we not try to do *something*?"

He scooted roast beef across his plate, catching a whiff of spices in the dark gravy. "If you can conceive of what that 'something' should be, pray, tell me, and I'll gladly do it."

"Perhaps...perhaps we should visit the Clanslands."

Jetekesh almost dropped his utensil. "You don't actually think that's wise, surely." A juggler's rapid motion caught his eye, and he watched without comprehending the acrobatics.

"Why not?" Rille asked. "Much of Dakarai's clan has been destroyed by who-knows-what. Isn't it possible *Erisyrdrel* is there?"

Jetekesh shifted to give her his full focus. "Did your dream give you any hint of that?"

"No. I only saw the darkness and you." Rille's brow crumpled. "And one other thing. Wings. I saw strange wings."

Sir Yeshton stirred. "You hadn't mentioned that before."

"I just now recalled it, Sir Knight."

Jetekesh plucked up his goblet to wet his lips. A single sip, nothing more. He swallowed and set the goblet down. “What do the wings signify, do you know?”

“No,” she said. “I’m afraid I don’t. My dreams and visions are often symbolic, and the meaning, even the timeline, doesn’t always make sense. I might learn more later on. Though sometimes...” her eyes tracked the nearest jester “...sometimes I never discover what something means—at least, not yet. Perhaps some visions are of a very distant future.”

“I don’t suppose your vision of *Erisyrdrel* is far removed from us?”

“No, cousin. I think not.”

Wind pricked Jetekesh’s skin as he stepped onto the balcony of his private suite. A bright waxing moon colored the stars and poured silvery hues over Kavacos. Silence pervaded the streets beyond the palace walls but for a dog’s cries somewhere in the shadows. Torches blazed upon the battlements, and the faint shapes of guards lent a deceptive kind of refuge against the chill night. The fragrance of dewy grass drifted from below, crisp and sweet, mingling with the perfume of hyacinths and daffodils.

Jetekesh clutched his sleeping robe close and stared out into the darkness, urging his mind to quiet enough to sleep.

The festivities had ended over an hour ago. The guests had been shown to comfortable quarters. Servants had doubtless begun cleaning up the throne room. Lord Father had bidden Jetekesh a peaceful rest, even as uncertainty dimmed the light in the king’s blue eyes.

The prince breathed in the solitude, glad of it, relieved to give in to his fears where no one could see how weak he felt. How drained the day had made him.

He slammed his hands against the balcony railing. His palms stung, but he didn't care. He welcomed the pain. Welcomed the physical manifestation of his turmoil.

Jetekesh slumped against the railing and stared at his right palm, painted orange in the distant torchlight. "Jinji, I need help. If we're to survive whatever's out there, I can't do it without help. I'm not strong enough yet. I still rely too much on other people."

He still ached for Mother, as horrible as she'd been, as stifling and treacherous as her choices were. He missed her. And he hated himself for that.

Light streaked across the night sky like a comet.

Jetekesh wrenched his gaze heavenward to watch the bright object—and backed away as he realized it shot toward him, aiming true like an archer's arrow. Jetekesh threw his hands over his face and stumbled backward until he struck the stone wall. Against his will, he peeked between his fingers.

The light had grown from a distant starlike orb into a sphere larger than Jetekesh. It burned like a white flame of blinding brilliance. As the light touched down on the balcony before him, Jetekesh tensed but couldn't look away. His heart raced. His breath rasped. Awe coiled over his body.

The flame shrank. The radiance dimmed. A figure appeared amid the light; tall, human in its form, with long hair of a strange white-blue color. As the glow reduced further, a face materialized, angular and fae-like, possibly male, with eyes of liquid silver.

"You are Prince Jetekesh, are you not?" The voice rang out, silken, clear.

Jetekesh lowered his trembling hands and nodded. "I am."

The glow fell away enough to view the ethereal man in

whole. He stood tall and willowy, perhaps twenty years old in appearance, clad in delicate armor of silvery white bearing the heraldry of two dragons in wheeling flight. The stranger inclined his head and pressed a hand over his breastplate. A thin scar ran down his right cheek and jaw.

"I am Kethalas, sentinel of the Jade Arch. I require your help, Your Highness."

Jetekesh gaped. Blood rushed in his ears, growing louder, louder. His bedchamber door burst open. Palace guards streamed into the room, swords and bows lifted. Jetekesh spun to face them. Among the helmed faces, he caught sight of his protector, Sir Lafe.

"Kesh!" Lord Father's voice cried out from the corridor beyond the open door.

Jetekesh held his hands out. "Wait! Stay back. He's not an enemy."

Nine long months ago, he'd heard the name Kethalas as he'd walked a road within Shinac. Jetekesh glanced over his shoulder and stared at the being standing on his balcony, sword sheathed, hands empty, eyes bright with concern.

"Let me through," Lord Father commanded.

The guards parted into two columns. The king walked between them, his blade glinting in the flame emanating from a torch a servant carried beside him. He still wore his banquet finery. His eyes burned in the torchlight, but his step faltered as he spotted Kethalas.

"Father," said Jetekesh, stepping toward him, "he's from Shinac. I believe he's an ally."

Kethalas stooped to one knee and bowed his head. "King Jetekesh the Fourth of Amantier, I am Kethalas, come from the realm of Shinac on a desperate quest. Knowing of your son's willingness to aid Prince Sharo's cause when Jetekesh visited our fae shores, and knowing him as a friend of Jinji Taleweaver, I seek his help once again in a matter most pressing."

Jetekesh's mind spiraled. *Him too? What can I possibly do?*

"What urgency compels you so?" asked Lord Father as he slid his sword into its sheath.

Kethalas stood. His eyes flicked to the guards gawking through the archway to the balcony. "I will tell you, Your Majesty, but not in such a crowd. I dare not."

Lord Father motioned, and the guards retreated in single file. Sir Lafe and the servant remained but stepped into the dark bedchamber, leaving the king, prince, and Shinacian visitor alone on the balcony. Lord Father strode to the railing, his stare never straying from Kethalas's face. The stranger returned his gaze steadily, a faint, strained smile hovering on his lips.

"We're alone now." Lord Father rested a hand on the stone balustrade. "Please explain your meaning."

Kethalas drew a long breath and dropped his gaze to the flagstones. "As I told your son, I am the sentinel of the Jade Arch. My vow was to protect it from any who may attempt to venture into your world from ours. Most creatures who try to cross over are of the darkest and most vile nature. Magic is not meant to enter Nakania."

Lord Father's eyebrows shot up. "Yet here you stand."

Kethalas nodded and looked up, his mouth a grim line. "Unfortunately, I failed to fulfill my vow. A fortnight ago, a dark and powerful entity attacked me where I kept watch. We battled for several days before it wounded me and broke through the Arch. I followed—but alas, between our joint magics passing through simultaneously, the Jade Arch shattered as we crossed the barrier. I am stranded in your world."

Prince Jetekesh stepped across the balcony, palms slick with sweat. "What happened to the creature you fought?"

Kethalas's silver eyes fastened on him. "To my everlasting shame, I cannot find it. I lost consciousness when I entered Nakania, and when I regained my wits I lay within the desert wastes among the debris of the Jade Arch, utterly alone."

"Could the entity have perished in the crossing?" Lord Father asked.

Kethalas shook his head. "Alas, no. Six days ago, I discovered its magical imprint upon the western shores of your country, not far from the Arch. It had seemingly fled into the waters and"—lines appeared across his face as his brows knitted together—"I fear it unleashed the demon *Erisyrdrel*." He bowed his head. "I despise what my ineptitude has done to Nakania, yet without the Jade Arch, I cannot hope to rectify my mistake by calling upon my brethren for assistance. All I could think to do was find you and ask for whatever help you might provide."

"What can *I* possibly do for you?" Jetekesh asked. His insides twisted.

"Help me to find *Erisyrdrel* and the dark force that unchained it. You know this world; I do not. And you are trustworthy. The Sigil of Truth rests upon you."

Jetekesh clenched his hands. He stared at Kethalas as his shoulders fell. "That's no kind of answer. That's not a plan at all. Truth-touched or not—whatever that even means—we've no guide, no direction to undertake such peril. I will help you, but only if we know how to go about this quest."

"My son speaks fairly, Lord Kethalas," Lord Father said. "How can we hope to track down these evils and stop them?"

"Fair words, 'tis true," Kethalas said. "Yet there is a fact about evil undimmed through all the ages of our two worlds: it cannot long remain hidden. Soon, one or both of these fell creatures will rear its head and shine like a dread beacon for all dark things to find. This, I do not doubt. And—"

Jetekesh's lungs hitched. "So your plan is to wait for them to appear? That's hardly a plan either. What horrible things might happen before we spot them? *Erisyrdrel* possesses people in order to work its dark will." His thoughts flashed to King Aredel of KryTeer—the heir meant to inherit the dread demon before Prince Sharo had interfered. If *Erisyrdrel* took control of the legendary Blood King, no kingdom upon Nakania stood any chance at all.

"All is not lost, fair prince," Kethalas said. "If we can find another Arch into Shinac, we may be able to call for the aid of my kin."

Jetekesh blinked. "Another Arch?"

The man smiled. "Certainly. I guard the Jade Arch. There are three more besides—that I know of—each guarded by my kith and kin in turns. I do not know where they are located on this side of the barrier, but should we manage to discover one of them, we are not without options."

A modicum of weight lifted from Jetekesh's shoulders. "That's something at least."

"So it is," said Lord Father, "yet Jinji sought an Arch into Shinac for years before he learned of the way through the Drifting Sands. If he could find none closer, where might they be?"

Kethalas shook his head. "Nakania is a strange land to me. Through the few stories I've heard from Prince Sharo and Lady Ashea, I know only the names of your larger kingdoms, and little else."

Jetekesh tapped a finger against his chin. "The most obvious possibility is that none of the Arches reside in Shing or Amantier, as both countries are where Jinji spent most of his time traveling. He couldn't sail easily to KryTeer and the Clanslands are too perilous for..." His eyes widened. "Dark things appeared in

Dakarai's village one week ago." He caught Kethalas's gaze. "When the Jade Arch shattered, would any other Arch feel the effects? Would they weaken at all?"

Fear glittered in Kethalas's silver eyes. "It is possible. The four Arches are connected. A surge might easily have rendered them inert for a matter of moments, perhaps longer. Upon waking in your desert, I feared invasion from Shinac. Yet nothing occurred." He inhaled. "But nothing could have occurred *there*. That Arch is destroyed."

Jetekesh's head throbbed. He rubbed his temples. *Rille was right.* "Lord Father, I think an Arch stands within the Clanslands."

Lord Father stared at a point in the night sky. "Yes, my son. I believe you're correct."

A breeze caught Jetekesh's long hair and flung it in his face. He batted it aside as the fragrance of roses tickled his nose. He felt Mother's presence beside him.

'Enough of this, Jetekesh. These matters are too weighty for you. A prince shouldn't run off in search of Arches and demons. Your place is here in the security of these walls. Let your father handle it. He's the king.'

Jetekesh set his jaw and closed his ears to her imaginary whispers. *You're dead. Leave me be.* "We should wake Rille. She ought to be included in this conversation."

"No need, cousin. I'm here." She stepped from the bedchamber and into the moonlight, pale blonde hair snarled from sleep, Sir Yeshton beside her. "I had another vision. This one concerned the Blood King of KryTeer."

CHAPTER 5
FLAMES

The night sky twinkled with countless stars, shimmering under the grueling heat of spring. King Aredel of KryTeer stood within his eastern courtyard and stared beyond the black ocean channel toward the hidden coast of Amantier. Water spilled from the fountain behind him, caressing his thoughts. Yet his mind reeled.

A voice had awakened him from slumber. A soft, insistent, slithering voice.

Aredel raked a hand through his waist-length black hair as he released a low breath. He dropped his hand and inhaled as his nerves tightened. *Why am I so afraid?*

Few things frightened the Blood King. He'd seen battles since he was four years old, riding behind Father on a great warhorse. Now, twenty-three years later, hardened and polished by countless conquests, no single man could unnerve him...save one.

Father is dead. 'Twas only a dream.

Yet the words hissing in his ear had unsettled him just the

same. *'I have not forgotten,'* the voice had said. *'I will not rest until you burn.'*

Aredel had bolted upright, flesh searing like he'd walked naked through the scalding northern desert of KryTeer.

He'd escaped outside for crisp air, but the season had turned hot early. *It will be a poor year for crops.*

"My Holy King?"

Aredel turned to find Artassa gliding toward him, wrapped in a silken robe. Her raven hair tickled her bare ankles as she stepped to his side.

He allowed himself a grim smile. "I didn't mean to disturb your rest, my wife."

Artassa's brown eyes caught the starlight and sparkled as she tipped her head back to stare up at him. Her full lips curved into a frown. "You are upset."

"I had a bad dream."

She nodded. "Shall I call for a soothsayer to interpret it?"

"No." He turned back to the black sea shrinking and growing under the waxing moon. "I would rather not feed it any strength to thrive."

Artassa tucked her arms around his elbow and set her cheek against his arm. "So cautious this night, my love. Do politics wear your patience thin and drive your mind into dark spaces?"

He grunted. "Always. But this is something else." He pulled away from her touch.

"Is it about Anadin?"

Aredel shook his head as his younger brother's face glimmered in his mind's eye. "No. That matter is settled. If he wishes to marry an Amantieran peasant, I shall leave him to choose."

"Your priests do not approve."

He shrugged curtly. "Do they approve of *anything* beyond the weight of their own purses? Kyella is a kindly lass. She'll do much to heal his mind—truthfully, she already has."

Despite years of torment and indoctrination at the hands of his father's priests, Anadin, at last, had free will to do as he wished. His attentions toward the farmer's daughter from Rose Province had proved the best of any treatment. There would always be risk. Anadin couldn't approach Aredel unless the king's men were certain he hadn't been drugged, or the prince would instinctively try to murder his elder brother due to the priests' brainwashing—but otherwise Anadin might one day mend from his madness. At least it remained a gentle strain, and Kyella's influence softened it more with each passing day.

"She's a heathen, my love," said Artassa softly.

Aredel studied her from the corner of his eye. "You disapprove as well?"

"No...if you find no fault in it." She pulled her robe tighter though the wind remained sweltering. "But already there is unrest. Already, your choice to return all conquered lands to their former sovereigns and"—she twirled her wrist—"revert the empire of KryTeer to a kingdom state is unpopular. Allowing Anadin's marriage to this foreigner will add fuel to the flames you have already been fanning."

He turned and caught her chin in his fingers. "And now my first wife lectures me on politics. Truly, KryTeer has changed."

Under the bright moon, her cheeks reddened. She pulled away. "I do not mean to overstep myself, Holy King. But you yourself thrived on conquering the civilized world. You were unstoppable. Born a god among men to bring the glory of our empire to every corner of Nakania. Yet now you are but a king of one continent. Bored. Irritable. Haggling over statecraft rather than bringing heathens to their knees. What can this fate have done to your pride, my love? What shall it do to your soul? Every day you weaken."

"Enough, Artassa." He held his hand out. "Enough. Save your impassioned speeches for another hour." He strode to the steps leading down to his private dock where his flagship, *Treshalaj*, creaked and moaned in the bobbing water. An ache passed through him. How he longed to sail. To escape this shrinking kingdom and find some new land where storytellers and bards and painters dwelt.

He bowed his head as Artassa's sandaled feet padded closer.

"You mourn the storyteller this night," she whispered. "I should have seen. I am sorry, my husband."

He angled away from her touch as he sensed it. "Leave me, Artassa. I do not desire company right now."

Artassa's warmth pulled away. Her sandals slapped the stones as she walked toward the palace, then her steps faltered. A gasp broke the stillness of the night. "My Holy King!"

Aredel whirled and stared upward. A coiling wreath of flame wheeled above the domed palace, its center expanding like a dark mouth as the fire descended toward the golden dome. Shouts rose as guards and Blood Knights discovered the same horror.

The flames expanded further, reaching toward the courtyard, fanning out to swallow the entire hill upon which the palace stood.

Aredel bolted to Artassa and caught her wrist. "Run!" He dragged her toward the nearest stairs as the heat of the blooming flames swept over them. Screams erupted from the palace—hundreds of them. Aredel didn't look back. He reached the first step and yanked Artassa down after him. She came willingly, silently, and he thanked the gods of war that his first wife had always been sensible.

Several hundred yards down, the stairs gave way to the docks. Salty wind tossed the scent and taste of fish and seaweed at them as Aredel sprinted to the flagship.

Its skeleton crew stood on the deck, eyeing the firestorm, until someone shouted, “Lower the gangplank! The Blood King is here!”

“Look!” cried another.

Aredel glanced up the hill toward the palace and found it ablaze, flames pouring from its bones to consume the hill and all structures upon it. Fire raced down the steps as though it *knew* where Aredel had fled.

He spun. “Abandon ship! Dive into the sea!” He dragged Artassa to the water’s edge. “Jump, now!”

She obeyed and plunged into the dark water. As savage heat reached for his back, singeing the ends of his hair, Aredel leapt into the cold ocean and let himself sink, down, down. Away from the wrathful flames. Away from the destruction of his home. Into the abyss.

He opened his eyes and found others swimming in the same silence, now lighted by the fire’s influence. Flames danced over the waves, perhaps seeking him.

The memory of the dread voice slithered back into his mind: *I have not forgotten. I will not rest until you burn.*

CHAPTER 6
FROM THE WOODS

Kajsa stepped outside Ingrid's turf house and patted her leg to call Raum over. She drank in a breath of frigid air as the wolf rose from his haunches, shook snow off his black and silver fur, and trotted to her side. He always visited in the mornings before Axel stirred in his own abode. She welcomed Raum's presence on her daily walk to the village proper.

The silence of dawn rang in Kajsa's ears as she patted the wolf's head. Pink light spread over the snowcapped peaks, tinged gold, casting a glow over the deep swells of snow covering the world like a woven blanket.

The wolf nuzzled his nose into Kajsa's mitten and whined.

"Shh, Raum." She pulled off her mitten to scratch behind his ear. "We mustn't disturb the Snowblinds." She cast a furtive glance toward the distant canyon between the mountains, caped in snow and crowned in ice. Avalanches were too common this time of year when the spring thaw loosened the sheets of rime.

With a large empty satchel dangling from one shoulder, she plowed her way to the cleared path leading toward the Elderhouse and surrounding turf houses. Smoke rose from the chimneys in dark columns. Beyond the nestled structures, Kajsa's eyes tracked the road trailing into the distant valley where Tild, the circular city-state of Frostfire Canton, winked like diamonds in the morning glow under its coverlet of fresh snow. Dark lines marked the roads spanning out to the surrounding villages like spokes in a wagon wheel, defining the Canton's reach.

Her stomach writhed. Ingrid needed supplies, and if the merchants didn't venture uphill today, Kajsa must brave the bustling markets of Tild. After that unseasonable blizzard, they likely wouldn't come.

Perhaps Axel will join me if I ask.

Her fingers sought Raum's neck, and the wolf bumped up against her leg to let her reach him. They neared the lodge where movement snagged Kajsa's gaze. A small crowd of villagers bundled in fur-lined capes gathered at the front doors as though listening to someone inside. Curiosity reeled Kajsa toward the doors, but as a villager glanced her way she flinched back and hurried down the street toward the market square, shoulders hunched, chin lowered, bangs hanging in her face.

An empty space met her where the merchants usually set up shop. She sighed as Raum keened a question.

"Nothing, Raum. Just means a trip into Tild. You can't aid me there."

She turned around to study the Elderhouse. More villagers huddled at the doors.

"Wonder what's going on." Should she retrace her steps to find out?

Don't waste time just to avoid the inevitable.

Her heart skipped a beat as she recalled the stranger in the death chamber. His peculiar gold eyes. The air of sorrow enveloping his frame.

"Morning, Ky."

She yelped and spun, slinging a hand over her heart. Axel stood behind her, slapping his mittened hands together to ward off the chill, bundled in an impressive fur coat and cap. His smile inspired warmth like a summer sunbeam.

He winked. "Didn't mean to scare you."

"Don't sneak up on a soul if you mean not to," she said, managing a glare.

He shrugged as his eyes drifted down to his pet wolf. "Raum, O treacherous friend. Why always this favoring of Kajsa, hm? I'll stop feeding you, you mooching cheat."

Kajsa chuckled. "He likes Ingrid's turf house for the rabbits. There are so many up there on the ridge."

"Doubt that's the only reason, eh, Raum?" Axel stretched out a hand, and the wolf trotted forward to receive an affectionate chin scratch through the mitten. As Axel straightened, a frown dusted his lips. "What goes on at the Elderhouse?"

"I really don't know." Kajsa let out a cloudy breath. "The crowd is growing."

"Let's go see." Axel started toward the lodge.

"Hold on, Xel. I must go to Tild for Ingrid's—"

"I'll come with you, but let's find out what's got everyone buzzing first." He continued toward the lodge. Kajsa caught up with him and matched his pace, though her chest constricted the nearer they got to the crowd. So many people...

A voice drifted through the open doors, deep, melodic, familiar.

Kajsa didn't need to stand on tiptoe and peer inside to know who had seized the attention of all. The stranger from the blizzard spoke in even, calm tones.

"...bent on conquering the world. I longed to escape before another tyrant rose in his stead. All the northern countries do is plan for war. It's all they've ever done since Cavalin the Great fell to Tallat's sword."

Murmurs hissed and flicked around Kajsa. Norvians well knew the casualties of that long-ago war.

Axel, tall for his eighteen years, climbed to his tiptoes and stared over the clustered crowd. "He's sitting with the council. Looks improved since last night."

Kajsa tugged on his sleeve. "Let's go, Xel. Ingrid needs—"

"Right." He rocked back to his heels.

"Wait. Boy." The stranger's voice was louder, and sharp as an icicle.

Axel froze, then rolled to his tiptoes again. "Me, sir?"

"Yes," said the stranger. "You are the one who found me in the storm."

The crowds parted to allow a line of sight between Axel and the stranger.

Axel grinned. "More like Raum did. He's my wolf. Raised him from a cub."

"Clever to train a wolf." The stranger smiled where he sat upon a lounge, wrapped in furs. Sorrow and loss capped that smile, and Kajsa's heart panged. The man lifted a hand from the furs and beckoned. "Come here if you would." His voice, soft, caressing, nearly pulled Kajsa forward as Axel trod into the Elder-house. She yanked herself back at the last second. When Axel reached the lounge, the man searched his eyes. "What is your name?"

"Axel, son of Treyo."

"I am Navolleth. I thank you for your service to me."

Axel shrugged. "Only a madman would've left you there."

A light flickered in Navolleth's strange eyes. They were truly gold. "Only a heartless madman—but that someone else *could* have doesn't diminish what you *did*." His fingers brushed Axel's sleeve. "I hope to return the favor someday."

Axel chuckled. "I hope that's never necessary."

"True." Navolleth's eyes slid to Kajsa. "A healer?"

Axel tracked his gaze. "Oh, yes. In training, at least. She's also a seamstress. Best in the Frostfire Canton."

Navolleth nodded toward her. Kajsa willed herself to smile back, longing to be on her way. In Tild, no one knew her. No one would demand she conquer her shyness and learn to communicate. The man's gaze lingered and Kajsa ducked her head. Raum whimpered at her side, and she bent down to pet him, glad of the distraction.

"I'd better get going. Heading for Tild this morning." Axel's voice sent a thrill of relief through Kajsa's soul.

"We will talk later, Axel," said Navolleth.

"I look forward to it." Axel's boots tramped across the floor and out onto the carved log porch. "Let's go, Ky."

She straightened up and nodded as she stepped onto the snowy road. "We'll need snowshoes."

They trudged to the carpenter's hut on the southern end of the village and fitted the long, webbed shoes over their boots.

As Kajsa tested her shoe straps, she glanced toward the Elderhouse. "He frightens me."

A lopsided smile crooked Axel's mouth. "Ky, *everyone* frightens you."

"Not you."

"I scared you just this morning."

She sighed. "You know that's different. Ready?" She stabbed her pole into the snow, gauging the depth of the drifts.

He stood up and waved his hand down the snow-driven path. "Let's go."

They walked together behind Raum who dove and burrowed

in the snow searching for rabbits and birds along the wide trail. The stillness of the woods to either side of the mountain path soaked into Kajsa's being. Sunlight danced between the naked branches above and painted patches across the sparkling snow before her feet. The crunch of the wooden snowshoes alone broke the quiet until Axel let out a sigh.

Kajsa peeked at him. A crease drew lines between his eyebrows.

"What's wrong, Xel?"

He shrugged. "Just restless. We all thought the storm would last for days, or we'd not have turned back. Of course, after discovering that Navolleth fellow lodged in a snowbank, I suppose we had no choice. He'd have died of exposure."

Kajsa frowned at her feet. "Perhaps. Yet there was nothing wrong with him—not even frostbite."

"He's lucky, then. Don't sound so disappointed."

Kajsa's cheeks warmed. "I—I'm not disappointed. I'm glad he's all right. It's not that..."

Axel chuckled. "Why does he bother you?"

She shrugged. "Just something." She reached out to brush one pole against a branch as she passed a listing fir tree. The faint aroma of pine curled around her face. "He looks very sad, doesn't he?"

Axel missed a step. "Sad, how?"

"His eyes."

"His..." Axel laughed. The sound sent a bird fluttering skyward. "Ky, you're the oddest girl. How could you see that in the dark last night or clear across the room just now? Your imagination's gotten away from you."

She fidgeted with her poles as her face grew hotter. "You're right. I—I don't know what I saw."

He lightly pushed her. Laughing, she staggered sideways

before she regained the path. They labored on, crunching snow, listening to the birds twittering overhead. Raum disappeared into the woods and returned soon with a bloody rabbit in his maw.

Kajsa flinched away when he dropped it at her feet.

"Good job, Raum." Axel stooped to scratch the wolf's ears. "Eat. Don't waste your breakfast."

Kajsa quickened her step to avoid watching the wolf eat. Axel caught up.

"Your trouble, Ky, is not sticking up for yourself. You need to be bold."

She shrugged. "You're bold enough for both of us."

He shook his head as a grin stretched over his fair face. "I might not always be around. Something might—"

"Don't." Her heart leapt into her throat. "Please don't."

"Sorry." He laid his mittened hand on her shoulder. "I'm not vanishing. I won't leave you alone."

She swallowed and barred the image of Father's corpse from her mind. "Thank you, Xel."

THEY TUCKED their snowshoes among the trees outside the Canton proper, and Axel commanded Raum to hide and wait for them.

As they entered the city-state proper, the clamor and bustle of Tild overwhelmed Kajsa's senses. Stringent aromas battered her nostrils. Shouts and laughter filled her hearing. Thankfully, Axel stayed close and at each wooden stall stuffed with wares he negotiated for the thread and needles, as well as the alcohol Ingrid needed for her tinctures, and bolts of cloth. Haggling over the cost of goods had never been Kajsa's strongest point.

Once Kajsa placed the last of the purchases into her satchel, Axel led her from the merchants' stalls, past the throng of Canton-dwellers, to the river rolling on Tild's quiet east side. The scent of mud and fish hung in the chilly air. Chunks of ice flowed along the lazy, slithering river whose banks overflowed in the season's first thaw.

"There, that's progress." Axel slipped his mittens off and pointed. "We'll end up with a kind of summer after all, no matter the weird weather."

"I hope so." Kajsa shifted the weight of her bundle. "But if we have another early freeze like last y—"

Axel whirled and poked her wrinkled brow with his finger. "None of your gloom. Not today. It's a pleasant morning and—" He cut off as waterfowl bugled overhead. "*See*? Geese!"

Kajsa lifted her eyes and caught the silvery flash of sunlight against the beating wings. The v-line of geese flew south toward the colder climes of Norva. She let herself smile. "That's a very good sign."

"That it is," said Axel. "So, stop fretting."

She ducked her head. "How do you always tell?"

Axel stooped and plucked up a stone. He tossed it into the sinuous water and watched it skip five times before he answered. "You're an open book, Ky. I can read you like I might a deer." He chuckled. "You're *a lot* like a deer."

She eyed the ripples in the river where the stone sank. "Is that good?"

"It's not bad." He angled to eye her and winked. "Just don't let me shoot you by accident." His fingers flexed and stretched like he held an imaginary bowstring and drew it taut. His fingers flew back, releasing the invisible string.

Kajsa smiled faintly. "If you shoot me, I'll come back as a spirit and haunt your every step until you apologize."

He leaned close and brushed a finger against her cheek. Her heart missed a beat. "I'd be glad," he said. "If I ever hurt you, I'd deserve it." His eyes darted to her lips, then he pulled away. "Hand me your satchel. We'd best get back before dusk settles in."

Kajsa glimpsed the sun, already sinking by inches toward the western mountains. By midafternoon little sunlight would remain to brighten the path. She nodded and offered Axel the bulging bundle. He accepted it, and the two walked toward the northern end of Tild where Raum waited beyond the city-state proper within the border of the woods.

At the northern gate, three guards leaned against the wall, chatting and laughing. Axel waved. They waved back while Kajsa tried to shrink inside her cape. One laughed.

"Be bold," Axel murmured, but Kajsa tugged him past the guards and out through the open gates.

The scent of sweat and hay gave way to the crisp aroma of snow and free wind. Kajsa took a deep whiff, glad to be away from crowds, from noise, from eyes. Raum crashed free of the brittle undergrowth and wagged his bushy tail. Axel clapped his hands and the wolf bounded to his side with a playful yip.

The three strolled along the thawing path until they reached the upward slope where snow had packed tight and slick. Shadows fell heavily over the road. Kajsa retrieved her snowshoes from the fallen tree where she'd stashed them and handed Axel's to him. They sat on the rotting trunk and strapped their shoes on with deft fingers. Finished, Kajsa rose and gathered up her poles.

A twig snapped deep within the forest.

Raum growled.

Kajsa's blood ran cold.

Axel sprang upright and turned to face the shadows. His

hand fell to his short sword. Another twig snapped. He dropped the satchel to the ground with a dull thud.

"Is it an animal?" Kajsa's whispered question hung in the air like a thread stretched too tight.

A cloud crept over the sun.

Something rustled in the trees.

Snap.

Axel shoved Kajsa back as he lifted his sword. A dark *thing*—large like a wolf—leapt at them from a cluster of firs, long beetle-black claws extended. Axel's sword caught the claws; he swung right, and the creature was flung into a naked oak with a nauseating *thunk.*

Two more creatures lunged from the trees.

"Axel!" screamed Kajsa.

He whirled, then danced back, flinching as a claw nicked his cheek when the creature flew past him. It landed on the path. It was like a canine, yet its body was misshapen, its chest too large for its long legs and small head. Matted black fur, dusted with snow, stuck up around exposed bones, as though the beast were fleshless. Its muzzle, long and narrow, stretched back to reveal bloody teeth, sharper than a wolf's. Eyes of molten fire glared at Kajsa and Axel. A rumbling growl exuded from the creature's unholy maw. Its claws, eight inches long, dug into the frozen earth as it hunched, preparing to spring.

The third creature lunged. Axel's sword scraped against bone as he answered. He grunted and slid backward, toward the second waiting beast.

Heart clambering, Kajsa wrenched her snowshoes loose and tossed them, then raced toward the creature just as it leapt at Axel's back. She swung one of her poles. It connected and cracked. The beast stumbled sideways.

"Ky, stay back!" Axel shouted.

She dropped the broken pole and adjusted her grip on the second. "I can't do that."

The first monster, lying under the oak tree, twitched. The beast she'd hit shook itself and stood, turning those blazing eyes on her as its ears fell back. The cloud fell away from the sun, highlighting fangs glistening with blood and drool.

Raum slammed into the beast.

"No!" Kajsa shrieked.

Axel fell backward with a cry. He clutched his sword against his chest—one palm flat against the blade—the creature pressed atop him. Its claws were lodged in his shoulders. Only his blade used as a shield kept the beast from mauling his face.

Kajsa swung her second pole. *Whack.* The creature snarled but didn't budge.

"Run!" Axel gasped out.

"No." She swung again, but a heavy weight caught the pole, and she stumbled back. The scent of rot rolled over her. She fell hard, then craned her head. The first creature held the pole in its mouth. It bit down, snapping it in two, eyes burning like hellfire.

Kajsa buried her head in her arms. *Mountain gods, spare us please!*

"*Jiavtek drio ooe*! *Quii dac*!"

The voice thundered over the sky, deep, rumbling. Full of might.

Kajsa dropped her arms and stared heavenward. Had the gods answered her prayer so directly?

Movement on the road seized her gaze. A figure in a cloak of deep blue velvet stood between the bowing trees, one hand lifted, a silver flame flickering above the open palm.

The beasts cowered, and one whimpered, its tail between its bony legs. As one, the creatures fled into the wood the way they'd come. Silence reigned. The cloaked figure held still as a stone. It rippled, then faded away.

The road stood empty.

Kajsa stared for several heartbeats, sweat trickling down her face, mind reeling.

A groan snatched her attention.

"Xel!"

She crawled through the snow to his side. He lay in his own blood; one shoulder glistened red in the gloomy pathway where slick blood seeped from an open wound around his torn coat. Kajsa dug into the pouch tied at her hip and grabbed a packet of powdered yarrow. She sprinkled it over the wound as she blinked back tears. Axel's face had lost all its color.

"Hold on," she whispered, stroking his cheek with her free hand. He moaned, eyelids fluttering.

Once she'd cleaned the wound, Kajsa wrenched open her satchel. She rummaged among the parcels, tossing several aside, until she found a bolt of cloth she'd bought for a new dress. She ripped strips off and soon had the wound bound. Finished, she pulled off Axel's snowshoes, wrapped his arm around her shoulders, then dragged him to his feet. His weight folded her forward, but she set her teeth and stumbled up the trail toward home, leaving her purchases behind.

A whimper sounded behind her. She glanced back and found Raum limping toward her, a red gash along the top of his matted head.

"Come on, Raum. Good boy." She shifted Axel's weight. "C'mon."

Raum reached her side and stayed near as they trudged up the path.

More than an hour passed. Kajsa's head pounded with every

step. Her lungs burned. In the growing gloom of dusk, she glimpsed flickering lights ahead, beyond the path.

Almost there.

Axel's breaths rasped near her ear. His flesh radiated heat.

This was no mere flesh wound. Had the beast's claws been poisonous?

The urgency of his plight lent Kajsa strength beyond anything she'd known. Sweat poured down her back, and hair plastered to her forehead in sticky clumps. One foot. The other. Step. Another step.

Don't give up.

Raum yipped.

Kajsa lifted her head and squinted into the shadows. A lantern bobbed toward her.

"Hallo!" she cried.

Footsteps crunched snow, and a figure materialized around a bend. "Kajsa?" The voice belonged to Frit, the carpenter. He sucked in air. "S'that Axel?"

Kajsa blinked back tears. Relief teemed over her limbs. "He's badly hurt. Please help me."

"Let me take him." Frit raced to her side and offered the lantern in exchange.

Together, they conquered the last several yards and entered the village. Raum trotted ahead, and Kajsa pinned her eyes on the wolf to keep her steps steady. Frit carried Axel straight to the Elderhouse where villagers gathered most nights, and Kajsa trailed into the warmth on his heels. A blazing fire thawed her stiff joints. She plucked off her cape and mittens as the fragrances of cooking pork and boiling turnips assaulted her senses.

"I need hot water," she whispered.

Footsteps darted off. Voices crowded Kajsa's ears, tones filled with questions, but she heeded none as Frit laid Axel on a fur-covered couch. Kajsa knelt before the couch and touched Axel's skin. So hot.

"What happened, Kajsa?" asked Frit, perhaps not for the first time.

She swallowed hard. "Creatures. In the woods. Attacked us. Dark things."

The voices droned on, worry mingling with disbelief. But they *should* believe her. Fa had died the same way.

Don't die, Xel. Live!

A hand fell on Kajsa's shoulder. She craned her neck to stare up into a strange face. The man from the snow.

He gently moved her aside and knelt before Axel. His slender pale fingers pried one of Axel's eyes open. He leaned near and murmured words to himself. Unraveled the makeshift bandages. Someone returned with water, and the man—Navolleth, wasn't it?—plucked up the sopping rag bobbing on the surface of the pot to dab at Axel's wound.

The boy hissed, then fell still.

"Let me work," said Navolleth. "Take the girl somewhere she might rest."

Kajsa resisted the hands trying to pull her to her feet. "I'm staying."

Navolleth's gaze found hers. His gold eyes danced in the firelight. "Kajsa, I will save him. Please rest."

A wet nose nudged Kajsa's hand. She gasped and looked to her right. Raum crouched on the floor, blood crusted on his head.

"Oh, Raum. I'm so sorry."

Navolleth spoke. "I'll see to the wolf as well. Someone, take the girl. She needs to bathe and sleep."

Strong arms lifted Kajsa. She stared into the face of the village butcher before her vision blurred. Her limbs grew heavy as a blacksmith's anvil. The scent of woodsmoke and blood mingled in her nostrils, so much like the night Father died.

"Lucky you thought to send someone out to find them, Lord Navolleth," Frit said from a distant place.

Lord? He's a lord?

"They had been gone too long," answered Navolleth. "Woods are dangerous at night, especially now."

Why especially now? Kajsa struggled to keep her mind alert, to hear on, but hues bled into blackness, and she sank down, down into colorless dreams.

CHAPTER 7
BORDER NEWS

"I won't stay behind, Lord Father." Jetekesh kept his tone firm.

The king eyed the prince seated beside him, faint lines etched into his brow. He cupped his hands before him at the head of the table. His blue eyes flickered in the glow of a dozen candles servants had lighted to banish the early morning gloom.

Prince Jetekesh clenched his fists to fight his stirring impatience. Rille and Sir Yeshton sat to his right, both intent and silent. Across from Jetekesh, left of the king, sat Kethalas. The Shinacian's slitted eyes had rarely left the prince's face since they had convened.

Father's hesitating too much. Say something. Back up your argument.

The prince drew a breath to steady his resolve. "We'll need two groups—one to travel to KryTeer, and one to search for the Arch in the Clanslands. I'll be among one of these companies." He leaned forward. "I just need that to be clear."

The king nodded slowly. "I understand. I won't prevent it,

though I'm reluctant to send my only son and heir into such danger."

Next to Kethalas, the clansfolk, Dakarai and Anenyasha, had claimed chairs after Lord Father had sent for them to join the impromptu council.

"He would be kept safe in my company, Your Majesty," said Dakarai.

Jetekesh glanced at the dark-skinned man and swallowed a protest. He didn't *need* to be protected. He needed to help. But Dakarai couldn't know that about him—couldn't know how much Jetekesh yearned to prove his mettle.

Better to show my ability than to argue the point with a stranger.

"I appreciate your offer, Dakarai," Lord Father said, "however, I'm not certain how far I can trust you yet. Wherever my son goes, his protector must also go."

Jetekesh bristled. A shadow lurked in the chamber's darkness behind him—a brawny, silent, bearded man in his late forties meant to take Tifen's place after the former protector had died. But Sir Lafe wasn't Tifen. He didn't have the man's quiet dignity. His reassuring presence. Sir Lafe had a hardened face pinched in a perpetual frown. Streaks of silver lined his brunette hair drawn back in a ponytail to trail down his thick neck. A trimmed beard contrasted with his dark blue eyes. He was an impressive, solid man, from a line of nobles who excelled in knighthood.

Rille shifted in the chair beside Jetekesh. She lifted a hand. "Lord Uncle, I wish to go with Sir Yeshton to KryTeer. I fear the warning in my dream comes too late—so my instinct tells me—and I worry for Anadin."

A chill climbed Jetekesh's spine. Rille had described a dream filled with fire and death. The great city Bahadronn had burned, and a dark clawed hand descended from the sky to claim the souls of the fallen. Jetekesh prayed it was a figurative vision, but Rille couldn't say one way or another.

Lord Father ran a hand over his face. Nearly a year had passed since his illness had been cured by King Aredel of KryTeer, but the man still showed signs of weariness. In moments Lord Father thought no one looked, his eyes bore a haunted mien. How much came from the poison, *traveria*, and how much was from years of marriage to the treacherous Bareene, Jetekesh couldn't guess. He wasn't certain he wished to know.

"Very well, Rille," said Lord Father in low tones. "I know better than to block you from something you've set your mind on. But *please* be careful. Losing your father is sorrow enough to bear."

"I understand, Lord Uncle." Rille stood. "I've plans to make; I'll leave you to make yours. Come, Sir Yeshton." She started for the door, then turned back. Her amber eyes softened as she met Jetekesh's gaze. "Farewell, cousin. We journey separately this time."

"Be safe," he said as his heart twisted.

The little girl and her guardian slipped from the room. The door snicked shut.

Sir Lafe moved a little closer in Rille's absence. The prince turned back to those seated at the table, ignoring his protector.

"With Rille departing for KryTeer," said Lord Father, "that leaves us to form the company meant for the Clanslands." His gaze fell on Jetekesh. "You will lead them, my son."

Jetekesh squared his shoulders. "Thank you, Lord Father."

The king turned to Dakarai. "Please guide him true. I sincerely hope you and my son will discover the Arch to Shinac within your homeland so that help from beyond can be obtained and all the dark magics seeping through may be purged. Saints go with you."

"If I may, Your Majesty." Sir Lafe stepped up to the table. "Why not have them journey with Lady Rille to KryTeer? Surely, her vision implies that another Arch stands *there*, and safety in numbers will be better guaranteed."

"I favor taking no chances, Sir Lafe," said Lord Father. "There may be an Arch in KryTeer. There may be an Arch in the Clanslands. Wouldn't it be better to find *both* rather than gamble on finding only one? We can't confirm the existence of either Arch. We can only hope."

Jetekesh drummed his fingers on the table. "I'd like to leave as soon as possible, Lord Father."

The king inclined his head. "Preparations will begin at once—but you'll not leave until I'm satisfied with each man picked to join your company. Rest for now, Kesh. This afternoon you'll be on your way."

Jetekesh climbed to his feet and considered Kethalas. "What of you, my lord?"

"I shall also rest before our journey if that is acceptable, Prince Jetekesh." The man stood, long hair rippling against his back. His scar stood out in the candlelight.

"Of course," said Jetekesh. "A room will be provided."

They left the council room together. A waiting servant led Kethalas toward another wing of the palace. As Jetekesh watched the Shinacian visitor depart, an ache clawed at his throat. If only he could return to those few precious days spent in Shinac alongside Jinji, days when he'd learned what friendship meant and how it felt to carry it.

Sir Lafe stepped up to Jetekesh's side. "Your Highness?"

Jetekesh grimaced and strode toward his chambers to sleep—if he could catch it.

'Do you really think you can survive the wilds, dearheart?'

Jetekesh squeezed his ears shut against Mother's bodiless voice as he skipped down the palace's front steps, taking two at a time. He struck the gravel drive and watched pebbles skitter away. He'd dressed in his plainest garb and a nondescript brown cloak he'd borrowed from his manservant. Hopefully, that would disguise his rank, at least.

Seven horses stood before him, saddled, along with a wagon filled with provisions. The clansfolk, Dakarai and Anenyasha, met Jetekesh at the bottom of the steps and eyed their borrowed mounts.

The woman murmured something foreign to Dakarai, who grinned and nodded.

Sir Lafe descended the steps next, along with Lord Father.

The king strode to Jetekesh's side and rested a hand on his shoulder. "Take no unnecessary risks, Kesh. Swear to it." A weak smile lifted his lips. "I'll not be called overprotective, but I *do* want you to come home safely."

"I understand." Jetekesh wrapped his arms around Lord Father.

The king held him in a firm embrace, then patted his back and released him. "I love you, son."

"And I love you, Lord Father." He drew back, swiped at his eyes, and turned to inspect the company. Aside from Sir Lafe, Kethalas, Dakarai, and Anenyasha, two Amantieran knights also in nondescript clothes stood near the horses, along with a wagoner. Not many. Good. Jetekesh didn't welcome the idea of drawing notice from people within the Clanslands.

Eight is still noticeable.

He frowned and turned to Lord Father. "I request the two knights remain here, sire."

The king shook his head. "No, my son. I'm inclined to place

my trust in all your companions, but I'll feel better sending you into the northern mountains with three strong Amantieran knights. Oblige me."

"As you will, sire." Jetekesh bowed. As he straightened up, his heart hitched. He must go off into the wilds of Amantier's northeastern border and beyond with naught but strange guides and a handful of warriors at his back.

I'm still much better prepared for this than my last excursion. A smile tugged at his lips, soft, edged with sorrow. *Jinji would go. He'd not even hesitate.*

Jetekesh swiveled and strode to his buckskin stallion. It tossed its dark mane and nickered as Jetekesh stroked its muzzle. "Let's ride true, hm, Hickory?" He swung up into the saddle. Leather creaked beneath his weight. The musty scent of the stallion drifted into his nose, strong and welcome. He angled himself to watch the others in the company mount. The wagoner, a thin man in his fifties, climbed onto his seat and took up the reins of his two horses.

Jetekesh found the king's face. "Farewell, Lord Father. I will return victorious."

"May the One God guard you, Kesh."

"Move out!" Jetekesh's voice rang across the courtyard. He took the lead, guiding the company through the palace gates and out into Kavacos as the sun bore down on his back. Children watched him ride past, ogling. A merchant halted his cart to bow his head. Two washerwomen darted out of his path and curtsied. Jetekesh smiled grimly before he rode on.

At the northern city gates, the watch raised the portcullis and saluted. Jetekesh waved at them before he urged Hickory out into the rolling hills. The Ruins of Glayn on the foothills before the Flute Mountains glittered under the bright, cloudless sky as

Jetekesh steered Hickory northeast toward the seldom-used mountain road.

Kethalas's mount came level with him and matched his canter. The man's silvery eyes glowed in the sunlight. "How far is it to these Clanslands, Your Highness?"

Dakarai answered from his horse behind Jetekesh. "Using this route, passing through Shing, will take us three weeks to reach the border to my country. If the weather is good."

Jetekesh narrowed a considering look on the Flute Mountains. Despite the lush green of their lower summits, dark clouds hid the highest peaks where snow fell three-quarters of the year. Few braved the roads of Bard Pass before midsummer. He glanced over his shoulder. "Was the weather good as you crossed the range?"

"We did not come this way," Dakarai said. "We traveled by ship across KriShen Bay and then crossed under these mountains through a tunnel. But though it is a faster route, it is not as safe. Better to travel this road."

Jetekesh's brow knitted. "I'd wondered how you made it to Kavacos in a single week. But I've never heard of any tunnels under the mountains."

"It is not spoken of outside the tribes. Forgive me for saying so, but Amantierans would not be welcome to enter it, nor would you relish the journey."

Jetekesh stared ahead and scowled. *If tunnels come into Amantier, we should know of them and be able to use them. I must tell Father when I return.*

The company raced the wind to the foothills and up an ill-kempt road. No villages stood in their immediate path; only one had been settled between Kavacos and Bard Pass, and that sat at the very roots of the mountain range. Its folk were considered the stoutest and most stubborn—and by some reports, even savage—of Amantier.

Moss Province.

Jetekesh had come this far north only once, despite its proximity to Rose Province. He'd been eight years old when Lord Father took him to meet the lord of Moss Province in the Keep of the Falls.

He'd never forget that singular experience.

Lakes dotted the earth and mirrored the sky as the foothills rose and fell under the hooves of nine horses. Soon the shadows of the Flute Mountains painted gray hues across the green grass. Jetekesh slowed his pace.

Clouds scraped the lower peaks, threatening snow. Jetekesh drew a warmer cloak from his saddlebags and clasped it at his throat, then sank his heels into Hickory's flanks. "Ha!"

The company flew up the rising slope. The ground leveled and revealed the village of Peat. Smoke rose from chimneys, and few villagers wandered the meager green. A well sat in the dead center of Peat, where a flock of sheep grazed under the watchful care of a little girl.

Sitting in the grass close by, three Shingese travelers ate bread and cheese. The foreign travelers eyed the company with interest while the little girl bowed low, then scampered toward a hut.

What are Shingese doing here this time of year?

The western trade season didn't start for another month.

A soldier bearing the heraldry of Moss Province sprinted toward Jetekesh's horse and bowed his head. "Your Highness?"

Jetekesh blinked. He wore nothing to distinguish himself, not a circlet or crest. How had he been so easily recognized? "Don't mind us. We're on our way to the Keep of the Falls."

"Yes, Your Highness. Do you require water? I'll fetch it for you."

"Thank you, no. We must be on our way."

Movement caught his gaze. One of the Shingese travelers stood and brushed her hands down her long tunic and short breeches. Jetekesh's heart twinged. Her features, so much like Jinji's, speared his soul.

She approached, cautious like a prowling fox, her dark slanted eyes keen.

Saddles creaked as the Amantieran knights reached for their swords.

A few feet away, the Shingese traveler pressed her hands together and bowed in Shingese fashion. "Forgive me, Prince Jetekesh, but if I may delay your journey a moment?"

Sir Lafe nudged his horse closer, his sword partially unsheathed.

Jetekesh glanced toward the shadowed pass, one league beyond Peat. "Say on."

"I have heard word of a distressing nature." The woman's tones were level and smooth. "It involves you, Your Highness."

He fought back a sigh. Now wasn't the time for distractions. "Oh?"

"I understand you imprisoned a storyteller called Jinji. He hailed from Shing."

Jetekesh stiffened and met the woman's black eyes. "That was over ten months ago."

"Yes, Your Highness. There are rumors that he was executed shortly thereafter."

Jetekesh swallowed against a lump in his throat. "Executed? No. Absolutely not." He gripped the reins tighter. "Jinji was...my friend."

The woman flinched. "*Was*, my lord?"

A desire for strong drink swept over Jetekesh. "Yes, peasant. He's dead. He died of an illness ten months ago." His voice cracked as his cheeks warmed with shame. *Don't take it out on her.* He loosened his grip and raked a hand through his long golden hair. "Forgive me. I shouldn't lose my temper."

"Nothing to forgive, Your Highness." The woman backed away. "I'm sorry to trouble you." She bowed and turned to walk back to her companions.

"Wait."

She paused and glanced back. A tear slid down her cheek. "Yes, Your Highness?"

"Why did you seek Jinji?" He nudged Hickory toward her. Lafe made a warning noise in his throat, but the prince ignored him. "Did you know the storyteller or only of him?"

The woman brushed the tear from her cheek. "I knew him, my lord, though not well. We met only once."

Jetekesh offered a smile. "That's usually enough to care about him. It...it took me a lot longer. I'm dreadfully stubborn." He halted his stallion beside the woman. "What is your name?"

"Song, my lord."

He eyed her companions: a young man near his age, and another boy of perhaps twelve or thirteen years. Jetekesh turned back to Song. "Why did you seek the storyteller?"

She grimaced. "For reasons no longer relevant." Her eyes dropped to the ground.

"Are you certain?"

She looked up. "Well...no, my lord. Not certain." She glanced at her two Shingese companions. The older one shook his head. Song turned back to Jetekesh. "It's rather a delicate matter."

"You needn't confide in me," Jetekesh said. "But if you, too, were Jinji's friend, I would help where I might." He glanced at the mountains. "Though I'm in a hurry myself." The clouds curled lower now. "If there's nothing I can do, I'd best carry on."

"Of course, Your Highness." Song bowed.

As Jetekesh lifted his reins to gently lash them, his gaze skimmed over the older Shingese youth. The stranger lifted his chin and stared back with intense defiance.

"Wait, my lord."

Jetekesh lowered his gaze to Song.

She padded nearer. "There is something you should know."

"All right?"

As she drew a breath, the young Shingese man sprang up. He darted forward and caught her wrist. "Say nothing. Would you betray your own?"

She yanked her hand free of his. "This concerns Amantier as much as Shing."

"They're our *enemies*."

Jetekesh scowled. "There has been a truce between our countries for eight months now."

The Shingese man glowered up at him. "Eight months have done nothing to heal our hurts from your occupation of over twenty years."

A blast of ire scored Jetekesh's veins. He leaned out of his saddle and stared into the young man's black eyes. "You and I weren't even *born* when that occupation ended. My father the king ordered all Amantieran soldiers out of Shing the moment he took the throne from his sire. Those grievances have nothing to do with here and now."

"Words mean little, Amantieran swine," the young man spat out.

"Liu, *please*." Song pushed up beside him. "Forgive his disrespect, Your Highness. He's headstrong and tactless."

Jetekesh squared his shoulders and let a breeze stroke his face as he stifled his roiling wrath. "You were going to explain your purpose in seeking out Jinji, I believe."

"Yes, Your Highness." She shoved Liu back as he started to protest, then met Jetekesh's eyes. Hers were earnest and steady. "We fear..." Her hands curled into fists. "We fear something terrible lurks in Shing. Something dark that can influence the very disposition of a man. Something inhuman. We'd hoped Jinji might understand and purge such a thing."

Chills spidered up the prince's back. "What makes you suspect this?"

Song hesitated. Pain brightened her eyes. "Your Highness, do you know much of Emperor Majinglee and the Lotus Court?"

"No, not beyond a history of the occupation years." He glanced at Sir Lafe and the two knights whose names he couldn't recall. All wore fierce expressions. "I've heard a few stories. That Emperor Majinglee is a just man. Doting, even. Some have called him weak-willed; that his desire for peace outweighs his love of country and that's why so many other countries have invaded during his long reign. I'm not sure what to believe."

Song nodded. "While exaggerated, these rumors bear some truth. Enough to appreciate that he means well, even if he is sometimes unwise."

"Your point?"

She tugged on her tunic hem. "Do you believe him capable of mustering an army to invade Amantier?"

"Certainly not. He hasn't the initiative—nor enough backing in his own court to manage it."

Liu's face colored, and his jaw set.

"So it has been, alas," said Song. "And yet...a force *is* being mustered, and Shing looks to invade your fair lands. Something has changed Emperor Majinglee. He isn't himself."

Jetekesh tensed and whipped his head around to find Kethalas. "Might it be?"

The Shinacian man frowned beneath his hood. "It is very possible."

Jetekesh turned back to Song. "When did this change transpire?"

"Just over one week ago," answered Liu.

Jetekesh ran a hand over his face. "Then it's likely linked to the same chain of events. You're certain an army is on its way?"

Liu took a step forward. "Perhaps not yet, but several days ago the emperor ordered it so, and many answered. Despite your insistence that he has no backing, more than a few Shingese knights are eager to even the score with Amantier—and, indeed, KryTeer. It would not require much of a push."

Jetekesh grimaced up at the mountain pass. He wrung his reins tighter. "Then war is coming, likely helmed by *Erisyrdrel*. The king must be warned." The Keep of the Falls lay unseen along the perilous mountain road hours away—but it was nearer than Kavacos now. "We must ride on. We'll push for Lord Emerin's fortress and there discuss the best course of action. If we delay any longer, we tempt the weather."

Song caught Hickory's saddle. "Your Highness, please, do you know the source of the emperor's condition?"

"Unfortunately, I suspect so."

"But you're not going to tell us?" Liu folded his arms. "We didn't have to explain anything."

Jetekesh arched an eyebrow. "No, and *you* didn't plan to." He glanced at Song. "How will you proceed?"

She frowned. "My village isn't far from here, just across the border below the Flute Mountains—but I hate to go home and wait for the coming conflict. If I might help in some way..." She stood on tiptoes and peered into his eyes. "If you knew Jinji as a friend, you know I can be trusted."

Sir Lafe coughed.

Jetekesh glowered at the man. "Excuse me for a moment, Lady Song." He backed Hickory up until he came level with the knight. "Yes, Sir Lafe?"

The knight leaned close. "My prince, that is no mere Shingese peasant. Long have the knights of Amantier kept an eye on her."

"Is she a criminal?"

"She's the Lady of Crimson Lilies."

Jetekesh jerked his head around to eye the young woman. *This* was the Lady of Crimson Lilies, the lone sword dancer who'd single-handedly killed a dozen Blood Knights nearly six years ago?

Song watched with a sad smile, a hand resting on her hip. Liu and the nameless boy stood behind her, the latter nibbling the remnants of his breadcrust. A quiver of arrows was strapped to the boy's back.

Jetekesh scratched his jaw and nudged Hickory toward the Shingese travelers. He halted the stallion and stared down at Song. "Come with us to the Keep of the Falls. We can better discuss everything within the safety of its ramparts."

She scanned the riders until her eyes landed on Dakarai and Anenyasha. A frown dusted her lips. "Thank you, my lord, but I don't want to slow your progress. Your mission looks urgent."

"Yet it ties into your own. Come. You and your companions can ride in the wagon."

The three travelers exchanged looks. Liu shook his head. Song shrugged. The boy gazed between them, offering no opinion.

Song turned. "We accept your generous offer, Your Highness." She walked toward the wagon as Sir Lafe trotted his mare to Jetekesh's side.

"Your Highness, she's dangerous," the knight whispered.

As Liu and the boy hopped into the wagon just after Song, Jetekesh allowed himself a wolfish grin.

"So are we. Very." His gaze drifted to Kethalas. He had a secret weapon on his side. "Remember, Shing and Amantier aren't at war—not just yet. If we can prevent conflict, we must. Besides, if their story and my theory converge into one truth, we just gained a serious advantage."

Sir Lafe lifted his thick brows. "My lord?"

Jetekesh fastened his eyes on the eastern mountain range, hiding the sprawling rice fields of Shing. "We had much more to fear not knowing our enemy's position. If *Erisyrdrel* truly dwells in the emperor's court, hidden within a feeble body, we don't have to seek him out."

"It doesn't give us the means to slay him, Prince Jetekesh," said Dakarai.

"No. But that's why we're seeking the Arch." He gathered his reins. "Let's ride."

As they trotted from the townsite, onlookers stared from their windows. The village girl returned to her sheep, her mother at her side. They curtsied.

Jetekesh grimaced for the umpteenth time. "Is it the entourage that gives me away, Sir Lafe?"

"No, my prince. It's your demeanor."

Jetekesh kicked his horse into a faster gait as his stomach churned. *Is that good or bad?* He didn't bother to ask. On his list of concerns, it didn't rate very high. He could find out more later—preferably after beating the growing storm to the Keep of the Falls.

CHAPTER 8
THE MARK

They chased the clouds. As the horses conquered the heights of Bard Pass, snow fluttered from the silvery sky, and a harrowing wind screamed in Jetekesh's face. He hunched over his saddle horn and huddled into his double cloaks. The higher he climbed, the gladder he was of Hickory's body heat. Darkness descended early among the sharp slants of the pass, and patches of snow slickened the road.

A fog crept down the rocky sides to pool around the horses' legs. The prince slowed his stallion with some reluctance. Jetekesh squinted to make out the path, and Sir Lafe slipped ahead without a word. The prince allowed it, even though annoyance pricked his chest.

Let him do his job. What else is he good for?

That wasn't fair. Sir Lafe was as honorable as any other knight in the king's service. It wasn't his fault Tifen and Sir Palan had died in KryTeer.

It's my fault alone. Don't take it out on others.

Jetekesh gritted his teeth and let the guilt pour through him.

He could use it. *Must* use it to grow stronger. To not repeat the mistakes of his past.

The wagon rattled behind him. Jetekesh glanced back but nothing looked amiss. Shapes formed and dissipated in the fog. The damp air seeped into Jetekesh's clothes and hair until his bangs hung lank. He wetted his lips and willed his courage to wax. It was only fog. No fell creatures would stalk them here.

This was Lord Emerin's domain. He would never allow such a thing.

Someone started to whistle a tune. Jetekesh twisted in his saddle to find Dakarai bouncing along just behind him, smiling like the sun still shone. He whistled merrily. Beside him Anenyasha looked as grim as Jetekesh.

"Must you do that?" asked one of the knights.

"No. I mustn't." Dakarai flashed a broad grin. "But I like to."

"Let him if it pleases him, Sir Knight," said Jetekesh.

The high notes rang off the canyon walls. Jetekesh imagined that the fog thinned just a hair. His skin warmed just a breath.

As true night fell, the company halted to light lanterns hanging from the wagon. The wagoner took the lead as they continued up the pass.

Jetekesh nixed the idea of making camp and urged them to press on until the Keep of the Falls appeared.

It finally did, a sprawling fortress hovering eerily above the thick fog. Torches illuminated the sturdy walls hewn into the rock of the mountain. Above the roar of the six waterfalls surrounding three sides of the keep, a trumpet sounded their approach.

Jetekesh claimed the lead as he approached the thick gates. "Ho, the watch!"

"Who goes there?" a baritone voice called down.

"Prince Jetekesh and company. Is Lord Emerin within?"

"That he is, Your Highness. Welcome! We've been expecting you."

Jetekesh blinked.

How?

The gates rumbled aside on a hidden windlass. Knights flanked the path beyond in two columns. Torches guttered in rows behind them. Jetekesh entered the keep with a pang of relief. The wagon rolled in after him, and the rest filed in, hooves clattering on the cobblestones.

Jetekesh guided Hickory across the bailey and over a bridge spanning the raging river. The mist of the falls kissed his face, and water collected on his eyelashes. He dismounted Hickory on the bridge's far side and stared up at the imposing fortress. The standard of Moss Province—a white fox on a green field—snapped in the high winds. In the long history of Amantier none had ever breached this keep, and under Lord Emerin's watch none would consider trying.

The fortress doors swung open, and a figure—tall, fit, caped, with a sword at his hip—strode from the lighted corridor beyond. Lord Emerin downed the steps three at a time, feet certain despite the standing water and smears of ice. He reached Jetekesh and bowed low as he clapped a hand over his chest.

"Welcome to the Keep of the Falls, my prince. My abode is yours." Lord Emerin rose. Blond hair settled around his shoulders. He looked to be in his mid-thirties, yet a kind of agelessness sparked in his green eyes and flashed in his cat-like movements. He considered the company. "Come inside and warm up." His voice was a low, growling tone. "The wagon will be seen to."

Song, Liu, and their silent companion hopped down from the wagon.

Lord Emerin looked them up and down but said nothing before he swept Jetekesh inside. Few men commanded a crowd so well, so effortlessly, as did the master of the Keep of the Falls. Lord Father said nothing but good about him, yet something in Lord Emerin's mien had always unsettled Jetekesh.

The keep lord led Jetekesh through the high, spotless halls of the keep. Tapestries depicting Cavalin the Third and his sainted daughter Vashi covered nearly every wall, and lit sconces lined the corridors.

That's right. Emerin is descended from the ancient hero's blood through Saint Vashi.

All nobility was related in one way or another, but Jetekesh considered few to be kin. Only the descendants of Cavalin had any true claim to the Amantieran throne. Lord Emerin's House stood among the few with direct ties to that great man.

The keep lord led Jetekesh up several stairwells to a posh bedchamber where an enormous bed stood against the distant wall. Rugs littered the floor. A massive hearth contained a cheery fire. A decanter of wine and several goblets were clustered at a table near the door. A bath crouched near the hearth, steam rising from the water.

"Change if you wish, Your Highness," said Lord Emerin. "Food awaits you in the dining hall below."

"How did you hear of our coming, my lord?" Jetekesh asked.

Lord Emerin grinned like a tiger. "No one passes through my mountains unnoticed." He shrugged. "And your father sent a messenger pigeon ahead of you. A servant will guide you to supper when you're ready, Your Highness." He bowed and shut the door behind him.

Jetekesh turned and found a nightshirt, robe, and slippers spread out on the edge of the bed. A manservant also waited to attend him.

The prince stripped and slipped into the tub with an appreciative sigh. His toes tingled in the sudden warmth. As he scrubbed the day's dust away, he tried to relish the soak. This might be his last civilized bath for some time, but duty urged him to hasten. He doused his hair in clove and lavender oils, rinsed well, and climbed out of the bath. His trunk hadn't arrived yet, so he reluctantly climbed back into his sodden clothes with the aid of the silent manservant. He wouldn't walk around in a borrowed robe.

A comb and brush sat on a stand beside a full-size looking glass, and Jetekesh allowed the manservant to attack the snarls in his long hair. Once he was finished, the servant led the prince from the chamber.

"This way, Your Highness."

Jetekesh followed the man down the passageway as he listened for sounds of the waterfalls outside. Was that wrathful dirge their song, or was the wind protesting the growing cold?

He reached a great hall lined with empty tables. At the head of the chamber, Lord Emerin sat before a feast spread across a long oak table. The imposing man stood and inclined his head.

"I hope you feel refreshed, Your Highness."

"I do. Thank you, my lord." Jetekesh glanced around for his companions. Sir Lafe slipped up beside him, also still clad in his wet clothes. No one else had arrived yet. Jetekesh took the carved wood wingback chair Emerin offered and breathed in the succulent aromas.

Steak, lamb, soups, bread, meat pie all garnished the table. He reached for the wine, took a single sip, and savored its warmth as it trickled down his throat. Then he deliberately set the goblet aside and tugged a platter of lamb legs nearer, unwilling to tempt himself into drunkenness. It would be all too easy to seek out an escape from the thoughts frothing in his head—from the fears he tried to keep pinned down. *Erisyrdrel* had returned, the Arch to Shinac within the Drifting Sands had been destroyed, and another monster—something Kethalas hadn't been able to defeat—had come into Nakania just beforehand. Now Shing threatened war.

And Rille had dreamt of KryTeer's impenetrable capital city burning to the ground.

How can we best such evils?

Scuffing footsteps brought his eyes from his plate. As he idly filled the dish with a variety of foods, the rest of his party entered through the right-side door. All still looked damp, but cleaner.

Lord Emerin directed them in turns to take places at the long table, and soon everyone was eating in silence. Jetekesh ripped meat from bone mechanically, tasting nothing despite the hunger he'd felt moments before. A pall settled over the room, thicker than the dense fog in Bard Pass.

The lord of the keep watched, eating nothing. His pale green eyes flicked from face to face.

When Jetekesh's hunger had been assuaged, he pushed back his plate. The rest followed suit, except Dakarai who ate a hearty soup with a contented smile.

How can he find any kind of enjoyment on the heels of his village's destruction?

He knew what Jinji would say. *To each man his own grief.*

Jetekesh inhaled. "We'd best explain whatever the king's message hasn't."

"Please do, Your Highness," said Lord Emerin. "The king explained only that you were traveling urgently and would divulge all upon your arrival. I suspect it's of a sensitive nature."

"Yes. It is." Jetekesh plunged into the explanation, trying to keep it succinct. He searched Emerin's face for doubt or shock as he explained about the Arch and claimed that dark magic invaded the world. The keep lord's neutral expression never faltered. His hands remained folded atop the table. His eyes held steady. When at last Jetekesh's tale wound down to the revelation of Emperor Majinglee and Shing, Emerin shifted.

"Reports from three days ago confirm Lady Song's story." Emerin's eyes pinned on her. "All able-bodied Shingese men have been summoned to Emperor Majinglee's court, and blacksmith forges are burning bright and hot across Shing. War is coming." He looked at the two knights sent by Lord Father. "Unless His Highness prefers it otherwise, I would ask you both to return to Kavacos. Alert the king of the impending attack. I will protect the prince in your stead."

One knight started to protest, but the other set a hand on his shoulder.

"Don't. Lord Emerin knows best."

The keep lord's lips twitched up into a smirk. "Often. Let's hope this is such a time." He shifted his focus to Dakarai and Anenyasha. "I've dealt with several of the tribes within the Clanslands—some are friendly, others aren't. How much can I trust you, I wonder?"

Dakarai swallowed a mouthful of soup and offered a smile. It touched his dark eyes and lit them up like warm coals in the candle glow. "I can offer every verbal assurance, yet I think none will suffice. Let my actions speak boldly and let your prince search the truth within his soul. He will not be led astray, touched by truth as he is."

Lord Emerin stroked his clean-shaven chin. "I'm curious what that means precisely. Both you and"—his eyes danced to Kethalas—"our illustrious Shinacian guest mentioned, upon meeting the prince, that he is touched by truth in some remarkable way. Why? What does it mean?"

Jetekesh sipped his wine, then pushed it away again, surprised he'd plucked it up.

Dakarai shook his head. “I only know what my watchwoman declared. All that it means, I cannot say.”

“What about you?” Lord Emerin tilted his head a little, eyeing Kethalas.

The Shinacian smiled faintly. “Me?”

“*You*. You specifically referenced a ‘Sigil of Truth’ by the prince’s report. What does that mean?”

Kethalas canted his head and considered Jetekesh. “Do you *not* see it plain as day?”

“His mien,” Sir Lafe said.

“Quite.” Kethalas’s long fingers stroked the air as he gestured toward Jetekesh. “How would you describe him, Lord Emerin?”

The lord angled his head to stare down at Jetekesh. “I thought as much.”

Jetekesh rapped his knuckles on the table. “Explain yourselves. What are you talking about? What do you see?”

“Forgive me, my prince.” Emerin shifted in his chair to face Jetekesh. “You’re radiant.”

Heat blossomed over Jetekesh’s face. “I—I’m *what*?”

“S’truth,” Sir Lafe said. “Ever since you returned to Kavacos from KryTeer.”

The two Amantieran knights murmured assent.

Jetekesh scowled. “What does that *mean*? Radiant, how? Why has no one told me this before now?”

“You’re touched by magic, Lord Prince,” said Kethalas. “It is not since KryTeer, I suspect; it is from your time in Shinac—and perhaps from Jinji’s tutelage. You might be said to glow. Some see it more clearly than others.”

Emerin grunted. “You look like a fae creature from that storyteller’s tales, no mistake, Your Highness.”

“I...I do?” He ran a hand down his cheek, his skin prickling.

Am I afraid or excited?

He lowered his hand. "Aredel—uh, the Blood King—he visited Shinac too. Is he also touched by truth?"

Kethalas gracefully shrugged. "Perhaps, but not all Arch travelers carry such a sigil. The Blood Prince—or King, as he now seems to be—is a man marked in different ways. His might not be by truth. And sigils are rare. You might call them gifts."

"Gifts." Jetekesh reached for his wine but halted and drew his fingers back.

Don't run. This isn't a bad thing.

"What *is* a sigil?" he asked.

"A marking. A magical rune only the gifted can see." Kethalas canted his head again. "Yours is emblazoned on your forehead. It radiates from you brightly enough, even the mundane can detect it on some level. It is brighter than a star, and greater than a king's crown."

Jetekesh brushed his fingertips across his brow as tears misted in his eyes. He bowed his head.

Did Jinji give me this?

Silence rang in his ears as he wrestled his emotions down. Finally, he lifted his gaze. "Then *that's* why everyone can recognize me."

Kethalas spoke. "You're too bright, too regal, to be anything less than a prince."

Jetekesh traced a knot in the table, then cleared his throat. "Well, enough on that subject for now. We must discuss more important affairs." He caught Lord Emerin's gaze. "If we send the two knights back to Kavacos, I assume you think it best for us to continue on to the Clanslands?"

"I do." Lord Emerin sipped from his goblet. "If there is an Arch there—and reason lends strength to that suspicion—we had best find it and summon aid, as Lord Kethalas suggests. Knowing two large magical threats have been unleashed upon our mundane land sets my soul on edge. We need the force of arms to stand against whatever they may do. Meanwhile, we must determine what other dark things slipped through and whether more might try."

"The dark things are dreadfully hard to kill," said Dakarai, the warmth in his eyes snuffed out.

"What did they look like?" asked Kethalas.

Dakarai stared at his empty bowl. "Wolves, almost. But with their ribs exposed, like the skin and fur have been melted off in places. Their eyes burn like magma. They are like creatures from the pits of Amantier's two hells, come in tangible form. Their claws and teeth carry a deadly venom."

Kethalas's brow drew together. "*Vashalan*. They are indeed like hounds from the underworld, said to be spawned from the lusts and hungers of the foulest fae and humans alike. They were born in the age of Cavalin, during the conflict when Tallat amassed the darkest forces to march against Shinac and Amantier. Tallat's thirst for Cavalin's blood and the slaying of that great hero became the catalyst to give these beasts their form."

Jetekesh shuddered. "How do we slay them?"

"They can be killed much like any other beast. Their strength lies in their endless numbers more than anything else. Kill one and two more fall upon you. The *vashalan* succumb most easily to fire or holy implements." Kethalas unlatched a silver flask from his sword belt. "Many faiths have such tools. This contains a flower extract produced by lake fairies within Shinac. It is imbued with their grace and blessed by the spirits of my realm. I understand Amantier has holy water blessed by your priests and through the grace of your saints."

"We do," said Jetekesh.

"I'll have my priest arm us with some on the morrow," Lord Emerin said.

Jetekesh eyed the lord. "Us, my lord? You intend to join my company personally?"

"Yes," said the keep lord. "As do Lady Song and her companions. I spoke with her briefly after I left you upstairs. We'll not take risks with your life, Your Highness."

"It's not just for you," Liu broke in. "Bard Pass is the quickest way back to Shing from here, and my emperor needs me." He hefted his chin. "I won't be denied the chance to save him."

The prince eyed the young Shingese man. He was obviously nobleborn, haughty and proud, just as Jetekesh had been not so long ago.

Was I truly that insufferable?

He knew the answer was a firm yes.

"It is also to protect you, Your Highness," Song said after tossing Liu a sharp look.

Lord Emerin took up her thread. "Especially after what Lord Kethalas has revealed of your"—he played his fingers over the air—"your gift. There are legends that Cavalin the Third was touched in a similar way. That he was in fact blessed by the fae of Shinac with a mark. The Red Mark, some called it. That sounds decidedly like your Sigil of Truth. I'll not chance losing the first of his descendants who has inherited something akin to that." He bared his teeth in a grin. "My House has long awaited the awakening of Cavalin's blood. Your father is a good and honorable king. I don't doubt that in the least. Yet *you* fulfill the hopes of this keep. Of my kin. A prayer, you might say, for the return of Shinac to these shores."

"You've always believed in Shinac, my lord?" asked Jetekesh.

Lord Emerin's grin stretched until he again resembled a tiger. "Oh, yes, my prince. We in the Keep of the Falls have never forgotten. When Jinji of Shing visited me here, I assure you he was treated like the fae kings of old. He told us many stories of Cavalin's daughter, Vashi—my ancestor."

Jetekesh smiled broadly at the image of Jinji grudgingly draped in silks and trying to stave off all the endless offers of succulent food. "I'm glad. If only he'd known such hospitality elsewhere."

Emerin rested a large hand on Jetekesh's narrow shoulder. "Doubtless now, out of mortal pain as he is, he does at last. Nothing vile can touch him beyond the grave."

Jetekesh's smile faded. "We buried him in the Drifting Sands, Lord Emerin. We placed a sea bell from KryTeer at his grave, and when it rang I witnessed Jinji's soul walking with Prince Sharo within Shinac. I don't know all it signifies...but I think Jinji Wanderlust labors on, even in death. He's not gone to dwell with the saints. Not yet. Not until the rightful king of Shinac returns and all dark things are crushed."

Lord Emerin chuckled. "That sounds exactly like him." He patted Jetekesh's shoulder and withdrew his hand. "Rest, my prince. We ride early tomorrow if that's agreeable."

"Agreeable or not, we must."

CHAPTER 9
HUNTED

The bones of the ancient palace of KryTeer pierced the red sky as the sun rose over the ocean. Aredel dragged himself from the sea, muscles sore, olive-toned skin wrinkled from the long inundation of the salty water.

Artassa plodded beside him, dressed in naught but her red shift. Her robe had been discarded in the bay to keep from sinking. She resembled a drowned cat, disheveled and trembling, dark eyes wide as she staggered along the sandy beach, clutching Aredel's fingers in her icy hand. She stumbled and he caught her shoulders.

"Steady."

She tipped her chin up and stared into his face. A tear wended down her cheek. "Aredel...What do we do?"

He tore his eyes from hers and swept his gaze over the remnants of upper Bahadronn. Buildings smoldered in the dawn light, and smoke scarred the sky. His heart constricted. "We find survivors."

The sailors who had joined them in the water followed

behind Aredel, sopping, silent. What could be said? The wreath of flame had covered the upper city tiers. Swallowed them. Screams had rent the air until the wreath vanished with the first light of day, and a palpable stillness had settled over the vestiges of KryTeer's heart.

Aredel turned to face the sailors. "Two of you will remain with Queen Artassa. The rest of you will follow me to the palace. Seek survivors. Leave the dead where they lie."

No one argued. A young, spry sailor and a wizened man remained with Artassa while the rest pulled ahead to flank Aredel. They traveled up the blackened steps and into Aredel's private garden, now mere ash and besmirched stone. Acrid smoke lingered on a hot breeze, and glowing coals littered the charred path.

Aredel guided the sailors to the husk of the palace. His lips lifted in bitter humor. How many fortresses and villages had he burned in his conquest of the world? How many lives had he stolen for the holy empire of KryTeer?

How many lives have I lost in return?

The palm trees surrounding the palace had fallen. The few still standing resembled black boulders, fronds gone and fruit shriveled. Aredel passed beneath these lifeless sentinels, his steps hammering through his soul like nails sealing up a coffin.

His mind's eye painted the memory of burying Jinji in the Drifting Sands. Jinji. His half-brother: born of Emperor Gyath and a Shingese noblewoman before Aredel had existed. Aredel's heart throbbed. If only he'd known sooner. If only he could have saved Jinji somehow. Had the gods now claimed Anadin as well? Would Aredel pay for his sins in a single night—to lose his beloved city, his harem, his younger brother, so shortly after losing Jinji?

Am I so depraved, judgment had to come with such wrath?

Once, Aredel and all his people had believed him to be a god come in the flesh to work the will of the war gods above.

What am I, really?

Structural beams hung like broken hafts, charred, stained black. As Aredel weaved around debris, the pungent odor of burned flesh met his nose. He steeled himself. How often had he provoked that smell? Why had it never bothered him before?

He knew—had always known—he was more beast than man. So Father had raised him. But until this moment, he hadn't understood just how far he'd fallen.

Jinji, what did you see in such a creature as me to accept me as you did?

Aredel was no better than other tyrants. His sins were as scarlet and vast as Gyath's, or Peresen's, or even Tallat's from ancient days.

The throne room's shell stood largely intact, though its furnishings and tapestries—its wealth of vases, rugs, gold lamps—all bore the mark of fire. A few bodies were slumped over near the tables. The drunken fools had slept through their deaths. The odor of smoke clung to the air, thick and oppressive.

The charred throne, standing high above the chamber, surveyed the splendorous ruin.

"What do we do, sire?" asked a sailor in a faint whisper.

Aredel squared his shoulders and whirled on the man, who flinched back. "What else? We rebuild."

THE BLOOD KING willed himself to find Anadin's chambers. The palace wing had suffered badly in the firestorm. Corpses lay in doorways where the blasting heat had struck them when they tried to flee. Aredel searched every single body for any identifying signs. Most were servants or guards. One, a priest.

He reached Anadin's sleeping chamber. Searching, he found no sign of a body in or near the remnants of the bed. The window stood open.

Aredel carefully stepped across the scorched room. He leaned out the window and found a tree untouched by the flames, protected by the wall's corner. The fronds swayed in the breeze. Aredel lowered his gaze. His heart stammered.

Two figures huddled beneath the tree, wrapped in blankets, faces hidden.

Aredel sprang from the windowsill and latched onto the palm tree's trunk. He shimmied down and dropped the last few feet, landing in front of the huddled figures. Loose fronds fluttered around him.

One huddled figure poked his head from the coverlet, face smudged with smoke, dark eyes wide. The figure gasped and flung the blanket away.

"Aredel!" Anadin leapt to his feet.

Aredel grasped his brother's shoulders. "I dared not hope you would survive."

Tears welled in Anadin's eyes. "Nor I, you. Gods be praised for this miracle!" Sobbing, he slumped forward and wrapped shaking arms around Aredel.

Aredel held the young man as tenderly, as tightly, as he would a toddler. In so many ways, Anadin had never grown up. The Blood King's eyes sought the second figure. Kyella of Amantier peered up at him, her pale eyes red-rimmed, freckled cheeks smeared, auburn hair loose and tangled.

Aredel drew back from Anadin. "It is a wonder you both found this spot."

"Kyella and I were walking the path over there when the fire bloomed. I climbed up the tree to grab this blanket before it was too late. How did that horrible flame come to be?"

"I don't know." Aredel frowned at the sky as it lightened from reddish gold to purplish blue. "More importantly, will it come again?"

Anadin tensed. "Might it?"

"Yes. I fear it didn't accomplish what it wished to last night."

"W—what did it wish?"

Aredel met Anadin's black eyes. "My death."

The prince's shoulders drooped. "But why?"

"There could be a hundred reasons. That can't matter right now. We must decide on our next course of action. Obviously, we should look for survivors. Gather at the ocean. Take stock of what remains of food and other necessities in the dockside warehouses. Then we must choose where to go from here."

"To Amantier," Anadin said. "We should find Sahala."

Aredel arched an eyebrow. "What has Rille to do with this?" His brother fondly referred to the little seer as his 'sparrow' in the Old Tongue.

Anadin shrugged. "Magic left Nakania when Jinji died. Why is it back? Perhaps Sahala will know."

"We cannot risk harm to our allies in Amantier." Aredel turned his gaze to the fronds swaying above. "We do not know if the wreathing flame will return and if so will it follow me?" His hands curled into fists. "First, I must confirm if my suspicion is correct. I will leave Bahadronn—alone. If the flame follows me, we will know."

"And if it doesn't?"

"Then I will return."

Anadin brushed his fingers against Aredel's shoulder. "But where will you go?"

"Most of the wharves are intact. I will borrow a boat. That will be easiest, as I can escape into the water."

"Won't you drown? The flame..."

"There is risk no matter my course. But I would rather know if I am hunted and why." Aredel placed his hand on Anadin's head.

Best not to mention my dream or the voice. He's worried enough.

"What if it *is* after you?" Anadin asked. "What then?"

Aredel folded his arms, brows pinching together. "Then I will flee from it until I develop a plan to foil its efforts. That is all I know to do at this point."

"I wish Jinji were here." Anadin's soft voice ran threads of pain through Aredel's soul.

"Yes," whispered the Blood King. "As do I."

THE FISHING BOAT bobbed in the black water, and the lapping waves beat against Aredel's ears. A sky full of stars shone like jewels, intensely beautiful, but cold and far away. Unreachable.

Like Jinji.

The morning had been spent gathering survivors. There had been far more than expected. Most of the fire damage had centered on the palace, and the outlying markets, docks, and warehouses of Bahadronn had suffered the least destruction. It was something.

Even near the palace and within it, Aredel and his crew had found surviving Blood Knights, servants, priests—all who had been clever enough to hide in nooks, in ponds, or behind barriers the flames couldn't destroy.

Throughout the day, thousands flocked to the shores where

Aredel had addressed them with promises to rebuild—but first he must defeat this new, unholy enemy.

Cheers had answered him. Faith had brightened the eyes of his people. To them, Aredel could slay any foe. Even a magical one. Even something intangible.

Can I?

He eyed the gleaming shores of Bahadronn four leagues away. His boat dipped and rose on a large wave.

"Gods of KryTeer, lend me your strength. Spare my people."

A sound like thunder grumbled above him. Aredel tipped his head back and spotted a flame growing above his boat.

'*I will not rest until you burn.*' The voice resounded in his head.

Aredel pushed to his feet, gripping his sword. A smile slid over his lips as wind picked up and tossed his long, black hair. "Try!"

The wreath stretched out to wheel above him. Heat stroked Aredel's face before he plunged into the ocean. Fire lit up the sea, but Aredel paddled his feet and watched the storm's wrath as a wild thrill blasted through his body.

Let us see which of us is strongest. At last, I will know if the gods have chosen me—or abandoned me.

He stifled an urge to laugh. Held his breath. Kicked against the current.

Watched the flames wrestle the ancient waters of Nakania.

Then he turned and swam hard for a second boat anchored away from the flames. He slid through the dark water, comfortable, unafraid. Fear for himself had died in long years past. He could handle an enemy on his tail, so long as those he loved remained safe.

He emerged from the water gasping and clutched the boat. He turned, pushed sopping hair from his face, and eyed the flames consuming the last bits of his former vessel. The wreathing fire circled wide around the debris, daring him to surface.

He allowed himself a dark smile and climbed into the second boat, slumped down, and rested.

Whatever magic this is, its precision goes only so far.

He could work with that.

His eyes narrowed.

You will not rest, but neither shall I. You have destroyed the holy city of Bahadronn. You have destroyed most of my House. You will pay.

CHAPTER 10
SCENT OF CHANGE

Kajsa pried her eyes open and stared at an unfamiliar log ceiling. Every muscle in her body screamed in her head. Something else screamed, too: a memory clawing its way to the forefront of her thoughts.

She bolted upright in a strange bed. Her heart slammed against her ribs.

Axel!

Kajsa flung the covers from her legs and found herself dressed in a homespun nightgown, not her own. A glance around the bare log walls of the room confirmed she slept in the Elder-house, likely on the second story where wayfarers sometimes stayed overnight.

With a steadying breath, Kajsa slid off the bed, then darted to the wardrobe where spare clothes hung for those in need. She changed into a nondescript woolen dress, ignoring her throbbing muscles, then she splashed her face and hands in the porcelain basin and tugged a brush through her long hair until every snarl vanished. Good enough.

She slipped from the little room and made her way down the tapestry-lined hallway to the stairs. Her legs burned as she descended, one hand sliding along the carved banister, but she kept a steady pace until she reached the last step and glanced around the wide common room. No sign of Axel or anyone else. Just a fire blazing in the hearth and shutters latched over the wide windows, keeping out the chill.

Kajsa crept to the kitchen beyond the large room where volunteers bustled about, preparing for the Elder feast tonight. One stout woman paused to eye Kajsa.

"He's in the death room."

Her heart faltered.

The woman softly smiled. "He's mending well, child. Go on. We're busy in here."

Kajsa tripped in her haste to reach the door to the death room. She rapped on the wood.

"Come in," said a voice like an angel.

Kajsa beamed as she stumbled into the bright room and spotted Axel sitting up in bed. Raum lay at his feet, groomed and curled up, asleep. In a chair on the bed's far side sat Navolleth, wrapped in a white fur cape. Light streamed in through the window behind him; its curtains had been drawn back, and the shutters were unlatched to let in fresh, chilly air.

"Hello there, sleepyhead," said Axel.

Kajsa shut the door behind her and trotted across the room to kneel beside the quilted bed. "You're alive. Thanks be to the mountain gods."

Axel grinned. "And to Navolleth."

Kajsa found the strange man's piercing eyes, then dipped her head. "Thank you."

"I owed him my life," said Navolleth. "I was honored to pay my debt."

Kajsa nodded and reached out to brush her fingers through Raum's soft black fur. The wolf stirred, cracked his yellow eyes open, and stretched his tongue out to lick Kajsa's fingers. Then he curled back up and shut his eyes.

"Raum'll be fine, too," Axel said. "He's just tired."

Kajsa blinked back tears, muscles loosening. Her shoulders drooped and her lungs eased.

"Ah, Ky." Axel's hand brushed her cheek. "You must've been terrified—but you were wonderfully brave. I don't know *how* you found the strength to fend off those creatures and bring me home."

She stared into his eyes and swallowed as the memory stained her thoughts. "I didn't fend them off. Someone else did. A cloaked man, I think. He disappeared after he—he called to them in a strange tongue."

"Are you certain you weren't imagining things?" Axel tilted his head. "It was quite a frightful moment, Ky."

She shook her head. "Were it not for him, we would be dead. Raum couldn't fight them all. The man—or whatever it was—called them away somehow."

"*Vashalan*."

Kajsa turned to Navolleth. His brow drew low over his eyes. His hands lay in his lap, fingers curled into fists, knuckles white. His metallic eyes lifted until they met her questioning gaze, and a smile like shattered glass brushed his lips.

What sorrows has he known to look so broken?

"Is that a word or a name?" asked Axel.

Navolleth dragged his stare from Kajsa to answer. "It is what those creatures are called, from how you have described them. They are unholy things, summoned by darkness, drawn to fear." His gaze shifted back to Kajsa. "Axel explained that you've seen them before. That they killed your father."

She flinched and stared at the floor. Her chest squeezed tight. She opened her mouth like words might spill out, but nothing did.

"Forgive me," said Navolleth. "I didn't mean to be cruel."

She shook her head as she blinked back hot tears. Her vision blurred and her throat ached. *Don't fall apart. Stay strong. Be brave.* She clutched the fabric of her dress and let the tears fall until her vision cleared a little, then she wiped the rest away. "I'm sorry." Her voice was a feathery whisper in her ears.

"Kajsa, don't apologize," said Axel. "You've got every right to grieve."

She looked up and pressed a smile to her lips. "I know...but I'm so tired of crying."

He leaned close and ran his hand down the side of her face. "Everything's going to be fine. Raum and I are safe, and no one else was hurt. I'm so relieved you're unharmed, too."

Her breath hitched as she stared into his pale green eyes. So kind, so reassuring and strong. "Thank you, Xel."

He dropped his hand to her shoulder, squeezed it, then turned to Navolleth. "Where do these creatures come from? How can we keep them away from our village?"

Navolleth rose from his chair and strode to the open window. The breeze stirred his long pale hair. "The cloaked figure whom Kajsa glimpsed on the path will keep this village safe."

Axel shifted. "Who—or what—*is* the cloaked figure?"

"That I cannot say. I haven't the words."

Kajsa had expected Axel to stay in bed for a few days, but he insisted on getting up after breakfast.

He moved around the room, as nimble as ever, a wide grin revealing his straight white teeth. "See, Kajsa? I'm healed."

She ought to feel relieved, but his recovery made no sense. "How is it possible?"

He shrugged but glanced toward Navolleth who had moved his chair to the window and stared out at the snowcapped world in silence.

How did Navolleth heal him so completely?

Kajsa's skin crawled. She scratched her wrist to banish the feeling and brushed her long hair back. "I'd best let Ingrid know we're back and safe—and that her purchases are scattered across the trail."

"I'm certain she knows," said Axel. "But you should check in on her just the same."

Kajsa paced to the door and slipped out into the main chamber. As the door shut, words drifted out, smooth as a polished river stone.

"She doesn't trust me."

"She trusts very few," said Axel. "A lot of the villagers think she's cursed."

Kajsa leaned near the wood to listen better.

"Do you trust me, Axel?"

"Yes, completely."

"Then there is something I would discuss with you."

"Anything," replied Axel.

Kajsa pressed her ear closer—but laughter from across the common room, near the hearth, jerked her back. Elder Viggo and the village midwife, Elga, stood near the flames, the latter's face red from the cold. Their words softened.

Kajsa trotted to the front door, plucked up her tattered cape and mittens from the pegs where they hung, slipped on her boots, and plunged out into the brisk morning air. A fresh layer of snow dusted the crusty footprints going to and from the Elderhouse. Kajsa took care to walk in the hollows and made her way up toward the crest where Ingrid lived apart.

What does Navolleth want to discuss with Axel? Why does the notion frighten me? Why am I always such a coward?

Her legs ached as she dragged herself the last few feet up the incline. A yip halted her, and she turned to find Raum loping toward her from the village, his ears perked and his tongue lolling. Kajsa crouched and let Raum launch himself into her outstretched arms. He dragged his tongue over her chin.

Kajsa laughed and buried her face in his fore chest. He whined an affectionate note and panted until she pulled back to peer into his eyes. "I'm glad you're better, Raum. I'd be lost without you close by." She scratched behind his ear, then climbed to her feet. "Let's see if Ingrid has a treat for you."

Kajsa reached the porch and pounded on the door, cringing at the noise. She entered the turf house upon the old woman's beckoning.

Ingrid stooped before the fireplace, stoking the logs into a brighter flame. She peeked over her shoulder at Kajsa. "Welcome, child."

Kajsa peeled off her mittens as Raum pushed past to curl up at the hearth. "How are you, Ingrid?"

"Better than yourself, I don't wonder." Ingrid hung up the poker on a peg. "Never mind the supplies. Frit told me all that happened and offered to find what remains of the parcels. I don't expect much, but it's only a small bother. Are you hurt?"

"Only a little sore," Kajsa said. "I'm very fortunate."

Ingrid hobbled to her rocking chair and quaked as she eased herself down onto the creaking wood. The mangy cat trilled and jumped up onto her lap. Ingrid chuckled and scratched at his scruffy neck, then her hand fell away, and she eyed Kajsa from the web-like wrinkles of her ancient face. "Tell me about the stranger—the man Axel found in the snow."

Kajsa toed the hearth ledge where the wood floor failed and the rock base rose. "I don't know much."

Ingrid snorted. "Tell me what you feel then."

Should I?

Of everyone, Kajsa trusted Ingrid most. She'd been the only proper maternal figure in Kajsa's life since Mother died ten years ago. Ingrid always listened. Reflected. Never judged. Didn't treat her like she was a bad omen because Fa had died so horribly...

Kajsa drew a breath. "I don't trust him. He frightens me." Heat slithered over her cheeks, but she didn't falter. "There's something very sad and almost *dark* about him. Like a nightmare flown too fast to recall."

Ingrid's head bobbed in thought as she stroked the cat. "There is a scent in the snow. A strange scent. Something sinister."

"The beasts in the woods?"

Ingrid's head tipped from side to side. "Yes and no. Yes and no." The old woman's faded blue eyes snared Kajsa and pinned her in place. "I dreamt that you must leave this village. You must cross the Snowblinds."

Chills raced up Kajsa's arms. "B—but why?"

"That I do not know. Nor when. But so I dreamt."

"You said your dreams weren't *real* anymore." Kajsa swallowed. "That ended nine months ago."

When Fa died.

Ingrid scratched the cat's chin. "So I did. Yet this dream was as in times before. It was real." Her gaze drifted to the window, and she rocked her chair faster. "Soon, you must leave."

Kajsa moved to the wardrobe and selected one of her finely embroidered dresses to change into so she could wash and return the plain frock. Though she didn't officially live with Ingrid, she stayed often enough she always had something to wear. Dragging the baggy dress over her head, she chewed her lip as a shiver tracked her arms and legs beneath her woolen shift.

Gods of the mountain, let her be wrong. I don't want to cross the Snowblinds. I don't want to leave Norva.

Whatever Ingrid had dreamed, only something menacing would send Kajsa away from her home. And hadn't the village suffered enough already?

She shook her fur-lined dress straight around her ankles, then plucked up her sewing kit and settled into a chair to finish the hem of the midwife's new skirt. Washing the frock would have to wait until after Ingrid's trade work was concluded for the afternoon.

Don't dwell on her dream. There isn't any point unless something happens.

She threaded her needle and bent to her work. The mountain winds howled over the turf house, scraping at the frosting of snow. It *was* just the wind. Nothing else.

CHAPTER II
DAWN

Jetekesh bolted upright in his bed. His nerves tingled as he stared into the gloom and listened hard for the sound that had awakened him.

A bell clamored outside.

He flung his coverlet aside and peeled off his borrowed nightdress. His trunk had been brought up while he slept, and he dug through it to find his plainest tunic and breeches. He slipped them on without ceremony, buckled his sword to his belt, and tied his hair back in a sloppy ponytail. Mother would hate his carelessness.

A knock rapped on the door.

"My prince?"

Jetekesh wrenched the door open. "Sir Lafe, what's the commotion?"

The man grimaced, thick eyebrows darkening his eyes. "We're besieged, Your Highness."

Jetekesh's thoughts careened to a halt. "Besieged? By Shing?"

"That I don't know, Your Highness." Sir Lafe's hand fell to his broadsword. "We must—"

Jetekesh pushed past him. "Where's Lord Emerin?"

"On the outer wall, I presume, Your Highness."

"With me, then." Jetekesh retraced his steps from the night before, listening for any footsteps or the crash of the gates. A handful of servants huddled at the bottom of the stairway.

"You." He pointed.

They spun toward him, staying bundled close together.

One woman curtsied. "My prince."

"Where's Lord Emerin?"

She glanced at the man beside her, then turned back to Jetekesh. "Outside, my prince. He stormed through here with his knights only moments ago." She pointed toward the front door.

"Thank you." Jetekesh trotted to the door and flung it open. Sir Lafe was on his heels. Another figure darted out behind him: Kethalas. The Shinacian's hair settled against his back, silvery in the ample torchlight and weak glow of approaching dawn.

Fog coiled through the bailey. Voices rose above the rattle of armor on the wall and the roar of the six falls. Sparks flew from torches, painting the fogbanks orange, casting undulating shadows over the ground. Jetekesh ran to the wall's stairs, visible above the thick vapors. He threw himself up the steps until he reached the battlements. Archers aimed their bows at the darkness on the outside, while Lord Emerin snapped orders in his growling tones.

Jetekesh crouched against the closest merlon and peeked down at the shadowed ground. Crouching shapes darted to and fro in the haze, their feral eyes burning with red light. He recoiled and bumped into Sir Lafe.

"Careful, Your Highness," the knight murmured.

Jetekesh gripped his sword hilt. "It's those wolf-like creatures, isn't it?"

"Looks that way," Sir Lafe murmured.

Jetekesh cleared his throat. "But surely they can't breach the—"

A howl rang out over the air. Otherworldly. Piercing. More followed. Not wolf-like at all; they were closer to anguished specters, moaning in the pits of the two hells.

"Here they come!" cried Lord Emerin.

What does that mean?

The wind held its breath, leaving only the rush of the waterfalls to fill the spaces. Jetekesh resisted an urge to peer over the battlements again. His heart thumped in his ears.

Claws caught the stone, breaking off bits of the wall. Jetekesh lurched back as a horrible, snarling, canine snout hefted into view. Molten red eyes bored into Jetekesh's mind to peel back every layer until it saw his soul. The creature lifted itself, back legs scratching against the stones, scrabbling for purchase.

It leapt this high? He ground his teeth, steeling his nerves. Now, right now, he need only worry about surviving. *Focus. Don't let the beast smell your fear.*

Cries filled the air. More horrible beasts dragged themselves over the crenels of the wall while soldiers stabbed at them with spears and swords.

The beast before Jetekesh growled. The guttural sound shook the prince's bones. Jetekesh licked his lips as he wrenched his sword from its sheath, but Sir Lafe shoved him back and charged the creature. The knight's sword rammed into its fore chest. The beast stumbled backward with a bloodcurdling scream as Sir Lafe wrenched his blade loose and staggered back.

"Torch them!" Lord Emerin shouted above the clank of metal and raging snarls.

Jetekesh darted to the nearest sconce and yanked the torch free, then wheeled and sprinted toward the closest soldier under attack. Sir Lafe beat him there, snatched the torch from his hand, and waved it toward the beast who whimpered and leapt from the wall to avoid burning.

"Stop interfering!" Jetekesh reached for the torch, but Sir Lafe danced back.

"Apologies, Your Highness. Your safety is my duty. Stay close."

Jetekesh clenched his hands into fists and dashed away to find another torch, ignoring his protector's protest.

How can I become stronger if no one will let me stretch myself?

Sir Lafe's footfalls pounded behind him. Iron fingers caught Jetekesh's arm and whirled him around. The knight's blue eyes blazed with a fury akin to the liquid fire in the beasts' gazes. "My prince, a time will likely come when we must fight together—but you serve only to hinder our victory at present. Please stay back."

Jetekesh's face and neck burned. His eyes narrowed into slits. "I won't forget this, Sir Lafe." He stormed down the stairs and plunged into the fog, grateful for the cool vapor against his flushed cheeks. Tears pricked at his eyes, but he banished them.

I will not cry. I won't!

The howls of the creatures rose higher. Talon-like claws scraped at the heavy wood of the gate, splintering it. Flames raced back and forth on the battlements while Jetekesh stood on the paving stones in the bailey and watched. Dawn came with an excruciating slowness. The sun stretched its fingers over the snowcaps and poured its beams over Bard Pass and the Keep of the Falls.

The beasts didn't vanish, though, somehow, he'd imagined they might. Didn't nightmares always dispel in daylight?

Lord Emerin's voice rang out as the sun burned away the fog. "Send men to the east side! Bring that oil!"

Archers showered flaming arrows over the wall and distant whimpers answered.

A scream slashed over the air.

"Stop it! Shoot it down!"

Jetekesh wrenched his eyes east. Against the swelling glow of morning, a dark shape lunged at him through the stubborn tendrils of fog. He threw up his hands. Stumbled back. Tripped.

Something sprang past him from behind. Pale, silvery-blue hair thrashed in the vapor as Kethalas collided with the beast. The crackle of ice whispered across the air as rime climbed over the beast's body, encasing it. The beast fell to the ground and shattered like glass.

No gore stained the glistening rime. The beast had been frozen through.

Kethalas stood above the pieces of the monster, panting for air. He turned, scar vivid in the sunlight, irises blazing white. "How do you fare, O prince?"

Jetekesh shook his head. "I...I'm well enough, I think."

Heavy footsteps thundered toward him. Sir Lafe appeared in the haze, eyes wide, jaw slack. "Are you wounded, Your Highness?"

"He is sound," said Dakarai, coming up behind Jetekesh. He smiled, flashing teeth. "You do not protect him alone."

Flames of shame raced through Jetekesh's veins, hot enough he wondered why the ground didn't melt beneath his feet to bury him.

Am I so helpless?

Dakarai shifted to peer down into the prince's face. "Your Highness, I will proceed to the wall and help fend off these creatures."

"Thank you," Jetekesh whispered. "Be careful."

The clansman bowed his head, pivoted on his heels, and strode toward the nearest flight of steps. Jetekesh studied his back, taking in the colors, the feathers, beads—and the bare feet.

Jetekesh shivered. *Must be tough as iron. Will I ever become so strong?*

A shape darted after Dakarai. Anenyasha. She slowed as she reached her companion, and her hands waved as she spoke in strange, clicking tones. Her spear glinted.

Jetekesh glanced at Kethalas. The Shinacian man stood a few feet away, eyeing the battle on the wall. Jetekesh paced to his side. "Aren't you going to join the fray? With your...gifts, couldn't you take them down easily?"

A strained smile touched Kethalas's lips. "I would, truly, but alas, I cannot."

"Why not?"

"I am recovering from several magical wounds."

"You're injured?" Jetekesh looked him up and down. "Should you sit down?"

The man smiled, and his eyes brightened. "No need. In this form, I am well enough off to stand. I cannot take my other shape for a few weeks more, I think, but I can still guard you."

"Are your wounds from your battle at the Jade Arch?"

"Yes." He pressed his hand against his side. "But fear not: I wounded my adversary as well."

"Good." Jetekesh jerked west as a scream broke over the sky. "Can we best these hellish fiends?"

"Your Lord Emerin is a capable and fierce leader. And I think the *vashalan* cannot long withstand the daylight. We must simply outlast them. When the fog is gone, they will flee into the shadows of the pass."

"Why are they attacking the keep? Where did they come from?"

Kethalas shook his head. "That I cannot say. *Vashalan* never venture forth without a master with whom they have made a pact. At least, that is the way in Shinac."

"Do you think *Erisyrdrel* is their master?"

Metal sang on the wall nearby. Another man screamed.

"Yes," said Kethalas. "I suspect so. In part."

The sun heaved itself over the eastern peaks and stared down into the bailey. Fog curled away from its merciless gaze.

Jetekesh tugged on his sleeve. "*Erisyrdrel* as well as the thing that broke the Jade Arch. Is that what you mean? You think they're allied?"

"Yes."

A howl crested the walls and the spires of the keep, cutting through the endless roar of the waterfalls. The clash of swords and the whistle of arrows faltered, then fell silent. Cheers broke over the battlements.

As the last vestiges of fog fled into the darkest corners of the keep, Lord Emerin descended from the wall, cleaning his sword on his silver cloak. His pale green eyes blazed in the morning light, and his shoulder-length blond hair hung loose and soaked with sweat. He strode across the bailey; dressed in boots, gray breeches, and a white blouse, its collar half-laced. His stained cloak fluttered as he issued orders to the armored man walking on his right.

"Make certain to gather those who fell over the wall first. I won't leave them for scavengers. Count the dead. Give me a full report."

"Yes, my lord." The man darted back to the gates.

Lord Emerin halted before Jetekesh. He bowed, then rose in a fluid motion. "We're victorious, my prince—for the moment." A grin flashed over his face before it died. "The cost has been high, but my men fought bravely."

"I commend them for that and congratulate you on your success, my lord. It was well executed."

Lord Emerin's smile reappeared, wry this time. "We had little choice, but I thank you for the compliment. I fear this incident will delay our departure a bit."

"You still intend to come, my lord?" asked Jetekesh. "Shouldn't you defend your keep in case it falls under attack again? Kethalas said the *vashalan* prefer darkness. They may return when true night falls."

The lord waved that away. "I rather doubt they'll return here if we proceed voluntarily into their present domain. Never before have they attacked this keep, and I suspect they did so now only to get at *you*, Your Highness."

Chills scurried like spiders across Jetekesh's skin. "Me, my lord?"

"I fear so. And with that suspicion wedged in my mind, I'll not remain here when my future king puts his life at risk to defend our kingdom. I will come."

"Why do you suspect the *vashalan* target me specifically?"

Emerin shrugged one shoulder. "If the forces of light seek you out—declare you marked—then how could the forces of darkness *not* learn of you? Not *fear* you? Why else would those hellish monsters attack? You're more important than a keep."

Emotions churned within the prince's chest. *Am I ashamed or grateful?* "Thank you, Lord Emerin. For your loyalty and your support."

The man inclined his head. "It's my duty and my honor. If you'll excuse me, Your Highness, I'll see to my dead, then begin preparations for our departure."

"Of course." As Jetekesh watched the lord stride away, his

mind raced over the journey lying ahead of him. He turned to Kethalas. "Will you be able to sense the Arch?"

The man looked eastward. "If I'm near enough to it, perhaps. I'm not certain how these Arches feel on the Nakanian side. Magic is everywhere in Shinac. It's like different instruments strumming and fluting over the air, recognizable and obvious. But in Nakania, magic must hide. What will that feel like, I wonder?"

A new voice answered. "Probably like Jinji."

Jetekesh whirled to find Song standing nearby. She clutched a sword in her hand and black hair clung to her face.

Even a foreigner fought, yet I'm not allowed.

The Shingese woman shrugged. "Magic is rare enough here, Lord Kethalas, I should think in some ways it will be easier to spot—if one knows to look."

Kethalas smiled. "So it may be."

JETEKESH SPENT the morning penning a letter to his father, enclosing all he'd learned and experienced in the single day and night away from home. He sent it with the two knights riding back to Kavacos. Lord Emerin included a missive of his own.

After that, the prince attended the brief services for Lord Emerin's fallen soldiers. The lord of the keep said a few simple, heartfelt words, then the soldiers' bodies were burned to purge them of any possible magical taint. The keep lord was certainly thorough.

The new company rode out of the Keep of the Falls after lunch, leaving behind its glistening waterfalls and solid ramparts. They headed east along Bard Pass. The sheer chasm walls hurled every sound back at the riders and shunned all direct light from the sun. Snow hunched in patches, bleeding out streams of muddy water to puddle along the narrow road. The company climbed slowly upward, past the timberline, where snow covered the ground like a lumpy blanket. The wagon dragged its way forward, leaving lines in its wake.

Jetekesh was positioned in the center of the company, Sir Lafe at his back, the wagon just behind. Lord Emerin had insisted the company surround the prince and provisions, to protect them from any outside attacks. It made strategic sense, so Jetekesh had agreed as his heart hung heavy in his chest.

Father left me in charge. The thought echoed in his mind like an unbidden chant, but he willed himself to banish it. *Sulking won't help you, stupid boy. I thought you'd grown up.* He clutched his reins and straightened his spine. *You've got little experience compared to anyone else here. Learn from them.*

Song, Liu, and the Shing boy, apparently called Yin, rode with them on borrowed mounts. True to his word, Lord Emerin had also come—yet Jetekesh was surprised that no other keep knights had joined them. When he'd asked Lord Emerin about it, the man had grinned like a cat and said, "I'll be enough."

The company halted at the top of a crest as the sun sank in the west and coated the world in dusky reds and oranges. Jetekesh let his eyes rove over the eastern slopes ahead of them, then unfolded his map to study the trail down the mountain slants. It would be another week before they left the pass and proceeded into the northeastern flatlands of Amantier. From there they would travel straight north before slowly curving east again. A fortnight from now they would reach the border of the Clanslands.

Jetekesh folded the map and tucked it into his saddlebag. He swung himself from Hickory's back, then eyed the large tent the wagoner and Song were setting up on the flattest bit of ground.

Liu looked on, while Yin helped Dakarai and Anenyasha unsaddle the horses. Lord Emerin stood at the back of the wagon with Sir Lafe, discussing dinner preparations. Kethalas studied the sun setting behind the Flute Mountains.

Jetekesh picked his target. "Sir Lafe."

The man turned. "Your Highness?"

"After dinner, I would like to spar with you." Jetekesh gripped his sword hilt. "I don't want to become rusty as we travel."

The man's brow creased. "So close to the keep, let us save our strength in case of another attack, Your Highness. We can spar another night."

That was reasonable, though Jetekesh's heart sank. "Very well, Sir Lafe." He padded closer to the wagon. "How can I help?"

"No need, Your Highness," said Lord Emerin. "Rest for now."

Jetekesh grimaced. "I'd rather help. I...don't want to burden anyone."

The two men eyed him, then Lord Emerin nodded. "Very well. Can you dice potatoes?"

Potatoes? Slimy, cold things.

Jetekesh nodded through a grimace. "I think so. It can't be too hard."

The lord dragged a large woven bag from the wagon's innards. "Here you are. And here's a knife."

Jetekesh sat on a large rock and carved his potatoes against one palm, as he had no board to dice them on, and using a dirty rock surface was out of the question. He worked at a slippery, painstaking pace, afraid to cut off a finger. Several times he had to chase down a stray vegetable after it slipped through his hands.

Sir Lafe sliced carrots beside him, while Lord Emerin built a fire and placed a pot onto a triangular trivet over the flames.

An hour or so later, the tent stood upright, and everyone

settled around the fire, seated on their saddles. They blew on their stew and said little. Stars appeared one by one overhead, and memories of Shinac swept through Jetekesh like a warm spring breeze. The fairy Ashea had sung to him his first night in that fae realm, her music like gentle rain and blooming flowers. It had been the first time he'd felt comfortable with people other than his father, and Jinji had been responsible for that.

Tonight, the silence was anything but comfortable. Small noises beyond the encampment tied Jetekesh's muscles into knots. Lord Emerin's pale eyes searched the peaks and fissures. Sir Lafe kept one hand on his sword.

"I will take first watch tonight," said Kethalas into the silence.

Jetekesh started to protest but stopped himself. No one else knew the Shinacian was injured. He plunged his spoon into the clay bowl and ate without tasting anything. The early morning and long ride weighed his bones down. He longed to curl up and rest.

"I'll take second," Dakarai said, as he prodded the flames higher with a stick.

Lord Emerin nodded. "I'll take last watch. We rise at dawn to break camp, if that's acceptable, Your Highness?"

"That's fine." Jetekesh scraped up the last of his stew and chewed it as he considered Kethalas. "Perhaps tomorrow night, Song, Sir Lafe, and..." his eyes flitted over the faces surrounding him "...Anenyasha might take the watches?"

"That's acceptable," said Song.

Dakarai clicked a few words to Anenyasha, who nodded. The clansman met Jetekesh's eyes. "She agrees."

"Very good," said Lord Emerin.

Liu tossed a log into the fire. "I'm capable of watching as well."

"And you'll get a turn the following night," Lord Emerin said.

Jetekesh bristled. *He's nearly my age!* "Do I also get a turn, then, my lord?" He kept his tones light, tossing his head.

The lord grinned but his eyes held no light. "Your part in this is different, my prince. Let us fulfill ours, hm?"

Jetekesh bowed his head. *He's no fool.*

He rose and handed his bowl to the wagoner, who had cleanup duty along with the boy, Yin, tonight. "I'm exhausted. Goodnight." He started for the tent.

"Goodnight, Your Highness," Lord Emerin called.

Dakarai piped up. "Pleasant rest, Prince Jetekesh."

No one else spoke. Jetekesh slipped inside the canvas tent and sighed as he unbuckled his sword. Thin, straw-stuffed mattresses for the whole company, covered in heavy furs, had been laid out above ornate rugs. Jetekesh's trunk sat beside the centermost mattress. He wended his way around the bedding and knelt on his own to dig through his belongings. He changed into his nightshirt along with fresh hosen in case he had to defend himself in the middle of the night. Finished, he folded the day's dusty wardrobe, tucked it into his trunk, then rolled onto the lumpish mattress. The sweet odor of straw tickled his nose.

He sneezed, then laughed. *This misery is nothing to my last excursion. What wouldn't I have given for a tent or decent bedding?* Instead, he'd slept under the stars with only his cloak to warm him.

He stared at the pitched roof. *I hope Rille and Yeshton are well.*

A week or so of travel would bring the two to the western shores of Amantier. There, they could charter a ship to KryTeer and arrive a week after that. *If only traveling didn't take so long. What if they're too late to help Aredel?*

He rolled onto his side and rested his head against his arm.

"Would I be sad?" The sound of his voice startled him. He chuckled. "Yes. Of course, I would."

Aredel was a war-hardened man prone to cruelty, but for Jinji—his half-brother and friend—he'd tried to change. The steps he'd taken since Jinji's death were enormous. No one would have wagered a single gold kana on him withdrawing his troops from every conquered country and promising restitution. Yet he had.

Does he hate what he's doing? Will it last?

Jetekesh shut his eyes and focused on his breaths. In. Out. In.

Sleep. Tomorrow will be another grueling ride.

CHAPTER 12
LOSS

Crisp mountain air slapped Jetekesh's cheeks when he opened the tent flap.

The horses stamped and snorted to keep warm while Lord Emerin brushed fresh snow out of the firepit. "Good morning, Your Highness. Not a peep from those devil hounds."

Jetekesh drew his heavy, fur-lined cloak closer and sank one boot into the snow. At least five inches had fallen during the night. "Morning, my lord. Maybe they hate snow as much as I do."

The lord chuckled. "Possibly so. Breakfast won't take long."

Jetekesh crunched a path to the horses and smiled as Hickory nickered a greeting. "Hello, my fine friend." He caught the stallion's muzzle and stroked between his eyes. "Hungry?"

Hickory lipped his sleeve before Jetekesh plowed his way to the wagon. He heaved several sacks of feed from the wagon-bed and plopped them down to fill the muzzle sacks, then he tied each to the eleven horses in turn. The work was monotonous, but listening to the munching animals felt oddly satisfying.

“Eat well. Soon we’ll be in greener lands, I promise.” Jetekesh returned the large, empty sacks to the wagon and brushed off his hands.

Will we have enough feed to last until we reach the end of the pass?

He plodded to the campfire, where Emerin, Dakarai, and Sir Lafe sat conversing in soft tones. Jetekesh dusted the snow off his saddle and flopped down beside his protector. He let out a breath that fluttered his bangs.

Lord Emerin caught his eye. “That was well done, Your Highness.”

“What was?”

“Feeding the horses. I didn’t expect you to expend yourself like that.”

Jetekesh blinked, then snorted. “I well believe that, after our first encounter in my youth.” He tipped his head. “Still, you’re a bold man, my lord, to say as much.”

Emerin stirred the frothing contents of the pot. “I speak my mind readily enough. But I don’t refer to your tantrums of years ago. I refer to more recent rumor and hearsay—which I don’t put much stock in unless it’s verified by my spies. Rumors of you were corroborated.”

Jetekesh tugged on a lock of hair. “I know I’ve been...difficult in the past. I won’t deny it. But I *am* trying to improve.”

“So I can see.” Emerin’s smile gentled. “Food’s ready.”

Porridge. Disgusting. Jetekesh held in a sigh and accepted the bowl Sir Lafe offered him as Lord Emerin dished out equal portions. It was tasteless but warm. The rest of the company joined them little by little, Liu coming last, a scowl deep against his brow as he drew his cloak closer to his body.

After breakfast they broke camp. Jetekesh helped the wagoner to saddle nine horses and harness the last two to the wagon. As they worked, he observed the wagoner's nimble fingers.

"What's your name?" asked Jetekesh.

"Harn, Yer Highness."

"Harn. I'm glad to have you along."

The older man's smile drew lines around his mouth. "Thank ye, Yer Highness. 'Tis an honor if I might be so bold as to say it."

"You may," said Jetekesh.

Mother's voice drifted like a shadow over his mind. '*Mingling with rabble, dearheart? It wounds this mother's soul to watch.*'

Jetekesh ducked his head and fumbled with the harness straps. *Ignore her. She's not real.* He raked back his hair with one hand and fastened the last strap with trembling fingers.

Harn peeked over his shoulder. "That'll do it, Yer Highness."

Jetekesh stepped back and examined the campsite. All but a few bedrolls had been reloaded into the wagon, and half the company had mounted their horses. He crossed to Hickory and swung up into the saddle, willing his heart to calm down. His nerves to quiet. His mind to settle.

When will Mother cease to haunt me?

Eyes pinned on him. Jetekesh glanced at the wagon. Loaded. He caught up his reins. "Move out!"

Lord Emerin took the lead. Jetekesh positioned himself just behind him, shooting Sir Lafe a *don't-argue-with-me* glower as the knight opened his mouth to protest. The others fell into formation behind him, and the wagon rattled and rocked along the narrow, slushy road.

SNOW FELL, soft and feathery, dusting the riders' shoulders. The sun hung low on the horizon behind the company as Hickory climbed the umpteenth rise along a perilous cliffside stretch of road. A gorge plunged deep to the right where snow buried most of a thick forest. The Nagali River cut its way through the bottom of the gorge, feeding the waterfalls surrounding Lord Emerin's keep. The river rapids roared through the mountains, fierce as a dragon's cry.

At least, I assume their cries are that fierce. Jetekesh glanced back at Kethalas riding close by. The man met his gaze and smiled. Jetekesh slowed Hickory until the two horses fell into an even pace, side by side.

"Prince Sharo told me a little about you when I was in Shinac," Jetekesh said.

Kethalas's smile slid sideways. "I can only think of one instance he might mention involving myself. Does he refer to the battle between the witch and Taregan?"

"Yes." Jetekesh tapped his jaw. "Is that scar from your battle against Sharo's dragon."

Kethalas chuckled and ran his fingers over the scar. "Yes. It is. I can't quite decide whether to feel shame or pride in having gotten it from my liege in combat."

"Sharo said you were bespelled by the witch."

"I was, yes. And Taregan set me free, spirits be thanked."

Jetekesh studied the man's angular features. "He didn't tell me you could change your form."

"It's not a thing we mention outside our clans." Kethalas shrugged. "But being within the realm of Nakania, and with my"—his voice dropped—"*condition*, I have little choice but to look human."

"You're not human?" Dakarai's amiable voice sent a jolt through Jetekesh's frame.

Kethalas glanced behind him to find the man much closer

than before. “Not strictly,” answered the Shinacian, his tones tight.

Dakarai lifted his hands in a shrug. “I do not mean to offend or provoke. But we have legends of Shinac within my tribe as well, and I am dearly curious about all you know and are. I would like very much to reach inside your mind and pluck out your knowledge, but only if it would not harm you.” He chuckled.

Kethalas stared at him until a smile broke over his face. “That is fair. There is much about Nakania and its many countries I should like to learn as well. Customs and stories—whether they are true or merely myths.”

“Perhaps when we camp, we might trade truths each night.” Dakarai clicked strange words at Anenyasha. The woman nodded and said nothing.

Jetekesh glanced between the two. “Does she speak the trade tongue?”

Dakarai shook his head, still grinning. “She refuses. Not out of disrespect. She has no love of speaking even in her native tongue. Why learn more words?”

Jetekesh glanced at Anenyasha. “Makes sense. Is she your sister?”

“No, no. We are betrothed.”

“For love or for connections?” Jetekesh started up, surprised by his own question. “I apologize. That isn’t my business.”

Dakarai laughed; a deep, merry sound. “Do not apologize. Curiosity is a gift, my tribe says. Anenyasha and I—we are in love. There is no better connection than that. Why else become betrothed?”

“Politics.” Jetekesh shrugged. “My parents married for the benefit of Amantier. They didn’t know each other well.”

Dakarai’s head bobbed as his dark eyes followed the gorge line. “I will not pretend I know nothing of how that ended. Your mother poisoned your father and sold out Amantier to the KryTeer Empire to save herself, did she not?"

"She did." His voice was smaller than he wanted it to be.

"So, in the end, it benefited Amantier not at all."

"Yes, that's true." The prince fiddled with his reins. "But how does one find love? How does one know what it is? Or do some never find it; only a lucky few?"

"Trust is the start of love." Dakarai cast Anenyasha a smile. "If there is no trust, there is no hope of more. I think love is possible for all people, and there is love enough if we seek it. But few are brave enough to trust first to find it."

"Trust can be broken." Jetekesh looked upward as a shadow passed over the ground. A hawk circled the air, then released a piercing cry before it dove for some far-off prey. "Placing your trust in the wrong person can get you killed. My lord father chose to trust my mother, and it nearly cost him all."

"Forgive me," said Dakarai. "I should have been more specific. *Mutual* trust is the key."

Jetekesh shrugged. "And what of unrequited love?"

"That is not true love. It is only a deep kind of affection. Love only reaches its truest form when it is returned."

"Maybe." Jetekesh shook his head. "I'm not inclined to believe you—nor to hope love finds me. Life is burdensome enough without that."

"You would prefer to marry outside the bond of love?" asked Kethalas.

Jetekesh grimaced. "I would rather not marry at all. But I know I have an obligation to find a queen and sire an heir. I suppose I'll leave the arrangement to the king. Him, I trust."

"Ah, but marriage is a long commitment," Dakarai said. "Yet you are young. There is time enough to change your mind and to heal from the wounds your mother inflicted."

Jetekesh shuddered. *Mother. Can I ever trust anyone enough to wed after all she did?*

As Jetekesh lifted a tentpole, shivers slithered down his arms. He paused and glanced over his shoulder.

"What is it?" asked Song, hoisting a corner of the tent canvas nearby.

He shook his head. "Just a feeling." He turned back to the pole.

Howls broke over the grim evening sky, ethereal and cold as a living corpse.

"To arms," Lord Emerin growled.

Jetekesh dropped the pole and slid his sword free of its sheath, trying not to make noise. He scanned the rocky crags surrounding camp. The hiss of loosing swords filled the air.

If they attack us, how can we survive until dawn?

"Caught out in the open like this, we're doomed," Liu put in, moving up beside Emerin near the wagon. "That fire has betrayed our position."

"Save your conflict for the fell beasts," Emerin whispered. "Or hide in the wagon-bed."

Liu flushed, then stalked away from the lord, drawing a short sword. His dark eyes snagged on Jetekesh, who offered a feeble smile as the howls rose higher. Liu glowered back, his mouth twisting in open disgust.

Could Jetekesh blame the young man? Shing and Amantier hadn't often seen eye to eye, and their history was a sordid one. *Perhaps I could use this journey to mend bridges.* Reluctance pressed him down; he didn't want to admit to Amantier's past mistakes, but surely Father would if he were in the prince's position. *I want to be like him, not Mother.*

More howls joined the chorus, and chills nipped at Jetekesh's gut as he shifted his stance, scanning the ridges for any sign of reflective, blazing eyes.

A single inhuman cry rose above the rest—not like a fell beast at all. The mournful sound pierced Jetekesh's heart and pricked at his eyes until a tear rolled down his cheek. His hands trembled.

What do we face?

The *vashalan* answered the melancholy note, lifting their voices to sing a dirge.

"What evil is this?" Liu whispered.

Lord Emerin padded to Kethalas's side. "Do you learn anything in this noise, Master Dragon?"

Jetekesh's heart panged. Lord Emerin *knew*?

The prince wrenched his eyes from the heights to stare at Kethalas, who merely blinked at the keep lord, then slowly shook his head. "I do not, my lord. It is a strange sound to me. A most disheartening one." He rested a hand over his heart. "What I can tell you is that the sorrowful voice belongs not to a *vashalan* but to something fallen from light. Far, far fallen."

Rille paused over the campfire, chills running up her spine as a heartbroken cry pierced the clouds far above the shadowed trees.

At the same moment, Yeshton dropped his armload of wood with a clatter. "What is that?" he whispered.

She shook her head as her chest throbbed. "I don't know, Sir Knight. But it hurts my heart."

Raum lifted his voice to answer the keening, mournful note upon the air.

"Hush," said Kajsa, drawing her shawl closer. She glanced toward Ingrid, whose chair had ceased to rock.

The old woman tipped her head to listen. "Such a lament I've never heard in all my days."

Kajsa wiped tears from her eyes. "What could make such a dreadful noise?"

Ingrid shook her head. "I can't say, child. Something not of this realm, that's certain. Not of this realm."

Silence fell in the wake of the heavens' cry. Aredel heaved himself into the longboat along Bahadronn's southern wharves, and grabbed the oars.

"You're still going out?" asked Artassa. "After that horrid sound?"

Aredel glanced at the rising moon. "Now, more than ever. No matter how sad that sound, it wasn't natural—nor does it strike me as the cry of wounded innocence. The magics stirring in KryTeer are dark, my wife. It might be attached to the wheel of flame hunting me." He met her brown eyes. "I will not risk my people."

Artassa reached out as if to stroke his cheek, though she stood on the dock too far away. "Be careful."

He nodded. "I won't let the fire claim me—nor any otherworldly noise. Untie my boat."

She unfastened the rope and tossed it into the longboat. "May the gods attend you."

He rowed toward open sea and his nightly ritual against the wreathing flames. *Gods protect my people.*

THE *VASHALAN* NEVER ATTACKED. Whether the desolate cry had scared them off or not, Jetekesh gratefully slipped into bed after a scant, hurried dinner, and fell into a deep but troubled rest.

He woke at dawn, sore, irritable, and hungry. After dressing, he stepped around his sleeping companions and out into a frosty world. He found Lord Emerin stirring the cookfire flames.

The horses shuffled and snorted, as uneasy and restless as Jetekesh's soul.

"Do you ever rest, my lord?" asked Jetekesh, plopping down on his frozen saddle.

The man's faint smile turned grim. "Rest and sleep aren't the same, my prince. I sleep, but I rarely rest."

Jetekesh stared at the boiling pot perched on the trivet. "How did you know about Kethalas being...you know?"

The lord scratched his stubbled chin. "There are reasons. I'm not really inclined to divulge them."

"Is that fair?" asked Jetekesh. "You divulged *his* secret."

Lord Emerin chuckled. "A valid argument, I suppose. Do I owe *him* an explanation, then, my prince?"

Jetekesh sighed and shrugged. "Do what you please, my lord. I'm in no mood to banter." He climbed to his aching legs and hobbled to the wagon to grab the horse feed and muzzle sacks. He'd spent the previous evening sparring with Sir Lafe after a full day's ride, and every muscle ached. He longed for a hot bath—or mulled wine—or anything to soothe his battle hurts and the leagues of travel.

I'm pathetic.

Jetekesh heaved another feed sack from the wagon-bed—and froze.

Burning red eyes stared at him from inside the wagon. Drool

dripped from jagged fangs as the *vashalan* rose on its bony legs. A pungent odor like rot and mildew rolled over Jetekesh's senses, and he choked.

Move. Move!

His legs wouldn't obey. His heart faltered, then thundered in his ears, deafening him.

The beast lunged.

Sir Lafe slammed into Jetekesh, knocking him aside. The knight crumpled as the beast bowled into him, and they tumbled to the ground together.

Jetekesh scrambled upright and fumbled for his sword. "Lord Emerin!"

The keep lord appeared from behind the wagon, then darted forward. He plunged his blade deep into the monster's ribs. The creature yowled and stumbled from Sir Lafe, dragging lord and weapon with it, until Lord Emerin yanked his sword loose.

Song and Kethalas raced to Lord Emerin's side, the former clutching her sword. Liu appeared behind them seconds later. Harn and Yin hung back.

Blood oozed from the beast's deep wound, but the creature didn't flee. It bared its yellow teeth and turned its feral gaze on Jetekesh. Frothy blood seeped between its fangs as it growled, and the coppery scent mingled with its putrid odor. Jetekesh's stomach lurched, but he resisted an urge to drop his blade and cover his nose.

"Your Highness, come this way, very slowly," said Lord Emerin.

The prince inched toward the keep lord. The beast's eyes tracked his movements, and the growls grew deeper, more guttural.

Jetekesh's heart struck his ribs. His head throbbed as ice slowed his blood flow. Slick sweat loosened his grip upon his sword, and he readjusted the hilt. Wind tugged at his hair and tossed strands in his vision.

The growls reached a basso rumble.

"Run!" Lord Emerin's voice shattered the sky.

Heart in his throat, Jetekesh bolted, blood pounding through his ears, boots kicking up grit. He flung himself behind the keep lord, crashing to the ground as the *vashalan* pounced. Jaws snapped shut on air where Jetekesh had been a second before. He drew himself to his elbows and craned his head.

The *vashalan* stood between Lord Emerin and Sir Lafe, pinned amid their blades, its hackles up, eyes burning with hatred.

"Take your shot!" the keep lord cried.

Jetekesh searched. There. Yin with a bow in his hand, arrow nocked and pointed. The boy unleashed it—and the arrow caught the *vashalan* between its eyes. With a harrowing, wraith-like yelp, the beast stumbled sideways.

Kethalas darted around Lord Emerin, a burning torch in hand. He jabbed the beast with the flame, and its fur caught fire at once. Howls rose into the sky as acrid smoke poured off the beast, carrying an odor like a rotting corpse bobbing on the surface of bog water.

Jetekesh turned away from the thrashing creature, stomach roiling.

"Pack up," Lord Emerin growled. "We'll eat on the road."

Most moved to obey, though Kethalas kept vigil over the torched beast.

Jetekesh started to climb to his feet, and a strong hand caught his arm and hauled him upright.

"Hurt, Your Highness?"

Jetekesh met Sir Lafe's eyes and shook his head. "Not badly. Just scrapes." He fought an urge to inspect his throbbing hands. *Mother would hate to see me so rattled and battered.* He smiled to defy the shame crawling up his skin. *Own it. Let her go.*

'*But, dearheart,*' cooed the spectral voice, '*you're so slovenly. Princes aren't meant to struggle like this. You've become so weak.*'

He gritted his teeth and pulled free of Sir Lafe's grasp. "Don't coddle me. Let's help get the tent loaded up."

Sir Lafe's expression held its stony façade. He nodded. "As you wish, my prince."

They carried the poles while Song, Dakarai, and Anenyasha rolled up the canvas. Yin stood near Kethalas, who watched the *vashalan* burn. Liu worked with Harn to saddle the horses, while Lord Emerin knelt in the wagon-bed and shifted barrels of food around, perhaps checking for more creatures.

The keep lord glanced over his shoulder as Jetekesh and Sir Lafe approached, a grim smile on his lips. "That boy's a good shot, but that was too near a thing to comfort my ailing nerves. How are you, Your Highness?"

Jetekesh shrugged. "A bit shaken but recovering, my lord." He shifted the weight of the poles. "It will be some time before I approach a wagon without feeling wary."

"Wary is the best way to feel right now." Lord Emerin's smile folded down into a frown as he took the poles from Jetekesh and positioned them inside the wagon. "My prince, as we carry forth, enemies will likely beset us on all sides. Between the *vashalan*, Shingese, and unfriendly tribes within the Clanslands, we must trust few and travel fleetly. Stealth is our objective." He took Sir Lafe's poles.

"I understand that, though it appears to be especially tricky to sneak," said Jetekesh.

The lord nodded. "You'll be hardest of all to hide." He shifted and dragged a black velvet cloak from behind him. "If you would consider wearing this, I'd be most grateful."

Jetekesh took the proffered cloth and fingered the soft fabric. The weave was unfamiliar. "I must stand out more than I thought."

"Like a beacon." Lord Emerin pulled a second cloak from a trunk. "I'll ask Lord Kethalas to wear one as well. He stands out almost as much."

Jetekesh started. "I stand out more than *he* does?"

Sir Lafe nodded. "Like a beacon."

With a soft sigh, Jetekesh draped the cloak over his shoulders, fastened the intricate silver clasp at his throat, then drew the cowl over his face. "Better?"

"Quite a bit, Your Highness." Lord Emerin tossed the second cloak to Sir Lafe. "Take that to Lord Kethalas if you would."

Sir Lafe nodded and strode away.

Lord Emerin seized Jetekesh's gaze with a sharp stare. "I heard about Sir Tifen, Your Highness."

Jetekesh inhaled a sharp breath. "Your point, my lord?"

"I knew Sir Tifen years ago. I looked up to him as he sought to become a knight. I heard about his father's wrongful disgrace and easily guessed the reason he left court. Forgive my bluntness, but in the Keep of the Falls, we well knew of your mother's affairs within the royal court. Her dalliances were legendary."

Jetekesh's cheeks scorched.

Lord Emerin scraped a hand over his stubble. "It's one reason I stayed away from Rose Palace. That aside, I heard about Sir Tifen's posthumous rise to knighthood. I heard how he and his father fell in the court of KryTeer protecting you."

Jetekesh stared at the ground, vision misty, insides churning. "*Your point*, my lord?"

"I understand why you won't let yourself trust Sir Lafe."

Jetekesh's head jerked upright. "Trust?"

Lord Emerin nodded. "You're afraid that to let him in is a

betrayal of Sir Tifen, and that you might one day lose him, too. Better to keep him at arm's length, hm?"

"...Perhaps."

The keep lord shrugged. "From my point of view, there are two ways to lose someone important to us. The first is to death. The second is to never know them to begin with. The latter is far sadder than the former, my prince, and much lonelier. Would you rather not have known Sir Tifen at all, Your Highness?"

Jetekesh pinned his eyes on the closest wagon wheel, neck burning. "Of course not."

"My prince, give Sir Lafe a chance." Lord Emerin shifted forward and jumped from the wagon-bed. "Otherwise, you'll carry a different kind of regret, should he perish in his efforts to protect you. I know Sir Lafe well from a time when he served under my father years ago. He's a good man. No sense of humor, mind. But a good man." He set a hand on Jetekesh's shoulder. "That's the best way to honor Sir Tifen's sacrifice."

Song, Dakarai, and Anenyasha reached the wagon with a rolled-up bundle of canvas between them.

"Ready to go, I think," said Dakarai. "Kethalas is certain the beast is dead."

"Good. I'll patch up the prince's hands, and we can head out." Lord Emerin's eyes flicked to the burning corpse. "I'd like to escape this aroma before we lose our appetites."

Dakarai nodded and led Anenyasha and Song toward the horses.

Moving to follow, Jetekesh lifted a hand to scratch an itch on his arm and flinched as his skin pricked. Blood smeared his palm. Grit had punctured his skin. *I didn't realize it was this bad. No wonder it stings so.* He turned back to Lord Emerin and, sighing, proffered his hands.

Lord Emerin doused a handkerchief with water from a water-skin. He cleaned Jetekesh's hands in turn, applied a salve from a tin in the wagon's herb kit, and wrapped his palms with bandages. "There. Keep an eye on those hands, Your Highness. We don't need them getting infected."

Jetekesh flexed his fingers to make certain he could grip his reins, then tugged gloves over the bandages. "I'll be careful. Thank you, Lord Emerin."

They strode together toward the waiting company, leaving the smoldering beast behind.

CHAPTER 13
WHITE LIGHT

Days of blistering work had been spent unburying the fallen in the palace of Bahadronn.

King Aredel stood before the graves heaped with fresh dirt. Among those who had died, six of his seven wives lay beneath the ground. Artassa stood beside him, silent, draped in a dark veil to hide her sorrow. Behind her, Aredel's protectors—Shevek and Ledonn—stood in perfect stillness in their bloodred armor. Their expressions were clouded with grief.

Anguish couldn't touch Aredel. There was no space for it beside his wrath. His body shook with bitter rage; his vision bled red. But he remained still, letting his fury build. Letting it permeate his soul.

He watched the sun sink toward the horizon.

Time to return to my boat.

He spent each night on the water, dodging the wreathing fire. But every time, the storming flames homed in closer and closer toward Bahadronn.

He mustn't let another attack happen.

How do I defeat such a plague?

Giving himself up was out of the question. His people needed him, and he wasn't ready to die. Not yet, not until long from now.

Aredel turned to Artassa. "I must go."

She dipped her head. "Be careful, holy husband."

He grimly smiled. "I will be clever, and that is far better." He squared his shoulders and started for the dock. Ledonn and Shevek flanked him as the crowds parted in silence. Eyes weighed down his frame. Faith-filled.

How can they still think me a god?

Since Aredel had learned the dance of death with his blade, most of KryTeer had hailed him as a god come in mortal form to conquer the civilized world. Even Lord Father's priests had declared him chosen, touched by divinity, more so even than the emperor. Aredel had worn that truth like he wore armor into battle. It was a grim reality, sobering rather than intoxicating. He had seen his divine role as a cold unbending fact—one that would require him to end Lord Father's life.

But in the end, he hadn't slain Emperor Gyath. Prince Sharo had done that. Did that make Aredel a failure? Were the gods displeased with his weaknesses? For years, he had sought to right the wrongs of the world in a swift, brutal motion. To end suffering by uniting all banners under the holy hand of KryTeer and its war gods. To protect the weak like Jinji from the bitter pains and injustices of life.

Yet Jinji had still died.

Intolerance, injustice, hunger, suffering... It all lived on.

To honor Jinji—to show his elder half-brother that he could change as Jinji wanted him to—he had given up his claims to other lands.

But nothing else had changed. All remained the gray hues of life's unfairness.

And now Bahadronn smoldered, a quarter of its citizens dead and buried.

Aredel reached the dock's brink and stared at the boat bobbing on the water. Wrath struck at his flesh like a den of serpents as his eyes skimmed the ocean sparkling red.

"Holy King?" Ledonn's voice hung in the air with a tentative note.

Aredel stirred and turned to his retainer. The Blood Knight bore several burns on his face, for he'd tried to rescue as many as he could from the flames consuming the palace on the night of the fire. Shevek carried similar burns on his hands and arms.

Ledonn held his gaze, probing. "You'll be clever, not reckless, yes, my holy king?"

Aredel sighed and pushed loose black hair from his face. "This cannot go on. I will face the flames tonight...but they will not win." His voice held an edge sharper than a dagger's blade.

Ledonn's eyes caught the light of the sunset as they widened. "But, Holy One, how can you beat fire?" He blinked and ducked his head. "Forgive my doubt."

Aredel turned back to the ocean. "Ledonn. Shevek."

"Holy One," they echoed.

"Do you believe me to be a god?"

"Yes, Blood King," they said.

"Do you believe the war gods of KryTeer have chosen me to protect our land?"

"Yes, Blood King."

"Do you believe those same gods will protect me in return?"

A pause, slight, merely a heartbeat. "Yes, Blood King."

Aredel let his smile grow into something real. A thrill sparked in his blood. "This night, I will test your faith. My faith. The faith of KryTeer." He lifted his hand and curled his fingers into a tight fist. "This night, I shall rise to my birthright or fall as a false god."

He removed his bejeweled vest, handing it off to Ledonn. Then he stooped, dragged the boat nearer to the dock, and stepped down into it. "Set me loose."

Shevek tossed the rope into the boat as Ledonn fell to his knees, armor clanking.

"Gods attend you in your trial." Ledonn's eyes were bright. "We shall await your triumphant return, Holy Blood King of KryTeer."

Shevek joined him on his knees and bowed his head.

Aredel turned from them. *What am I, Jinji? Only you knew, and you have abandoned me to this colorless life.*

His rage flared, but it couldn't touch the place in his heart where Jinji's memory dwelt. How could he blame the storyteller for dying? Nakania was too small, too cruel a world, for such a man to stay within its borders. He had joined Prince Sharo in Shinac, as he ought.

I was lucky to know him first.

Aredel rowed the boat into the open waters far from KryTeer's shores and tossed an anchor into the sea. It sank into the depths and vanished in darkness. He sat and waited for the first stars to appear in the purpling sky. Red stripes stained the deepening shades of night, and clouds clutched the last threads of woven gold like covetous dragons.

An ancient song slipped into his mind, and he sang it softly to himself while he sharpened his weapons on a whetstone as the stars caught the light of the rising moon.

Hours crept away like a thief. Aredel's skin pricked as the moon reached the midnight heights. He sheathed his dagger and pocketed the whetstone. In the swaying boat, he carefully rose as the whoosh and spark of fire sounded above him in the night sky. He tipped his head back to watch the wreath of fire bloom across the air. Light and shadow pitched over the surface of the water and cast undulating shapes in the boat.

Aredel raised his arms over his head. "Here I am! Consume me if you dare, flames of Hell!"

The wreath stretched and brightened as it spun faster and hotter. The boat rocked forward, and Aredel dropped his eyes to find a figure, featureless, standing before him. Translucent tendrils poured off the colorless shape, like water spilling from a maw in the side of a mountain.

"What are you, fell creature?"

The watery shape sputtered and turned into black sand, then shifted into the form of Emperor Gyath as he had been in Aredel's youth—muscular, tall, with sharp eyes and a deep smirk.

"My son," thundered the powerful voice.

Aredel's eyes narrowed. "You are not he. You are the demon who has possessed our line since the days of Cavalin and Tallat. But you were banished back to the sea by Prince Sharo. How are you free?"

Gyath's face shifted as black sand poured over it, and the figure shaped into the watery silhouette of a faceless woman.

"I am not so easily bound," a female voice gurgled.

Aredel narrowed his eyes on *Erisyrdrel*. "A lie. Prince Sharo declared you would stay bound for many years. Someone has released you."

Laughter babbled from the rippling head. "Does it matter? I am free."

"And you have destroyed my palace and swallowed up many of my people. Now you torment me...yet you reveal yourself rather than kill me. Why?"

"The fire is a curse left by your late father, Blood King," answered the watery specter. "But I can spare you further harm and loss."

"How and why?" Aredel crossed his arms.

"Allow me to reside within your mortal shell," she burbled. "I will make you truly a god upon Nakania."

"I refuse. Possession makes me no more than a tool. Why work to gain my consent?"

The watery shape bubbled, sighing. "I cannot force possession of one so strong-willed—and my unceasing presence requires a contract." She lifted watery fingers toward him. "Together, Blood King, we can rule this world as you have always dreamed. I need a body, and you would gain long life and great powers beyond what you can imagine."

Aredel chuckled. "Is that what you promised my father? Yet he was dying of a weakened heart."

"Seeing your greatness, I hungered to possess you, and so I did not sustain him in his gluttony."

The Blood King snorted. "And if another comes along with greater potential than myself, will you not abandon me to the same fate?" He dropped his arms to his sides. "Tempt me not, vile sea demon. I'll not sell my body and soul to a fickle creature chained to her own appetites."

The watery form trembled and frothed. "You would rather I slay you?"

Aredel took a step forward. "*Try.*" He lifted his chin. "But I am no mere man—I am the kin of Jinji of Shing, he whom you feared above all."

"I did not fear Jinji!"

Aredel bared his teeth in a grin. "Liar."

The demon let out a scream like breaking waves and a rising tempest. The wreathing fire exploded over Aredel's head, and blazing balls of flame raced toward Bahadronn. His heart lurched, and he reached for the flames as though he could catch them.

"No!" His cry cut over the air, and he whirled on the demon. "Coward!"

A burbling laugh answered. "You fear not for yourself, but what of your kingdom? Your greatest weakness is your love of KryTeer and its pathetic people. Watch them burn, O Blood King. Watch and accept your mortality. You are no god."

Aredel spun back toward the city blazing with torches as the flames approached its shores. His heart sank.

I have no power, Jinji. When it counts most, what good am I? I don't want to be a god. I just want to be a king able to protect what truly matters.

Cold fear surged up his back, and down his arms. The demon's laughter pattered against his ears like rain in a growing storm. Waves lapped at his boat, and he stumbled but steadied himself.

The first fireball struck the harbor, and firelight blanched the sky.

Aredel gripped his sword and whirled as he unsheathed it. "Cease this destruction, demon!"

Light beamed from Aredel's sword as pristine white smoke poured from his hand and arm. Aredel stared, then dragged his eyes up his arm and down his torso. The white smoke curled off his frame, wisped off his feet, illuminating the interior of the boat, shining off the black waves.

Erisyrdrel's laughter cut off. "What are you doing? What is this?"

Aredel's instincts pushed him. He lunged at the watery shape, and *Erisyrdrel* broke into a million droplets that scattered out of the boat and into the depths.

"I think not." He stabbed his blade into the water.

A streak of white lightning pulsed through the depths, and an unearthly wail ascended as waves rolled and rocked the boat.

Aredel stumbled back and caught himself on the boat's lip, sword clattering to his feet. He glanced toward land. The fireballs had vanished. None but the first had struck the city, and the flames on the docks had evaporated. Only a smear of smoke stained the sky above the twinkling harbor.

As the waves stilled and the boat steadied, Aredel sighed and pawed his hair away from his face.

A breeze tickled his cheeks, cool and welcome.

'*We're not finished, Blood King.*' The voice burbled into silken silence.

Aredel let a savage grin stretch across his lips. "I certainly hope not, you foul monster. I yearn to hunt you down." He spotted his sword at his feet, lightless. He flipped his hand back and forth, but the light had extinguished.

"Was that you, Jinji?" he whispered. "Did you beseech the gods on my behalf?"

He laughed, long, deep, too relieved and stunned to stop himself.

Aredel, king of KryTeer, terror of the world, had few things to fear—but boredom had always been one of them. Now, an enemy had appeared, something to hunt down and destroy...and he had somehow tapped the power to accomplish it. He plucked up his sword, sheathed it, then settled onto the boat's seat and caught up his oars to row toward shore.

Would *Erisyrdrel* return to battle him again, or would she flee and cower someplace far away?

Whatever her course, I won't allow her to remain free. Jinji paid too high a price for that.

CHAPTER 14
THE ARCHON

"Good morning, Axel!"

Kajsa trotted around patches of snow to catch up to her friend while Axel turned to wave at her. When she reached him, puffing for breath, she leaned her hands against her knees and swallowed hard.

Axel chuckled. "Why the haste?"

She shook her head and straightened from her crouch. "Didn't want to slow you down. Where are you going?"

He pointed to the Elderhouse. "Lord Navolleth has invited me to join the meeting of elders. He's speaking."

Kajsa's brows shot up. "Why did he invite you?"

"Likes me, I guess. We have a kind of—a bond. I saved him; he saved me."

As words gathered in her throat, Kajsa pressed her lips together. *But I saved you, too.* She wrestled against the urge to say it. Clasped her hands against her tailbone and rolled back to balance on her heels. "What is he speaking to the elders about? Navolleth, I mean?" She flattened her feet.

Axel's eyes sparkled. He leaned close and tapped his lips with a finger. "Can't tell you. Not yet. But, Ky, it's going to change *everything.*"

Gooseflesh danced up her arms. "Why should anything change?"

He winked. "Talk later. I don't want to be late." He caught a strand of her long, pale hair, and tugged it lightly. "Meet me at the creek for lunch?"

"A—all right." She hugged herself and stared after him, watching his platinum hair flounce as he sprinted across the icy path. He ducked inside the Elderhouse and shut the door. She slapped her mittens together and blew breath over them to warm her fingers. "Let it go, Kajsa. It's likely nothing."

But Ingrid's words pattered through her thoughts, seeping into her mood to dampen it like rainclouds. *'Soon you must leave.'*

Kajsa trotted to Frit's turf house a few buildings down from the Elderhouse.

He answered on her second knock and offered a tight smile. "Here for Ingrid's packages?"

Kajsa nodded.

"Some of it couldn't be saved. The food was all gone."

"I thought it would be." Kajsa accepted the satchel bulging with supplies. "Thank you for fetching the rest."

"Happy to help the old woman."

She swung the satchel over her shoulder.

"Tell Ingrid hello for me." He shut the door.

Kajsa turned and made her way back up the path toward Ingrid's solitary home. As she shifted her load, the trill of birds slowed her feet. Two robins winged overhead and settled in a birch where they built their new nest. Kajsa smiled.

Looks like spring really is coming.

She set the satchel on Ingrid's porch and brushed a finger

against a carved depiction of Ingrid's family tree on the door. Kajsa's heart twinged. Poor Ingrid had never married—her line would end with her.

Will that be my fate?

Fluttering wings beat against the air, and Kajsa turned to watch a dozen birds flee into the open sky. Silence fell across the ridge, and she stared into the dense thicket of firs several yards from the porch. Her skin prickled.

Did blazing red eyes watch her from beneath the evergreen boughs?

Kajsa backed up and thumped against the door. Growls reverberated in the thicket, and a branch snapped. Kajsa's fingers pawed for the knob. Grasping it, she unlatched the door and stumbled backward. Slammed it shut. Leaned against the wood and panted for breath as her body shook.

Her vision swam, but she blinked back the tears.

What good does it do to cry? You're safe. They won't come in here. They're probably not even real.

Her spine stiffened. She'd left the satchel out there.

With quaking limbs, she slipped to the window and pulled aside Ingrid's heavy curtains to peer through the distorted glass pane. No sign of wildlife. No indication of terrible eyes in a monstrous face.

Kajsa glanced over her shoulder and found Ingrid napping in her rocking chair. The cat lay curled up on the hearth stones, undisturbed by Kajsa's imaginary attackers.

Drawing a breath and leveling her shoulders, Kajsa inched the door open and dove for the parcels, then slithered back inside and snapped the door shut. No sound. No threat.

Why are you so silly, Kajsa? It's broad day. Stop acting like a little child.

She deposited the parcels on the table and set about making

bread for Axel's lunch. As she kneaded the dough, her tension bled away. Those horrible beasts wouldn't come near the village. Not with so many hunters about. Not with the sun high in the sky and no shadows to hide in.

Her fingers fumbled. *But they attacked us before in daylight. Why?*

KAJSA TOSSED pebbles into the burbling creek while Axel nibbled on a wedge of fresh bread. Birdsong floated on the crisp wind, and the fragrance of mountain snow stroked her senses.

"I'm leaving, Ky," Axel said.

The pebble she tossed struck a log and ricocheted before it plunked into the water. "Where are you going?"

"Lord Navolleth and Elder Viggo want me to attend a meeting in Tild. We're going to see the Archon." He shifted on the moss-covered log to grin at Kajsa. "*Me*. Can you believe it? Lord Navolleth says I've got my head on right for someone so young. He sees a bright future ahead of me. Isn't that something?"

Kajsa pressed a smile onto her lips. "That's amazing, Xel. When are you leaving?"

"Tomorrow."

Her heart plummeted into her churning stomach. "It must be very important."

Hair flounced in his eyes as he bobbed a nod and leaned close. "'Tis." His mouth snapped shut, and he leaned his head to one side. "I'm not supposed to talk about it though. It's very secret. Almost no one knows. Just the elders and Lord Navolleth —and myself." His eyes sparkled like stars, and he laughed. "Ah, Ky. Can you believe it? All my life I thought I'd have to hunt and trap for my living. Never make ends meet. But now— Ahh, now I can *be* somebody."

"You *are* somebody, Xel. Somebody wonderful." She caught up a mitten on her lap and wrung it. "But I'm happy for you. You're gifted, Axel. Everyone knows it. I'm not surprised Navolleth can see it, too."

Axel's grin crooked. He wrapped an arm around Kajsa and pulled her close. His scent was like pine needles and woodsmoke. "Thanks, Ky. You're special, too. You've seen the best in me for years—even back when everyone thought I'd just be a troubled whelp all my days."

"Well," she flopped the mitten onto her lap, "being a *boy*, that's likely true. But you're growing into someone fine. You don't need lords and elders to make it so."

Axel's grip slackened. He tipped his head forward to eye her sidelong. "But it helps, Kajsa. A lot. Most of us are apprenticed to one trade all our days. You're lucky the wisewoman favors you—you get to choose whether to embroider or heal. Maybe even both. I never thought I'd get a choice."

Kajsa's gaze fell to the stream. A fish darted in its shimmering depths. "What would you choose if you could do anything?"

He turned to stare into the woods. "To fight. Fight for change."

"That means nothing. What change?"

He shrugged. "The kind that makes a difference, gives us something better."

She tossed another pebble into the water. It plunked and sank to the stony bed. "That still doesn't mean anything. Anyone can fight. A hunter, a weaver, a baker. What do you want to do that you can't do if you're stuck in a trade?"

He blew out a breath. "Why're you like this? Why do you

always have to prod for meaning? I don't *know* all that it means. I just feel an itch. A—a craving for something more than gutting deer and trapping rabbits. I want to, I dunno, to *matter.* To be someone others can respect and revere."

"You want power?" The words slipped from her lips unbidden.

Axel jerked back. "No. *No*. Not like that. Just to make a real difference—and I can now. I will. Lord Navolleth has plans for me. Big plans." He raked his pale hair back. "Watch me. I'll become someone you'll be proud to know."

"I'm already proud to know you, Xel." She shifted to face him. "I—I already care."

He flashed a smile warm enough to melt bones. Her heart fluttered.

"Ah, Ky. Listen to you." He leaned forward, tilted his head, and brushed his lips against her cheek. "Careful now. You'll steal my heart."

Breath caught in her windpipes. Her face burned, and she dipped her head. "Don't tease me, Axel Hunter'son!"

He laughed, long and light, caught her fingers in his, and squeezed her hand. "Can't help it. You're too much fun." His eyes darted to her lips. Before she could think, he leaned in and caught her lips with his. His hands slipped around her waist as he deepened the kiss. She let him, too frightened, too stiff to move.

Does he mean it?

He drew back. Laughed again. Stood and brushed moss and twigs from his pants. "I'd best get back to help my Fa repair his gear. He won't let me travel to Tild unless I do, since I'm missing the next hunt."

Kajsa found air and drew it in. The cold breeze tickled her throat and seared her lungs. "Axel. Did you mean that just now?"

He cocked his head. "Mean what?" A mischievous grin flashed over his lips, then he spun away. "Gotta go. See you tomorrow."

She watched him, immobile, numb to the growing chill as the sun ducked behind a heavy bank of clouds.

"Bye," she whispered.

CHAPTER 15
BRIGHT FIRE

Jetekesh huddled in his black cloak and tugged his collar tighter to his throat. The summit of the pass was drenched in snow so thick, the wagon couldn't break through. Lord Emerin had called a halt and swung from his horse to examine the drifts that sloped up between the sheer cliffs, hiding the road.

He eventually tramped back and shook his head. "No good pressing our luck, Your Highness. We'll not break through so early in the season."

"Do we return to the Keep of the Falls?" asked the prince.

"No." Emerin pointed to a gap between the rock walls a few yards back down the pass. "There's a lower road that veers north and tends not to get as much snow. It adds a day or so onto our journey, but it's better than freezing right here or turning back entirely. What say you, Your Highness?"

Jetekesh eyed the gap, then nodded as a shiver snaked up his limbs. "Let's take it. Better a day later than not at all."

"Very well." Emerin trudged back to his horse and moved to speak with Harn on the wagon.

Turning the company around took time in the slick conditions, and sleet started up again, soaking Jetekesh through his cloak. He hunched down to soak in Hickory's warmth, trying to ignore thoughts of what Mother would say.

'Ah, and I would say plenty, dearheart. Your posture is everything. Straighten up. Be regal.'

Grimacing, Jetekesh refused to sit straight until the wagon had been guided back down the pass. The company followed and squeezed through the gap—the wagon scraping the rocks as it passed through the natural opening. Harn expertly guided his horses, and soon the company was rolling along.

All the shuffling had put Jetekesh behind the wagon, and he rode near Liu and Song, with Dakarai and Anenyasha in the rear. Unwilling to force his way back to the front in the slick, biting sleet, Jetekesh contented himself with recalling the stories Jinji had told him of Shinac.

"You must be miserable, Highness." The voice belonged to Liu.

Jetekesh glanced at the Shingese nobleman. "Why, because it's cold and wet?"

"Aren't you more accustomed to life inside a palace?"

Jetekesh looked ahead again as the wagon jostled over a rough patch in the old road. "Of course. But I did get my first taste of adventure last summer. It taught me a little about a life of travel."

Liu coughed—or was it a scoff?

Jetekesh refused to let the young man's derision eat at him. Instead, he glanced at Song. "How are things in Shing—beyond this ugly business with the emperor? I know my father has been making great strides toward a new peace pact. We'd welcome a new season of open trade with Kyon Taro."

"I'm afraid I'm the wrong person to ask, Your Highness," Song said. "Liu here has more knowledge of matters in the capital. But if you seek the view of the common folk of Shing, we welcome peace in any season and pray to the earth it lasts forever. War is hardest on farmers and herders. We gain nothing and lose much."

Jetekesh's mind flitted over his tutor's lessons. "Not always, Lady Song. Sometimes wars are the only means of bringing about change. A sad fact, but an honest one." He tightened his clutch on Hickory's reins. "I doubt this is one of those wars, though. Not with a demon involved."

Liu brought his horse level and fell into pace beside Jetekesh's mount. "You presume to understand common folk, Your Highness? Interesting. I'd understood you to be indifferent."

A grimace tugged at Jetekesh's lips, but he resisted the start of a retort. "That's not quite true. I wasn't indifferent. I was"—the word formed on his tongue, bitter like an herb—"repulsed by anything common." Shame crawled up his neck, scorching. "I thought myself better than them, superior because I'd been lucky enough to be born a prince."

Liu pinned him with a narrow stare. "And now it's different? You're miraculously changed?"

"I—I'm beginning to change." Jetekesh stared hard at the rolling wagon. "I *want* to change."

"So, you still see yourself as superior?"

A breath shuddered down Jetekesh's throat. "No. Not that. More answerable as a leader making decisions for his people, perhaps, but not superior. If anything, I..." As he sought the words to express his desires, a faint, howling song rose above the storm. He stood in his stirrups, straining his ears as he slowed Hickory.

At the same moment, Kethalas rode around the wagon. "*Vashalan*, close. We need to circle up to fend them off if they attack."

Those riding at the rear of the wagon squeezed one by one between the conveyance and the close rock wall. Circling up would prove impossible along the narrow pass, but Emerin directed everyone, except Yin and Jetekesh, to shift boulders into a kind of barricade, while the prince and youth tied off the horses by the wagon. Protecting their mounts would become Jetekesh's priority, keeping him away from the main fighting if the *vashalan* appeared, whether he liked it or not.

Howls floated closer, cutting through the slush fall, chilling Jetekesh to his center. His close encounter with one mere days ago flared up in his mind as his hands throbbed. He glanced at Yin, huddled close, arrow nocked and ready to fly despite the sleet in his eyes.

Jetekesh slid his sword loose, ignoring his protesting scrapes. The hilt slickened before he could tuck it under the shelter of his cloak. He wiped it dry as best he could while wet snow seeped into his leather boots.

Snow clung to his eyelashes. The clouds scraped close, swirling in the wrathful winds, whipping strands of loose hair across Jetekesh's face.

The chorus of *vashalan* song swelled higher, nearer. Haunting and angry.

Someone near the barricade of stone lit a torch. It flared bright and warm against the darkening storm. Kethalas, probably. The man-dragon had been the one to torch the last beast.

Jetekesh rubbed water from his face several times while he

crouched, waiting in the wailful deluge. Would the *vashalan* strike or only prowl close and delay the company more?

If I really am like a beacon, they'll keep hunting us. Can I turn this light off? Can I hide what I am? Is the cloak doing anything?

He squeezed his eyes shut, clutching his sword closer.

Jinji, how do I deflect them? How do we survive their attacks?

A frigid wash of helplessness doused him as the wind picked up, punctuating his emotions. Nothing had really changed since his strange journey from Amantier to Shinac to KryTeer—not really.

He was still the same foolish child who had caused the deaths of Tifen, Palan, and then Jinji. Yes, the storyteller had been dying already, but Jetekesh had chosen to goad him into action. To force him to his feet one last time to face the Bloody-handed Emperor, Gyath. It had been Jinji's triumph. He'd summoned Prince Sharo of Shinac to cut down the tyrant where he stood.

Jetekesh had still been the one to push Jinji into action—action the storyteller hadn't had the strength to endure.

Bowing his head, Jetekesh resisted the tears burning in his vision.

Don't focus on the past, or you won't survive the here and now.

A piercing howl rose above the others—not the sad, keening note from that strange night, but a hungry, razing cry. The others joined it. The wind died all at once. All fell silent until the faint patter of tiny flakes kissed the prince's ears.

"Make ready!" Lord Emerin called.

Above the barricade, red eyes winked. A black mass sprang from the rocks, and the torch danced across the air, bright, mesmerizing. Kethalas moved like a hurricane, forcing the beast to scamper back up the boulders. Other inhuman eyes winked into sight, catching the fire glow, but Kethalas jabbed his torch at them and shouted out strange words bursting with power.

At the same moment, Lord Emerin and Sir Lafe leapt up onto the barricade and slashed at the *vashalan*. Close by, Dakarai and Anenyasha swung their spears against another clutch of canines.

Yin unleashed an arrow and struck true. A *vashalan* whimpered and tumbled over the shallow barricade. Still, more of the creatures climbed over the stones, their bony forms imposing in the storm's gloom.

Liu and Song met a pack of beasts away from where Lord Emerin, Sir Lafe, and Kethalas answered the majority. Gritting his teeth, Jetekesh jumped to his feet and raced into the fray as more *vashalan* appeared around the two Shingese fighters. Another of Yin's arrows hit its mark, right between a beast's disturbing eyes. It lurched back and writhed.

Jetekesh raced toward another brute as it scrambled over the barricade. Its eyes settled on him, and the beast bared its teeth in a grin that oozed with delight. Hefting a breath, Jetekesh tried to quiet his mind, to slip into the easy motions Master Ivam had drilled into him over the past few months. Step, swing forward, aside, aside, inward slice. His blade caught the beast's flank, tearing through matted fur to bite thin flesh.

I won't run. I'm not afraid.

Lies. Fear flooded every spare inch of him, but it filled him with something else: a fire, a reason to hold his ground. To prove to the imaginary voice of Mother that he could fight, even triumph, despite his fear.

A coward caves to his fear. A brave man faces it and wins. Something Sir Palan would say.

The beast recovered and lunged at him, maw wide open. Jetekesh stepped back to gain ground. Sleet caught his boot, and he slipped under the beast's attack. The *vashalan* landed and skittered on the frozen ground.

Jetekesh jammed his sword into the earth and shoved himself

upright, yanked his sword loose, and charged the creature before it could gain proper footing. The *vashalan* curved to face him as Jetekesh swung his sword hard and sliced into the beast's neck.

The sword sank deep, but the prince didn't have enough strength to cut clean through and sever the head. The beast jerked—jerked again—then sank down, eyes flattening.

Jetekesh wrenched his sword free, panting for breath as he whirled to seek another foe. Two more canine monsters climbed over the barricade, their eyes fastened on him. He quivered under their palpable hunger. The storm rose again and daggers of sleet stabbed at Jetekesh's exposed flesh.

He hoisted his sword. Shifted his grip. Slid his feet into a solid stance.

The *vashalan* pounced in unison—but a figure darted from the right, slamming his full weight against one beast.

Sir Lafe.

Jetekesh waited a single heartbeat as the *vashalan* flew at him, all fangs and claws, then he sidestepped and cut across, his bones rattling as he made impact. The beast whimpered, then staggered aside with a snarl, wobbling on the ice.

Jetekesh pressed his advantage and jammed the sword straight through the *vashalan*'s ribs. A high whine answered, then the beast slumped to the ground. Jetekesh freed his blade with a tug, satisfaction prickling through him. Another victory.

He turned again, legs trembling. He wasn't used to exerting himself under such harsh conditions.

Don't stop.

Sir Lafe straightened over the second *vashalan*'s corpse, a glint in his deep-set eyes. Yet more beasts poured over the barricade. A never-ending army.

The horses whinnied. Jetekesh spun toward them as Yin unleashed arrow after arrow, felling as many of the encroaching demonic canines as he could. Jetekesh lurched toward him, Sir Lafe on his heels.

A patch of ice caught Jetekesh's boot. He crashed against the frozen road, sword clattering from his numbing fingers. Breath exploded from his lips in a cloud. Sleet stung his eyes, hammering around him, intensifying. Unless this blasted storm let up, he'd soon be unable to discern friend from enemy.

Strong arms hooked his underarms and hefted him upright. Sir Lafe pressed Jetekesh's sword back into his fingers.

"The horses," the man shouted above the lashing gale.

Slipping and slithering over the road, Jetekesh made his way toward Yin.

We can't win like this. They won't stop coming.

Yin pointed his bow straight at Jetekesh, arrow nocked. He unleashed it with deft fingers. Jetekesh winced as the arrow whistled past his head and struck something behind him. Without glancing back, Jetekesh reached the Shingese boy and turned alongside Sir Lafe toward the infested battleground, keeping their backs to the frantic, tethered horses.

Despite the sleet, Kethalas's torch bobbed and whisked around in the frenzy, and Jetekesh's heart thawed several degrees. Hope hadn't died yet.

What can we do? How can we win?

"Kethalas, the torch!" Lord Emerin's call rose above the clash of sword and claw, and Jetekesh tracked the bobbing flame in the darkness.

Hard to believe it's afternoon somewhere below this pass.

The torch ceased to bob, then seemed to grow brighter, brighter. Blazing like a small sun. The wind quieted as if the flame tamed its tantrum. The sleet slowed until mere snowflakes fell from the sky. The torch blazed on, brighter still, held up by a figure Jetekesh couldn't identify.

Whimpering, the *vashalan* drew backward, crouching low, fangs bared as they issued low growls.

The flame burst upward into a column, reaching through the clouds, cutting through the gloom. Clutching the torch, Lord Emerin stared upward, green eyes glowing with some inner flame that fed the fire.

Jetekesh stared. *Am I dreaming?*

The storm rolled back in every direction as the fire broke through the last dregs to find the bright blue sky. Dropping his chin, Emerin glowered at the *vashalan* and spoke in a voice like thunder. The words were unfamiliar, foreign. Ringing with power.

The *vashalan* turned tail and scampered over the barricade in a flurry of fur, each trying to climb over another to flee first.

Moments passed. Adrenaline still pounded through Jetekesh. The storm retreated until the sky hung blue and wide above the narrow road.

Lord Emerin let the torch droop in his hands as the pillar of flame died. Heaving a sigh, he turned a faint smile on Kethalas. "That's quite the torch you have."

Kethalas took it from the lord, eyeing it like a critical swordsmith inspecting his latest masterpiece. "So it is." His tone was bemused.

Lord Emerin scanned the battleground, every canine corpse, and every human. No one in the company had fallen in combat. His smile stretched into a grin. "I stand among fierce comrades." He wobbled, then crashed to his knees before Kethalas could catch him.

"I'll be fine," the keep lord whispered, but his voice rang out with residual thunder. "Just a little weary."

"Rest," Kethalas said. "I will protect the prince."

With a grunt, Lord Emerin collapsed to the frozen earth, making his fair hair a tousled pool around him.

Jetekesh staggered close, adrenaline cooling to a weary numbness. "Kethalas, did *you* summon that pillar of flame?"

The man-dragon shook his head. "Not I. I am no fire wielder." His eyes gleamed as he stared at Lord Emerin upon the ground. "Fierce companions indeed." He whirled. "Harn, please help me get the mighty lord inside the wagon. I do not think he'll stir again this day."

CHAPTER 16
FAIRY SONG

The next morning, Jetekesh rode Hickory along the slushy mountain road near the back of the wagon. Lord Emerin still lay unmoving within, wrapped in a blanket. He hadn't stirred at all during the night, but Kethalas had assured everyone that the lord was sleeping, nothing else.

Now, as the sun slid toward the tor of the sky, Lord Emerin moaned.

Jetekesh straightened in his saddle. "Stop! Stop the wagon, Harn."

With a cluck of his tongue, Harn rolled the wagon to a halt. Jetekesh dismounted, flung his reins at his protector, and swung up into the wagon-bed.

Lord Emerin cracked his eyes open as Jetekesh leaned over him.

"How do you feel, my lord?" the prince asked, keeping his tones soft.

The man eyed him for a long moment, as though he didn't recognize Jetekesh. Then he blinked several times and inhaled a long breath. "Ah." His eyes took in the wagon interior, then he settled his gaze on the prince. "Your Highness, are you well?"

"Well enough." Jetekesh smiled. "And you?"

"Well enough," was the lord's murmuring echo. "How long was I asleep?"

"Through the night and longer. It's nearly noon now."

Lord Emerin pushed upright on one elbow and squinted out at the broad light of day. "So it is. Quite the fire trick Kethalas used, wasn't it?"

Jetekesh held still. *He doesn't want me to know* he *summoned the bright flame. Very well, I'll leave it be for now.* "So it was," he said aloud. "It appeared to rob you of most of your strength."

The lord grunted, then ran a hand through his blond tresses. "And left me with a ravenous appetite. Nearly noon, hm? Time for a quick respite then, wouldn't you say, Your Highness?"

"Definitely." Jetekesh heaved himself out of the wagon and sprinted to Kethalas and Dakarai who were waiting at the head of the column. "He wants food."

Dakarai chuckled. "What man doesn't? I will cook." He swung from his horse and clicked a few words at Anenyasha, who nodded. "It will not take us long."

"Thank you." Jetekesh raced back to the wagon and poked his head inside. "Won't be long before your appetite is sated. Have patience, Lord Emerin."

The man flexed the hand he'd held the torch with. "I can wait. I'm not wilting away."

Jetekesh grinned, then let his smile fall. "Quite a blessing, that fire trick. Without it, we'd all likely have died."

"Possibly," Emerin replied, not meeting Jetekesh's eyes. "We'll need to confirm it, of course, but I doubt the good dragon will be able to conjure up such a trick again any time soon. We must be careful until we reach the lowlands." Lines etched around his eyes. "And even then..."

Yes, even then. So close to Shing and headed for the Clanslands, what enemies might strike?

We'll be exposed on the grasslands.

Aloud, Jetekesh said, "We'll make do. What other choice do we have?"

Lord Emerin shifted to meet his eyes. A smile shaded his lips. "You really have grown, my prince. You give me new hope for Amantier." He caught Jetekesh's wrist and brought it up until the prince's ring flashed in a ray of sunlight. "If I may, Your Highness, I wish to extend my oath from father to son. My life is yours." He kissed the air above Jetekesh's signet ring, then straightened, releasing his wrist. "Now, let's see about food."

Jetekesh tracked the man's movements out of the wagon. Emerin gave no indication he was still weakened by his fire trick, nor wounded from his tussle against the *vashalan.*

Praise the saints.

Jetekesh stepped from the wagon after the lord. The rest of the company had gathered around a cookfire as Dakarai stirred the roiling contents of the pot resting on its trivet.

As they approached, Dakarai raised his head, dark eyes glittering in the bright sunlight. "Good rest, my lord?"

Lord Emerin grinned. "Far more than I'm accustomed to, but I'll survive."

Dakarai chuckled and turned back to the grain porridge. "I'll be glad when we leave the high pass. Good hunting lies lower in these mountains. I could use fresh meat."

"Aye," said Harn, nursing a small flask. "So could we all."

Jetekesh sat on a boulder beside Sir Lafe, glad the knight had taken the time to brush off the snow and spread out a spare blanket. He nodded at the man.

Eyeing the group huddled close to the fire's warmth, the prince smiled. "I'd be glad of some mulled wine myself."

Sir Lafe grunted his appreciation of the notion.

"I did hear you were partial to drinking," Liu said, turning his hands to warm his palms. "Indeed, rumors reached Shing that you weren't often sober."

Jetekesh stared into the flames. "Yes, well, rumors are rarely worth their weight against the truth."

"You don't drink to excess then, Highness?" Liu asked.

Song tossed her companion a needled stare. "Enough of that, Liu. Don't let our companions think civility is dead in Shing."

"It's fine." Jetekesh shifted to a more comfortable position on the boulder. "I don't get drunk, not anymore. In the past, I did on many occasions—but I wasn't perpetually intoxicated."

"I see." Liu's sneer gainsaid his words.

Dakarai stirred his porridge with one hand while batting aside steam with the other. "What about a song while we wait? I know a good one."

"Please," Jetekesh said above the murmurs of approval. "One from your own country, my lord?"

Dakarai's grin widened. "Naturally."

He lifted his voice in a pleasing basso roll, clicking strange sounds that lifted in a peculiar but pleasant melody. After a single stanza, Anenyasha joined him. Her higher tones melded into a flawless harmony, dipping down, then soaring to a height that left Jetekesh breathless.

As the music ended to general applause, the mountains seemed to pick up the refrain, carrying it higher, until Jetekesh imagined the sky sparkling with fairies who repeated the stanzas in their own tongue as they winged in circles.

Dizziness struck him, and he slumped forward.

"Your Highness?" whispered Sir Lafe, his hand hovering close.

Jetekesh shook his head. "Just a little lightheaded. I'm especially hungry, I think."

Across the fire, Liu scoffed.

Jetekesh straightened up and glanced toward the sky again, but the vision of fairies had vanished.

'*Poor dear,*' cooed Mother's voice. '*The mountain air isn't good for you. You're wasting away on this foolish quest. Turn back now, my boy, while you still can. Leave the chores to the men—that's what they're good for.*'

Jetekesh softly shook his head. *And what am I if not a man?*

He pushed Mother's illusory influence from his head and eyed the food. "Is it ready yet, Dakarai?"

The clansman grinned. "Just now, yes, Your Highness. Dig in."

CHAPTER 17
SMOKE AND FLAME

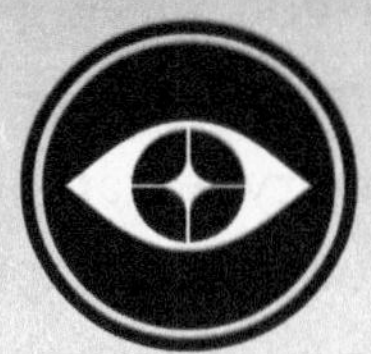

Rille trod up the gangplank while searching the water lapping against the ship. Sir Yeshton strode behind her, carrying their meager baggage. Wind snapped the KryTeer pennant overhead and howled up the channel between Amantier's shores and the distant, unseen lands of KryTeer. Sailors busied themselves with ropes, while crowds milled along the port below the ship's bobbing structure.

The captain, an olive-complected KryTeeran man, stocky but trim, caressed his curly black beard as he observed Rille step onto the deck. She cut a path to him, forcing a sailor to dance out of her way, then she curtsied as she arrived.

"Thank you for agreeing to take us to your country, good sir."

The captain stroked his beard. "I know what you are, Lady Rille." An accent curled around his words.

She tensed. A faint chink sounded behind her, and she imagined Sir Yeshton gripping his sword hilt, ready to decapitate the man.

The KryTeeran captain chuckled. "Relax. I run under Prince

Anadin's orders. I know how fond he is of his little Sahala. I would not dream to anger that man nor my emperor."

Rille let her shoulders relax though her heart hammered in her ears. "Don't you mean your king, Captain?"

The man grinned broadly. "The Blood Emperor may call himself whatever pleases him. But I know better than to think of him as less than he is: a god among men." He shrugged and craned his head. "Jisha, come here!"

A gangling, adolescent KryTeeran boy bearing an abundance of pimples shuffled into view. "Aye, Captain?"

"Lead the lady and her knight to their quarters. Don't pester them, mind. The shadow bird favors her." The captain's eyes pinned on Rille. "We'll leave with the next tide."

"Thank you, captain." Rille turned to Jisha. "Lead on."

Jisha nodded and swaggered toward the decks below. "S'way, milady." His accent was more tangled than the captain's. He hunched his shoulders and guided Rille and her protector past the mizzenmast and down a trap door to the officers' quarters. He let Rille and Yeshton slip past him and into the room. "Anything you need 'fore I go?"

Rille took in the tidy, compact room fitted with several cots, then shook her head. "That's all. Thank you, Jisha."

"S'all right. Good day, milady." He dipped his head, then shut the door after himself.

Sir Yeshton set the baggage on the wooden floor. "I confess, sailing isn't my favorite mode of travel, my lady."

"Nor mine, Sir Knight." Rille padded to the window and stared out at the gleaming sea under the noon sun. "But until we can sprout wings, it's all we can do."

A knock pounded on the door.

Rille spun. "Yes?"

The door creaked open, and the captain poked his head

inside. "Forgive me, Lady. Word just reached me. Thought you should know."

Rille studied the strain around the man's eyes. "Know what, captain?"

He drew a breath. "Battered ol' ship just limped into port. Bahadronn has fallen."

Rille's heart missed a beat. "How? To whom?" Her voice rose higher than she'd intended.

The captain shook his scraggly head. "Strange reports from the battered vessel say it was fire pouring from the heavens. Dunno what that means."

A tremor raced up Rille's limbs and spine. She leaned against the windowsill and sucked in air. "It's already occurred? The warning came too late."

The captain's eyes narrowed. "You dreamt this?"

She nodded faintly. "Before, my dreams came earlier than the event. I had time to warn people... But now they seem to come to me even as it's occurring." Tears filled her eyes. "I hope Anadin is well."

The captain cleared his throat. "We're leaving almost at once, milady."

"Thank you." She turned to the window and sought out some sign of the distant shore as the door clicked shut. "Oh, Yeshton."

He strode to her side and rested a hand on her shoulder. "I'm here, Rille."

She closed her eyes. "Thank you for that. It's some comfort to me."

THE WIND FAVORED THE *DAJANYAN*. The man-of-war raced under clear skies to the shores of KryTeer.

Rille rarely left the cabin she shared with Sir Yeshton. By the knight's report, rumors spread throughout the vessel, declaring her everything from witch to shapeshifter. Yeshton took it upon himself to deliver her meals, wash her clothes, and discuss the details of travel with the captain. Rille let him. She had always preferred solitude to the superstitions of common folk, and she suspected sailors were even worse.

Four days at sea brought the *Dajanyan* into Bahadronn's scorched harbor.

Rille swept down the gangplank with determined haste, soaking in the sight of people milling about amid the intact sections of the ancient city. Above the higher tiers of debris, the palace stood, a mere blackened husk. The sight sent chills up Rille's flesh.

It looks so much like my own broken estate...

The captain followed her and Sir Yeshton from the man-of-war where he bade them farewell with a few words. He barreled off toward a guardhouse, likely to learn what he could of the fate of his king. Rille turned away, cringing against a heart pang.

Loss is part of life. He'll learn to cope, as we all must.

She strode toward the surging crowds, but Sir Yeshton caught her shoulder.

"A moment, my lady. Look."

She glanced at his eyes and followed their path toward a column of Blood Knights marching through the throng along the main road. Her lungs expanded on wings of hope. At their head, dressed in his customary billowy black silks and beaming like the sun, trod Prince Anadin. His arms lifted as he approached. Rille ran to him and let him swallow her in a strong embrace.

"Greetings, my Sahala. A carrier pigeon told me you were arriving today, though I doubted it at first."

"Hello, Anadin." She pulled back and stared up into his deep black eyes. "I'm relieved to find you well."

He laughed, a sound like springtime and lark song. "As I am glad to *be* well. But what brings you to Bahadronn? Surely, you didn't race all this way for a hug."

"I dreamt of the fire, Anadin."

He blinked. "Did you?"

"Yes. From what I can ascertain, I dreamt of it the very night it occurred."

He chuckled. "What use was that? You couldn't possibly warn us in time." He cocked his head. "But you said your Sight had faded after—after, you know."

"Yes." Rille nodded. "I'm confident that when Jinji left this world, all magic failed in Nakania, yet—" She glanced around as she realized hundreds of eyes watched her. "Perhaps we should discuss this privately. Where are you staying?" She hesitated. "And how is your lord brother?"

"Ah, Aredel. *That* is an interesting tale as well. He's alive, though you likely didn't doubt it. How could anything slay that man? We're staying at an inn we've transformed into our temporary headquarters. This way, Sahala." Anadin spun on his heels, and the Blood Knights pivoted with him. Rille and Sir Yeshton stayed at the prince's back, moving fast to maintain Anadin's lengthy gait.

The sprawling inn stood a few blocks from the harbor, overlooking the vast southern ocean. The red and black flag of KryTeer, bearing the Winged Sword, streamed against the sky. Guards in bloodred armor surrounded the five-story edifice, grim and still as statuary in a cemetery.

Rille passed them by with a shiver. Much had changed since the forces of KryTeer had destroyed her home and murdered her father, but the fear and grief of that night would never depart from her soul. She had reconciled with King Aredel. Someday, she might even find it in herself to forgive him. But for now, she tolerated those bloodstained hands. Peace mattered more than private grievances.

The Blood King sat at a desk in what had been the inn's lobby, garbed more simply than she'd ever seen him in a plain silk vest and baggy *sirwal* pants. The space around him was crammed with officials, knights, scribes, and servants, while the innkeeper was nowhere in sight.

"Ah." Aredel's eyes found hers. "Welcome, Lady Rille. This is unexpected."

Anadin walked to the desk and leaned against the ornate wood surface. "Aren't you pleased, *shaqin*?" The term of affection meant 'older brother' in the Old Tongue. Anadin had explained that early in their lives, the brothers had adopted *shaqin* as well as *shaqel*—meaning 'younger brother'—to maintain a secret affection in defiance of their father's will. Gyath had set out to quell all loyalties among his kin, afraid that united they might rise against him. In the end, they'd done exactly that.

"Should I be pleased?" Aredel glanced at the scrolls and parchments scattered across his desk. "Ledonn."

The king's protector stepped up to the desk. "Yes, Blood King?"

"Finish these reports. I'd best learn why the seer has come to KryTeer with such haste. She looks grimmer than normal." He stood up.

"As my holy king commands." Ledonn took the king's place in the wingback chair.

Aredel motioned to a private chamber adjacent to the lobby. He slipped through the door, then crossed the ornate room to settle on a window seat overlooking the wide western bay. The thick fragrance of floral incense permeated the air.

Rille chose a plush chair that creaked as she sat. Prince Anadin settled on an area rug and crossed his legs, staying near Rille.

"What news do you bring from Amantier?" asked Aredel.

"Strange tidings." Rille sighed and folded her hands on her lap. "Most importantly, I dreamt of your city burning as it happened."

"Did your dream tell you how or why it transpired?"

"No...but I already suspect the answer."

"Go on." Aredel shifted on the window seat, and his hand settled on his jeweled sword hilt.

"*Erisyrdrel* has been released from the sea," she explained. "I dreamt so the week preceding the burning of your fair palace. At once, I rode for Kavacos to warn my lord uncle and cousin." She shook her head. "And there, even as I dreamt of Bahadronn's destruction, a Shinacian appeared to Prince Jetekesh and asked for his aid against a threat that has escaped into our world from beyond the Arch in the Drifting Sands."

Aredel gripped his sword. "Do you think this threat has allied with *Erisyrdrel*?"

"I fear so. But either way, we now have two threats. My lord cousin travels at this moment to the Clanslands in search of another Arch, with two clansfolk as his guides."

"Why another?"

"Because whatever fought against the Shinacian sentinel brought enough force to bear, it shattered Jinji's Arch." She traced the embroidered patterns in her skirt. "Now we must find another Arch to ask for aid against our magical foes." She lifted her eyes. "How else can we defeat them?"

The Blood King wore a grim smile. "We are not without hope." He held up a hand. His fingers glowed white. "You alone do not wield magic in Nakania now, young seer."

A keen pang of jealousy shot through her, but she stifled it at once. "Lord Kethalas—that's the Shinacian sentinel—he said my lord cousin has been touched by truth due to his time in Shinac. It seems likely you have experienced a similar transformation, Your Majesty."

"So it does." His fingers curled together as his smile widened. "Kethalas, you say? I know the name. Prince Sharo mentioned it whilst we traveled the road to a dark keep to stop Lord Peresen and his *Unsielie* army from crossing into this realm."

"Do you trust Kethalas?"

"Yes, certainly. He's a dragon allied with Sharo."

Rille straightened. "*Dragon*? Well. That should come in handy."

"Indeed. Does he travel with Prince Jetekesh?"

"Yes. Though he looked human to me—mostly." She reflected on the man's strange hair and slitted eyes.

Anadin scooted closer on the rug. "What should we do, Sahala? Shall we sail to Amantier?"

"We have our own problems, *shaqel*," said King Aredel. His dark eyes speared Rille. "Each night following that first assault, I've been plagued with a fiery visitor—until a few nights ago. At that time, she revealed herself to be *Erisyrdrel* and threatened my people unless she was allowed to possess me. When I refused, she threatened to finish what she had begun. That is when my magic stirred. I've heard nothing from her since, but I can't well go traipsing off if she might level what's left of Bahadronn meanwhile."

"That doesn't have to stop me," Anadin said.

King Aredel arched an eyebrow. "As fond as I am of you, *shaqel*, you haven't a fleeting hope of fighting any magical foe, powerless as you are."

Anadin's mouth snapped open, then shut, reminding Rille of

a turtle. The prince shrugged as he sighed. “He’s right, of course. He’s always right. But I’d like to help somehow.”

Rille reached for his hands, and he interlaced his fingers with hers. “You can, Anadin. I’ve come here for a second reason.”

“Which is?” asked King Aredel.

“To find a third Arch into Shinac if it exists.” She held the Blood King’s skeptical gaze. “I need to know your legends. If such an Arch hides in KryTeer, we must discover it.”

CHAPTER 18
ACCUSATIONS

Green hills rolled on forever, speckled with yellow and purple wildflowers. A honey-sweet gust swept over the grass, and it shimmered like velvet brushed by gentle fingers.

The warmth nearly drove Jetekesh from his cloak, but he resisted his instincts and shifted the soft material to let the fragrant breeze beneath. Bees hummed past his head, and the horses whinnied, as glad of the greenery as the company was. When Jetekesh glanced back to eye the snowy peaks of the Flute Mountains, a pang caught his insides. Had he really passed through those mighty tors unscathed? He, such an insignificant speck?

"The going will be easier now," said Lord Emerin, glancing over his shoulder. "Should we rest the horses and cook something, Your Highness? It's only a few days more 'til we reach the closest village. We can restock our supplies there."

"Please," gasped Jetekesh, tossing back his cowl. He slowed Hickory's gait. "Is there a bathhouse in the village?"

The lord reined in his horse. "This near Shing? Absolutely." Lord Emerin swung from his steed and arced back in a long stretch. "A natural hot spring feeds it, too."

"Good." Song slid from her saddle and patted her horse's neck. "I'm glad *this* part of Amantier is civilized." A smile twitched over her face.

"Believe it or not, Southern Amantier has bathhouses as well," said Jetekesh. He dismounted and removed Hickory's bit and reins to let him eat. "Jinji made sure we used one once. We Amantierans like our pleasures as much as anyone in Shing, I'd wager."

Liu snorted. "We will discover the difference in those pleasures soon, I think, *Your Highness*. Your god doesn't allow you quite the same level of indulgences. I suspect your bathhouses aren't so grand as those in Shing either."

Dakarai chuckled as he hauled wood from the wagon bed. "Who needs a bathhouse? Give me the surrounds of nature for my walls. I'd just be grateful for the hot spring in its natural pools."

"I *like* walls," Jetekesh said. The idea of all and sundry watching him bathe marched chills up his spine. He unstrapped the buckskin's saddle and hefted it from Hickory's back. "Though I suppose it's purely cultural. Jinji would call us a 'band of welcome variety' or some such thing. How can we stretch ourselves if everyone around us is exactly the same?" He dropped the saddle and tracked the sun against the hazy blue sky.

Something massive wheeled overhead, wings beating over the air. Jetekesh threw up his hand to shield his eyes and squinted.

Nothing. Just the sun in the heavens.

He leaned against Hickory, who nickered. *I must be weary, that's all. I could've sworn that was a dragon.*

A shadow crossed Jetekesh's feet. He looked up and found Kethalas close, studying his face with drawn brows.

"You look...bright."

Jetekesh blinked. "I what?"

"Your glow... It brightened. It is still so. The same thing happened several days ago, during Dakarai's song." Kethalas looked him up and down, brow knitting more. "Do you feel strange at all?"

"Tired?"

The Shinacian shook his head. "Beyond that. We are all travel-worn."

"Well." Jetekesh glanced skyward. "I thought I saw a dragon. But as I said, I'm tired. My imagination ran away from me for a moment."

Kethalas looked upward, intent, hungry. "This imagination of yours, Prince Jetekesh—has it ever run so far into the realm of fae things?"

"Well, no. But since traveling to Shinac, I suppose I've imagined fairies and Sielie more than once. Never dragons though, until now."

Movement caught Jetekesh's eye.

Lord Emerin had abandoned building his fire and trotted over. "What are you two discussing? Lord Kethalas looks ready to eat you."

Jetekesh glanced at the dragon in man form. "I don't know why, my lord. I'm just weary."

Kethalas's lips split in a fanged grin. "We shall see." He turned to the lord of the keep. "He thought he glimpsed a dragon overhead."

Lord Emerin lifted his eyes and scanned the sky. "Is that an omen, a daydream, or a reality we should be concerned about, Lord Kethalas?"

Kethalas's silver eyes flicked back to Jetekesh's face. He breathed in, long and slow, then let out a whispering sigh. "It's too soon to say. My instinct tells me this is nothing alarming." He rotated to face Lord Emerin again. "The one assurance I can offer is that I would know if a dragon were near in truth."

Jetekesh toed the ground with his boot. "I'm tired, my lords, nothing more. A bite to eat and a moment to rest will bring my mind back to Nakania."

Kethalas's grin stretched wider.

A prickling surge of temper flashed through Jetekesh. "Is something funny, Lord Kethalas?"

The Shinacian shook his head. "Not funny, Prince. Remarkable."

Jetekesh's brows shot up. "Remark—Never mind. It's obvious you're not going to explain."

"I think I shouldn't. Not yet." Kethalas lifted his chin and scented the air as a fox might. "There's a brook nearby. I shall catch us some fish."

Dakarai jumped from the wagon-bed, spear in hand. "I will come with you. I welcome the exercise." Despite his earlier hopes, he'd found no good hunting in the lower ranges of the Flute Mountains.

Kethalas nodded, and he and the clansman strode south toward a line of grass far greener than the rest. Did Jetekesh imagine that the man-dragon limped a little?

I can't forget he's injured. He mustn't push himself too much.

Jetekesh's gaze strayed to Dakarai's back and his frown deepened.

"What's wrong, my prince?"

Jetekesh glanced at Lord Emerin, then gestured toward the retreating forms. "How can he smile like that?"

The lord's eyes stalked the prince's waggling fingers. "Which?"

"Dakarai. He's always smiling, often laughing, yet his village was all but destroyed. I'd be a broken shell."

"What good would that do?" asked Lord Emerin.

Jetekesh flinched. "*Good*? What has that to do with feelings?"

"Very little, Your Highness. But I suspect Dakarai is the sort of person who handles his emotions with great respect. He'll grieve but not where anyone can watch. Meanwhile, he won't burden others with his sorrow."

"Grief isn't a burden, my lord." Jetekesh's hands curled into fists. "He has every right to show how he's feeling."

Lord Emerin's eyes flashed, and his voice lowered to a rumble. "Yes, my prince. But that same inborn right gives him the *choice* to mourn alone. Perhaps every smile heals a fragment of his heart. Maybe it's how he cries." He sighed and ran a hand down his stubbled chin. "Forgive my curtness, Your Highness."

Jetekesh let his eyes drop to the ground before his feet. "Nothing to forgive, my lord. Your assessment is fair. I shouldn't judge his actions by my own." He swallowed against a lump in his throat. "What are we eating?"

Lord Emerin glanced over his shoulder to eye Song, Anenyasha, and Yin crouched around a cookfire. "Rice, I think. Lady Song offered to make it." He shrugged. "It beats roots, I suppose." He turned back to Jetekesh and thumped a hand against the prince's shoulder hard enough that Jetekesh's feet bit into the earth. "It goes two directions, Your Highness. No one here could rightly weigh your pain. And from what I can see, you bear it markedly well for one your age." His hand fell to his side. "If it brings any comfort, know you can talk to me. I've suffered a loss or two myself. I can empathize."

"Thank you, Lord Emerin." Jetekesh looked away and cleared his throat. "Shall we check on the food?"

They walked together to the hunched bundle of cooks. Song looked up, dark eyes probing. "Food is well underway, Prince Jetekesh."

"Good." He spotted his saddle among the circle surrounding the fire. Sir Lafe sat beside it upon his own saddle. Jetekesh took his seat and watched Song stir the cauldron of rice above the flames. He shifted his feet away from the heat. "I know a bit of your story, Lady Song. Enough to respect your skill and courage." Away from the pass—with its biting cold and screaming wind—conversation was easier.

She looked up with a strained smile. "Thank you, Your Highness."

Jetekesh pointed at Yin. "Your brother, I assume?"

"Yes."

"What of you?" Jetekesh settled his eyes on Liu. "You look—and act—nobleborn."

The young Shingese man jutted out his chin. "I am."

"He's a prince of the House of the White Lotus, Your Highness," Song said. "Son of the emperor's nephew."

Jetekesh arched his brows. "So illustrious a person came to find Jinji?"

Liu shifted upon his saddle in the grass, a light sparking in his black eyes. "I am trusted and not without skill."

"I apologize for not asking sooner." Jetekesh caught a strand of golden hair and twirled it around his finger as his stomach squirmed. "I felt a bit overwrought in the pass, what with the *vashalan*. But that's no proper excuse. Forgive my slight. It wasn't intentional."

A smiling sneer climbed Prince Liu's face. "It's a small matter. We in Shing are well accustomed to Amantier's slights."

Song whapped Liu's leg with her rice-dotted ladle. "That's no excuse for poor manners, Your Highness. Besides, you're not dressed like nobility if you recall."

"That *hurt*." Liu's face colored.

"Not as much as your shame ought to pain you," she said. "Despite bringing word of Shing's invasion, we have been treated with civility and equity by Prince Jetekesh and his knights. Yet your courtesy appears to be absent. What would your lady mother say?"

Liu's scowl deepened. "Out of respect for your past service, I've put up with a great deal of your insolence on this excursion, Lady Song. But now you go too far."

Song's eyes narrowed. "Oh? Shall I be punished, Your Highness?"

Jetekesh lifted a hand as he drew breath to interject—but Lord Emerin coughed and shook his head. The lord wore a broad grin. Jetekesh creased his brow.

Would he have me stand back if it comes to blows?

Liu's hand fell to his sword. "You don't know how tempted I am to show you your place, Lady Song. The Blood Knights underestimated you. How else could you kill so many? And you know as well as I, that accursed Aredel patronized you when he let you walk away."

Song shot to her feet, hand clutching her ladle like a sword. "Unsay what you have said, my prince, before I prove to you how wrong you are. I would hate to have to maim you for your misplaced pride."

Liu sputtered and lurched to his feet.

Lord Emerin opened his mouth as he started forward.

"Enough." Jetekesh stood. "We both know her threat isn't an idle one. She could use that ladle against your sword and win, just as she could against most of us here. Sit down, Prince Liu, and let that be the end of your outrage for one day if you please. Aren't you weary?"

Liu stared at him, gripping his sword hilt, knuckles white. His jaw flexed as he wrestled with something inside himself. His shoulders relaxed, and he flounced back down upon his saddle. "She's not *worth* it." His eyes collided with Jetekesh's. "I know all about you, Prince of Amantier. Don't preach to me about control. Don't command me like I'm one of your whipped dogs." His lips lifted in a jeer. "They say you're not even the king's son."

Jetekesh flinched back, stung as though Liu had thrown a stone at his face. The faint chink of drawing swords caught in his ears, and he wrenched his gaze from the hazy ground and blinked to find Sir Lafe and Lord Emerin standing before him.

"Liu, you're a fool!" Song snapped.

"That will cost you your life, Shingese filth," growled Lord Emerin.

Whatever the lord's expression, it must've been extraordinary—or perhaps Liu recalled the pillar of fire Emerin had wielded against the *vashalan*. The Shingese prince's face paled to the shade of thistledown.

Song dropped to her knees, then folded forward until she was prostrate before Jetekesh. "Please accept my humblest apologies on behalf of Shing for this egregious insult, Your Highness. Liu's accusations are unwarranted and groundless. I beg of you not to let one boy's hot temper destroy the peace we are seeking to build between our two lands."

Lord Emerin glanced at Jetekesh, still gripping his sword. "Give the word, and I'll cut the filthy cur down, Your Highness."

"N—no," whispered Jetekesh. "It's fine. I...I'm not offended. Stand down. That's an order."

Lord Emerin hesitated, then sheathed his blade. "As you command, my prince." The tension bled from his muscles.

"Thank you for your forgiveness, Prince Jetekesh." Song straightened up and glanced at the pot. "The rice is nearly cooked."

The keep lord and Sir Lafe sat, and soon heaping bowls of plain rice passed hands until all ate in tense silence.

Jetekesh stared into his bowl, throat swollen, mouth dry. His vision shimmered like reflections on a mountain lake beneath a brilliant sun. How had he never considered Liu's accusation before? How could he not have wondered if he had the blood of kings flowing in his veins? He'd learned well enough that Mother had enticed many lovers to her bed. That few escaped her clutches.

What if I'm not the rightful heir of Amantier? What if Father isn't my sire?

His gaze dimmed. His bowl slipped from his fingers and crashed at his feet.

"My prince?" Sir Lafe's voice fell against his ears like distant gales—faraway and immaterial.

'You're my *son, dearheart,'* Mother whispered in Jetekesh's mind. *'That's what you know. That's what matters.'*

Tears rolled down his face, burning his flesh. *Don't. You can't fall apart. You're stronger than that...*

Hands clasped his wrists. "Prince?"

He looked up. *She* stood before an expanse of darkness engulfing his field of vision. Mother.

Who am I?

Her lips curled in a cruel smile. *'You are all mine, dearheart. Forever.'*

"Prince Jetekesh?" someone called.

He shut his eyes and buried his face in his hands. "I'm fine. Leave me alone." The words scratched his ears, rough and broken.

Why did it matter how he'd been born? Didn't he love Father enough to let that go? To resist an ugly possibility? Yet somehow...it did matter. Mother had won after all. The only truth he could rely on, could fully believe, was her claim to his blood.

I'll always wonder. I'll always fear the truth.

'*Dearheart.*' She loomed before him, a haunting specter, more real than anything else.

He lurched back, and plunged into blackness.

CHAPTER 19
HEART TROUBLE

W*hat happened?*

Jetekesh stared at the canvas ceiling of the tent. His throat throbbed, hands clutching the coverlet like he'd clung for dear life to a pitching boat in a storm.

His body floated, hollow, while his heart beat a faraway rhythm out of reach.

"How do you feel, Prince?"

Jetekesh rolled his head to one side. Dakarai sat cross-legged beside his bedroll. The man wore his customary smile, though it was gentle rather than playful.

The prince sat up and tightened his grip on the coverlet as the world tottered. "Did I...faint?"

"Dead away." Dakarai's grin stretched a little wider. "Likely, it was fatigue combined with hunger. You ate nothing, I understand."

Jetekesh stared at his hands. "It was more than that."

"Oh?" Dakarai shifted to pluck up a bowl beside him. "It's cold, but eat it anyway."

Jetekesh pried his fingers loose and accepted the rice. He took a bite and swallowed it down with a grimace.

The clansman leaned forward. "What was this *more*, Your Highness?"

"Liu... He inferred..." The prince cupped the bowl in both hands. "That's not right. He boldly suggested that I'm..."

"That you're not legitimate? So Lord Emerin told me." Dakarai paused. "This bothers you."

"Of course it does! He's called into question my birthright. My bloodline. Everything that defines me!"

"These things define you, Your Highness? Not your own soul? Your own feelings? These do not matter more?"

Jetekesh groaned and dragged a hand through his hair. "I don't want the possibility to change me, but how long has my father's court wondered the same thing? How many..." He choked down a swallow. "How many men at court wonder if *they* are my father?" His tongue tasted like sand. Tears welled up in his eyes. "How can I ever face them again and not wonder?"

"Probably, you cannot."

He blinked and angled to face Dakarai. "Do you not understand?"

Dakarai shrugged. "My father took to wife a woman who already carried me in her womb."

Jetekesh stared. "He did?"

"Yes. It was not her choice, you understand. She had been raped."

The prince dropped his eyes. "Oh. I—I'm sorry."

"No reason to be sorry, Your Highness. It was not my fault. It was not her fault. My father was a good man who raised me as his own son. This, he didn't need to do. He *chose* to treat me no differently than any good father treats his offspring. The man who is my real father is a terrible man. A criminal. This fact bothered me for many years until I finally decided it didn't matter. It *could* have, but it didn't, because I preferred to love, honor, and become like the man who raised me instead. Blood is good. Claims are good. But so is love that transcends these things." Dakarai shrugged. "Your father has probably wondered if you are his son. How could he not? But he loves you, nevertheless. And that says more for his love than someone who loves out of obligation."

Jetekesh spread his palm before him. "Yet, if I'm not his son, I have no right to become king."

"Why?"

"I...I wouldn't be descended from Cavalin."

Dakarai chuckled. "Neither was Cavalin."

"What do you mean?"

The clansman raised his hands in a wide shrug. "What makes a king? Had Cavalin the Great descended from kings from the beginning? Or were his actions what made the people *want* him to be king? We all come from humble roots, Prince Jetekesh. Our choices and abilities define our character, our rights, our accomplishments. Tallat of KryTeer was a fisherman before he was a tyrant. Aredel was emperor before he chose to become a lowly king. You are perhaps illegitimate, but what makes someone legitimate? Your Highness, which would you prefer to win out? Your mother's lusts or your father's love?"

Tears spilled down Jetekesh's cheeks. "I want to heed your words. I want them to be enough."

"Soak them in, then. Let them take root somewhere in your soul—and when you doubt these words, reflect on them, *want* them like soil wants water. They will bloom in time if you give them strength to grow. Faith is a powerful force when we let it in, small at first but able to flourish. But keep in mind, it takes less effort to water doubts, for they are like weeds feasting on the darkness inside each of us."

Jetekesh studied the man's dark face. "How old *are* you?"

Dakarai flashed a grin. "Twenty-six autumns, Your Highness."

"You *can't* be that young."

"Do I sound too wise? I'm only repeating the words of a wiser man than I. My father taught me these things."

"He sounds a great deal like Jinji." Jetekesh's heart clenched. "He—Jinji—was illegitimate, you know. He didn't know his father until nearly the end of his life. He was the son of the bloody-handed emperor of KryTeer. I—I can't imagine learning *that* if I feel as I do about my mother. How could he not want to rip off his own flesh?"

"We are not our fathers nor our mothers, Prince."

"I know...and yet it still hurts. Still plagues my mind." He laughed; a low, bitter note. "Will I never grow?"

"If you are hurting, you are likely growing. If you are comfortable, that is probably a sign you are shrinking." Dakarai stood up. "I will let the others know you are awake. We have chosen to make camp here tonight, as it's close to evening now. The stream is a slow one, and clean. You might try bathing."

Jetekesh tracked the man's feet. "Dakarai."

At the door flap, the clansman turned. "Yes, Prince?"

"I didn't know what to expect of someone from the Clanslands. But you're kind. Thank you for that."

Dakarai smiled. "Those in the Clanslands are as varied as anyone in your own kingdom, Your Highness. Some are kind. Some are cruel. I hope someday *all* shall be kind." He bowed his head. "I take my leave of you, Prince."

A breeze drifted in as Dakarai slipped outside. Light stretched, then snuffed out.

Jetekesh took a second bite of rice as tears started again. *Am I happy or sad? I can hardly tell the difference these days.*

CHAPTER 20
BLIND

"I knew you were stubborn and prideful, but I didn't take you for a dishonorable man."

Liu's cheeks flamed with heat, but he whirled toward Song in defiance, nonetheless. After Jetekesh had collapsed by the fire, the Shingese prince had stalked away, too disgusted to witness the Amantieran heir's theatrics. Standing near the stream, Liu had stared into the gurgling water, his mind reverberating with the words he'd flung at the spoiled brat.

I said nothing I didn't believe.

He jutted out his chin and met Song's black eyes with a glower. "I won't apologize. I meant everything I said—and you know as well as I do that he's probably illegitimate. You cannot tell me *no one* has wondered about his birthright."

"He hadn't." Song's voice was low. "Even a privileged life is full of heartache and loss. No one escapes from that."

Liu scoffed. "If he never considered the possibility, he's more of a fool than I thought."

"Yet your unkindness—what did it accomplish?"

"What kindness do I owe to Amantieran scum?" Liu jabbed a finger at the distant tent where Emerin had taken the boy. "Perhaps *you* are content to bury our country's sorrows—to hide in your sheep-ridden province and forget the world—but I am not. Not yet. I'll never forgive Amantier *or* KryTeer for what they've done to us. Especially not to my Lord Uncle! He's given every moment of his life to spare our people the worst hardships during one occupation after another. I'll not sit by and watch that pampered *boy* ascend the rotten throne of Amantier only to march in—with his precious Shinacian Mark—and occupy Shing all over again. I'll defend my country and my emperor if I must do it entirely on my own!"

Song clapped a fist to her chest. "You think I cower in the countryside and forget the bloody history of our people? You think I hold no fealty to Emperor Majinglee? Fool, fool, three times the fool. I love my emperor. I love the ancient soul of my homeland long blessed by the earth spirits. I love our roots—and I ache to protect our future. Do not mistake my quiet for surrender, nor my associations for treachery. I know as well as you do what price our people have paid over the years—but I'll not be blinded by pride and hatred. I will embrace *any* chance for peace —true peace—whether it comes in a shepherd's cloak or a velvet Amantieran robe.

"Do not forget Cavalin, once High King of *all* Nakania. We were united—all different banners and different races—but wielding one fearless heart. Right now, Jetekesh represents the best hope for that alliance to be reborn. Already, his actions—as well as Jinji Wanderlust's—have collapsed the tyranny of KryTeer. What might this prince accomplish going forward? What can *we* do together if we help him?"

"Your faith is ill-placed," Liu sneered. "Mark my words, Lady of *Sheep*: Prince Jetekesh will do *nothing* to aid us. He's a sniveling pig in royal britches, nothing more. I refuse to believe he's anything else!" His voice rang out across the grasslands, higher pitched than he'd ever sounded before, almost shrill. The foreign noise startled him.

"Blind. Foolish." Song's mouth twisted in disgust. "Very well. Be stubborn, Your Highness. Refuse to see what is uncomfortable, no matter how true. In the end, we will all witness who is truly nothing and who is much more. Truth will not long stay hidden. Will you be able to face yourself then or turn away, I wonder?"

Heat scored Liu's veins until he shook with suppressed wrath. "How dare you insinuate..." He stepped toward Song, visions of strangling her slashing across his mind. His fingers flexed.

Don't. She's still Shingese.

Turning away, Liu kicked at a stone. It plunged into the stream. "Leave me alone. It's obvious that your fealty can be purchased at any price, and as a loyal prince of Shing I'll not associate with turncloaks."

Her reply was a quiet scoff. The crunch of her retreating footsteps filled his ears. Liu sniffed and tugged hard on his coarse tunic, searching the far bank for any distraction from his growing shame. The grass downstream rustled. A second later, Yin stood up, a bow and arrow in his hands. He eyed Liu with quiet disdain, then moved away, his sounds almost silent.

Was he spying? Did he mean to shoot me if I...

The blood drained from Liu's face.

How close did I come to death?

CHAPTER 21
ATTACKS OF THE MIND

"Your Highness?" Lord Emerin's voice rolled into the tent chamber like swelling waves.

Jetekesh swiped at his eyes. "Come in." He stuffed more rice in his mouth.

The lord of the keep entered, the portrait of regality, from his newly washed hair and shaved face, to his fresh travel clothes, to his stance and polished sword. In the man's green eyes, did pity or worry burn strongest?

"How do you feel, my prince?"

Jetekesh drew a quick breath. "Better. I—I think the heat overwhelmed me."

Lord Emerin's lips twitched. "I would've suspected Prince Liu's stupidity had been the cause. It certainly sent my head reeling—as well as my temper." He crossed to stand before Jetekesh's bedroll and lowered himself to one knee. "Forgive me. I should have intervened in their argument before you had to involve yourself. I confess, I'd wanted to witness Lady Song in action—but that was reckless."

Jetekesh snorted. "I can't blame you for the desire. But your judgment was perhaps poor under the circumstances. Tension is high enough between Amantier and Shing right now. Best we don't let squabbling tear our company apart."

"You're absolutely correct, Your Highness. I'll not let myself become caught up in impulsive decisions again." He searched Jetekesh's eyes. "May I be blunt?"

Heat crawled up the prince's cheeks. "If you feel it's necessary, my lord."

"'Tis." Emerin shifted to kneel on both legs and settled back on his heels. "You suffered earlier from an intense onslaught of raw emotions. I've seen others suffer similarly after war and other ugly dealings." His eyes darted away. "In truth, Highness, I've experienced the same before. Once you experience an overwhelming series of horrors...sometimes it's too much to bear. Your mind panics. Your heart feels close to bursting."

His keen eyes caught Jetekesh's again. "Don't be ashamed, Prince Jetekesh. The bravest warriors I've known deal with such things. It's like a scar that doesn't quite heal right. Sometimes it flares up." He rubbed his smooth jaw. "After what your lady mother put you through since your infancy, no one who understands will condemn you for your reactions."

Jetekesh bowed his head. "I will. I do. My suffering has been minuscule compared with those of Jinji or Tifen. And I've never even been to war."

"Did you not wrestle against your mother's overbearing reach every single day, Your Highness?"

Jetekesh managed a slight shrug.

Lord Emerin sighed. "Forgive me. It's not my place to tread over your pain. I brought this up only to make you aware that you experienced an attack within your mind, and that it's not something to fear. It's something only to understand."

"Will I suffer more such attacks, my lord?" Jetekesh hated how small his voice sounded.

"Yes, likely so. I'll try to walk you through them if I can."

Jetekesh traced his spoon handle with one finger. "You said you experience them? These attacks?"

"I used to. Not so much now." Lord Emerin offered a melancholy smile. "We all have broken moments. Moments that change us forever. Losses we can never gain back." He sighed. "I told you I came on this quest to protect you. That's true. But it's not my only motivation." His eyes glinted in the dim light. "I want to reach that Arch, Highness. I *need* to find it."

Jetekesh stared into the man's eyes. "Why?"

Fury burned in those green depths. "To find what I lost. To get it back." His jaw set. "No matter what it costs me."

CHAPTER 22

THE CALL OF WAR

Kajsa stood on tiptoes in the slush to catch a glimpse of Axel beyond the crowd. Raum whimpered beside her, and she glanced at the wolf. "I know, I'm eager to find him, too." She flattened her feet to scratch behind Raum's ear, glad he was with her in the pressing throng. "I'm sure he's looking for us as well."

The noise of the crowd grew louder.

She leapt to her toes again and craned her neck. There. Axel rode into Tuksa on horseback like a knight of old, grinning from ear to ear, pale green eyes dancing in the broad sunshine. Beside him, smile soft as a feather, rode Navolleth. A cloak of deep blue velvet, lined with fur, draped his shoulders, lending him the appearance of a regal fae king from legends of Shinac.

The village chandler brushed past Kajsa, and she staggered until Raum caught her with his wet nose. Kajsa stroked the wolf, then steered around the outskirts of the chattering crowd. Voices rose with questions. Rumors had been spreading since yesterday when word came that Navolleth, Axel, and Elder Viggo would return from their week-long absence. They'd met with the Archon of the Frostfire Canton.

No one in Tuksa had ever done that before except Ingrid when she'd been a small girl.

Kajsa reached the Elderhouse and slipped around to the back entrance. Smoke plumed from the kitchen chimney and from the main chimney. Doubtless, a great feast would be laid out in celebration once Elder Viggo explained *why* he'd gone down to Tild to meet the leader of the city-state.

Kajsa glanced at the wolf near her heels. "Stay, Raum."

She sneaked through the back door and ducked as she made her way through the bustling kitchen. Voices rose and fell, tossing and catching orders as the baker and a slew of volunteers juggled trays of breads, slabs of meat, and myriad other foods whose fragrances made Kajsa's mouth water.

Once free of that madness, she padded down the corridor, past a set of stairs, and cracked open the door leading to the main hall. Navolleth and Axel stood to either side of Elder Viggo before the hearth, where a platform had been set up. Villagers packed the chamber, except where Kajsa crept, since access to the kitchen must be kept clear. The roar of voices bombarded her ears as she stole through the doorway and took position behind a log pillar near the tables where food would soon be set.

Elder Viggo raised his hands. "Settle down. Quiet, please."

Noise drained away, slow, reluctant.

The elder smiled. "Thank you. I know there've been a lot of rumors surrounding our audience with the Archon. I'd like to dispel most of them now. We're not overrun with these strange wolves we've heard of. The attack in the forest was an isolated incident. Nor are we forced to flee our village due to fights with our fellow Cantons. All within Norva is peaceful."

Murmurs swelled and receded like a tide.

"That said," the elder continued, "Lord Navolleth tells a different story of the people beyond the shield of our mountains —and I'd like you to hear him out as the Archon himself has. Please, my lord." Elder Viggo stepped back and allowed Navolleth to stand at the platform's center.

"Thank you, Elder Viggo." Navolleth's voice drifted over the room, serene as a lake on a windless day, yet his words carried to every corner in the wide chamber. "My new friends, I thank you for attending this meeting, for hearing me out. Take my words and hold them in your hearts before you accept or reject them, I urge you." He drew a long, soft breath. "I am recently come from beyond the mountains, from a land teeming with greed and war. It is an ancient custom there to squabble over boundaries and cut down those of other races or creeds. They are a barbarous lot, soiling the very earth with blood and tears."

He paused, shutting his eyes. Silence hummed. After a moment he stirred. "Forgive me. My own losses weigh my soul down as I consider their blindness, as well as their lust for death and mayhem." Navolleth pressed a fist to his heart. "What grieves me most is to watch their dance of destruction mar the fertile earth 'neath their feet. While you, all of you, in this cold country, struggle day by day to till your ground and plant your crops, to battle against snow and avalanche, never knowing when you shall see sunshine again. While you endure *all* this, just beyond your northern mountains, nestled under a welcoming sun and four bright seasons, the peoples of Shing, Amantier, KryTeer, and other, smaller nations, squander their blessings and wreak havoc.

"You would not sow such hatred into such precious ground. You, who understand the struggles of survival, have long known better than to bruise your fellow beings for the mere sport of it."

Kajsa shifted her weight. *What is he getting at?*

The pop and hiss of the fire in the hearth could be heard above the quiet of the chamber.

Navolleth went on. "Dear friends, I needn't paint a vivid image of your suffering. You know it far better than I. But I must paint for you the contrast which lies beyond these sacred mountains."

He stretched out his hand, eyes lifted as though he could see the peaks beyond the ceiling. "Rivers flow in green dells rarely touched by snow. The snow atop the mountains vanishes by the middle of summer and doesn't return until autumn bids the northern climes farewell. Snow falls enough to bless the crops but rarely harms them. They can plant fruit trees which blossom each spring. Their cattle and sheep are soft and plentiful. Occasional frosts might threaten the harvest, but it is rare, and the further north you journey, the warmer and more fertile the earth. There are places where snow never falls. Islands bursting with fruits you've never dreamt of."

When he spoke in those gentle, caressing tones, Kajsa could almost *feel* warmth on her skin and the fragrance of strange blossoms on a pleasant breeze. Her heart ached to taste the strange fruits. To see mountains not crowned with snow.

Navolleth's eyes dropped to face the crowd, and his fingers curled into a fist. "My Norvian friends, the peoples of the North do not deserve these blessings left to them by Cavalin the Great. They have abandoned the peace he offered them. They have defiled the very land he died to protect—and the *vashalan* attacks are evidence of this. Are you not also descended from that great king? Yet you were banished to these lands in the struggle for Cavalin's throne, then forgotten by your long-ago kin over time. They don't even appear to remember you. These lands are hailed as the Snow Wastes where none would dwell.

"It is your responsibility and your privilege to band together, all of you. Not just this Canton, but *all* the city-states of Norva. Join your strength together. Stand and march with me into the North. Let us take back your ancient birthright. Let us cleanse Nakania of its bloodlust once and forever. Turn your back on these unwelcome wastes. Take back Shing. Amantier. KryTeer. Punish those who have defiled Cavalin the Great and all he stood for—and bring peace to the shores of Nakania."

His eyes brightened as he leaned forward. "Your Archon agrees. He has ordered Axel and me to journey to every Canton of Norva and speak with each Archon in turn. To muster an army the like of which your northern neighbors have never seen. Do not fear—we also have a strong ally hiding in Shing, gathering a force of those who wish to aid us. We will join with them and spill tainted blood, that we may cleanse the soil of all past injustices. Will you join us in this honorable task?"

Silence. Glances. The pop of wood in the hearth.

"I will," said Frit, stepping forward. His jaw was set. "I'm weary of cold and hunger. Of wondering whether spring will come each year. Tired of burying my frozen neighbors. I will join you and take back what belongs to us. I will stir the ancient warrior blood of my forebears to purge the taint of Nakania!"

Other voices joined him.

"I will!"

"And I!"

"I'll join, Lord Navolleth."

"Hear, hear!"

Cheers erupted. Kajsa slinked back to hide in the shadows. Her heart thumped against her ribs.

Go to war? Against so many? We haven't the might for that, nor the right to steal others' lands.

She darted through the door, past the kitchen, and outside into the greening world. Patches of snow dotted the path before her, and Raum trotted from the trees beyond the grounds of the Elderhouse, snout flecked with blood.

Kajsa crouched and stroked the wolf's nose. "Oh, Raum. It's far worse than I thought. We're going to war." A tear streaked her cheek. She let it fall. "So many will die. For what? A home that's not ours? I love Norva. I love it here."

Raum tilted his head and whined a question.

Kajsa patted his neck. "Axel can't really want this. I'll speak with him. I'll implore him to talk the others out of war."

"Hi, Ky."

She whirled to find Axel standing at the open door. A smile brushed his lips, hands cupped behind his back.

She rose.

"I saw you run out. Navolleth's words must've startled you."

Kajsa nodded faintly. "Xel, this isn't right. We shouldn't start a war over the mountains. It's...ludicrous."

He scoffed. "So is staying in Norva. Ky, the snows are getting worse. We're starving. Think of all the people we've lost just this past winter."

"By the will of the mountain gods—"

"No, Kajsa." Axel strode forward and seized her shoulders. "It's not normal to lose so many. It's not right. We've struggled long enough in these forsaken lands."

"But we chose them." Kajsa's voice hung low, soft. "Our ancestors *left* the North to cultivate this land. They wanted to come here."

"No, we were exiled. Robbed. And now we want to leave."

Kajsa pulled loose. "Through bloodshed? Why can't we travel north and ask to join them?"

Axel snorted. "You think they'd let us? You really believe they'd allow all of Norva to enter their lands? Take some for ourselves?"

"We could ask."

"Do you *know* how crazy you sound?" asked Axel, laughing. He ran a hand down the side of his face. "No one is going to let us *in*. We'll have to fight."

"We can only try, Xel. Warfare is wrong. We'd be *stealing*—"

Axel groaned. "Enough, Kajsa. I understand. You're scared—and you should be. War is ugly. But think about what we've endured. Think of what we're missing. Think of the world Lord Navolleth described. That could be ours. Warmth, Ky. Sweet fruits and fields that are green longer than white. We deserve that."

"At what cost?"

"They're already killing each other. You should hear Lord Navolleth's stories. KryTeer is an overreaching, greedy empire of corruption, slaughtering all in their wake. And Amantier puts to death any who don't believe in their One God. Now Shing is rising to wipe out all others. It's madness, Kajsa. But we can end it—forever!"

She shook her head. "Then *we* become no better, Axel. For all Navolleth's pretty words, he forgot to mention the most important thing: the innocent. Surely there are children there. Too young, too weak, to be part of the problem. What should we do with them? Slay their parents, take their homes, and then what? Let them grow up hating us? Or do we kill them, too?"

Axel stared at her. "I hadn't thought of that."

She squared her shoulders. "Ask your Lord Navolleth about *that*, Axel. Ask him about the children."

His eyes darted between hers. A soft smile climbed his lips. "You know, Kajsa, I've never seen you like this before. I thought you as timid as a mouse."

Tension bled from her shoulders. "You told me to be bold."

"So I did. I'll ask Lord Navolleth. I'm certain he has an

answer. But, Ky. This is big. Bigger than you and me and this suffocating village. The Archon told us about the struggles of all the villages with these long winters . We're dying off. Norva is shrinking. We can't stay here. If it comes down to us or those in the North, you'll have to choose. Which will it be, Ky? The children in the North, or your own people?"

Kajsa ducked her head. "I don't want to choose."

"You'll have to."

She sucked in cold air. "There's another option." She looked up. "We should send a delegation. Meet with the leaders beyond the mountain. Ask for help. We're descendants of the same great man, aren't we?"

He scrubbed a hand over his brow. "Stubborn girl. Why would they listen? They're out to destroy each other. Who would you speak with? The KryTeer tyrant? The self-righteous king of Amantier? The angry Shingese emperor?"

"Any. All! We must try peaceful solutions before we go to war."

"Okay. All right. Enough." He lifted a hand to bat down her words. "I'll address your concerns with Lord Navolleth, but it'll make little difference. The Archon is preparing for war. It's going to happen."

"Will you fight in the army?" Kajsa whispered.

"Yes."

She met his eyes; strong, glowing with fervor. Her heart thrummed.

Axel took a step forward. "Kajsa, I love my people. I'll do whatever it takes to protect them."

Kajsa inhaled, a surge of strength straightening her shoulders. "Come with me. Let's travel north to meet with the Shingese Emperor. Let's try talking first."

He barked out a laugh. "You're mad! *Us*? What good would

that do? You can't even speak to the butcher or the chandler. You?"

"That's why you must come." Her heart twisted. "Help me."

"No. Forget it. Let the Archon and Lord Navolleth guide us. They know best. Ky, we don't have to be nobodies anymore. Lord Navolleth has made me his aide. I'm traveling with him to all the Cantons. We can muster a force the like of which has never been seen in the North."

"But we're not strong enough!"

"But we *are*. And we have allies over there—you heard Lord Navolleth. Besides, he isn't—" He glanced over his shoulder, then back to Kajsa. "He's not normal. He wields *magic* like something out of the tales of Shinac. He healed me with a touch. Saved my life. Our army will be invincible. No one will defeat us."

A shudder coursed through her limbs. "If he's that powerful, why doesn't he change our weather? Give us warmth? Let us stay here in Norva?"

"You're impossible! He's not all-powerful. He's not a god. But his magic can aid us, help us win."

"What more can I say?" She lowered her gaze to stare at her feet. Nausea churned in her stomach.

He sighed and brushed a finger against her cheek. "Sorry. I know your nature. You're a healer. War is hardest on you. But sometimes it must happen just the same. Don't despair. I'll protect you, always."

Her shoulders slumped. Tears gathered in her eyes until the world blurred like paint under a deluge of water. "Oh, Xel. What has he done to you?" She whirled and fled, running into the woods, away from the whispers of war and the bloodlust tainting Axel's tones. Away, far away.

But no matter how she ran, Ingrid's words chased after her. *'You must leave this village. You must cross the mountains.'*

"I don't want to!" she cried. "I want to stay in Norva."

Her foot caught a branch. She hurtled forward and landed hard against the frozen ground. Air exploded from her lungs. Wheezing, she rolled over as her ears rang. Tears burned her face.

Alone. She was all alone. Losing Fa had been so horrible, but she'd still had Axel. Now he stood just out of reach, eddying in a sea of ambition.

A twig snapped. Kajsa craned her head as blood pumped faster through her veins.

Raum whimpered and trotted into view.

Her muscles melted into a puddle. "Oh, come here, Raum. Good boy."

He padded over and curled up beside her, smelling of wet fur and loam. Kajsa buried her head in his scruff and let the sobs come.

'You must leave this village. You must cross the mountains.'

"Not yet, Ingrid," Kajsa whispered. "Please not yet."

CHAPTER 23
A NEW PATH

A faint glow snared Jetekesh's gaze. He glanced left along the grassy slope.

Was that a fairy?

Whatever it was, it had vanished.

The horses around him trotted on. No one else reacted to the sight; he must have imagined it. Jetekesh turned his gaze forward again, glad of the clouds covering the sun, even if they threatened rain.

Rain is better than snow.

Kethalas guided his horse to Jetekesh's side. "Oh. Forgive me, Prince Jetekesh. You seem deep in thought."

The prince shook his head. "It's nothing important. What's on your mind, my lord?"

"The wind is against me," said the dragon, "but I'm catching a strange scent on the gusts from time to time. It tastes of iron and hatred."

Shivers crawled up Jetekesh's spine. What did hate smell like?

"What does it signify?" he asked.

"That I cannot yet determine. It might be from very far away. I would take flight to discover its source and distance, but I do not wish to risk my healing just yet." Lines appeared around Kethalas's eyes.

"Don't push yourself." Jetekesh glanced toward Lord Emerin. "Should we alert the others?"

"It might be best. We should stay vigilant in case it is another threat to our company." Kethalas nudged his mount. "I'll let Lord Emerin know." He guided his horse to the lord's side, and they conversed in soft tones.

A heaviness tugged on Jetekesh's heart. *We're close to the borders of Shing. But surely, they can't guess we'd be so near, nor could they ascertain our quest or even who we are.* He drew his hood lower over his head. *Unless...*

Kethalas moved through the mounted company, whispering his warning. Shoulders straightened. Hands settled over swords. Yin unhooked his bow from his saddle.

Thunder rumbled, and a cord of lightning tinted the grim clouds in hues of silver and white. Rain plunked off armor as the company hunched under the growing deluge. Mist settled along the rolling hills.

Kethalas trotted back to Jetekesh's side. "In this storm, I'll catch no scent."

"Doesn't matter. We'll discover in time what it is, or we won't."

Two days had passed since Jetekesh's panic attack. Since then, the company had been unsettlingly quiet as they aimed for the closest village and the promised hot springs. Lord Emerin claimed they'd reach it by the next day at noon or sooner. Few in the company would meet Jetekesh's eyes, and when they did, they quickly looked away. Liu ignored him entirely. Apart from

Emerin, only Kethalas and Dakarai seemed immune to the discomfort.

The rain was a welcome distraction, even though it soaked Jetekesh's clothes and chafed his skin where the saddle rubbed. Blisters were better than the pity and scorn that must've developed in the hearts of his companions.

A sound like fairy song tickled his ear as thunder rumbled across the earth. Jetekesh looked south. Something glinted beneath the rain, across the plains, atop a hill.

"Kethalas?"

The Shinacian followed his eyes. Then stiffened. "Run!"

The horses broke into a gallop, and the wagon lurched forward. Jetekesh tossed a glance over his shoulder. Dark shapes took form in the mist. Hundreds of them, armored, thundering toward the company on horseback.

The white lotus of Shing adorned the sodden blue flag streaming above the army on their heels.

Jetekesh tore his eyes from the sight and willed Hickory to gallop faster. Faster. Over a hill, down a grassy slope, northward.

How can we hope to escape?

Arrows whistled past his mount. Lodged in the ground. Vanished in his wake.

Someone cried out. Jetekesh twisted in his saddle. Harn was slouched forward, reins slack in his hands. The wagon careened to one side and tipped, dragging its horses down.

"Keep going, Your Highness!" shouted Lord Emerin.

"I will help Harn," Dakarai said, already slowing his mount.

Jetekesh wrenched his eyes forward, heart in his throat, blood racing with fire. An arrow whistled, then an immense force slammed into Jetekesh's shoulder. He cried out, slumping sideways.

"Your Highness!" Kethalas's voice.

Jetekesh slipped from Hickory's back, still clutching the reins. His arm looped the stirrup. Hickory dragged him over the bumpy ground as grass whipped his face. His legs burned against the earth.

"Take hold." Kethalas's horse pounded the ground. A hand appeared in Jetekesh's vision, clawed fingers spread wide.

Jetekesh reached for those fingers. Missed. He sagged against the stirrup, teeth grinding. The taste of dirt and blood branded his tongue. His shoulder throbbed like a pincer had scored his flesh.

"I'll get you free, Prince. Hold on!"

Jetekesh spat out dirt. "H—hurry!" The jolting earth battered his bones, and consciousness quavered. The arrow bit deeper into his shoulder.

Kethalas's voice rose about the scrape and jolt. "Whoa, Hickory! Whoa!"

The horse slowed. The ground's relentless assault lessened. Stopped. Jetekesh hung from the stirrup, trembling, mind reeling. His limbs quailed as Kethalas knelt and pried the reins from his numb fingers, then the dragon slipped the prince's arm from around the stirrup.

"Quickly, Your Highness. Ride with me." Kethalas dragged Jetekesh to his feet and stood the prince before his stallion. "Please mount."

Jetekesh staggered forward and caught the saddle. Pain wracked his shoulder. He hissed out a breath and tried to lift himself. Thunder rumbled in his ears.

"Never mind, Prince. Hold fast."

Jetekesh looked southward towards Kethalas, Song, Yin, and Sir Lafe. All of them surrounded by the Shingese army. Dakarai, Anenyasha, Emerin, and Liu were nowhere to be seen. Had they been cut down already? Was Harn dead?

The Shingese commander trotted forward, a wicked grin on his round face. "Surrender." He spoke in the trade tongue.

"Not so fast, my lord." Song wheeled her horse to face him. "We are a company of peace on our way to the Clanslands. By what authority do you run us down?"

The commander's smile slipped. "Shingese, are you?"

"Some of us," said Song.

"But some are of Amantier." The commander's eyes settled on Jetekesh. "And royal by the looks of it."

Curse it all, I forgot my cowl. Too late now. Jetekesh sank against Kethalas as dizziness overtook him. The dragon held him steady.

"And so?" Song's voice rang out, clear and light. "These lands belong to Amantier."

"They did, but no longer. We have conquered this province." The commander nudged his mount forward. "And we heard a rumor that a certain prince rode this way through Bard Pass along the Nagali River."

Jetekesh swallowed down a lump. *What do we do? If they capture me, I'll be used as leverage against Lord Father.*

Kethalas's fingers tightened on Jetekesh's arm. "Does open war now wage between your two countries?" asked the dragon.

The commander's eyes widened as he absorbed the strangeness of Kethalas. "What are *you*?"

"Never mind that, Commander." A threat edged the dragon's voice. "Answer my question."

Jetekesh glanced into Kethalas's eyes. His pupils were mere slits, catlike. His teeth were bared, revealing fangs.

The commander's horse snorted and backed up a pace. "Steady." The commander patted his mount's neck as his eyes darted between Kethalas and Jetekesh. "You're prisoners of the Empire of Shing. Surrender and no harm will befall your company." He nodded toward Jetekesh. "We'll treat his wound."

Jetekesh swayed. "Best...listen. Otherwise, we'll be slaughtered, my lord."

Song climbed down from her horse and approached the commander. "I am Song of the Crimson Lilies. Will this knowledge bear any weight in persuading you to let us depart?"

The commander eyed her. "I honor you, Lady Song, but it matters not. My orders are to bring the Amantieran prince to our emperor's throne. But you, my lady, are free to do as you please."

Song glanced toward Jetekesh. She sighed and gazed up at the commander. "I will ride with you and plead his case before Emperor Majinglee."

The commander shrugged. "Do what you will, Lady. You always have."

Kethalas's grip on Jetekesh tightened enough to form bruises. He hefted his chin. "You will treat us with the courtesy befitting civilized countries, or I shall personally rip your troops apart."

A few Shingese officers laughed, but the commander's eyes narrowed, and he nodded. "We will honor the codes of war established by King Cavalin of old. No harm shall befall you in transit to Kyon Taro."

Kyon Taro. The capital of Shing. Jetekesh smiled to himself.

Like Jinji, it seems I will travel from one capital to another.

The commander motioned with one hand. "Bring a healer to treat the prince's shoulder."

"Yes, sir." An officer barked something in Shingese, and soon a female healer arrived on horseback, black hair braided, dark eyes sharp as needles.

She swung from her saddle, clothed in the pale colors of a Shingese physician, clutching a satchel. Kethalas moved aside a little, and she prodded the arrow in Jetekesh's back.

"This will hurt somewhat." Her accent was thick.

Jetekesh nodded and squeezed his eyes shut as the healer tore his shirt away from the wound and worked to dislodge the barbed arrowhead. The process took several long, anguished moments. She cleansed the wound, applied a salve, and bound his shoulder with bandages.

The healer stepped back. "Good enough until we make camp." She turned to the commander and spoke in liquid Shingese tones. When he responded, she bowed and remounted her horse, then rode back into the ranks and out of sight.

He eyed Jetekesh. "Mount, Prince. We ride now for Kyon Taro."

Kethalas squeezed his arm. "I will help you."

"Thank you." Jetekesh limped to Hickory and let the Shinacian boost him up into the saddle. His arms and legs throbbed. Scratches bled openly. He hardly felt them as his head spun. His ankle ached most now that ointment numbed his shoulder. Despite it all, he took up his reins and wheeled Hickory around to face the commander. "I am ready to ride."

The commander searched his face. Doubtless, the man had heard all the stories of Jetekesh's delicate upbringing. Of his spoiled fits of temper. Of his discourtesy toward foreigners.

I'm not that prince any longer. I will show this man, and all of Shing, that Amantier is gracious and honorable.

The commander shouted in Shingese, and the army surged southeast toward Shing, away from the plains of Amantier and the northward trail to the Clanslands. Away from the Arch.

Every hoofbeat thrummed through Jetekesh's bones, rattling his willpower. But he rode on, Kethalas and Song flanking him. Sir Lafe rode at his rear, Yin beside him.

"Where are the others?" asked Jetekesh softly.

Kethalas scented the air. "Close."

Jetekesh nodded and concentrated on keeping astride. It was all he could do.

For now.

CHAPTER 24
WINGS OF HOPE

The Shingese commander called a halt one hour before dusk to Jetekesh's great relief. The armed force, fifteen hundred strong, had crossed the border into Shing several hours before. They seemed to relax as they set up camp, chattering and laughing as though they'd won a great victory.

Kethalas helped the prince from his horse, then they were led to a heavily guarded tent, where a comfortable bedroll beckoned Jetekesh. He collapsed upon it and let the aches of the day roll over him with a faint moan. Every inch of him throbbed. His shoulder had begun to bleed several hours before, then crusted over. The bandage tugged against his wound, causing it to burn.

Sir Lafe took up a corner of the tent. Where Song and Yin had gone, Jetekesh didn't know.

"Here, Your Highness. Drink."

Jetekesh lifted his head and found Kethalas holding a water-skin. The prince dragged himself upright and accepted it with murmured thanks. The water soothed his throat and settled in his empty stomach, cool and welcome.

"Better?" asked Kethalas as Jetekesh lowered the skin.

"A bit." He wiped his lips with a sleeve. "This is quite the predicament."

Kethalas nodded. "We must only endure it until I'm well enough to take my proper form, Your Highness. After that, I will free you."

Jetekesh sighed. "That's some comfort. I only wish we had a feasible plan to defeat *Erisyrdrel*. It appears we'll face the demon without Sharo's aid."

"Alas, you may be right."

Rolling onto his back, Jetekesh flinched. He lifted his eyes to the pitched tent ceiling. The foreign style and fabric underscored his distance from home. Even the material beneath him, the scent of the ground, the clatter of the camp outside—all pointed to the cold fact: He was a captive in Shing. "Will Emperor Majinglee execute me, do you think?"

"No."

Jetekesh shifted his head to find Kethalas's gaze. "You sound confident."

The man-dragon shrugged. "The emperor is likely not himself. *He* will do nothing, but of *Erisyrdrel* I am less certain."

Jetekesh huffed out a breath. "So much for comfort."

Kethalas chuckled. "Apologies, Your Highness. I didn't mean to mislead you."

"It's fine. I should've known better than to ask such a question. How could you know how this will end?"

"None can know."

"Rille might." Jetekesh imagined his young cousin: her amber eyes and strict bearing, hands on hips, a pout curling her lips downward. He laughed to himself.

"Is something amusing, Your Highness?"

Jetekesh sat up and hissed as his shoulder throbbed. "Oh, not really. Well, it shouldn't be. My cousin—the seer—she's been a thorn in my side since I met her nearly a year ago. She kidnapped me, you know. Dragged me into Jinji's company against my will." He sighed, grinning. "She called me rude names and chastised me regularly. I despised her."

Kethalas knelt beside the bedroll. "You sound fond of her now."

"I think I am. I never knew what having a cousin meant. We'd never met before that night in the dungeons of Kavacos. We did nothing but bicker as we traveled toward the Drifting Sands—and then, I think she resented me for visiting Shinac without her." A smile touched his lips. "I don't know how she feels about me, and I've no idea when my feelings changed, but somehow I've begun to view her as a friend."

"Ah." Kethalas ran a claw along the patterns of the blanket. "That is what cousins are meant to be, I suspect. My own kin and I have always been close." Pain flashed in his eyes.

Jetekesh leaned forward and rested a hand on Kethalas's arm. "Are your wounds agitated?"

Kethalas lifted his eyes from the bedroll. "I am well enough under the circumstances. I merely thought of something painful."

"Your family? Have you lost someone dear?"

The Shinacian shrugged. "In a way, yes. I am estranged from my clan."

Jetekesh tensed. "But *why*?"

"I am dishonored."

"For what? Being bespelled by a witch?"

"Yes... For that." Kethalas smiled, eyes bright with sorrow. "Fear not, O prince. It is only for a season." He looked away. "Although now, perhaps not."

"What do you mean?"

Kethalas sighed, shoulders wilting. “My failure at the Jade Arch is a second disgrace. I might not be able to return to my kin henceforth.” His eyes darted around the room, lingering on nothing.

“Neither incident was your doing. That’s unjust.”

Kethalas blinked and turned his gaze to Jetekesh. “But dragons are just beings. My kin know best.”

Jetekesh scoffed. “Always?”

“Well. Usually.” Kethalas laced his fingers together and stared at his palms. “Lord Taregan will know what is fair.”

“I’ll speak for you,” the prince said. “I’ll meet with Prince Sharo as soon as we find the Arch and reach Shinac.”

“Shall we find it...do you suppose?”

Jetekesh shifted onto his knees, ignoring his thrumming shoulder and the protest of his ankle. “Aren’t *you* the one who declared this a fleeting setback? Didn’t you threaten the Shingese commander? As soon as you’re recover, you will set us free.”

“That may be weeks yet, Your Highness.” Kethalas dropped his eyes. “What might happen meanwhile?”

“We’ll survive. Simple as that. Don’t forget, Lord Emerin is in our company—or, well, he’s close by. You don’t know his reputation as I do—but in Amantier he is called the Lord of Thunder; the only knight who could duel the legendary Sir Palan and keep his feet. He’s a marvel. My lord father admires him very much. What he lacks in brute strength, he balances with sheer force of will and the speed of a lightning bolt.”

“You admire him quite a lot, yourself, Highness.”

Jetekesh laughed. “So I do. My point, Lord Dragon, is this: We’re not defeated yet. By the will of the One God and the purpose of our company, I’ll not let this end in Shing—unless it’s to our favor. Take heart in that promise.”

The dragon’s smile reappeared, like sunlight on water.

"Thank you, O prince. I shall draw strength from your courage and better arm myself against fear and doubt."

AT DAWN, the Shingese army broke camp, and Jetekesh remounted Hickory. The buckskin looked groomed and fed.

At least they're not brutes.

Jetekesh stroked Hickory's mane. "How fare you, my friend? Do you enjoy seeing the world? Have you ever been so far from home?"

The stallion nickered and tossed his head.

"My thoughts as well." Jetekesh patted his neck, then straightened. He flinched as his shoulder pulsed. The healer had rebound his wound that morning and wrapped his ankle for good measure. She hadn't thought it broken, only badly twisted.

Kethalas and Sir Lafe rode beside him as the company traveled east along a wide, lazy river. Still no sign of Song or Yin, or even the rest of the broken company.

"I'm certain Lady Song and her brother are well," said Kethalas as he caught Jetekesh glancing around.

"I hope so."

"Surely the Shingese would not deal falsely with one of their own."

Jetekesh nodded but doubts crowded his thoughts. If dragons could banish Kethalas for a circumstance beyond his control, if Lady Mother could sell out Amantier to save herself, what weren't people—and beasts—capable of?

Keep faith, Kesh. For all the vile characters in this world, there are people like Father and Jinji, too. Not everyone is refuse.

As he traveled, Jetekesh unfolded the map in his saddlebag and traced the army's progress. The Shingese capital Kyon Taro was nestled in the middle of the vast, lush country. The river they followed must be a branch of the grand Tindo River. He ran a finger along the waterway.

"It will be at least a week and a half before we arrive in the capital, at our present pace," he said.

"That is helpful," said Kethalas. "What time I can take to mend will benefit us a great deal."

Jetekesh smiled. "That's the spirit, my lord."

Kethalas lifted his head and scented the air. "The deeper we plunge into this country you call Shing, the stranger the air smells. There is a...a darkness in the wind."

"Is it *Erisyrdrel*?" asked Jetekesh.

Kethalas shook his head. "I think not. It is another scent. Perhaps even the foe I fought at Jade Arch."

Jetekesh tightened his fingers on his reins. "Both of them in Shing? I suppose darkness gathers darkness to itself."

"Yes, as light attracts both light and darkness." The man-dragon's silver eyes drifted upward. "It will rain again very soon."

Jetekesh sighed and pulled the hood over his face. "Perfect. Now my blisters can spawn more blisters."

Sir Lafe snorted.

Jetekesh glanced at him. "Lord Emerin said you have no sense of humor, Sir Knight. But that sounded dangerously like a laugh."

"'T'wasn't, Your Highness." Sir Lafe rubbed a finger under his nose. "I sneezed."

The prince lifted an eyebrow. "Whatever you say, Sir Knight."

Did a smile twitch on the man's lips, or did Jetekesh only imagine it?

They rode in amiable silence, despite traveling as prisoners surrounded by soldiers of Shing, separated from most of their company. Jetekesh found himself grinning as he imagined Jinji riding beside him, humming a merry tune.

What have you done to me, storyteller, that I can find the silver lining in this situation? I'm ruined forever.

He chuckled.

'*What a doting fool you've become, pet.*' Mother's voice broke into his reverie, tearing the sunshine warmth in his soul.

The sky rumbled and unleashed rain in a dense torrent, as though at the specter's silent command.

Horses whinnied and soldiers cursed.

Jetekesh squinted to see ahead in the column. His thick cloak saved him from the deluge for a minute or two before water soaked into his clothes and trickled down his back. He hunched forward until his back ached.

Focus on the rain. Don't let Mother in. She's dead. She's gone.

'*But you're part of me. My son, dearest, you'll never be free of your blood.*'

He choked down a whimper and swallowed hard. *Ignore her. Don't let her poison words enter your heart.*

Her laughter flooded his mind, deranged, high-pitched.

His teeth ground together, and he throttled his reins. "Kethalas."

"Yes, Prince Jetekesh?"

"Speak with me. I—I can't abide this silence."

"What should I say, Your Highness?"

"Tell me what it's like to be a dragon."

Kethalas chuckled. "I've never been otherwise. How shall I define the differences?"

"I've never flown." Jetekesh glanced at him. "Tell me about flying."

"Ahhh. There's nothing like it. Have you ever fallen from a great height?"

Jetekesh nodded. "When I was small, I stumbled from my father's horse. At the time, it seemed a great distance."

"You know that sensation in your stomach? That fluttering?"

Jetekesh nodded. "The *terror* of it?"

"Yes. But imagine the thrill without the terror. That lightness in the hollow of your stomach just before you understand you're falling. Imagine climbing. Up, up, toward the sun. Weightless. Airborne. The wind catches you, holds you like a parent's gentle hands as you take your first steps. Sometimes, the wind will drop you. Let you tumble. But your wings catch you and thrust you upward again. There is no great fear. Only great, wondrous flight. You breathe in the clearest air, crisp, and it fills your being with light. Ah, prince, there is nothing else like it in all the world."

Jetekesh breathed in the loamy breeze. "It sounds wondrous. You're able to fly as you are now, aren't you? You flew to Rose Palace in this form."

"Yes, if I'm careful. My side and one wing are wounded, but I risked the flight to reach you swiftly."

"You've said you're unacquainted with Nakania and its countries, so how..."

Kethalas tossed him a sidelong glance.

Jetekesh's cheeks warmed. "Ah, right. A beacon."

"Yes, Your Highness. A beacon."

Jetekesh loosened his grip on the reins and tugged off his glove to glance at his hand. It appeared normal. No glow. No mark. "Then, that's how the Shingese army found us, even cloaked as I was?"

"I'm afraid it's likely."

Jetekesh swallowed. "I hope Harn is alive. If my presence caused his death..."

"Calamities will happen, O prince. You can do little to spare others from them. And you couldn't know how brightly you shine."

Jetekesh grimaced. “You might have told me how bad it is, my lord.”

“Would it have stopped you from pursuing the Arch?”

“Well, no.”

“Then why harbor regrets? Especially with Harn’s death unconfirmed. Life is filled with enough loss and guilt, there’s no sense burdening yourself with imagined shame.”

“You’re right. I shouldn’t dwell on it.” *But it’s better than listening to my dead mother’s taunting slights.* He swiped water from his forehead. “What do dragons eat, my lord?”

Kethalas chuckled. “*Meat*, Your Highness.”

“I guessed that much. Do you...do you eat people?”

“Some dragons do. But they are few and specialized. I prefer venison above all other meats—most of my kind do. Some enjoy kine or sheep nearly as much, but I find them too tame.”

Jetekesh blinked. “Cows are *tame*?”

“Lazy, coddled. You know. Domesticated.”

“So, you don’t eat horses?”

“Certainty not. Horses are noble.”

“Are deer not?” Jetekesh glanced at the man-dragon.

Kethalas shrugged. “It’s different. They are *meant* to be our food.”

“I see. But not horses.”

“No. Horses taste wrong—though I’d eat one if I must.”

Jetekesh nodded. “In this form, you’ve been eating our fare. Does it bother you?”

“Not when I look like this. My mind and soul adapt to the shape I take. Some dragons live out their days in human form and eat as all humans eat. Though we’ve a strong preference for meat.”

“Do you like fowl?”

“Yes. Well enough.”

"But not more than venison."

Kethalas's fangs showed in his smile. "Not more than venison, no."

Jetekesh shook water from his gloves. "I'm glad I'm not a dragon."

"Why is that, Your Highness?"

Jetekesh shrugged. "Because I like variety in my diet. Fruits, breads." He waggled his fingers. "*Desserts.*"

"To each their own, Your Highness. To me, venison *is* dessert if prepared properly."

Jetekesh grimaced. "I like sugar. And wine." He pulled his cloak closer. "I'd love some mulled wine, piping hot."

Sir Lafe grunted.

Kethalas sighed. "Ah, the blood of a hart is hot when—"

"Enough. Stop." Jetekesh batted his words back with his hand. "None of that, Lord Dragon. Spare me the details of your diet."

Kethalas's grin widened. "As you wish, Prince Jetekesh. It's just as well. I'm hungry thinking of it."

Jetekesh's grimace deepened as he rolled his eyes. "Oddly, I'm *not.*"

Sir Lafe met his wandering gaze and grunted again. His complexion looked a shade paler.

CHAPTER 25
FAREWELLS

The night sky sparkled like ice crystals, cold and aloof. Kajsa stared at the stars from the open window, longing for the short summer still so far away.

She sat upon her bed, alone in Fa's turf house on the south edge of the village. She seldom stayed here these days; instead, she rolled out a fur and slept near the hearth in Ingrid's abode, where life and warmth surrounded her. But tonight, she'd craved solitude. She'd needed to think.

She tore her gaze from the heavens to find the Elderhouse lit up with torches, music swelling from within. Her heart ached. The feast had commenced at nightfall and might well carry on until dawn. Few would be sober by now. Likely the village would appear vacant through most of tomorrow.

She bowed her head and stared at her lap. *How can they celebrate a coming war?*

Did Axel revel with the rest? Did he drink and laugh over the coming loss and bloodshed? Did the village girls flirt with him?

'Soon, you must leave.'

She twisted the fabric of her embroidered skirt. "I don't want to go, Ingrid. Why must it be me?"

The old woman's voice drifted from across the dusty room. "Because, my child, no one else in Tuksa repudiates this war."

Kajsa whirled toward the unexpected voice with a faint yelp.

Ingrid stood in the gloom, caught in a strand of feeble moonlight. "You desire peace. You alone must seek it."

Kajsa rose. "But Ingrid, I must stay and care for you. I can't leave."

The old woman laughed. "I'm well enough, Kajsa. Nothing will harm me now."

"Even so, I'm too—too weak. I'm not made for such journeys." She pressed a hand to her chest. "What can I possibly achieve beyond the mountains? How can I stand before royalty and beg them to spare my people?"

"Child, fear not." Ingrid's voice held strong and steady, as though she weren't a woman of ninety-seven winters. "Seek out the Marked Prince. In all things, stay with him. He will help you. You will help him."

Kajsa clutched her blouse. "Ingrid, please. I wouldn't even know where to begin my search. The North is unknown to me—I can't go alone."

"If you take another, you will lose them. Go. Be brave, dear Kajsa. The gods shall attend and guide you."

"But—" She stepped forward. In the gloom, Ingrid's silhouette had vanished as suddenly as it had come. Had Kajsa dozed off and dreamt of the old woman?

Even so...

Kajsa let her shoulders fall. She shivered. "I'm not strong enough, Ingrid."

After dawn, Kajsa trudged to Ingrid's isolated turf house and stomped the bits of snow from her boots on the porch. The warming weather had melted most of the snow in the village, but here on the ledge, it held on, stubborn as the old woman.

"I'm here, Ingrid." Kajsa stepped inside, surprised by the cold within. No fire blazed in the hearth. She glanced toward the rocking chair, and her heart stuttered. The chair had been shattered to bits before the open window. Ingrid lay among the wood debris. Blood pooled around her. The stench of death clung to the air.

Kajsa started forward, then halted as she caught a glimpse of the gore ripped from Ingrid's stomach. Just like Fa.

A scream tore from Kajsa's lips, and she slumped to her knees. "Please, no! No, no!"

A yowl sounded behind her. She staggered upright and whirled around. She expected to meet the vicious beast who had killed Ingrid, but instead the mangy cat stood on the windowsill opposite Ingrid's resting place. Its back arched, and its tail stuck straight up as it spit and hissed at Kajsa.

"Oh, Tatters, poor thing. How did you survive?" Tears stung Kajsa's cheeks. She reached toward the cat. "Come here. I...I won't hurt you."

The cat whipped out claws and batted at Kajsa's fingers. She drew back before the claws connected.

"Don't be mean, you poor thing. I'm a friend." Water dripped from her chin. "I...wouldn't hurt you...for anything." She slipped to her knees, striking the floor hard. Sobs ripped up her throat. "Oh, Ingrid. How could I not come here last night? I failed you. I'm...so sorry..."

A faint trill reached her ears, and soft fur brushed her fingers.

Kajsa looked down and found the mangy cat rubbing against

her. A wild glint still flashed in its eyes, but it meowed and rubbed against her knee again.

She scooped it up and held it close. “I won’t hurt you, poor thing. Poor, poor thing. I’m glad you’re not killed. Thank you for not dying. Thank you.” She leaned forward and wailed in the silence of the room.

“I’M SORRY, KAJSA.”

She turned to find Axel behind her among the trees on the edge of the village green. Biting her lip, she wheeled away and wrestled fresh tears. Her eyes lingered on the pyre in the center of the green where Ingrid’s remains awaited the Firing ceremony.

Footsteps crunched the newly fallen snow. A warm hand fell on her shoulder.

“You’ve lost so much, Ky. I can’t imagine your pain.”

The tears fell. Kajsa let them. “Do you see? This is why I can’t let this war take place. I know what it is to lose kin.”

He sighed. “Let’s not go into that right now, okay? You’re distraught. I don’t want to fight with you.”

Kajsa drew a shuddering breath. “Sorry, Xel. But I’m leaving.”

“Leaving? The village?”

She nodded.

“Where will you go?”

Her eyes lifted to stare at the northern mountains standing like a sentinel above the village. “I’m going to Shing.”

Axel’s fingers clutched her shoulder, digging in. “You’re not serious. Look at me.”

She turned, lifting her chin. Her eyes held his evenly. “I’m perfectly serious. I must go. I must *try* to find a peaceful solution, and if the Archon has already made up his mind, I must plead with your enemy for mercy."

"Do you hear yourself, Kajsa? That's madness. It's Ingrid's death that's making you talk like this. With those beasts roaming the forest, you can't actually—"

"It's what Ingrid wanted me to do. She came to me, Xel. After she died, she came to my house and told me to find the Marked Prince. He'll help me. I don't want to—and I'm frightened—but I'll honor her request. It's all I can do to atone for her death."

Axel shook his head. "That's ridiculous. The dead don't come back with messages, Kajsa. You imagined it."

"But I didn't." She took his wrist and pulled his hand from her shoulder. "I'm going, Axel. Alone."

"Don't. Please." He leaned close. "What about *us*?"

Her heart quickened, but she pulled away from his hypnotic gaze. "I'll come back, gods willing. And I'll bring word that we can take a bit of the North for ourselves. We don't have to stay here, and we don't have to fight. Let me try, Axel. Please."

He wrenched free of her grip. "You're a fool. You'll not make it over the mountain. No one can for another fortnight, at least."

She shuddered. "Navolleth did."

"Barely, and he's—" His voice dropped. "He's *magic*, Ky."

"It doesn't matter. I'm *going*."

He ran a hand through his pale hair as he groaned. "See reason." He turned and stared at Raum. "Kajsa, I beg you not to go. But if you won't change your mind...take Raum. Let him protect you."

Her lips parted. "I can't—"

"*Please*."

She studied the wolf, who eyed her back, tail thumping the ground. "All right. I accept."

Axel took a step forward and gripped her arms. "You don't have to do this. It will change *nothing.*"

"You don't know that."

"But I do." His fingers dug into her skin. "Don't. Do. This."

"I'm leaving after the Firing, Xel. Don't tell anyone. Don't stop me. It was Ingrid's wish that I go—and I'm going."

His head ducked as his arms quavered. "I can't stand to lose you, Kajsa. What if those monsters murder you too?"

Her lip trembled. "I'm frightened."

Axel's head whipped up. "Then—"

"No. Don't ask again. Let me go, and let's stop bickering. My heart hurts too much already." She stood on tiptoe and brushed her lips against his. "Goodbye, Axel."

His eyes gathered darkness, and he stepped back like he'd been struck. "*Fool.*" He pushed past her and marched toward the village green.

She watched his rigid back and shivered in her cape. "I love you, Axel."

CHAPTER 26
KITH AND KIN

Rille stood atop the hill overlooking Bahadronn, the KryTeer palace corpse teetering behind her. Anadin and Sir Yeshton flanked her like sentinels.

"What does a Shinacian Arch look like, Sahala?" asked Anadin. He pressed a hand to his brow to shield his eyes and squinted at the city.

"Nothing, at first." She angled to scan the western horizon. Rolling hills of sand dotted with palm trees. Highways streaming with caravans bringing supplies to the crippled city. Far beyond that, the sea gleamed, its expanse endless, its whispers timeless. "In the Drifting Sands, it revealed itself in darkness under a starry sky."

"Ah, yes. Aredel described that to me," said Anadin. "He said pillars of sand rose up, twining toward the heavens, flanking the path to a glowing archway. Quite a charming image. I'd love to see that. You don't suppose it *needs* sand for all the twining pillars, do you?"

"I don't think it's necessary." Rille sighed. "I wish I could sense it somehow. We need clues. If only your library hadn't burned down."

Anadin shrugged. "Nor our palace and two-thirds of its residents, alas."

Rille winced. "I'm sorry, that was thoughtless of me."

"It's quite all right." Anadin patted her shoulder. "You're learning."

She sighed and stole along the scorched stone pathway that circled the ruins. "Let's search the northern side. Keep talking, Anadin. It might trigger a vision. That can sometimes help me to see something important."

He skipped along behind her, merry as a child. Sir Yeshton lingered in the rear, silent, searching.

They came around the palace remains to view the northern horizon with its slopes swelling around a great river.

Anadin raced ahead, pointing to the serpentine water. "Oh, Sahala!" He whirled to face her, black eyes bright. "There *is* a legend from the north of KryTeer. I just remembered. 'At the head of the great Mahadri river, where once the breath of life flowed free, find the Way to Paradise, and there return—return to me.'" He shrugged. "It's better in my native tongue, but there it is."

"It's pretty," she said. "But what does it mean?"

His shoulders bobbed in another shrug. "It's an old folktale about a god who fell in love with a mortal. It's a bit convoluted now. So many versions exist. But the gist is the god wishes to wed a mortal woman, but his fellow gods forbid it. She's not worthy, they say. He courts her in secret nonetheless, and she falls in love with the god in return—until his brother, a jealous being, catches them and informs the rest of the pantheon. They banish her to the desert wastes of KryTeer—which long ago were entirely without water or vegetation.

"The woman despairs, but the god finds her—and being

unable to help her directly, he blesses the desert with a great river. From that springs up oases to give her respites from the grueling heat. He sends a message by animal—depending on the version, it might be a camel, a tiger, or a mystic bird. Whichever it is, the message is: 'At the head of the great Mahadri River, where once the breath of life flowed free, find the Way to Paradise and there return—return to me.'"

Rille smiled. "That's a pretty story, Anadin."

"Isn't it? I've always liked the old legends about the birth of KryTeer—before the tyrant Tallat rose to power and changed all that." He turned north. "The trade tongue turned the folktale into a nursery rhyme. In my tongue, 'way' is actually the archaic word *tahadi*. A more literal translation for that is 'secret doorway.' Do you think it might mean something? Might refer to the Arch into Shinac?"

"It might." She doubted they were so lucky, but it was a lead. "We can search if there are no more obvious paths to take." She reached his side and turned to Sir Yeshton. "What do you think, Sir Knight?"

Yeshton stared at the wide river flowing from the north. "All legends carry truth of some kind or other. I think Jinji would seek the head of the river."

"You're right. So he would." She laced her fingers together. "Well, then. North, we go."

"I'm coming, Sahala."

Rille smiled up at Anadin. "I'm glad."

THE BLOOD KING eyed Rille for a long time from his chair in the inn's lobby, seeming to weigh her plans. "I will come as well."

She blinked.

I didn't predict that response.

"That isn't necessary, Your Majesty. You're needed here—"

He shook his head. "If I remain, I endanger all of Bahadronn. Should *Erisyrdrel* still wish to either possess or destroy me, it is better I'm far away from here." He lifted his hand and flexed his fingers. Light sparked like white embers, following the path of his hand. "And I should like to test the nature and might of my fledgling magic."

No one moved. All eyes stared at the king's hand arcing light across the air. Several onlookers inhaled sharp breaths.

Rille sighed. "You'll do what you think best, Your Majesty, so I won't waste breath arguing with you. I'd like to leave at dawn."

"That can be arranged." The Blood King motioned, and the red-clad Blood Knight, Shevek, bent down to listen. King Aredel's words were too soft for Rille to catch them.

With a nod, Shevek straightened and slipped away from the hovering officials.

King Aredel caught Rille's eye again. "I will see you at dawn outside the inn."

"Very well." Rille took Anadin's hand.

"This way, Sahala." The prince led her to a set of stairs, and she followed him up five stories and onto a flat roof.

A woman sat on the edge of the building, draped in colorful layers of KryTeeran clothes. As Anadin pulled Rille closer, the woman turned and smiled. Her auburn hair stirred in a warm breeze.

"Kyella!" The seer darted to her side and knelt to hug the Amantieran farmer's daughter.

"Hello, Rille." Kyella pulled back to study her. "You look well."

"I'm well enough." Rille studied the fair, freckled face before her. "I heard you intend to marry this child." She glanced at Anadin who grinned back. "Did he blackmail you?"

Kyella chuckled. "If love is a form of blackmail now, then yes. Somehow, he's won me over these many months."

"Hello, Kyella." Sir Yeshton's voice floated over, soft and low.

Kyella stiffened, then rose from the ledge. "Yeshton!" She raced to him and threw her arms around his neck. "How are you, you senseless, elusive man?"

The knight grinned. "Better than you, for I'm not marrying a lunatic."

She laughed and dropped her arms. "Look at you. A knight at last. I know how you've ached for it—and you look so dashing in your fine clothes."

Yeshton's gray eyes swept up and down Kyella's foreign apparel. "You also cut a fascinating figure, my lady."

Her cheeks bloomed pink. "No formalities, please. We're like family, aren't we?"

Rille stood and straightened her skirts. She'd first met Kyella when she had fled with Sir Yeshton, Jinji, Jetekesh, and Tifen from Kavacos, on the heels of Queen Bareene's treachery. They'd sheltered in the humble house of Farmer Drinel and his daughter.

At the time, Kyella had harbored romantic feelings for Yeshton, but the knight saw her like a little sister. It was good to see the young woman happy now, even if Anadin was a peculiar choice. He'd taken a fancy to her when they met on the docks of Kilitheer en route to KryTeer, and Anadin had rarely left Kyella's side since. He'd even helped locate and rescue her father, who had been sold into slavery.

Anadin moved to Rille's side, chuckling. "What a funny little family we make, Sahala."

She blinked and glanced up at him. "Family?"

His smile widened. "The knight and his two *sisters*, don't you remember? When I marry Kyella, I'll be part of your little circle."

Rille grinned; she couldn't help herself. She and Yeshton had claimed kinship when Emperor Gyath sought her gift. Upon meeting them, Anadin had seen through the deception at once but hadn't divulged his findings to the emperor's priest or soldiers.

She took Anadin's hand again. "I find that a welcome thought."

CHAPTER 27
ONWARD

The villages and towns of Shing looked nothing like the boxy structures and towering turrets of Amantier's quaint cities. As they passed through a flourishing town one afternoon, Jetekesh eyed the elegant curved rooftops and red pillars, the lotus ponds, the cherry blossom trees. He marveled at the variety of cultures and landscapes in Nakania.

He'd seen the Holy City of Bahadronn in KryTeer months ago, with its domed roofs, chiming sea bells, and depictions of elephants, tigers, and strange gods on tapestries and stone surfaces. The air had tasted of spices that burned his tongue while the merciless sun scorched his skin.

Compared to that harsh clime, this eastern land, with its green hills and frequent rain felt like a paradise.

I'm still a prisoner, scenery notwithstanding.

Song had found Jetekesh's tent three nights before to reassure the prince that she and Yin were well. He'd slept easier since then, but captivity grated on his soul. He wasn't ready to face the demon *Erisyrdrel*. He needed to reach Shinac, find Sharo, and bring back an army of dragons.

He shifted in his saddle, wincing as blisters flared up and muscles throbbed.

Hooves rumbled to Jetekesh's left. He craned his head to watch a Shingese rider gallop up the ranks. The sun, peeking through the storm clouds, glinted off his armor. The cavalry guarding Jetekesh and his companions didn't falter, but a few riders exchanged looks.

Five minutes later, a halt sounded, then hooves resounded from the front of the line.

The Shingese commander—named Hon—descended upon Jetekesh. Hon reined in his steed. With his dark eyes narrowed, his countenance matched the louring clouds.

"Hello, Commander." Jetekesh was careful to keep his face blank. He wouldn't show fear or uncertainty before an enemy. "Have you at last decided to let me go?"

"We have a problem, Your Highness."

Jetekesh raised his chin by a centimeter. "Do we?" His mind raced. He and his companions had been careful to create no trouble. They'd eaten, bathed, halted, slept, and ridden upon command. Once, he'd tried to explain the urgency of his quest without mentioning the Shingese emperor, but Hon had cut him off and walked away.

"Those of your company who escaped have been tracking us this past week," Hon said curtly. "For two days now, they have taken to untethering our horses, and just now they killed three of my soldiers and absconded with two of our supply wagons. This harassment is infuriating and must cease."

Jetekesh worked his mouth to battle the grin that twitched at his lips. *So, you didn't catch them after all.*

He shrugged. "What am I supposed to do about it?"

"Call them off," barked Hon.

"How? If you can't find them to stop them, I can't do better—nor do I wish to. I'm your prisoner, but I'm *their* prince. If you want your wagons back, you'll have to free me. Choose."

Hon's scowl deepened as Jetekesh spoke. The commander yanked on his reins. "Very well. But if I or my men spot your shifty conspirators, we will shoot to kill."

"That's your duty, I presume." He let his smile loose. "Best of luck."

The commander wheeled his mount and galloped back to the head of the column, adjutants in pursuit. Murmurs filled the ranks, and half a dozen Shingese soldiers studied Jetekesh from the corner of their eyes.

He ignored them as he nudged Hickory onward.

"Lord Emerin is a bold man, isn't he?" said Kethalas.

Jetekesh chuckled. "No doubt of it. I visited the Keep of the Falls when I was eight. My lord father took me there to meet the new lord of the keep. It was an experience I shan't forget in all my days."

Kethalas canted his head. "What happened if I may ask?"

"Well..." Jetekesh's grin weakened a little. "There was a lot of unrest at the keep. I understood very little of it, being so young, but I recall a lot of angry people. And looking back, I can guess why. I think my father went there to settle the disputes surrounding Lord Emerin's succession."

"But why? Is he not the rightful heir of the keep?"

Jetekesh nodded. "His father, Lord Kayvar, ruled Moss Province well and long. Lord Emerin had been missing for several years just before his father died. Many had presumed the young lord dead—until he returned one day, mere weeks before Lord Kayvar succumbed to an illness that had long ailed him."

"Where had Lord Emerin been?" asked Kethalas.

The prince shook his head. “He wouldn’t say. There was a lot of speculation. Some thought he’d defected to Shing. There was an outcry when he stood to rule the Keep of the Falls. Not within his own kin—they’re the most close-knit family among all the Amantieran nobility—but neighboring provinces were outraged. They demanded he explain himself and prove his loyalty. Some even alleged he’d killed his father, which was baseless and absurd. In the end, the king sanctioned him, but not before a disgruntled nobleman stood before the assembly gathered in the Keep of the Falls and accused Lord Emerin of treason.”

“What happened?”

Jetekesh’s lips curled into a broad smile. “He and Lord Emerin dueled. There was no help for it if Lord Emerin wished to preserve his honor.”

The prince’s mind snapped back to the memory of clashing swords; the scent of sweat and beeswax in the long audience chamber; the dry, hot day. “Until I later entered Shinac, I’d never seen the like of what I witnessed. Lord Emerin moved like a windstorm, light and devilishly fast. He toyed with his enemy, danced around him like a torrent as he grinned like a maniac. The nobleman had no chance at all. Lord Emerin cut him down in moments, though it felt longer, like we’d been caught outside of time. The only other warrior I’ve ever seen fight like that is King Aredel of KryTeer when he faced Lord Peresen in Shinac. But that fight was more equal.”

Jetekesh rubbed his thumb along the leather reins. “Honestly, Lord Emerin seems like a different person when he’s fighting. And...” His cheeks warmed as he recalled his stupidity.

“What is it, Your Highness?”

Jetekesh managed a sideways smile. “Just before that duel, when we’d been about to enter the assembly hall to discuss Lord Emerin’s rights, I’d complained of the heat to my lord father. It’d been a sweltering day, and Mother used to scold me for sweating. She wasn't there, of course—she never traveled to the Keep of the Falls—but she always had a way of remaining in my head even in her absence."

Jetekesh ducked his head. *She still does.*

He drew a breath. "Lord Emerin heard me complaining. I'd even stomped my foot and refused to enter the hall. He crossed the corridor, turned me to face him, and told me in quiet, deadly tones to respect my king. I'll never forget his eyes. They...weren't human."

Kethalas scratched the bridge of his nose. "Oh, he's definitely human. But there is something odd about him, even beyond his fire trick."

"You think so, too?"

Kethalas nodded. "Being what I am, I've seen all types of people and creatures, Your Highness. They usually stay within their species in terms of habits, smell, demeanor, and so forth. That's not to say they aren't individuals, but collectively, there's a sameness. A familiarity. Few cross lines far enough to make one question their origin. Lord Emerin, however, isn't *tame*. There's an otherness to him. A transcendency."

He eyed Jetekesh, eyes slitted and shining in the sun. "You are the same, though not in a wild sense. You are grounded—or nearly so—in your otherness. Safe. Comfortable. Meanwhile, Lord Emerin is intense. His quiet is unnerving. There's a kind of instability within his soul."

That didn't weave into Jetekesh's perspective of the man—except when he remembered the feral light in Lord Emerin's eyes when he'd chastised Jetekesh all those years ago—and again when he'd wielded the pillar of fire.

He told me he'd struggled against severe trauma. That sometimes he panicked, as I did mere days ago. Is that what he meant?

What did he experience when he vanished from his home for so long?

Jetekesh uncurled his fingers from the reins and studied the calluses on his hands. He'd shed his sopping gloves earlier to prevent worse blisters.

Emerin said he lost something—something that has to do with a Shinacian Arch—and he'll do whatever it takes to get it back. Did that occur when he vanished? Did he enter Shinac? Surely, he'd tell me if he knew where an Arch was.

A shadow fell over Jetekesh's palm. Thunder drummed over the sky, and soon the rattle of rain against metal sounded above the squelch and splash of hooves on the muddy road. He drew his cowl over his head and hunched forward with a grimace.

Endless days of rain and riding tumbled into fatigued rests at night. Jetekesh's mind wandered far as he trotted ever nearer to the capital of Shing. The deeper into these foreign lands he rode, the more Jetekesh ached for one last glimpse of Jinji, alive, smiling—those turquoise eyes probing into Jetekesh's soul.

Jinji had been Jetekesh's only friend. Mother had never allowed him to have any—and he'd come to think himself above such things.

What a fool I was.

The friendship of that peculiar storyteller meant more to Jetekesh than kingdoms and crowns. To have it back, Jetekesh would muck out stables and eat moldy bread.

That sounds melodramatic, even in my own head.

Yet as he urged Hickory through a deep, puddled rut in the road, Jetekesh smiled, for he knew he meant it.

If Lord Emerin and the rest of the errant company still

plagued Lord Hon's troops, the Shingese commander didn't let on. Kethalas reported their scent nearby between rainfalls, but those reprieves were few. The past two days, the rain hadn't let up and conversation had withered to nothing.

A few more days of this deluge and I'll sprout saplings from my limbs.

But Jetekesh would reach the capital before that. Considering what he'd calculated on his oiled sheepskin map, and the growing restlessness of the soldiers surrounding him, it couldn't be more than two days more before he reached Kyon Taro.

There, he would meet Emperor Majinglee.

Or rather, *Erisyrdrel.*

Lord Father had spoken about the Shingese emperor before; he called him a kindly old man, worn out from constant foreign invasion and occupation, but proud of his ancient heritage and bloodline. Majinglee would rather spend his days reading and walking the illustrious halls of the Lotus Palace than politicking or warring with his neighbor countries.

How do I free him of the demon possessing him without risking his life?

Jetekesh rubbed his thumb along his reins until the leather drew a line in his flesh. He looked up and peered ahead into the storm. If Kyon Taro stood within sight, the mists embracing the earth were too close to let Jetekesh have a peek at the grand old city. He wiped water from his brow and dredged up an old song to hum to himself. Anything to keep his thoughts from swirling like the rivulets under Hickory's hooves.

The words to the song bloomed in his head, and he softly sang it to himself as he shivered in the growing cold.

"Cavalin of ancient oath,
High King in days of yore,

Stood bright and well upon the field,
Before he joined those gone before.

"His noble mien and daring deeds,
His heart so bright and bold,
Shall ne'er be lost to time, 'tis said.
His sacrifice was as foretold.

"He fell, he fell, but all's not lost.
He lived before he died!
He lived, and lives again, they say,
Beyond the place he said goodbye."

Jetekesh clutched his reins tighter. "'He lived, and lives again, they say, beyond the place he said goodbye.'"

"A pretty song, Your Highness." Kethalas's voice sliced through the rain. "'Tis said in Shinac, those who sacrifice themselves to save the world of Nakania enter the fae realm as heroes, never to taste of death again."

"Have you ever seen him?" Jetekesh's stomach fluttered. He angled to eye the dragon. "Cavalin the Third?"

Kethalas shook his head. "Not I. But if such a hero did truly enter Shinac, it would be to the Hold of Valliath he would go. And there he would dwell, hailed as a hero, preserved for the days when all heroes are called forth to battle one last time before the True King of Shinac returns."

Jetekesh looked ahead as he mulled over Kethalas's words. "I've seen him, my lord."

"Cavalin?"

"No. Ehrikai. The rightful king of Shinac—the lost heir."

"Truly?" Kethalas's horse quickened its pace until it came level with Jetekesh's. "When? How?"

"It was after we defeated Lord Peresen. Jinji had sacrificed himself to slay the man and bring us back to Nakania—and as he lay dying, the Shinacian king appeared. He healed Jinji and charged him to stand before Emperor Gyath in KryTeer."

Kethalas drew a long breath. "What is he like, Prince Jetekesh? Please tell me all."

The prince closed his eyes. "It's a sight I'll never forget. He was light and darkness in perfect balance—a figure carved from both; sinister and beautiful. His voice had the power of lightning. His eyes were a pale, striking blue, and his hair was the pale sheen of platinum. I—I couldn't breathe when he looked at me. I'm afraid I'd demanded that he save Jinji, and he reprimanded me for my impatience. Had I thought he'd truly come, I wouldn't have shouted so—so—boldly."

Jetekesh expected a laugh from the dragon at that, but Kethalas remained silent. The prince glanced at his companion to find the dragon's brows knit together as he stared ahead. Droplets of water sparkled like ice against his silver-blue hair.

"Are you unwell, my lord?"

Kethalas blinked and turned his silver gaze to Jetekesh. "No. Merely envious." He sighed and rubbed the scar on his jaw. "I'm twice dishonored, fair prince. First by a witch's spell that caused me to terrorize the world I most cherish. That my liege lord had to rescue me, and that I wounded him in the process, shames my soul to its core." He lifted his eyes skyward, ignoring the rain freezing upon his face. "And then, again, at Jade Arch, I failed to defend my post when that post was my means of returning with restored honor to my clan. I fear I shall never be able to face my kin again. Nor can I hope to gaze upon the True King of Shinac when he returns to his throne."

"That's rubbish." Jetekesh shook his head. "Does your clan

feel this way, or is it merely your own convoluted perspective that drives you to avoid them?"

"It...is custom, Your Highness. I must restore my honor—"

"So, then, restore it. Isn't that what you're doing right now? Trying to help Nakania?"

"It is my fault your world needs saving."

Jetekesh snorted. "We needed it well before all this. Or hadn't you heard, we of the mundane realm tend to hurt ourselves best? We don't need shattered Arches and demons from the depths of the sea to find any excuse to unsheathe our blades and dominate the world."

"You have so little faith in your own kind."

Jetekesh shrugged and stared ahead. "Faith is built upon strong groundwork. What can I find for a foundation?"

"You."

Jetekesh glanced at him. "Me?"

"Aren't you a prince? Don't you have more sway than most? And after all that happened through Jinji's efforts, you are allied with KryTeer against all odds. The Blood King has revoked his claim to the world and reinstated the rulers to their rightful stations. That is a start of something new, something strange among countries and provinces, is it not? You, who have the blood of Cavalin of old, might restore to Nakania all that the High King fought and died for: a new kind of world, not so mundane, but bright and hopeful. That is something I should choose to put my faith in, and how much more wonderful is it to know *you* might help to shape that new world?"

Jetekesh bowed his head and listened to the rhythmic thud and squelch of hooves around him. *Can I manage all that?*

"That's quite a weight you've tossed at me." He looked up as the hammering rain quieted to a drizzle. "Do you think... Might

Shinac return to Nakania's shores if we *could* reach that new, bright future you paint?"

"Perhaps. It would certainly be more possible than it presently is."

It's something to aim for. Something perhaps only I—I and my father and Aredel—have the power to attain.

He squared his shoulders. "I'd like that, Lord Kethalas. More than anything. I think it would be the best tribute I could pay to my storyteller friend."

And if Jinji somehow dwells in Shinac, if that vision was real, perhaps I'll see him again.

THE RAIN EASED off at last.

Jetekesh dragged his sopping hood back and lifted himself in his saddle to eye the lush valley cradling Kyon Taro, where the Lotus Palace gleamed after its days' long bath. The palace stood in the center of the rambling city, guarded by high walls of white stone and red pillars. Rice fields surrounded the city proper, and beyond those fields, an army camped—a hundred-thousand strong at least—a black and grim stain beside the fair streets of Kyon Taro.

Jetekesh's heart faltered. *War is coming.*

"Steady, O prince." Kethalas's voice drifted to him like a welcome breeze. "You are not alone, and what we accomplish here may spare your country—and Shing—from pointless carnage."

Blood pounded in Jetekesh's ears, but he nodded. "I'm glad you're here."

An accented voice spoke. "You also have my sister."

Jetekesh glanced left to find young Yin riding alongside him, eyes pinned on the valley ahead. The boy turned his dark eyes to Jetekesh, and a smile tugged at his mouth. "The Lady of Crimson Lilies is nothing to scorn."

Jetekesh's eyes drifted to the horse behind Yin's. Song rode in silence, jaw set, eyes fixed on the path ahead.

"What will you do, Lady Song?" Jetekesh asked.

"Whatever is right, Prince Jetekesh."

"May the One God guide us to know what that means."

CHAPTER 28
THE SUMMIT

Snow reached Kajsa's thighs as she plowed up the mountain trail. Raum loped alongside her, tongue lolling like this was a delightful game, uninhibited by the pack strapped to his back. Blissfully unaware of the magnitude of their undertaking.

Kajsa shifted her own pack and trudged on. With each step bitter snow seeped into her boots, leggings, and woolen skirts. The heavy cape she wore did nothing to protect her against the mountain winds that shrieked like ghouls. Her fingers were numb and red beneath her mittens. Her lips were chapped and cracked.

Three days ago, she'd dressed warm, packed light, and sneaked out in the dead of night. No one had stopped her. Only Axel knew her plan, and he'd not bothered to reappear, to try a final time to convince her not to go. She was glad, really. She might not have had the strength to argue her point again—not when every nerve in her body screamed against this course of action. Not when tears leaked from her eyes at the very idea of leaving the village, and all she had ever known, to cross over the unforgiving mountains and seek out a prince who might not even exist. Even if no one was left in Tuksa to notice her absence —except for Axel.

Even Ingrid is gone now...

Had she imagined the old woman coming to her? Had she dreamt her up?

No. Why would I? I'd rather stay home.

Besides, she would never forget the sight of Ingrid torn up, the same way as Fa. Dead. She couldn't stay in the village after that.

Tears froze on her cheeks as Kajsa slogged a few more steps before she sank down between snow drifts and shivered. "How can I do this, Raum? It's suicide to go on."

But she'd already traveled several days up the mountain pass. To turn back might still mean death. Wind howled in her ears through her fur-lined hood, and she shrank under its barrage. The crisp fragrance of snow taunted her senses.

Raum slumped down beside her, pressing his heat against her frame. She folded herself over him and shuddered. Had she been right to do this? Or had she gone mad? What difference could one girl make against the tides of war?

Move. It's better than dying here.

She climbed to her feet, shook snow clusters free of her embroidered skirts, and slogged on. Raum took the lead and plowed a sort of trail in the snow, tail high and hopeful.

Toward evening, Kajsa staggered. Her toes were too numb to gauge her steps. She slumped against a large, ice-crusted rock, and peered ahead where Raum burrowed in search of dinner.

It's so cold. If I stop, I'll never move again.

"Kajsa."

She started up, heart thumping, and turned to find Ingrid

standing just beyond the rock. Swirls of snow were visible through the old woman's frame. She looked as she had in life, yet a new kind of vitality brightened her eyes and smoothed her wrinkles.

Ingrid pointed off the path. "There is a cave. Come."

Kajsa stumbled to her side, and the wisewoman led her to a cave glowing as though a fire blazed within. The cave was small, tucked against the sheer rock of a rising peak, and free of snow. Sure enough, a cookfire sparked and hissed, lighting the chamber. The aroma of meat and herbs rose from a pot held above the flames by a trivet.

Kajsa stared. "How is this possible?" She lifted her eyes, but Ingrid had vanished.

Raum slinked into the cave and shook snowflakes from his fur. He padded to the fire, curled up, and licked his bloody mouth.

Kajsa warmed herself as she quietly wept between bites of a hearty rabbit stew.

THE SAME MIRACLE occurred each night as Kajsa made for the summit of the pass. Ingrid appeared at dusk, led her to a makeshift camp sheltered from the snows, where warm food simmered, and then the old woman vanished without any explanation.

On the sixth day up the mountain, Kajsa halted on the frigid heights of the Snowblinds at eventide, gripping her cape close, stamping snow from her boots. She stared at the leagues spread before her. So many.

But we've already come so far.

Clouds hugged the path ahead, hiding any hope of viewing

Shing, but she knew it lay there somewhere, green and lush. Warm. Real. She wanted to see what Navolleth had described.

"We're close, Raum. We can do this."

Unholy howls pierced the sky.

Kajsa whirled as Raum let out a low growl, ears pressed against his skull.

The howls lifted again, sending shivers through Kajsa's flesh, biting deeper than the cold.

"Oh, Raum. What are they doing here?" She slid the pack from her shoulders and dug out the hunting knife she'd taken from Ingrid's turf house.

Raum's growl pitched up, tail lowered, hackles raised.

"Easy, boy. Maybe they won't find us. Maybe—"

A hellish beast darted over the snow along the path she'd blazed moments before. Hands shaking, Kajsa slid the hunting knife from its sheath. "Stay back!" Her voice cracked in the frozen air. Her breath plumed out in a cloud.

The chorus of howls lifted again, chilling, horrible, like a dirge.

"Gods of the mountain, spare me." She clutched the knife before her, point forward.

Another canine monster leapt from a ledge above, fangs bared, saliva dribbling, red eyes burning with hatred. Kajsa shrieked and stumbled back as Raum sprang at the beast. They collided with snarls. Claws and teeth ripped into each other.

Kajsa looked on, knife shaking in her grasp. *What do I do? Raum is going to die!*

She tightened her grip and raced toward the bundle of fur and growls. Raum yipped in pain and staggered sideways, a line of blood dripping from his muzzle. Kajsa tripped past him and rammed the knife into the mangy beast's throat. Its eyes latched onto her, and a gurgling growl issued from its maw as a putrid odor permeated the air. Kajsa wrenched the knife loose and backed away.

Those lurid eyes bored into her, animosity blazing. Then the beast shuddered, slumped over, and lay still.

Growls surrounded her, playing dark music against the throbbing of her heart.

She rose. A bead of blood fell from the knife's tip, dyeing the snow crimson. Energy surged through her limbs, keeping her upright. "Stay back, or so help me, I'll slay every last one of you! I swear it on Ingrid's pyre and by the wrath of the mountain gods!"

Ingrid materialized before her, holding an intricately carved staff in her hands. She stood in a defensive stance. "Go, child. Flee! I will delay them."

Kajsa snatched up her pack. "Come, Raum."

They darted down the northern side of the mountain where the snow didn't pile so high. As the snarls and screams grew behind her, Kajsa hunched her shoulders forward and let her feet pound the icy earth. Her bones jolted with the impact.

She ran. On and on.

Her lungs burned.

Her heart thudded against her ribs.

She wouldn't stop.

Raum loped along beside her, never faltering.

They ran for what seemed like years. At last, her legs gave out and she collapsed, rasping for air. Her body shook, sweat pouring down her back, limbs burning.

Raum settled beside her with a whimper. He nosed her cheek.

Kajsa peered at him through tangles of pale hair as she swallowed between pants. "I—I'm...all right." She dragged herself to her knees with quaking hands. "Did...we lose them?"

Raum tilted his head and whined.

Kajsa wiped perspiration from her face, then peeled off her sweat-soaked mittens. "Got to keep...moving, Raum." She pushed to her aching feet, limbs quivering, head splitting. "C'mon."

They staggered down the mountain together, trying to put as much distance between them and the beasts on the summit. Adrenaline pulsed deeper through Kajsa's limbs, and she kept moving, moving.

Don't stop. Never stop.

ICE CRYSTALS SPARKLED red upon the trees as Kajsa stepped over the timberline at sunset. Ahead stood ranks of firs and naked aspens, guarding the mountainside like the gods' protectors. She stared up at the ice baubles ornamenting a stately fir, stunned by its beauty.

Raum nosed her hand.

She blinked and gazed down at the wolf. "You're right. We should keep moving."

Raum trotted ahead. Kajsa watched him, and her heart panged.

He's limping. I should treat his wounds.

She shook herself, willing her mind to uncloud.

Think, Kajsa. Those beasts carried poison. Raum needs your help.

"Let's stop a moment." She sank to the ground and rummaged in her pack until she found a poultice meant to draw out infection. "I need a fire."

"Kajsa."

She looked up and found Ingrid standing before her. "Not here, child. Keep moving. Just a little further."

Tears collected in Kajsa's eyes. "I can't. Please."

Ingrid shook her head. "Down the mountain. Walk just ten minutes more, and you'll reach a safe camp."

Letting her tears fall, Kajsa repacked her poultice and staggered upright. "Come, Raum. Just a bit longer."

The wolf limped at her side, and in the waning light, Kajsa could see the wound around Raum's muzzle. The gash oozed yellow pus mingled with blood.

She reached down and stroked the wolf's head. "Just a few minutes more."

Raum whined and wagged his tail.

What seemed an age later, they reached a campfire tucked between large, icy boulders. The light reflected off the rime, adding warmth and color to the darkness of the mountain woods. Soup simmered on the trivet like always.

Kajsa slumped before the fire, dragged the pack from her shoulder, and detached Raum's pack. A hole had been torn in the cloth, and half the contents were gone. Food. Extra water.

Ingrid's been providing those. We'll be fine.

Kajsa set her canteen near the fire to warm the water, then fed herself. She gave the rest of the soup to Raum and fixed up the poultice.

"This will sting, Raum." She pressed the poultice over his maw as he licked his chops clean. Raum endured it, yellow eyes pinned on Kajsa, trusting her.

She stroked his back and hummed a song. In the darkness around her, shadows creaked and moaned as the wind whispered threats. After a while, she removed the poultice and cleaned Raum's leg where a bite mark had swollen the furry flesh. The wolf growled as she bandaged it but allowed her to work.

"There. Finished. Good boy." She scratched under his chin,

and his hind leg thumped the frozen ground. Kajsa laughed. "Best get some rest before those beasts reach us."

She unrolled her bedding and curled up, shivering. Her legs pulsed with their own heartbeats, and her head pounded in her ears. Raum pressed his slender body against hers. Fur tickled her nose. She snuggled closer, grateful for the warmth.

"Thank you, Raum. I'm glad you're here."

He whined as he yawned and nestled closer. His tongue licked her cheek. They dozed off together.

Morning spread dazzling colors through the beads of ice hanging from the fir needles.

Kajsa rolled over and stared at the treetops. Raum still pressed against her, cold from a faint dusting of snow covering the world.

"C'mon, Raum. We must keep going." She sat up and winced as her muscles protested. Fortunately, she didn't feel fevered despite her exertions of yesterday. She ran her fingers through Raum's fur. So cold.

Her hand recoiled.

"Raum?"

She angled to find his face tucked into his forelegs. Kajsa shook him. He lay so still, stiff, not breathing. She let out a sob and leaned closer. Raum's eyes stared straight ahead, flat, lifeless. Bloody drool had frozen to his maw and nose.

"Oh, no. Please no. Please no." She shook him again. "Come back to me. I'm so...so sorry. I'm so sorry." She slumped back, drew her knees to her chest, and huddled into herself. "Please. Please don't leave me alone. Oh, I'm so, so sorry. I should've stopped sooner. Forgive me, Raum. Forgive me."

"Kajsa, child, you can't stay here."

She lifted her eyes and found Ingrid standing before her. "He's gone, Ingrid. My dear little friend is gone."

Ingrid's eyes glowed with compassion. "So he is. That poison is deadly. You couldn't do anything to stop its course."

"He should have stayed behind. I shouldn't have brought him with me, Ingrid."

"Ah, child. That wolf loved you too much to remain with Axel. He gave his life to protect you. That's why he came."

Kajsa lowered her head and sobbed. "I can't do this. Not without Raum."

"You must, Ky. Otherwise his sacrifice is meaningless. If you turn back, you will die on the summit. Shing is mere days ahead of you. Walk on, child. Stay the course."

Kajsa's shoulders trembled. Her heart might burst, and her lungs ached. Slowly, she nodded. "I'll keep going. I'll not give up." Her eyes found the still wolf. "But how can I just leave him?"

Ingrid took a step nearer. "He's not here now, child. He's with me. This is merely his shell. Walk on. The earth will care for its own." She vanished.

Kajsa stumbled to her feet and numbly broke camp, unwilling to glimpse at her friend again. Heart quaking, she aimed north and refused to look back.

"Goodbye, Raum. Thank you."

CHAPTER 29
MAHADRI

A week's journey into the northern desert of KryTeer brought Aredel and his company to the Rabahan Oasis. There, he set up camp and ordered the company to remain for several days to rest the animals and servants.

Within his private tent, he spent the respite studying the scrolls and tomes salvaged from the palace library, seeking any hint of an Arch at the head of the Mahadri River. The gods hadn't granted him any luck yet.

Aredel sighed and pushed back the heavy tome he'd been perusing. He stood and strode to the netted doorway to stare out at the spring surrounded by palm trees and reeds. Rille and Anadin stood ankle-deep in the water, while the latter laughed and splashed the girl. Rille endured it, then retaliated with a triumphant laugh of her own.

Aredel's insides knotted. He rarely felt lonely; he'd always been too busy to bother reflecting on his lost childhood. He'd had to grow up fast to survive. But after he'd met Jinji, he'd begun to see the world as more than land to be conquered. He'd looked into faces and found souls staring back. Feelings. Wills.

But even so, he stood apart. Now, with the borders of his domain shrunk down to the single continent of KryTeer, he might find time to learn who and what he was. What remained of Aredel elvar Gilioth d'ara KessRa.

That thought frightened him far more than combat or injury ever had.

What remains of a soul who has spent his life slaughtering the innocent?

Anadin's laughter sang over the air. Despite an existence spent oppressed by priests, disdained by his father, and disregarded by his people, Prince Anadin glowed with life. With dreams. With a future. He'd fallen in love.

In love.

So had Jinji, though he'd lost his true love without ever gaining her.

Aredel shifted to study his wife, Artassa, seated on a rug on the far shores of the spring, toes dipped in the clear water. Servants shaded her from the brutal noon sun.

He had never fallen in love. His seven wives had been chosen for political advantages of one kind or another. Even Artassa, wed to him when he'd turned seventeen years old, had become a friend but never his great love. She revered him; perhaps even adored him. Worshiped him as a god. But he saw her as no more than a subject, faithful and beneficial.

What is love? Is it a mere fancy? A delusion discovered in one's search for purpose?

Certainly, Lord Father had never loved his wives and concubines. Nor even his children. He'd only loved himself.

Jinji wouldn't deceive himself in such matters.

Aredel would rather believe Jinji right than the deceased emperor of KryTeer.

Then I am the broken one.

Artassa raised a hand to wave at Aredel. "My holy husband, join us!"

"Yes, come, *shaqin*!" called Anadin. "It's perfect weather for bathing!"

Rille doused the prince with water and Sir Yeshton laughed from the shore.

Lady Kyella had remained in Bahadronn, but Artassa had insisted on coming on this mad journey. Why she chose to subject herself to the heat and blisters of travel, Aredel couldn't understand. She'd always been safe in the palace, kept out of pain, pampered as the First Princess and then the Queen of KryTeer.

Aredel drew aside the netting and slipped out into the heat. He trod to the spring across the sand and circled the little pool to stare down at his first wife.

Artassa lifted her brown eyes and smiled. Her painted lips were glossy in the sunlight, even through her sheer veil. "Hello, my holy husband." She shifted to give him room on the rug. "Relax. You work too hard, always."

Aredel knelt before her, his sandaled feet hanging off the rug to dig into the sand. Servants moved the awning to shade him better. "Wife," he said. "Why have you come?"

She tipped her head sideways. "To support you, my husband. Why else?"

"Support me how?"

"I just wish to be near you, my king. I cannot abide the idea of that fire consuming you in the northern wastes and I not know it for weeks or months. I would rather stay close."

He searched her face, probed at the light burning in her eyes; the set of her jaw; the flare of her nostrils, challenging him to question her sincerity. Aredel sighed. "Do as you will." He twisted to settle on the rug and eyed Anadin and Rille in the water. "But you worry for nothing, wife. I have power now as I have never had before."

"So you do," she said. "And I believe you are capable of destroying any foe before you—but accidents may still happen. You bleed as other men. And you say that the fire was conjured by a curse left from your father. How can I accept that idly?"

"Should I perish, Artassa, you won't face execution. That law is no more. No need to fret."

Artassa's hands clutched her silken skirts. "Do you truly believe that is my reasoning, Holy King?"

He glanced at her. "I wouldn't blame you if it were."

"Why are you goading me, my husband?" Her face pinched, muscles in her neck taut.

He looked away. "Because I don't understand you. I know you revere me; that I've never doubted. But that's no reason to put yourself in harm's way or—"

"Please don't make me say it!" She gasped and clamped a hand to her lips. "Forgive me, my holy husband. I forgot my place." She curled forward, bowing her head.

"None of that." Aredel brushed a finger against her veiled cheek. "I shouldn't probe you. It's rude. Arise."

She lifted her eyes to find his. "You may do as you please, my husband. But I ask you to spare me your scorn if you can. I don't deserve your censure."

"No, that's true. You don't." He stared at the ripples cascading over the water. "Are you lonely, Artassa?"

"My king?"

"Your sister wives are gone. You alone remain."

"You'll gain more wives in the future, Holy King."

He grimaced. "Should I?"

"Don't you want to?"

He shrugged. "I haven't decided." He'd barely known those he'd since lost. He'd always been off conquering lands. These past months as king, he'd not known how to interact with the people closest to him. Anadin was easier than most. His brother pushed himself upon others, demanding attention, earning affection with his unguarded, peculiar ways.

Artassa stared at her feet.

"What is it?"

She shook her head. "Nothing, my husband."

He sighed. "Speak."

"You've changed."

"And?"

She twisted to face him. "Once, you were the proud prince of an empire. A man without equal—far superior to your gluttonous father. You shone like the sun as you toppled kingdoms and claimed all for the glory of KryTeer."

"Yes. And?"

She dropped her gaze, shoulders shaking. "What are you now? You've given up all you gained, all you were, for what? Some foolish storyteller who is dead?"

Aredel's eyes narrowed and his skin prickled. "Artassa."

She looked up. "I know he was your brother. That you loved him. These things I understand—but not how he could change you. Forgive me, but I must speak my heart, even if the cost is death." Artassa's eyes flashed with an inner fire. "Where is your pride, my king—my *emperor*! You were changing the world, and now you have abandoned it. You lost yourself when Jinji died, and none can find you, none can help you. You pace like a caged tiger in the night. You wander in the day. And even with your newfound gift—" She caught his hand and lifted it. "Even with divinity shining through your skin, you flounder. How can I help you, my husband? My holy god. How can I guide you back to your greatness?"

Aredel wrenched his wrist from her grasp. "Enough. You've said your peace, now heed your king." He stood up and stared down at her. "If I am lost, it changes none of the choices I have made for KryTeer. Our wealth is ample, even without the slaves and tributes from other lands. The continent of KryTeer is vast, Artassa—larger than Amantier by far. Larger than Shing. Nearly as large as both combined. We have plenty without oppressing others. Without robbing from them. Why waste our wealth on keeping them beneath our thumb?"

He sighed and folded his arms. "Yes, Jinji changed me. And perhaps I do flounder in this new age of peace—but I will not rescind the oaths I made when first I took the throne. We cannot be what we were under the commands of tyrants going back to Tallat. We must return to our roots, learn from them, and find a new way to define our land. I will not rob from another man any longer unless he first robs me. This is who I am, Artassa. I am not lost."

Her body shuddered. Tears rimmed her dark lashes. She searched his eyes. "Is this the will of the gods, my holy husband?"

He nodded. "I believe it is. I believe the gods brought Jinji into my life to show me the greatest path for KryTeer. Before you condemn me, wife, share my vision. See if it is not good."

Her gaze lowered. "But what of Bahadronn? Its greatness is lost."

"It will be rebuilt. It will be a symbol of New KryTeer and all we can become under its banner." Aredel turned and found Anadin, Rille, and Yeshton watching him from the spring. Servants looked on. Ledonn and Shevek stood near the camels, smiles wide on their usually impassive faces.

"Yes, Holy King." Artassa's voice quavered. "Forgive my doubt."

He crouched and rested a hand on her shoulder. "It was kindly meant. Look at me."

She obeyed, eyes shimmering with unshed tears.

He tried a gentle smile. "You *can* aid me, Artassa."

"How, my husband?"

"By standing beside me. By not hindering my work. We must learn peace together, you and I. We must strive to understand it better."

The edges of her lips lifted. "As you wish, my husband."

THE HEAD of the Mahadri River cascaded from the slick rocks, its roar filling the sky. Rille flopped down on a red boulder and fanned herself as she caught her breath from the hike, over-heated despite the lightweight KryTeeran-style dress she wore. Somehow, she hadn't pictured mountains in KryTeer, though these were certainly different from Amantier's lush ranges. Red rock and scrub painted the hues of this bald mountain height. A few palm trees stood defiantly around the waterfall.

Anadin dropped onto the boulder beside her, cheeks flushed from exertion, hair plastered to his face. "Well, there it is."

Rille nodded. "So I surmised." She spotted Yeshton kneeling in the mud downstream to take a drink.

As Queen Artassa slumped against a fallen palm tree, King Aredel prowled to the pool gathered beneath the waterfall. Shevek and Ledonn stood behind him, red armor glistening with droplets formed from the mist. The rest of the caravan had remained at the base of the mountain.

Aredel stared into the crystal depths. "How do we tell if an Arch stands here?" He turned to eye Rille.

She shrugged. "I had hoped I would sense it."

His eyebrow lifted. "Nothing?"

"Nothing." Rille stared at the stream rushing down the mountainside. It had taken two days of scaling the crags to reach the head of the Mahadri. Now what? She lifted her gaze to the rainbow painted above the frothing pool.

If only Jinji were here to tell us if the Arch exists.

"Oh." Anadin straightened. His black eyes probed the shadows beside the waterfall where two palms leaned over each other to crisscross before a cave.

"What is it?" Rille squinted into the gloom but sensed no magic entrances.

"Someone is standing there." He lifted a hand to jab it at the darkness.

Rille looked again. At the same moment, something in the shadows stirred. A humanoid figure emerged from the cave, unnaturally tall and slender, cloaked in black tatters, face pale as death, eyes like a storm. Delicate black lace-like wings became visible as the fae creature approached, deadly in its beauty, graceful as a blade.

Aredel strode forward, unsheathing his sword. "What do you want, *Unsielie*?"

The creature eyed him, revealing no emotions. "Art thou the Blood King of KryTeer?" Its voice rolled over the company like a whistling wind through the grasslands of Amantier, high and low in a strange harmony of tones.

"I am," said Aredel. "But you haven't answered my question."

The creature turned to survey the rest of those assembled. Its stormy eyes speared Rille. "Art thou the child scryer?"

Rille lifted her chin. "And if I am?"

The creature glanced at Anadin. "Art thou the Empathist?"

Anadin tossed a bewildered glance at Aredel. "Um. No?"

The fae creature turned to the Blood King. "Thou must come with us." It gestured toward the cave.

Aredel stood his ground. "Where and why?"

"Thou must come with us." Its singsong voice hummed lower. "Now."

Two more fae beings stepped from the cave, similar in demeanor and appearance. Their lacy wings fluttered. Their eyes scanned the group.

Anadin leaned toward Rille. "This is a guess, mind, but I think we *did* find the Arch."

Rille frowned. "So it seems."

A song welled up from the dark fae, sorrowful, heartrending; they lifted their hands in unison, and Rille found herself stepping toward them, feet light, her mind screaming against her body's actions. Anadin joined her. The pull grew stronger, dampening Rille's reluctance.

"Enough!" Aredel's voice thundered through the gorge.

The spell on Rille's limbs broke. She shrank back and tugged Anadin with her. Together they backed toward the streambank.

Aredel's sword glowed white as he leapt at the fae things. Their song pitched higher as wings lifted against his assault. The blade struck black lace, but the wing was stronger than it looked. It held.

Aredel stumbled back.

The lead fae canted its alien head. "Thou hast come into strange powers, Blood King. But we must collect thee nonetheless."

Artassa screamed.

Rille spotted a fourth fae fluttering into the cave. Artassa was cradled in its long arms. They were swallowed by darkness.

"Artassa!" cried the Blood King.

The song pitched higher, magically seizing Rille's limbs again. She trotted toward the cave mouth, and with each step, worry bled away until she smiled.

I'm going to Shinac. How wonderful!

Anadin darted ahead of her and vanished inside the cave. She rushed to catch him, laughing, freed of burdens and fear.

"My lady, please stop!" Yeshton's voice rang in her ears as the ground gave way and she fell—fell into an abyss of darkness. Wonderful darkness.

I'm going to Shinac!

AREDEL SPRANG backward as the *Unsielie* swiped a dark wing at him.

Sir Yeshton battled a second of the fae creatures even as he cried out for Rille. His sword hummed when the wing thwacked it. Another strike and the sword cracked. Yeshton stumbled down the bank and splashed into the water before leaping upright.

The compelling *Unsielie* music pitched higher, and Aredel wrestled the pull on his frame. *Keep your thoughts. Stay still!* But his foot took a step forward. Another. He ground his teeth and tried to pull back.

The lead fae hooked his gaze. "Come, O dark king." Its voice toned in his mind, clear as a crystal chime, beautiful, so beautiful.

Artassa and Anadin are beyond. Should I keep resisting, or find them?

The answer was simple.

His eyes darted to Shevek and Ledonn combating the last *Unsielie*. "Remain here," he commanded. "Aid Sir Yeshton. Find

Prince Jetekesh and his dragon and help in their quest! I must enter Shinac once more."

Aredel dropped his arms and let the fae magic weave around his limbs.

Find me beyond, Erisyrdrel, *if you can.*

He strode to the cave maw and stepped inside. The ground collapsed beneath his feet, and he plummeted into obscurity.

CHAPTER 30
BLACK SAND

The palace gates loomed ahead, carved with a complicated lotus design and bold foreign scrawl. Commander Hon led the way, while an armed guard flanked Jetekesh, Kethalas, Sir Lafe, Song, and Yin.

They entered the main courtyard where cherry blossom trees and dragon statuary stood in orderly rows. The sweet fragrance of spring infused the air. A path lined with red pillars led the way to the palace proper, and Jetekesh approached with mounting appreciation. No building older than the Lotus Palace existed in Nakania, not since Shinac had vanished from the southern lands leaving desert behind. The palace was a wide, square, three-story edifice with a red roof curving up on the ends.

The ornate palace doors swung aside. Jetekesh squared his shoulders and curled his hands into fists before he strode into the grand corridor, fragrant with strong incense, and lined with round pillars draped in red cloth and golden tassels. Dragons carved in gold ornamented the ceiling. The floor was of polished black stone veined with gold and silver.

Servants swathed in crimson silk embroidered with the white lotus bowed as the company passed down the corridors. Then the servants moved toward the front of the palace where Jetekesh presumed the throne room stood. Rather than follow them, Commander Hon led the prisoners to a residential area, and some of Jetekesh's nerves quieted. They weren't going to be tossed into a Shingese dungeon, then?

Beyond more double doors carved with scrawl, a massive antechamber spread before the prisoners, smelling of a different incense. The room showcased the lush, elegant red silks, low furnishing, and golden reliefs Shing was known for. The craftsmen of this country spent their lives perfecting their art, some spending years on a single piece of wood meant to decorate a hidden corner of some noble's estate. And they were honored by that single accomplishment few would ever recognize. Was it any wonder Jinji had sprung up from such a society of contradicting opulence and humility?

"Wait here," Commander Hon ordered. "The emperor will summon you when he is ready."

Jetekesh turned toward the man and inclined his head. "We'll wait. Thank you for escorting us."

The commander stiffened and scanned Jetekesh's face, perhaps seeking mockery. His lips pinched thin, and he exited, taking all but two soldiers with him. The remaining two guards slipped out after a moment and presumably stationed themselves outside the doors.

With a sigh, Jetekesh strode to a nearby chair of twined bamboo. He eased into it, uncertain how tough the strange wood was. It held well, and he settled back, sighing again. Incense prickled his nose, and he sneezed. "I'll never understand why people burn that odious stuff."

Kethalas chuckled. "It has healing properties."

Jetekesh tracked the man-dragon across the room, where Kethalas studied a painting of a lotus pond framed in gold. Considering what Amantieran legends said about dragons and their penchant for hoarding wealth, perhaps the Shinacian was studying the frame itself.

Song and Yin seated themselves on a lounge-like furnishing. They stayed silent while Yin's eyes danced from one priceless object to another.

Sir Lafe positioned himself beside Jetekesh's chosen chair. "What do we do now, Your Highness?" the protector asked in low tones.

"We wait." Jetekesh brushed back his hair. What he wouldn't give for a bath. "We can't do anything until we meet *Erisyrdrel* face to face."

"And then?" Sir Lafe asked.

"We denounce him," Kethalas answered, turning from the painting. "We expose him for what he is."

"We need to be careful," Song spoke up. "The emperor mustn't be harmed."

Memories of Gyath's court wrenched through Jetekesh, and he leaned forward to press his hands to his face. This was so much like the last time, waiting in agony for some solution, some way to defeat *Erisyrdrel*. Caught in the enemy's net. Three good men died that day, not so long ago.

I can't let that happen again.

"All will be well," Kethalas said, his voice drifting nearer.

The prince lifted his head to stare into the Shinacian's metallic eyes. A calm had descended on the dragon-turned-man.

Jetekesh smiled at him. "Have a plan, do you?"

Kethalas shook his head. "But you are marked, Prince

Jetekesh. Marked by the storyteller true. I came to you because I knew you could help. And you will. You can defeat *Erisyrdrel* if any Nakanian can at all."

"Small recommendation." Jetekesh straightened up in his seat. "We're not magical here, and *Erisyrdrel* isn't alone. Do you sense the other one—the one who shattered the Arch?"

The Shinacian frowned. "I do not. But I'm not sure I could even if he stood close. Not as weary as I am." His hand hovered against his side.

He's more injured than he's letting on.

Silence settled over the prisoners. Jetekesh weighed the hopelessness of their quest. This wasn't how things were supposed to end up. They'd been seeking help from Shinac.

I can't face Erisyrdrel like this, in company with so few. Maybe if Lord Emerin were here with his fire trick...

Something flickered in Jetekesh's periphery. He glanced over, but nothing stood beside him.

'Give up, dearheart,' cooed Mother's voice. *'There's no sense in wasting your life this way. Surrender and Erisyrdrel may spare you. You would have power, purpose, glory.'*

Jetekesh pushed his palms to his eyes, blackening his view until the voice fell silent. What good were those things? He'd seen Mother always discontented, even miserable, though she wielded power, purpose, and glory like her personal banners. Gyath had wielded them, too, and still his son deposed him. Aredel had also had them and ultimately gave them up to honor his half-brother, the humble storyteller. Jinji, who had neither power nor glory, had been happier than all three combined, wielding only purpose as his herald.

Jetekesh dropped his hands and stared beyond the black marble floor at his feet, probing his soul for whatever it was that Jinji had marked inside him.

Guide me, Jinji. Help me. I can't do this without you.

A knock sounded at the doors, then both swung inward, and a servant in lotus robes bowed. "The venerable Emperor Majinglee summons you."

Jetekesh rose, nerves fluttering, insides twisting. He wasn't ready; he had no plan, no answers. "Lead on." His voice rang out, clear and steady, betraying nothing of the truth.

Is this it? Like Jinji in Gyath's court, is this the hour of my death?

THE ROBED SERVANT and the two guards met Commander Hon in the corridor, who then guided the prisoners down long corridors to a great chamber as splendorous and plush as any room Jetekesh had ever seen. Every surface was covered in cloth or gold or images of dragons and lotus flowers.

A low dais cradled a lacquered throne covered in golden cushions. Above it, the ceiling held a network of crisscrossed wood, defining squares where, according to the prince's tutors, ancient writing told the hallowed history of the oldest empire in Nakania. Tall windows lined both sides of the chamber, letting in ample light to glint on the gold surfaces. A few Shingese magistrates stood near the throne, eyeing Jetekesh with undisguised sneers.

The emperor was absent.

A servant slipped from the side of the chamber and bowed. "Emperor Majinglee is on his way, Commander Hon. Please wait."

"Thank you." The commander eyed Jetekesh. "I presume you have enough manners to treat our emperor with the respect he's due."

Jetekesh nodded. "Yes."

"Good."

Silence reigned. A door opened to the right side of the chamber, and an elderly man with a long thin white beard stepped into the room. Guards flanked him, and servants trailed in his wake. Despite his age, the emperor stood tall and walked with easy grace in his black silk dragon gown. He moved to his throne, eyes never scanning the room until he sat upon the golden cushions.

"Bring them forth, Commander Hon." His voice quavered with age but carried through the chamber.

At Hon's gesture, Prince Jetekesh strode toward the throne. He padded over the embroidered rug, clicked his heels together, and bowed at the waist.

"Your Imperial Majesty, it's an honor to meet you." He straightened and caught the emperor's gaze.

A chill coursed up his spine.

Erisyrdrel stared back through those cold black eyes. A smile dusted the old lips. "Welcome, Prince of Amantier, to the Lotus Court."

Drawing a calming breath, Jetekesh chose his words carefully. "May I ask, Imperial Majesty, why I've been captured from my own lands and forced at a grueling pace to travel across Shing to stand before you now? Are we not allies since KryTeer freed both our countries?"

"So we have been," answered the old man. "Yet Shing cannot so easily forget the many grievances inflicted upon it. First, KryTeer swallowed us up in secret—then Amantier occupied our lands and stripped us of our pride and wealth." His eyes narrowed. "And then, KryTeer revealed itself to the world and crushed us. Would *you* forget these slights, Your Highness?"

Jetekesh shook his head. "Not easily, I admit, Majesty. By the same token, there is a history of Shing's crimes against

Amantier. Yet did we not stand together against the tyrant Tallat after High King Cavalin fell upon the field? Does that count for so little?"

Emperor Majinglee's eyes narrowed. "What thanks did you offer Shing after we came to the rescue of your brittle kingdom at that last great battle?"

"Much, I should think." Jetekesh waved his hand. "My point, Majesty, is this. Let us forget the past pains of our peoples and focus instead on preventing further pain going forward. Can we not rise to a better place *now*, learning from the mistakes both our countries made long ago?" He pressed a hand to his chest. "That's the dearest wish of my heart."

"Oh?" The emperor sneered. "This from the treacherous queen's son?"

Jetekesh flinched but steeled himself. "No. *This* from the heir of a noble king who has sued for peace during every moment of his reign."

A grin stretched over the emperor's face. "So brave." He stood, and his eyes gleamed. "But peace has reached its end for now. We shall revenge ourselves against those who have destroyed our lands, our culture, our prosperity. You shall be the first to fall in this new age of conflict, young prince. And then we shall see if your father still sues for peace."

Jetekesh's heart stuttered. "You intend to execute me?"

"Oh, yes, Prince Jetekesh. I have not forgotten our dealings in KryTeer." The black eyes flashed blue like water. "I *know* that you see me."

Jetekesh glanced around at the magistrates, the servants, the guards. Eyes darted away.

They know. Or they suspect. Yet they're too afraid to act.

Could he blame them? Jetekesh stood before the demon, powerless, captive. *What difference can I make?*

'None, pet,' cooed Mother's disembodied voice. '*You're weak. You've always been weak.*'

His fists clenched tighter. *Saints guide me. What can I do?*

Lady Song strode in front of Jetekesh and bowed at the waist, palms pressed together. "I beseech you, my emperor, to stop this call to war. Shing is free to thrive. Let us not chain her through senseless bloodshed."

The emperor's gaze lowered to Song. Did he hesitate? Did a flicker of affection brighten those black eyes? Hard lines traced his mouth as his jaw set. "Ah, the traitor. Rise, Lady of Crimson Lilies."

She straightened.

The emperor stepped from the dais and stood before her. "You're brave to come here."

Song held his stare. "You pardoned me for my offenses against KryTeer, Your Majesty, if you remember."

"Ah. So I did." He lifted a hand to cup her chin. "Yet your actions anger me."

"*You*, Majesty, or the creature inside you?" asked Song.

Murmurs hummed through the chamber.

The emperor smiled. "Once again you will betray your own, will you?"

"I shall stand with Shing against all who would oppress her—even her own ruler." Song pulled free of his hand.

The emperor recoiled. His frame shook. "I..." He gasped and staggered backward.

Steps echoed in the chamber as servants and knights scurried forth to help their liege lord, but the emperor lifted a hand. "I am well. Stay back." His teeth clenched together. "This is... nothing." His dark eyes darted to Song. "Lady, *end* this. Please. I beg you..."

She bowed her head. "I understand." Like a bolt of lightning, she sprang at him, unsheathed a dagger, and plunged it between the emperor's ribs.

"No!" Jetekesh cried.

Mother's laughter flooded his mind. *'Too late, dearest pet.'*

Black sand exploded out of the emperor's mouth as he slumped to the ground. Song stood over him, mesmerized by the dark pillar coalescing above her. The rush of windsong filled the chamber as the last wisp of sand abandoned the old man's body to float on the air. It churned near the ceiling, surveying those below.

Wind brushed Jetekesh's cheek and whispered in his ear. **Let me in, O prince. You wish to become strong. Together, we shall be mighty.**

'Yes, my dear son, let the magic in. Become strong as I always wanted you to be! You shall rule Nakania!'

Jetekesh quailed and stepped back. "No. I won't."

Do not be a fool! The wind howled and raked claws through his hair. **Either you shall become my host, or you shall die!**

Jetekesh held himself erect, even though his heart thundered in his ears. "I refuse to choose either. I'll not become a slave to your vile will."

Black sand coiled, then burst asunder to fill the room. Tendrils of sand lunged at Jetekesh and shot into his mouth. He hacked and gagged as it rammed down his throat, dry, bitter, tasting of tar and blood. He stumbled back and fell. The sand pulsed in his body. Every foreign particle burned within him. He screamed and clutched his head as wind filled his senses, deafening all else, racking his frame.

Succumb or I will consume you.

Won't you consume me either way?

Flames rolled over the room. Shouts filled the space around him.

Arms caught him.

Dragged him upright.

Lord Emerin stood in his vision, shouting words Jetekesh couldn't hear above the rising torrent in his head. Beyond the lord of the keep, Dakarai, Anenyasha, Sir Lafe, Song, and Liu dueled against the royal guards.

Swords glinted.

Spears flashed.

Yin shot an arrow into a Shingese knight's eye.

Lord Emerin pressed a dagger to Jetekesh's throat, eyes vivid, feral. He shouted—and his words penetrated the screaming wind. "Release the prince, *Erisyrdrel*, or I will kill him myself to spare him from your evil!"

The biting sand dug in deeper. Jetekesh screamed.

Give in, boy!

Never! Never!

A frustrated howl bellowed in his ears. Jetekesh let out a sob as sound muffled, and hot blood oozed from his ear. Black sand erupted from his body, spilling from his mouth, ears, eyes. He slumped in Lord Emerin's arms, strength spent, body convulsing.

"I have you," breathed the keep lord in Jetekesh's uninjured ear.

"Look out!" someone shouted.

The keep lord whirled, bringing Jetekesh with him. The prince looked up as the pulsating sand lunged at Song.

Kethalas's body morphed as he dove in the way. Scales dotted his flesh, and his frame grew and shifted, until a great dragon stood within the Lotus Court. His reptilian body sparkled like ice, shimmering with pearlescent colors, a mane of pale blue draped down his long, lithe neck. Horns sprouted from his magnificent head as silver eyes—slitted, inhuman—fastened on the twisting sand.

The metallic odor of copper wafted on the air. A red gash on the dragon's breast seeped blood where several scales were missing. One wing was torn and smeared red.

The black sand rebounded off the dragon's scales.

"Give in, *Erisyrdrel*," rumbled the dragon. The chamber shook. "You have lost."

The sand screamed and twined around itself, writhing.

Not yet! It burst across the air again to fill the room. Tendrils shot toward Dakarai, Lord Emerin, Yin, and Liu.

It filled them all in the same moment. Lord Emerin released Jetekesh and stumbled as he clutched his throat. His eyes turned black—no pupils, no irises. Just blackness.

"No!" Jetekesh cried out.

The dragon let out a roar that shook the rafters.

Dust puffed over the air and glittered like motes in the sunlight.

Magistrates, servants, and guards cowered.

Jetekesh staggered forward, pressing a hand to his wounded ear. Blood stained his fingers. He raced toward the sand while his friends wrestled against *Erisyrdrel*'s possession.

"Leave them be, demon!"

The sand changed direction, then poured down to form into a woman's frame cut from water. She pulsed like a burbling fountainhead, and when she spoke, her voice gurgled. "Give yourself to me, Prince Jetekesh. Do that, and I will spare your faithful companions. Surrender, and I will not drown all of Shing."

He inhaled to quiet the hum of his nerves and the pain in his throbbing ear. "And then what? Will you make me kill them all? Will I level Shing myself?"

A bubbling laugh escaped her translucent lips. "Ah, prince. So mistrustful. Yet think of all we might do together—how the world will bow at our feet."

"I don't want the world." Jetekesh's gaze scudded over the fallen emperor. "Certainly not the world you're trying to establish."

"What *do* you want; the power to protect those dearest to you?" She stepped closer. "I can give you that, Jetekesh. You will never be subject to tyrants again. You'll have the power to protect or destroy according to your just heart."

Jetekesh snorted. "You think I'd believe your lies? I know what you are: death, destruction, and slavery. I've seen your handiwork as KryTeer has run over the world. I want none of that."

"You did not scorn such things mere months ago."

Jetekesh lifted a brow. "Perhaps not, but nor did I embrace them. I'm *not* my mother."

Gurgling laughter scraped over his good ear. "But you're wrong. *I* know the truth. *I know who your father is.*"

Jetekesh's spine tightened. A lump shaped in his throat. Breath rattled through his lungs as he fortified himself. "It doesn't matter. It's possible I'm not royal by blood—but I won't choose you over my father's affections." He curled his hands into fists. "*Erisyrdrel*, I will do all I can to stop you, never to help you. I swear this on Jinji's grave and by the magic of Shinac!"

His voice rang throughout the chamber, and a tingle ran up his arms. A chime sounded in his head, and a warm breeze breathed through his hair, soft, fragrant as blossoms and dewy grass. As he eyed *Erisyrdrel*, the world shifted. Colors brightened. Figures stood around the room; glowing; translucent. The ghost of Emperor Majinglee stood above his fallen body. Lady Mother cowered close by, shielding her eyes from Jetekesh while a black and silver wolf stood over her, keeping her pinned in place. She was real. Dead, but still a specter.

And there.

Jetekesh's heart fluttered.

Jinji Wanderlust stood beside the ice dragon, turquoise eyes bright, a smile like a sunbeam on his face. He strode toward Jetekesh, and the water demon shrank away to cower near Mother.

"Jetekesh, my friend." Jinji reached out and clasped a hand to the prince's arm. Despite his translucence, his grip was solid and strong. His long hair, once black streaked with white, was now entirely white, like freshly fallen snow. "You have come into your calling."

Tears gathered in Jetekesh's eyes, but he blinked them away to stare into his friend's warm face. "I thought I'd never see you again. You died before I could—could say goodbye and apologize for all the horrible things—"

"Hush, Jetekesh. None of that." Jinji laughed. "I have only a little time. Let us focus on all you have accomplished. You've grown so much. I've been watching you. Ah, Jetekesh, I'm so proud to call you my friend."

"Thank you." A tear rolled down the prince's cheek.

Jinji turned to face *Erisyrdrel.* "It is no longer enough to bind this creature to the deep ocean. She must be destroyed."

Jetekesh swiped the tear away. "But how?"

Erisyrdrel tossed her watery head. "There is none who can destroy me!"

Jinji turned and pressed something into Jetekesh's hands. "Use this, my friend. None can destroy her but by the will of the True King of Shinac." His body flickered and faded to near indistinctness. "Believe in your strength!"

The prince uncurled his fingers and peered down at a golden medallion bearing the True King's crest. Words tumbled into his mind, and he witnessed what he must do. He lifted the crest before him, mimicking the vision. "*Erisyrdrel*—"

Jetekesh slammed to his knees under an intense pressure as the crest weighed him down. A heaviness pressed against his soul, threatening to crush him. The immensity of power contained within the medallion threatened to tear him asunder.

Erisyrdrel laughed. "The little prince isn't worthy. Too bad!"

He tried to speak again, but his body quaked. Power throbbed through him, searing. Cutting.

His friends wrestled against a cluster of Shingese knights who had taken the opportunity to attack. Anenyasha's spear flashed and danced across the air. Dakarai cut a man down.

Yin had taken a blow. He clutched his leg, trying to staunch the blood. Song knelt beside her brother, tears running down her cheeks. Somehow, Jetekesh could feel her grief over killing the emperor as though it were his own. Every emotion in the chamber—raw fear, deep resentment, wretched grief, clawing greed—filled him up.

Somehow Jetekesh must stop this madness. If he failed, everyone would die. *Erisyrdrel* would ravage Nakania. Shing would become a second KryTeer.

The medallion grew heavier.

Jetekesh slumped forward. *I...can't...*

Jinji watched him, smiling.

Such faith. Had anyone beyond Jetekesh's father ever believed in the prince so much?

The two people who have the most cause to hate me. One who must suspect I'm not his son. The other who died because I goaded him to action against an impossible foe.

Yet Jinji trusted Jetekesh to wield this power. Immense, fathomless.

I must.

"D-demon..."

Wind tore at his clothes.

Erisyrdrel tossed her rippling head. "Admit defeat, pathetic child. You have lost. Your mark means nothing against one such as me."

To believe in my strength, I must prove it.

"*Erisyrdrel.* Demon...of the dark waters of Shinac..." Jetekesh gritted his teeth and dragged himself to his feet. His muscles burned. "By thy name, I banish thee...to...the court of Lord Ehrikai"—the words gained strength as power rumbled through him—"within the realm of Mahkeen, where..." he hefted his chin "...where thou shalt be judged for thine offenses!"

The weight fell away. The medallion burst with golden light.

No! The demon's sightless eyes widened. **Curse you, child of Cavalin! Curse you!**

Droplets ruptured. Sand fizzled and vanished with a spark of flame. The rushing of wind and fire roared in Jetekesh's good ear, then died away. The exultant cry of long trapped souls—across hundreds of years and leagues of earth—resounded through the chamber.

In the same moment, the visible specters—Mother, the emperor, and the strange wolf—vanished. All but Jinji's faint outline.

The storyteller cupped Jetekesh's hand. The crest evaporated from the prince's fingers.

"Well done, Jetekesh," Jinji said. "Only the truest and most loyal subject of Shinac's rightful king can invoke his power with his crest, and fewer still with such command. Ah, my friend. I am so glad we met again." His hands squeezed Jetekesh's. "Now, my prince, you shall be my successor within Nakania. Look for truth, Jetekesh, and you will find it." His smile softened. "Farewell for now."

Jetekesh swallowed hard. "Please, Jinji. Stay."

“Oh, how I should like to heed your request, but that cannot be. I am borne away from these shores for now.”

“For now, Jinji?”

“Until Shinac returns.”

Jetekesh shook his head. “Will I see that time?”

“I hope so. I truly hope so. Goodbye.” Jinji faded to a mere whisper.

“Goodbye, Jinji. Goodbye, my friend.”

The storyteller disappeared.

CHAPTER 31
RESTLESS

No one stopped Jetekesh from moving to Lord Emerin's side.

The lord of the keep sat on the ground, legs spread before him, a bewildered look in his eyes. He tipped back his head to eye Jetekesh. "What happened?"

"She tried very hard to possess you." Jetekesh helped to hoist the keep lord to his feet. "Can you stand?"

The lord nodded, wobbling a little. "Think so."

Once he was certain Emerin could stay standing, Jetekesh left him to check on Song and Yin. "Are you both all right?"

They nodded in unison. The blood had stopped flowing from Yin's leg, and the wound was bound.

Song's red-rimmed eyes darted to the guards standing in shock around the chamber. "What are they waiting for? Shouldn't they arrest us?"

"I think they dare not move." The prince nodded to Kethalas in his mighty dragon form.

Song's eyes tracked his gaze. "That makes sense. I'm a little reluctant myself."

"He doesn't eat people," said Jetekesh, smiling. "He prefers venison."

"Good to know." Her lips rose in a limp smile that fell at once.

Sir Lafe darted to his side. "My prince?"

"I'm well enough, Sir Knight. Yourself?"

"Not possessed." Sir Lafe rolled his shoulders. "That's good enough."

Jetekesh chuckled. "I can't disagree."

He glanced around and found Dakarai helping Anenyasha up. At her feet, her spear lay in two pieces.

The clansman glanced toward Jetekesh and nodded. Unharmed. Jetekesh nodded back. "We're very fortunate, Sir Lafe."

"So we are." The knight surveyed the crowd of Shingese officials. "What should we do now?"

Liu strode to the fore of the chamber, still clutching his sword. "All of you witnessed what has occurred," he said. "You know as well as any of us that Emperor Majinglee"—his voice broke—"Emperor Majinglee was possessed by a demon from the sea. Never would he sanction open warfare on the heels of signing treaties of peace with Amantier and KryTeer. That was never my lord uncle's way."

Liu's eyes scanned Jetekesh's face. Something between a grimace and a scowl twisted his face. "We must thank Amantier's prince for defeating the demon, and we must pardon Lady Song for freeing the emperor of his tormentor through death." He bowed his head. "Both have done all they could to spare Shing from shame."

Jetekesh stared. How much did those words cost Liu to state? At least the haughty prince knew when to set aside his bias for the sake of his country. Respect stirred in Jetekesh's chest.

"Prince Liu," said a magistrate, taking a single step forward.

Kethalas rumbled.

The magistrate flinched. "My lord, these goings-on are strange indeed. Are we to ignore the directives of our emperor?"

Liu narrowed his eyes on the man. "Which directives, Lord Tu Pan? Those assigned during his final days in control of himself—or *after* a demon possessed him?"

The magistrate dipped his head while a second official stepped forward.

"We must issue a declaration and order the armies of Shing to stand down. Many already march on Amantier, my lord prince."

"Dispatch riders," Liu barked. "Stop those armies. We will *not* go to war."

Jetekesh let his eyes close as he sighed. *We've avoided the worst of the bloodshed.*

He glanced up at Kethalas gleaming in the sunlight like a mountain of ice. The dragon eyed him back, his fierce expression alien and unreadable. Yet something of Kethalas remained in that stare.

Lord Emerin rested a hand on Jetekesh's shoulder. "One enemy less to worry about, Your Highness. But the war isn't won yet. We must still locate an Arch leading to Shinac. We still need to get Kethalas home—and we might still need that dragon army."

Jetekesh nodded. "At least we have bought a little time, saints willing. I'd like to start for the Clanslands within the next few days—but not until I'm confident things are stable here."

"Harn is well, by the way." Emerin flashed him a grin. "He's a stout fellow—and the arrow only grazed him.

"Thank goodness." Jetekesh smiled.

We're all relatively unscathed. I hope Rille and the others are as well.

He turned toward the lord of the keep with a crooked smile. "I hear you hassled Commander Hon quite a bit."

Lord Emerin chuckled. "It was a pleasure, my prince."

"Of that, I've no doubt." His eyes flicked to the wide windows where the lush lands of Shing were framed under the southern snow-capped mountains leading to the uninhabitable Snow Wastes. "I wish I could rest easy, my lord. But my nerves are taut, and my spirit feels restless."

"Mine as well." Emerin shrugged. "Though my spirit is restless by nature."

Jetekesh followed the distant lines climbing those mountains. "He's close, somehow, Lord Emerin."

"Who, my prince?"

"Whoever wounded Lord Kethalas at the Jade Arch and unleashed the water demon. With *Erisyrdrel* gone, I feel him like a presence at my back. If I can trust these feelings, I fear him far more than her."

Jetekesh's mind rolled over what Jinji had told him.

'Look for truth, and you will find it.'

He sucked in a breath. *If that's the case, I must prepare myself. Not all truth is wholesome.*

CHAPTER 32
A VISION

Nightmares drove Jetekesh from his bed.

He stumbled from the blankets and padded to the open balcony overlooking the ancient city of Kyon Taro, a hand pressed against his throbbing ear. Howls filled the air, and he understood the source of his bad dreams.

Vashalan.

A bloodcurdling howl rose near the palace wall. Jetekesh flinched, broken eardrum throbbing again.

"Your Highness?"

Jetekesh didn't look behind him. "They're becoming very bold."

His protector strode onto the balcony and stared out into the moonless night, searching. "I had hoped they would disappear when you banished *Erisyrdrel*."

Jetekesh's mind flashed to the confrontation with the water demon four days ago. His ear ached more, and he pressed his hand harder against it. "No, these came with another. They're a tool for whatever Lord Kethalas fought at the Jade Arch—just as *Erisyrdrel* was."

Sir Lafe sucked in a breath. "Then, do you think this faceless foe ordered the demon to start a war between Shing and Amantier?"

Jetekesh shrugged. "Possibly. Or *Erisyrdrel* acted on her own in a way that furthered the other being's objectives while still satisfying her own thirst for vengeance." He sighed, and his bangs fluttered. "I'm afraid we have no choice but to find out."

He'd planned to leave for the Clanslands days ago, but reports of the *vashalan* closing in on Kyon Taro had delayed the journey. Besides, Kethalas had reopened his wounds when he'd transformed in the Lotus Court, and soon after he'd reverted to his human shape and collapsed. They couldn't go anywhere until the Shinacian was recovered, at least somewhat.

Jetekesh let out another soft breath and leaned over the balcony railing. "We can't just let them terrorize Shing while we sit here, Sir Lafe."

"Agreed, Your Highness. But they're blasted hard to slay."

The memory of their burning stench curled Jetekesh's lip as he wrinkled his nose. "We should send out archers armed with flaming arrows."

Sir Lafe leaned against the railing beside him. "We've no power to command Shing's forces, Your Highness."

Jetekesh scowled. "I *know* that, Sir Lafe. But it's a better plan than sitting about."

"So it is."

The prince glanced at his protector and studied the man's profile in the light of the torches lining the palace façade. He looked solemn, with his heavy brow drawn close over his rugged features. "Sir Lafe?"

The man shifted to face him. "Yes, Your Highness?"

"My lady mother... Did she ever—" Jetekesh pursed his lips and dropped his gaze to the courtyard below his borrowed bedchamber. The sound of a trickling fountain floated on the air. He inhaled. "Did she ever attempt to—to seduce you?"

Sir Lafe blinked like an owl. "No, Your Highness." He turned to face the night. "I wasn't her preferred style of lover. Not young and impressionable enough. Nor pretty."

Jetekesh cringed. *He's a blunt man, isn't he?*

The prince traced his fingers along the polished wood railing. "I'm glad she...left you be."

Sir Lafe grunted. "So am I. She'd be a hard woman to resist."

Jetekesh's cheeks burned.

"And," said Sir Lafe, "my wife'd likely flay my flesh were I ever to fall into sin."

Jetekesh blinked. "You're married?" He chuckled. "That shouldn't surprise me. But somehow it does."

A smile bobbed across the man's lips. "I don't blame you." He shrugged his hands. "I'm not what most call approachable."

Jetekesh bit back a question, but it tumbled out. "Are you in love?"

"Yes, Your Highness."

"So many of you are." Jetekesh lifted his gaze to the starry sky.

The knight snorted. "Makes the bad days bearable."

"There are still bad days even when you're in love?"

"For all, Your Highness."

A howl rolled over the palace wall. Jetekesh's heart clenched, and he curled his hands into fists. "It's a horrible noise." He patted his damaged ear. "Made worse by my wound."

"It may heal with time, Your Highness. I knew a man who lost his hearing in one ear and gained it back years later."

"I hope so. Either way, it's better than the alternative."

Jetekesh could've been possessed. He might have become the host to *Erisyrdrel* and been compelled to conquer the world.

Now I face a new foe, less known, perhaps far more dangerous. Will it try to enslave or vanquish the world?

A shooting star streaked the inky sky. Jetekesh watched it vanish beyond the black heights of the distant southern mountain range. A tingle started in his hands, and his vision shifted.

The world lightened. Dawn painted soft light over the snowy peaks, and the buildings of Kyon Taro fell away. Lands spread before him, and the mountains drew closer in a rapid motion like he flew toward them. And there, lying in a pile of leaf debris, huddling against the night's chill, a girl tried to sleep.

Long pale hair sprawled down her shoulders and back, hiding her face. Strange, embroidered fur-lined clothes hung off her slender frame.

Feelings flooded Jetekesh's soul: *She needs help. She's cold and alone and desperately frightened. Find her. She seeks you.*

Jetekesh stumbled as the vision closed like a rope snapping in two. He stood upon the balcony, breaths clipped, body shaking.

"What happened?" Sir Lafe's voice hung low, rough.

The prince shook his head. "I..." He sucked in several breaths. "There's someone who needs my help. She's at the roots of the southern mountains near a branch of the Tindo River, I—I think."

Sir Lafe's brows knitted together. "You *saw* her? Just now?"

Jetekesh managed a hurried nod. "Yes. I did." He closed his eyes, willing his heart to slow and his mind to still. *Gather yourself. Be calm.* "She's seeking me, and she's hungry and alone. I need someone to find her before the *vashalan* do."

The knight nodded. "I'll speak with Lord Emerin. Someone will be sent at once. What does she look like?"

Jetekesh described what he'd seen. "She's coming this way. Find her. Help her. Bring her to me."

Sir Lafe set a hand on his shoulder. "It will be done, my prince."

"Thank you." Jetekesh leaned against the railing as strength bled from his limbs. Cold seeped into his bones and he shivered.

Is this what it means to be your successor, Jinji? Will the magic that killed you slowly sicken me? Will I die?

Sir Lafe had left. Silence screamed in Jetekesh's good ear.

He slumped to the balcony floor and stared at the space before him, unseeing, the prickle of fear racing up his flesh.

I don't want to die, Jinji. I want to help Nakania, but not at that price.

CHAPTER 33
THE HEART OF SHING

Kajsa stumbled along the muddy road, cape gathered close, hood draped over her head to stave off the worst of the rainfall.

Rain. It's raining here, not snowing.

The country of Shing rolled before her; green, lush, *warm*. She'd seen lush seasons before, of course. Norva turned green during the final thaw, but it was a much smaller, closed-in land than these open, rolling fields, lined by trees bursting with pink and white flowers. So many rivers and streams cut across the earth, and reeds clung to the banks, strong and abundant.

Only now, seeing the wealth of Shing, did Kajsa understand Lord Navolleth's perspective. He had told the Archon and Axel and all the villagers what the people of Norva missed in their harsh clime, yet none of them could imagine what he described. Not quite. Yet even so, Kajsa couldn't agree that Shing's prosperity justified Navolleth's scheme.

Find the Marked Prince. Find the Marked Prince. Stay with him.

The words rolled like a chant through Kajsa's mind as she

trudged north toward the heart of Shing. Toward the hope for help.

Hooves thundered along the road ahead. Kajsa ducked her head and moved to one side, away from the worst of the puddles along the rutted highway. She expected the rider to gallop past—to spray her with water and not even notice. Such had happened twice already.

But the hooves slowed to a trot. Then halted. A voice barked down at her in a strange tongue.

Kajsa jerked her head up.

Is he angry? What have I done wrong?

The man was Shingese with dark, slanted eyes and sleek black hair tucked up in his ornate helm. Plated armor glittered in the rain. He wore a bemused smile rather than a glower.

Perhaps he's only asked a question?

Kajsa shook her head. "I'm sorry. I don't understand your language."

The soldier blinked, then leaned toward her. "You speak the Old Tongue?" His accented voice tripped over the words.

Kajsa gasped. "Yes! I—I seem to, at least."

He eyed her for a long moment. "From where do you hail?"

She pointed. "Over the mountains. In Norva."

His eyes skimmed the ridges, brows pinched together. "Why are you here?"

"I seek the Marked Prince. Do you know him?"

The man's eyes widened, and he scraped teeth over his lower lip. "Marked Prince? Could you mean Prince Jetekesh of Amantier?"

Kajsa's skin tingled. "I—I don't know." She wrung her sopping mittens.

The man grunted. "Come. I will take you to Kyon Taro. You

will meet with Prince Liu and Prince Jetekesh. We shall see what you are about."

Kajsa hesitated. "How did you know to find me?"

The man lowered his hand. "Come. Ride with me." He offered a smile, softening his features. "Prince Jetekesh sent me to find you. I am Sir Kousa, a knight of the Lotus Court."

This is what I came for.

Kajsa took his hand and let him hoist her into the saddle behind him. She wrapped her arms around his waist and marveled at the world from this vantage point. She'd seen horses before but never ridden one.

"Hold on tight."

She obeyed and pressed her face into the man's cold armor as the horse wheeled and lurched into a gallop. Kajsa kept her eyes shut for several moments before she willed them open. The world flew past her, green, vibrant, smelling of sweet blossoms and growing things.

The storm rolled away as she rode for the Marked Prince in the heart of Shing. *I'm almost there, Ingrid. I've almost completed my quest.*

THREE DAYS' grueling ride brought Kajsa to the fair capital of Shing. Peddlers and horsemen passed her by in the streets with no more than a cursory glance. Sir Kousa cantered straight to the walls of the Imperial Palace with its red pillars and curved rooftops. The gates of the palace swung aside, and the horse trotted into the courtyard where ornamental trees and dragon statues lined a paved road to the front steps of the grand building.

Kajsa had never seen such a magnificent sight in all her life.

Even the Archon's palace in Tild back home had nothing on the intricate architecture of this building.

Shing is the oldest country in Nakania. It makes sense it would look and feel so very different.

Sir Kousa halted his mount. "We walk from here." He swung down and offered his hand to her.

She accepted his help, muscles stiff and burning.

A page trotted from the gatehouse and took the horse's reins from Sir Kousa, then the knight led Kajsa up the paved pathway toward the palace proper. Her nerves hummed in her ears as she dragged her sore legs toward the steps.

I'm about to meet the leaders of Shing. What am I supposed to say? I can barely talk to the people of my own village.

Yet she couldn't turn around and flee. Norva was leagues away, over a snowy mountain pass crawling with monstrous creatures, and Ingrid had guided her steps to this country, to sue for peace. To *try* to prevent war.

I can't turn back. Not after Raum's sacrifice.

Thoughts of the brave wolf lying so still on the mountain shot pain through her limbs like lightning scorching her veins.

For Raum, for Ingrid, I will not *give up so close to my goal.*

She set her jaw and curled her fingers into fists.

The ornate wooden doors swung aside to admit her and her escort. Sir Kousa strode ahead, comfortable, straight-backed, and Kajsa hunched into herself to follow along the pillar-lined interior.

Strong incense tickled her nose.

She sneezed.

The Elderhouse in her village and the longhouses of Tild would have echoed the noise back to her a hundred times—but the rugs, tapestries, and hanging fabrics of the Shingese palace cradled the sound to soften it.

Silk draped the servants who shuffled about beyond the pillared space. One slinked to the door looming ahead and drew it aside to let Sir Kousa and Kajsa into the throne room beyond. The chamber's wide, tall shape filled Kajsa's lungs with dread as her breath deflated. Several people stood below the short dais at the head of the room, conversing among themselves. They turned to consider her as the knight led her toward the throne.

A young man bearing the distinctive traits of his Shingese line, draped in gold and white silk, glanced between Sir Kousa and her with an arched eyebrow. Beside him stood a man with similar features, likely a relative, older, with silver threads at his temples and streaking his long raven tresses. He wore a silken burgundy robe with intricate embroidery. Kajsa's fingers itched to stroke the complicated pattern of swirls and strange writing, to study its design.

Beside them, with coloring and clothes of a different civilization, stood a slender young man perhaps Kajsa's age. His shirt, vest, hosen, and boots bespoke a culture meant for warmer climes. His hair hung long and straight, golden in color, framing turquoise eyes like the deep pools in the lowlands of Norva. Something in his bearing, or perhaps his eyes, pierced Kajsa like someone far older than his years. He glowed, as though the sun had let some of its beams drape over him like a mantel. On his forehead, blazing like a brand under a blacksmith's iron, a symbol kissed his flesh.

Kajsa drew a breath to stifle the tears welling in her eyes.

I've found him. I've found the Marked Prince.

She nearly sank to her knees but managed to stumble ahead, then halt as Sir Kousa stopped. The knight pressed his palms together and bowed at the waist. Kajsa started, then dipped into a curtsy beside him,

Of course he's bowing! These people are royal.

She risked a glance at the Marked Prince. He eyed her, a faint frown on his lips, gaze probing.

Sir Kousa unfolded himself, and Kajsa drew a breath as she straightened.

The knight gestured toward Kajsa and spoke in the Old Tongue. "Prince Jetekesh, as requested I've brought the waif. She speaks the Old Tongue of Cavalin, and for her sake, I do so as well."

"Thank you, Sir Knight," said the Marked Prince, speaking the Old Tongue fluidly.

The young Shingese man lifted his brows higher. He spoke a different language, its cadences similar but too rapid and changed to catch more than a few familiar words: *Filthy waif* and *Prince*. His tone finished like a question.

The prince nodded and spoke in the Old Tongue. "You can hardly blame her for her haggard appearance. She traveled through *vashalan*-plagued lands in rain and mud. You didn't look much better after traveling over the Flute Mountains, Prince Liu. None of us did."

As the Shingese prince colored, footsteps slapped the floor to Kajsa's right. She glanced over and froze as a tall man with dark brown skin approached, black hair beaded and colored green, pink, and orange in streaks. He halted a few paces away and smiled warmly.

"Hello," he said in clear, even words, also using the Old Tongue. "I am Dakarai of the Clanslands. You must be hungry." He held up a red fruit. "Please, partake."

Kajsa's stomach roiled. She flushed and ducked her head. "I—I can wait. Thank you. I must first deliver my message to the Marked Prince."

The room held its breath. Kajsa cast a furtive glance toward the dais, toward the Marked Prince called Jetekesh. He measured her, saying nothing.

Kajsa looked at the tall, dark man.

Was that rude? Should I accept?

The man's smile grew, and he padded forward, took her wrist, and rested the fruit in her dirty palm. "Eat. There is no haste so great that you cannot first accept this gift."

"After that, you might bathe," offered Prince Jetekesh. "We'll have a warm meal prepared, and afterward, you can deliver your message. Is that too long a wait, my lady?"

Kajsa blinked. *Why does he call me his lady?*

She risked a look toward Prince Liu.

He rattled off a command to a servant, then turned to eye her as the servant bustled away. His gaze still maintained an aloof, disdainful air, but it had lessened somewhat. "The bath is being prepared. Kazuko will take you."

A woman approached, clad in a layering of embroidered robes pulled tight to her frame, a wide, strange belt wrapped at the waist, tied in a stiff manner at her back. Her hair twisted in a strange, high coif, and an ornate comb stood like a crown on her head. She smiled and beckoned.

Kajsa's heart clambered in her chest as she whirled toward the throne. Toward the Marked Prince. She squeezed the red fruit in her hands, willing its cool, firm surface to ground her emotions. "I am very grateful, Your Eminences, both for your concern and hospitality—but this message cannot wait a moment. I have traveled from the southern realms of Norva, and lost a dear friend along the way, to bear ill tidings." Her heart skipped. Would they believe her? Would they view her as an enemy when she explained?

It can't matter now.

She inhaled, then released her breath. No one stopped her, no one prodded. Silence hummed in the grand chamber. "War comes to you from the south. An army is being raised in Norva to march over the mountain and conquer Shing, Amantier, and KryTeer. And likely, all others."

Prince Liu rattled off words in that strange tongue. Kajsa caught none of them.

Prince Jetekesh glanced at his fellow royal with a frown, then his light, clear eyes stabbed her. "We had no notion of any country beyond the mountains southward. By every Amantieran map I've ever seen, the Snow Wastes are uninhabitable."

Snow Wastes. An apt name.

She nodded. "That comes as no surprise, Your Highness." She took a step toward him, eyes locked on his. "Norva is a small circle of realms, established when our ancestors fled during the black days after Lord Cavalin fell to the Serpent's sword. They wished for a safe haven. But Norva isn't as bleak as it sounds. And we have had peace since the Cantons were established."

"Cantons, my lady?"

She nodded. "City-states. I came from the northern city-state called Frostfire. The city proper is Tild. Small villages surround Tild, some for farming, some for fishing, some for hunting. My village is a hunting village which supplies Tild and the other villages with meat for the harsh winters."

The prince strode toward her and stopped two feet away. "Does your city-state have a king, my lady?"

Her nails bit into the fruit's flesh as she lowered her gaze. "I am Kajsa, Your Highness. That is my name. I am not a lady."

"Kajsa." His voice caressed the word. "Please answer the question, Kajsa."

She bobbed a nod. "Yes, a kind of king. We call him our Archon. Each city-state in Norva has an Archon."

"Archon." The prince inhaled. "And your Archons, they all desire war? Why?"

She stared down at the red fruit as she rotated it with her fingers. "A...a stranger appeared in our lands over a month ago. He is a strange man, quiet, and very sad. He—he began to speak about the prosperity of the North and how little we have in the Cantons of Norva. He stirred up unrest and greed in my village... and then he and Axel went to meet the Archon in Tild. The Archon agreed we must come here to take these fertile lands for our own."

"Who is Axel?" asked the prince.

Kajsa's vision wobbled. "My...my friend."

"The one you lost on your journey here?"

"No. Another." Her voice cracked.

"I'm sorry, Kajsa." His tones were velvety soft. "You've had a very hard passage, it seems. But why come here, and why alone?"

"I...I knew I could do nothing to dissuade my people. They wouldn't listen to me. But the idea of...of war...it was too dreadful." She looked up, and her breath hitched as her eyes met the prince's. "Children are hurt the most in wartime. I couldn't abide standing by..."

She chewed her lip and stared down at her feet, cheeks blazing. "That's not entirely true. I didn't want to come at first. Ingrid—she is...she *was* the wisewoman in my village—she asked me to come. To warn you. I didn't want to, but after she died...I had to. Someone had to, and no one else would. Raum—he's my wolf friend—he came with me and defended me against those horrible monsters on the mountain. Then he died of their poison."

Fingers brushed her shoulder. She lifted her eyes until she met Prince Jetekesh's. His smile looked awkward but sympathetic.

"Thank you."

She blinked. "W—what?"

"Your warning is worth more than you know. Tell me of this stranger, please. The one who stirred up so much unrest."

Kajsa's mind flickered over the memory of the sorrowful man. "He's called Lord Navolleth. Everyone calls him a lord. I don't know if he is...but they believe he is."

"You said he's quiet and sad."

She nodded. "But strangely persuasive. He doesn't need to speak loudly to snare attention. He looks strange, too. Pale, like all my people, but his eyes are golden." She drew a breath. "When he speaks, it's as though he bespells you."

"Did he say where he hailed from?"

"Here. The North. He calls all of you wicked and violent. He told a terrible story of KryTeer conquering the world."

A breath fluttered from Prince Jetekesh's mouth. "He's not entirely wrong, but it seems he's tried to skew the truth to serve his own ends. Has he ever manifested strange abilities? Unexplainable things?"

Kajsa started to shake her head, then froze. "Yes. He healed Axel after he and I were attacked by the beasts in the woods above Tild. Axel and—and Raum were wounded, but when we reached the village, Navolleth healed them. I didn't see it happen, but Axel told me he could use magic. He must have. The poison is deadly otherwise." She wiped at a tear on her cheek.

The prince's eyes flicked past her. "What do you think?"

"Definitely sounds like he might be the one," said a strong, clear, rumbling voice.

Kajsa peeked over her shoulder to find a tall, straight-backed man with long fair hair and keen green eyes standing several paces away, a wrist draped over a sword hanging at his hip.

He caught her eye and smiled grimly, then focused on the

prince. "We should ask Lord Kethalas if the description matches what he knows—if he saw enough."

"Agreed." The Marked Prince turned to a solid man standing to one side of the dais, until now unnoticed. "Sir Lafe, will you relay this information to our invalid dragon?" A smile glimmered at the prince's lips. "He'll be grateful for the distraction, I suspect."

Sir Lafe bowed and trod to a door on the side of the chamber. He slipped out and shut the door with a faint snick behind him.

Kajsa looked back at the Marked Prince. "Do you know Navolleth?"

"Perhaps *of* him." Jetekesh folded his arms and tapped a finger against his silk sleeve. "If he's the same fellow we've sought, then we've already handicapped him in one regard. A minion of his recently had control of Shing, but we took care of that."

Kajsa tensed.

He sounds at his ease, as though slaying an enemy is no great matter. Is he as violent as Navolleth has claimed? Did I make a mistake in coming here?

The prince's eyes roved across the ceiling as strain lined his face. "How large will his army be?"

Kajsa's muscles tightened more. "I don't know, Your Highness. I've heard little about the forces of the other Cantons, and only slightly more about our own. But we were once a fierce people. We fought hard in the age of Cavalin."

The prince's eyes dropped from the ceiling, and he considered her for a moment. "You're the Vykyis."

Kajsa blinked. "I've never heard the word before."

He nodded and unfolded his arms to clasp them behind his back. "Seafaring warriors in ancient days. My tutors told me you were the first to sail to this continent from the High North and discover Shing—and presumably Shinac. That was a thousand years ago, maybe more. The Vykyis began our exodus from the Broken Paths to new, lush shores. The Amans followed—which brought my people here.

"We settled Amantier together when Cavalin of Amantier joined his House with the Vykyis's ruling clan, after Cavalin became High King. It's said that after Cavalin's death, his second son and a large portion of the Vykyis traveled south and disappeared over the mountains. Scholars believe they died in the cold climes." A smile twitched at his lips. "Evidently, they were wrong—just as they were wrong about Shinac being only a legend."

"Scholars are only mortal after all," said the man called Dakarai, "and therefore fallible. Whatever the case, I think the young woman has told us what is most important, and now she should rest and bathe."

The Marked Prince blinked. "Right. Yes. I apologize for neglecting that. Please, be comfortable, and if you're inclined, join us for dinner. I'm afraid that if we're to prepare a proper defense against your people, we'll need to know whatever information you can give us."

Kajsa wrung the fruit. "Will you fight against my people?"

He held her gaze. "Only if we find no other way. I swear it. I have no desire to go to war."

She exhaled a soft breath. It seemed those living on this side of the Snowblinds weren't as violent as Navolleth had claimed. Her mission hadn't been a waste. War might be prevented.

Raum, we did it.

CHAPTER 34
THE NEXT MOVE

Perched atop the great heights of the Snowblinds, Navolleth peered through the swirling ice crystals that thrashed his long, pale mane. He considered the distant lands of Shing. A frown touched the edges of his mouth.

Erisyrdrel was defeated.

It was a small loss. The water demon was a vile thing; one Navolleth had been loath to ally with in the first place. Yet to reach his ends, he would do what he must.

The next step was unavoidable, though equally loathsome.

If fear of the *vashalan* and the threat of war would not discourage the boy, then Navolleth must take a more direct hand.

He must stop the Marked Prince, no matter the cost, or all would be lost.

A loathsome task, yes. But unavoidable.

The story continues in...

Book 2: The Marked Prince

Join my newsletter to keep up to date on my latest projects. You'll also gain access to exclusive short stories, including *Jinji's Curse*—the account of a certain storyteller meeting a certain blood prince for the first time.

Visit www.mhwoodscourt.com to sign up!

GLOSSARY

PEOPLE

Anadin [ANN-uh-din] — Prince of KryTeer and Aredel's younger brother.

Anenyasha [ON-enn-YAW-shuh] — A female warrior from the Clanslands.

Aredel [AIR-uh-dell] — Blood King of KryTeer.

Artassa [Ar-TASS-uh] — Queen of Kryteer. First Wife of Blood King Aredel.

Axel [axle] — A village hunter in Tuksa within Norva.

Bareene [buh-REEN] — Prince Jetekesh's mother and former queen of Amantier. Deceased.

Cavalin [CAV-uh-linn] — Once High King of Nakania, he died defending his lands from a demon-possessed tyrant. He is the ancestor of Prince Jetekesh.

Dakarai [daw-kaw-rye] — A male warrior from the Clanslands.

Ehrikai [AIR-ihk-EYE] — The True King of Shinac.

Elga — The midwife of Tuksa Village within Norva.

Emerin [EM-er-inn] — The Lord of the Keep of the Falls of Moss Province in Amantier.

Erisyrdrel [eer-iss-SEER-drel] — A water demon who possessesed Emperor Gyath of KryTeer until she was banished by Prince Sharo.

Frebe [freeb] — Captain of the Guard of Rose Palace in Amantier.

Frit — The carpenter of Tuksa Village within Norva.

Gyath [GYE-uth] — The deceased Emperor of KryTeer. Father of Aredel and Anadin.

Harn — A wagoner from Amantier.

Hickory — Prince Jetekesh's buckskin stallion.

Ingrid — The wise woman of Tuksa Village within Norva.

Ivam [EYE-vam] — Prince Jetekesh's sword instructor.

Jetekesh [JET-eh-kesh] — The Crown Prince of Amantier.

Jetekesh the Fourth [JET-eh-kesh] — Reigning King of Amantier.

Jinji [JIN-jee] — A storyteller from Shing.

Jisha [JEE-shaw] — A cabin boy on the *Dajanyan*, a KryTeeran man-of-war.

Jung Tep [joong tep] — Prince Liu's father in Shing.

Kajsa [k-EYE-suh] — A village healer-in-training in Tuksa Village within Norva.

Kayvar [kay-VAR] — The previous lord of the Keep of the Falls. Emerin's deceased father.

Kazuko [kaw-zoo-koh] — A Shingese servant.

Kethalas [KETH-uh-LASS] — A traveler from Shinac.

Kilith [kill-ith] — An Amantieran saint.

Kousa [koh-suh] — A Knight of Shing.

Kyella [k-EYE-ell-uh] — A farmer's daughter from Amantier. Engaged to Prince Anadin of KryTeer.

Lafe [lay-f] — Prince Jetekesh's protector.

Liu [lee-YEW] — A prince of Shing.

Majinglee [mah-JING-lee] — Emperor of Shing.

Navolleth [nuh-VOLL-eth] — A stranger who appears in Norva.

Norgric [nor-grik] — An Amantieran saint.

Palin [pal-inn] — A legendary knight in Amantier. Deceased.

Peratha [per-AH-thuh] — An Amantieran saint.

Raum [r-ow-m] — Axel's tame wolf within Norva.

Rille [rill] — Prince Jetekesh's cousin. She is a seer.

Sharo [SHAWR-oh] — A fae prince of Shinac.

Song — The Lady of Crimson Lilies from Shing.

Tallat [tuh-LOT] — A KryTeeran fisherman-turned-tyrant. He allowed Erisyrdrel to possess him in order to gain power. Ultimately he killed High King Cavalin in combat.

Tifen [TEE-fin] — Prince Jetekesh's former protector. Deceased.

Treyo [tray-oh] — A hunter of Tuksa Village within Norva. Axel's father.

Tu Pan [too PAWN] — A magistrate of Shing.

Vashalan [vash-uh-lawn] — Wolf-like canines made from dark Shinacian magic. They carry a deadly venom in their teeth, and similar poison in their long claws.

Vashi [VAH-shee] — An Amantieran saint and High King Cavalin's daughter.

Viggo — The Elder of Tuksa Village within Norva.

Yeshton [YESH-tun] — A knight of Amantier. Rille's protector.

Yin — Song's younger brother. A competent bowman.

PLACES

Amantier [ah-mawn-teer] — The country where Prince Jetekesh lives. Its people are the Amantierans.

Arch — A magical portal into Shinac.

Bahadronn [baw-hah-dron] — The capital city of KryTeer.

Bard Pass — A pass in the Flute Mountains leading from Moss Province in Amantier to the eastern realm of the country. It is one route to the Clanslands and Shing.

Broken Paths — The old lands before the various races sailed to Nakania and discovered Shinac and Shing. It is said the Broken Paths are no longer inhabitable.

Clanslands — A jungle country with many tribes. Few outsiders venture there due to its many dangers.

Flute Mountains — The northernmost mountains of Amantier.

Frostfire Canton — A city-state in Norva.

Karanki [kaw-ron-kee] — Dakarai's tribe in the Clanslands.

Kavacos [kav-uh-koh-ss] — The Rose City. Capital of Amantier.

Keep of the Falls — Lord Emerin's keep in Moss Province of Amantier.

KryTeer [kr-EYE-teer] — An arid western country ruled by Blood King Aredel. Its people are the KryTeerans.

Kyon Taro [kee-on tar-oh] — The capital city of Shing.

Mahadri River [maw-HA-dree] — The oldest river in KryTeer. It runs north to south.

Mahkeen [maw-keen] — A realm outside of Nakania and Shinac. Details unknown.

Moss Province — The northernmost province of Amantier. Lord Emerin's duchy.

Nagali River [nuh-GALL-ee] — It runs from the Clanslands, through the Flute Mountains, and into Amantier.

Nakania [nuh-KAWN-ee-uh] — The civilized world. Also called the mundane world.

Norva [NOR-vuh] — A country hidden in the Snow Wastes south of Shing. Its people are the Norvians.

Rabahan Oasis [ruh-BAH-hawn] — An oasis north of Bahadronn in KryTeer.

Ruins of Glayn [glay-n] — Old ruins north of Kavacos in Amantier.

Sage Province — A western province in Amantier. Rille's duchy.

Shinac [shee-NOCK] — The realm of the fae and magical. To most, it's only a legend. Prince Jetekesh knows better.

Shing — An eastern country, considered the oldest known civilization outside of Shinac's borders. Jinji's homeland. Its people are called the Shingese.

Snow Wastes — See *Norva*.

Tild — The common name of the city-state proper of Frostfire Canton.

Tindo River [tin-doh] — A river running through Shing.

Tuksa [took-suh] — Kajsa's mountain village.

Valliath [VAL-ee-oth] — The Hold of Valliath is the realm within Shinac where the True King was born. Also see *Ehrikai*.

TERMS

Amans — The ancestors of the Amantierans.

Archon [ark-on] — The king of Norva.

Dajanyan [dah-jawn-yawn] — A KryTeeran man-of-war.

Driodere [dree-OH-deer] — Grim Death itself. An Amantieran term, derived from the Old Tongue, for the spirit of death who guides the deceased to their final resting place.

Holy Nocturne — A festive Amantieran holiday that takes place at the Winter Solstice.

Sahala [suh-HALL-uh] — An old KryTeeran word meaning 'sparrow.' Anadin's term of affection for Rille.

Shaqel [shaw-KEL] — A KryTeeran term of affection meaning 'younger brother.'

Shaqin [shaw-KEEN] — A KryTeeran term of affection meaning 'older brother.'

Treshalaj [tresh-uh-LOJ] — The Blood King's flagship in KryTeer.

Unsielie [un-seel-ee] — A form of dark fae in Shinac. Cousins to dark elves.

Vykyis [v-eye-k-EYE-us] — The ancestors of the people of the Snow Wastes. Also see *Norva.*

Watchwoman — A seer within the Clanslands.

Wisewoman — The village healer in Norva. She is a seer.

Acknowledgments

Deepest appreciation to my family and friends for cheering me on and believing in my vision. You'll never know how much it truly means! Special thanks to my parents, as well as my sisters, Heidi and Tawnee, for reading every story I type, no matter what shape it's in. You're brave souls indeed!

Heartfelt thanks to my alpha and beta readers for boldly plunging into a wild manuscript to help me tame it. Beba Andric, Laura A. Barton, Brigitte Cromey, R. K. Goff, Mandi Oyster, and Heidi Wadsworth — you're all as mighty as dragons!

Stupendous thanks to my *epic* editors, E. L. McNicholas and Sarah B., for applying those last touches that properly shape a story like clay on a potter's wheel. Your keen eyes are truly heroic!

To my amazing Kickstarter backers: Thank you for taking a chance and helping me soar!

A, Amelia Anastasi, Amena Jamali, Amy Murdock, Andy F, Angela Morse, Ashley Bathory Araujo, B.A. Williamson, Bradley Hamm, Bree Moore, Brian Bondurant, Cam Inglis, Cathryn deVries, Chris Edgerly, Christa Niehot, Clarissa Gosling, Ellysa Hermanson, Emma Adams, Erin DeBiase, Felicitas Odemer, Gina Mistura, Giselle Jeffries Schneider, H Anderson, HCM, Heidi Wadsworth, Helen Febrie, Hope Terrell, J & G Sugden, Jamie Dockendorff, Janice Muehle, Jennifer Klütsch, Julianne, K.

Hendrick, Katherine Shipman, Katie Cherry, Kristopher Ecklof, Laura Jacobs-Finch, Leslie Twitchell, Logan Kallander, Mandi Oyster, Marshall, Matthian, Merrie Destefano, Nolan Barrett, Peter Younghusband, Rebecca Hill, Rebecca L. Garcia, Renee, Robert Zangari, Rosa Thill, SARLE, Shabana, Sonya Bramwell, Steven and Scott Sobotta, Tawnee Wadsworth, Tessa, Thann Shira, Thomas Bull, Tiger Hebert, Tim, Vickie Grider, Xolotl.

I would be remiss if I didn't also thank my Lost River community for the tremendous support its members have shown since I first published in 2020. I'm overwhelmed by your enthusiasm and dedication, and I'm blessed to live among you!

Most of all, I thank my Father in Heaven for giving me a deep-rooted love for stories, and the ability to tap that love to tell my own.

—M. H. W.

Special Acknowledgments

To those who went above and beyond to back my Kickstarter at the highest tiers, you are the absolute best of the best.

Thank you!

Dragon Tier:

Meredith

Sean P Brady

Seamus Sands

Gryphon Tier:

Lauren Freeman

Lisa Papi

Nick Frank

Scott Casey

Elf Tier:

Brian Healy

Dudley Pajela

Gerald P. McDaniel

Leeta Song

Steven Streeper

About the Author

Writer of fantasy, magic weaver, dragon rider! Having spent the past two decades devotedly writing fantasy, it's safe to say M. H. Woodscourt is now more fae than human.

All of her fantasy worlds connect with each other in the Mithrinn Universe, forged with great love and no small measure of blood, sweat, and tears. When she's not writing, she's napping or reading a book with a mug of hot cocoa close at hand, while her quirky cat Wynter nibbles her nose.

Learn more at www.mhwoodscourt.com

Also by M. H. Woodscourt

MARK OF VALLIATH

High Fantasy/Young Adult

The Storyteller True

The Shattered Arch

The Marked Prince

The Blood Fountain

RECORD OF THE SENTINEL SEER

Science-Fantasy/New Adult

Prince of the Fallen

Rule of the Night

Song of the Lost

Paths of the Broken

Heart of the Sentinel

WINTERVALE DUOLOGY

High Fantasy/Young Adult

The Crow King

The Winter King

Paradise Trilogy

Portal Fantasy/Humor/Young Adult

A Liar in Paradise

Key of Paradise

Beyond Paradise